Long Journey Home

D0112946

Sharlene MacLaren

Publisher's note:
This novel is a work of fiction. References to real events, organizations, or places are used in a fictional context. Any resemblances to actual persons, living or dead, are entirely coincidental.

LONG JOURNEY HOME

Sharlene MacLaren
www.sharlenemaclaren.com

ISBN-13: 978-1-60374-056-2 / ISBN-10: 1-60374-056-2
Printed in the United States of America

1030 Hunt Valley Circle
New Kensington, PA 15068
www.whitakerhouse.com

Library of Congress Cataloging-in-Publication Data
MacLaren, Sharlene, 1948–
Long journey home / Sharlene MacLaren.
p. cm.
Summary: "Recently divorced from her abusive husband, single mother Callie May meets new neighbor Dan Mattson and strikes up a volatile relationship that, by the grace of God, turns into romance"—Provided by publisher.
ISBN 978-1-60374-056-2 (trade pbk.)
1. Single mothers—Fiction. I. Title.
PS3613.A27356L66 2008
813'.6—dc22 2008021470

1 2 3 4 5 6 7 8 9 10 11 12 16 15 14 13 12 11 10 09 08

To Gavin Mark Tisdel...

Keeper of the key to your
Grandma's heart.

Dan Mattson pushed the speed limit on Highway 6, feeling wild and reckless. With both windows down, radio blaring, map stretched out on his lap, he sped past a sign reading OAKDALE: 10 MILES and breathed a sigh. *Not far now,* he told himself. With his back muscles aching and his stomach (and gas tank) nearly empty, he was more than a little anxious to reach his destination.

Along the way, he had noted several large farms, their rickety fences lining the roadside. Here and there, cows and horses huddled in groups, grazing on thinning, grassy knolls. Restless and impatient, he ran his fingers through his thick, black hair, then reached down and turned up the volume on the radio. At the sounds of a familiar country tune, he began humming along with the radio until his cell phone started vibrating. He yanked it from his pocket, flipped open the cover, and spoke a hurried greeting.

"Danny, where are you?"

He should have known his sister would inquire after him before the day was done.

"Hi, Sam. I'm not far from Oakdale."

"Well, I miss you." It was hard to ignore the pouty tone.

"Already? I just left this morning." He forced a smile. Lately, it took a lot for one to come naturally.

"It doesn't matter. Things are not going to be the same around here without you."

"Things have not been the same for a long time, Samantha," he corrected.

Had it really been more than a year since his life took a sharp, screeching turn? Even now, the past memories tangled with his present senses.

"That's true, but did you have to move away? These things take time, Danny, and the constituency did give you six months to rest up and collect yourself," she said.

Collect myself? Is she kidding? Six months had barely been enough time to shake off the numbness before reality set in. He swallowed down an angry retort. "We've been over all this, Sam. It's for the best."

"Leaving your congregation was for the best?" she asked.

"Sam…"

"Folks were just starting to heal. I don't think you gave it enough time."

Sam was nothing if she wasn't forthright about her feelings. Of everyone in the family, she'd been the most adamant about him sticking it out with his congregation. Did she think this last-minute conversation might convince him to turn around? It was almost enough to make him chuckle.

"I did what I had to do. Hanging around wasn't doing my parishioners any good."

"Do you know that for sure?"

He heaved an enormous sigh. "I was their pastor, Sam, but I was the one who needed shepherding."

"God uses imperfect people all the time."

"Maybe so, but a church needs strong leadership. What kind of pastor stands in front of the pulpit Sunday after Sunday and offers nothing more than a few babbling words? Shoot, Sam, even *I* had trouble following my sermons."

Samantha giggled. "I have to admit, they were going from bad to worse."

"There you have it," he murmured, mindlessly reading passing billboards.

"I was kidding."

"No, you weren't. Did Mom put you up to this phone call, by the way?"

"Nope. In fact, she told me to leave you alone."

"Smart woman."

A tiny pause silenced Sam for a moment. "When are you going to stop blaming yourself for the accident?"

At her question, he tightened his grip on the steering wheel. "Who said I was?"

"It's pretty obvious, although why you would is a mystery to me. You weren't even with them when it happened."

"Precisely. That, my dear, should explain my guilt."

"So, you're saying if you'd been with them it wouldn't have happened? That's silly. And what about this? If you'd been driving, you might all be dead. That was a treacherous storm."

"I gotta hang up, Sam. I'm getting closer to town."

"Dan, answer me this," she persisted.

"What?" He gritted his teeth against his growing perturbation.

"Besides blaming yourself, do you also blame God?"

He sighed. "I am so tired of talking about this."

"Just answer me."

"I don't know." Some things were just too hard to put into words.

"Shall I discount all your past sermons about trusting God even through the tough times? I still remember you preaching at John Farhat's funeral. You looked straight into his wife's eyes and said, 'We would never see the stars, Ellen, if God didn't sometimes take away the day.'"

A ball of guilt formed a tight knot in his chest. How many people had he hurt in his leave-taking? Worse, how many had he led astray? "Let it go, Samantha."

"I suffered, too, you know. I lost a sister-in-law and a precious niece. And think about Mom and Dad...." Her voice drifted off as Dan watched the road ahead.

"Gotta go, Sam. I'll call you soon."

He clamped the cover of the receiver down hard and stuffed the thing back in his pocket, then quickly yanked it back out, opened it up, and hit the off button.

Oakdale City Limits

Dan breathed deeply when he passed the familiar landmark. He'd visited Oakdale only briefly before, but something about its tranquil setting brought a sense of peace and belonging. Its rambling old oaks, fields of wild flowers, ageless pines nestled on faraway hillsides, and timeless brick homes surrounded by flower beds held a kind of idyllic appeal.

He passed an ancient cemetery and instinctively slowed, its sight only adding to his pensive mood. Cemeteries did that to him.

Andrea… Her name shot out of nowhere.

He pushed the accelerator. "God," he muttered, "what were You thinking? Taking my family away from me was a rotten trick."

Dan flipped the turn signal at the entrance to Oakdale Arms Apartment Complex, his new stomping ground—at least until he got a grip on himself. He saw the large moving van sitting in the parking lot. It contained a minimum of furniture, enough clothes to get by, and only those memorabilia that wouldn't cause undue pain. He'd already made payment to the moving company, and the driver had said he would be back for his truck in a couple of days. Moving companies didn't often operate that way, but since the driver was an old friend, he'd made special arrangements.

Dan parked the car, got out, and stretched. Oakdale looked like a nice enough community—quiet and pleasant, with a friendly aura. Its appeal was almost tangible. Maybe this would be his answer to finding some much-needed peace.

He would go into the apartment he'd leased, then make a call to his old high school friend who'd offered him the construction job. He took in the sights and smells around him, felt the warmth of the summer sun on his back, and believed in his heart of hearts that he would find answers right here in this lovely little bedroom community on the outskirts of Chicago.

∽

A hair-raising scream roused Callie May from her sleep-drugged state at precisely six fifty-six on Sunday morning. "Nooo," she groaned, burying her head beneath her pillow. Hadn't she just closed her eyes five minutes ago? *Just give me another hour, Em.* But as the screams rose in decibels, she surrendered to the fact that her eight-month-old baby was hungry and needed attention.

On her way to the nursery, she adjusted the thermostat. Early sun reached its spindly fingers through the half-drawn blinds, sending shafts of light through the kitchen window. *Looks like another sunny day,* she mulled. Too bad she couldn't say the same for her spirits.

Emily's pouty sob gave way to instant smiles when

Callie walked through the door. "You're a stinker, you know that?" she chided while lowering the bar on Emily's crib and lifting the baby into her arms. "Waking Mommy when she had just fallen asleep." Emily smeared a wet, warm kiss across Callie's face, making Callie chuckle in spite of herself. "You think you can win me over with your kisses?"

After a hasty diaper change, Callie hoisted the baby on her hip and headed for the kitchen. "Ba-ba-ba-ba," Emily chanted along the way, oblivious to her mother's less-than-chipper mood, her recent "B" sounds coming out in an attempt to say "bottle." Of course, Callie's father begged to differ. "She's trying to say 'Grandpa,'" he claimed.

Pulling open the fridge door, she spotted a bottle of formula and snatched it off the shelf, then pushed the door shut with her hip. "Cold or hot?" she asked, holding the bottle under the baby's nose. Emily reached for the bottle and steered it to her mouth. "Guess that answers that," she said, tipping Emily back in her arms while the baby suckled.

As she reached for a mug for tea, a sudden racket in the hall outside her door sparked her interest. Yesterday, someone had started moving into the vacant apartment across the hall, but she'd been too self-absorbed to pay much attention. Now, however, she found herself padding across the room for a peek through her peephole.

At first, she saw nothing through the tiny hole in her door. But then, a tall, strongly built man emerged from the apartment, large crate in hand. He looked to be about her age—perhaps in his mid- to late-twenties. He paused just briefly, as if pondering something, giving her a chance to study his handsome, sober face with its clear-cut lines, generous mouth, and thick crop of black hair. An unexpected shiver scampered up her spine. Even through the tiny opening, she sensed his angry mood; she saw it in his crinkled brow and clenched jaw.

He looks mad enough to spit poison. Who is he?

A squirming Emily forced her away from the door. She told herself that the man was of no concern to her, and not to mind his dark and dangerous appearance, never mind that her marriage to an abusive man had ended mere days ago and she was feeling vulnerable. She had enough things to worry about without adding a dodgy-looking character into the mix.

Dropping into a soft chair, she gathered her baby close and blew out a loud breath. While Emily finished off the last few ounces of formula, Callie leaned back and closed her eyes. If the stranger held down the noise, she might be able to catch a few more winks before getting ready for church.

∽

"What? You're pregnant?" he screamed. "You finagling witch!"

An angry fist shot out and hit her square in the jaw, knocking her to the floor. Pain seared her face like fiery talons while a gasp of air pushed past her lungs. She skidded across the hardwood floor and slid up against the wall.

"Don't hate me, Thomas. I—I didn't mean for it to happen. Please…"

"Shut up!" he ranted, reaching for a fistful of her hair and yanking her head around till it snapped. "You're gonna get rid of that mistake in your belly, you hear me?"

The urge to retch consumed her. Mistake? Timidly, she raised her face to him.

"I—I can't do that."

"You can and you will," he wailed, pulling her hair until it nearly ripped from her scalp. She screamed with pain. Sneering, he dropped his hand and tramped to the door.

He wrenched his coat from its hook and pushed his arms through the sleeves. "I'm going out! I can't stand the sight of you!"

When he slammed the door behind him, she lowered herself, exhausted, into a rumpled heap on the floor.

☙

Her own sobs and the beads of sweat that dotted her forehead were what roused her from the nightmare. It wasn't the first time she'd dreamt it, and it was unlikely to be the last. Shaken but relieved, she swabbed her brow with the back of her hand. Thomas was in Florida. She was in Illinois. The marriage was over—as was the abuse. Now, if she could just rid herself of the terrifying memories.

Two o'clock. Dan stared at the clock for a solid minute, allowing the leather chair to swallow him up. The worst of the moving was over, thanks to a husky kid who'd been about to set off on a morning jog when he saw Dan struggling with the sofa and had offered his muscle. Now it was just a matter of hauling down a few boxes of trash, bringing up some miscellaneous items from the truck, and getting his apartment in order. With his motivation tank running on empty since arriving yesterday, he'd accomplished little.

Rubbing his hands together as if the friction might somehow boost his energy, he hauled himself up and stretched, then approached the boxes he'd stacked against the wall. "Destination: dumpster," he muttered, bending to retrieve a carton full of trash and maneuvering his way through the door and into the hallway.

At the bottom of the stairs, he reached for the doorknob, only to have the door swing toward him, opened from the other side. A woman with a baby on her hip started to scoot past him, and, in the process, knocked him off-kilter, sending most of the trash—several magazines, a local newspaper, a squashed milk carton, and a partially consumed can of tomato soup—in various directions.

She jumped back, blue eyes wide with surprise. For some reason, her reaction annoyed him. These days, it didn't take much.

"I'm sorry!" she squeaked. Her urgent apology didn't appease his grouchy spirit. In fact, he had half a mind to brush past her, and he might have, too, if he hadn't feared toppling her fragile frame.

"No problem," he replied sourly, bending to retrieve the strewn items and noting the speckled wall where the remains of tomato soup had splattered.

While he collected the mess, his eyes strayed to a pair of sandaled feet, toes freshly painted in bright pink polish. Chagrined for having noticed, he released a sigh.

"Sorry about that," she said, apologizing for the second time. The baby let out a squeal that erupted into an impatient sob. He glanced at it and noted the "it" was a girl. *Blast!* Were these his new neighbors?

He straightened and gave the woman a sideways glance, noting certain wariness. Not for the first time, he rued the fact his years of ministerial experience had made his senses keener than most.

He cleared his throat. "Excuse me, may I get past?"

"Oh!" She stepped aside, and her baby's cries escalated.

He wanted to blow her off, but something about her pale, petite features, wispy blonde hair, pert little nose, and big round eyes made it impossible. And the baby girl didn't help matters. Smaller and younger than his Chelsea had been, she still bore a striking resemblance. The woman, however, looked nothing like Andrea. Frozen in place, he gawked for what must have been a full thirty seconds.

"I—guess you're moving in, huh?" she sputtered.

He nodded and angled his gaze at the stairs. "You live across the hall?"

She bobbed her head. "I've—we've—lived here for a while now." If it hadn't been for a painful memory, he might have studied her pixie face—and that of her baby. Instead, his defenses shot up.

"Your kid's about to cut loose."

A red, splotchy glow moved over her face, and he knew he'd either embarrassed or offended her. *Well, too bad.* He had neither the time nor the energy to care.

"She's—ready for a nap. It's been a busy day."

He gave her a curt nod, knowing he should have been more genial. Considering he was the new kid on the block, he might have tried a little harder to act neighborly.

She lifted her chin a notch and forced a smile that didn't come near to reaching her eyes. "Well...," she expelled a huff of air, "...have a good day, then." That said, she pushed past him to climb the stairs, baby on one arm, diaper bag on the other.

He nodded and watched her go, giving himself a mental reproof for noting the gentle sway of her body as she climbed the stairs.

∾

Callie unlocked the door and pushed it open with her hip, relieving herself of the diaper bag first by dropping it to the floor before shutting the door behind her. "Shh," she soothed her squalling child. "You are one sleepy baby, and that strange man didn't help the situation."

Retrieving a pacifier from the diaper bag, she stuck it in Emily's mouth. She quieted immediately, taking to it like a starving pup, even though she was anything but hungry—she had just downed a jar and a half of baby food and a bottle of formula at Callie's parents' house.

"What a grumpy man, huh?" Callie mused aloud, as if the baby comprehended. Emily's droopy eyes indicated imminent sleep. "Well, we'll just put him right out of our minds."

Of course, saying that and doing it were two different things. Even as she laid the baby in her crib, threw a light blanket over her bare legs, and smoothed down a few rumpled wisps of blonde hair, she thought about the man whose dark eyes betrayed bitterness and some sort of deep-set pain. Did he also hold a volatile temper in check? The notion made her shiver unexpectedly.

Hadn't she just escaped a man with a temper? Would her new neighbor also pose a threat?

While Emily slept, Callie sorted through closets and drawers, emptying their contents of anything reminding her of Thomas and their former lives. In haste, she tossed several pictures into a waste container, saving only a couple for Emily's sake.

"God, help me be enough for her." It was a rusty, halfhearted prayer, the kind that followed on the heels of desperation. Whether He'd actually heard her plea was another story. It wasn't that she didn't believe; she'd actually invited Christ into her heart as a young girl and had attended church faithfully ever since. So, yes, she was a Christian. But a committed one? Not by a long stretch.

The sound of the doorbell cheered her spirits, especially when she discovered who had come to visit. "Hey, Lisa!" She greeted her best friend with delighted surprise, grabbing her by the arm and ushering her through the door.

Lisa grinned and headed straight for the kitchen. "I'm dying of thirst. It's hot out there."

Callie closed the door and propped herself against it, watching while Lisa filed frantically through the refrigerator. "There is the faucet, you know," she teased.

"Not the same," Lisa mumbled, pushing aside the milk and juice and laying hold of a bottle of water at the back of the fridge. Unscrewing the cap, she guzzled down several swigs before coming up for air. "Ah, that's good," she said. "I don't like your faucet water. It's much too..."—she turned up her nose—"cityish."

"Cityish?" Callie laughed. "And inferior to your 'countryish' well water, I suppose?"

She took a few more swallows, screwed the cap back on, and smiled. "There are advantages to living in the country, and fresh drinking water is only one of them."

"Not to mention the fresh smell of cow manure and pig do-do," Callie countered, pushing away from the door.

"Neither one for which you can hold us responsible. Now, if you're talking the flowery fragrance of rabbits and chickens...well, that's something else altogether. Speaking of rabbits, I swear—if Luanne gives birth to one more bunny, I will personally ring Louie's neck."

"Louie?"

"Her happy husband," Lisa retorted, kicking off her sandals and plopping down on the sofa. She tucked one bare foot under her, fell back into the soft cushions, and pointed her gaze upward.

"Why don't you separate them?"

Lisa popped her head up and stared at Callie as if she were missing a few screws. "What? And take away Louie's reason for living?" She took another swig of water before setting the bottle on the sofa stand next to her head.

Callie giggled. Deciding to take the chair opposite the sofa, she dropped into it with a flourish. If anyone could give her a quick mood lift, it was Lisa. They'd been fast friends as junior high cheerleaders and had remained close ever since then.

"So—it's over, huh?" Lisa mumbled.

"I'm afraid so. Friday at noon, if you want to be exact. Mom took us out for hamburgers—not to celebrate, mind you, but to keep my mind occupied. Over lunch, she stated more reasons than Bayer has aspirin why Emily and I should move in with her and Daddy."

Lisa folded her hands across her middle and angled her with a speculative glance. "You're considering it?"

Callie shook her head. "No way. I've had my independence too long to move back home. Besides, my dad's not well. I think it'd be too much for him having Em underfoot all the time. It's enough that we visit every few days. He loves her to pieces, but, well, she's as busy as a butterfly—flitting from one thing to another. I can barely keep up with her myself. I can't even imagine what it'll be like once she starts walking."

Lisa giggled softly and gave her shoulder-length brown hair a single backward swipe. Her blue eyes sparkled. "Well, you'd better start training now. When that baby starts toddling around, you'll never catch your breath."

Callie curled her feet up under her and gazed toward the kitchen window, distracted by the sound of water splashing in the community pool outside.

"Want to do something later?" Lisa asked. "Maybe go out for a bite to eat? I could get a sitter for Emily, or we could bring her along."

"Not tonight, but thanks for the offer. I really need to make a grocery run."

Her friend gave a quiet nod. At the pool, a mother issued an order, and a child wailed in protest. The refrigerator hummed, the dishwasher heaved into its next cycle, and the clothes dryer purred in the other room, tossing fresh-washed sheets and dish towels.

"He hasn't called, has he?" Lisa asked.

Callie studied a tiny spider making its way across the ceiling. "No, and he'd better not. Last I heard, he was running around with some woman down in Florida."

Lisa clicked her tongue disapprovingly. "You went beyond the call of duty with that one, Cal. Lord, forgive me, but that cheating fool hardly deserves to shine your shoes."

A foreboding ache gnawed at her stomach. "I kept thinking we could work things out. Crazy, huh?"

"It's hard to rehabilitate an abusive alcoholic, Cal. Especially one who's happy with his life as it is."

"He's not happy."

"He's also not in any big hurry to get help. He's dangerous, Callie. I hate to say it, but I'm glad he's out of your life. He's been trouble from the very beginning."

"And I was blind for not realizing it."

"You were young and in love."

"Old enough to know better. I was one of those

ignoramuses who believed marriage would make him a better person." At this, she laughed outright, not so much at the humor in her remark, but at the absurdity of it.

"Hey, stop blaming yourself. You loved him, baggage and all," Lisa said with a grimace. "He had a rough life, and because of that, had no idea how to be a husband or a father. But that's over now. End of story. He's not your responsibility. You need to let God heal you."

A tiny sob welled up in Callie, but she quickly swallowed it, hoping Lisa hadn't noticed. "I am nothing but a bother to God. He must be shaking His head at me about now." A cynical chortle leaked out.

Lisa sat up with a jolt and shook her head. "Listen to you. God loves you more than you know, Cal. If we were perfect, we wouldn't need a Savior. He understands everything you're feeling and knows your pain. You can trust Him."

Unadulterated shame pinched her in the side. "I know you're right. It's just—it's been a while since I last prayed. I don't feel worthy at the moment."

Lisa pulled herself to a sitting position and downed a couple more sips of water before standing. "Weren't you listening to the sermon this morning, young lady?" She walked to the sink to drain the rest of the liquid. "Pastor Tim talked about that very thing. None of us is worthy of God's love, but He freely gives it anyway. That's where the whole issue of having faith and trust comes into play."

Lisa took up a dishcloth and wiped down the counter, even though Callie didn't think there was a crumb to be found.

Not wishing to hear two sermons in one day, she breathed a sigh of relief when Emily whimpered from the nursery. She started to get up from her chair, but Lisa whirled and stopped her with a hand. "Uh-uh—she's mine."

Callie grinned and settled back into her chair, watching as Lisa set off down the hall. While Lisa sweet-talked Emily for the next few minutes, Callie took advantage of the opportunity to close her eyes.

"Get ready for a night on the town next Saturday—we'll do dinner and a movie," Lisa called from the nursery.

"Huh?" Callie asked, popping open one eye and angling it at the baby's room.

"Call a sitter. I'll pick you up around six." Lisa poked her head out, a diaper-clad Emily in her arms. "And I won't take no for an answer."

Callie entered Mason's Food Mart dressed in soiled shorts and torn T-shirt, baby riding on her right hip. Nabbing a grocery cart with one hand, she hoisted Emily into it, secured the strap, and handed Emily her cloth doll before pushing off down the aisle, filling her cart with necessities and listening to her baby's nonstop jabber. On a whim, she tossed in a bag of peanut M&M's, her mood dictating a deep need for chocolate.

In one aisle, she looked for her favorite brand of salad dressing, chagrined to discover two lone jars on the top shelf, far beyond reach. "Great," she mumbled. With care, she used the bottom shelf as a step stool and stretched to her limit, gratified when her fingers grasped the desired object.

"Need some help?" asked a low-timbred voice.

Whether from hearing an unexpected voice or feeling guilty for having been caught climbing on store property, she was startled and tottered, dropping the jar, which hit the tile floor with a loud splat and shattered. The red, oily substance spread and puddled across the aisle. Emily started to whimper.

"Well, now you've done it, haven't you, neighbor?" came that same voice, this time conveying mock disdain. She needn't have turned to identify its source, so it annoyed her that she had. "A little accident prone, are we? You run into a neighbor, and now you're destroying store merchandise?" He shook his head. "My, my, you're dangerous."

Callie felt her eyes narrowing on her subject. Tall and daunting, he wore a lopsided grin she'd have wiped off his mouth had it not been for his intimidating aura. He gripped a grocery basket filled to the brim with various items—a quart of milk, a loaf of bread, a jar of peanut butter, a box of Cheerios, and a razor and pack of blades.

"You again?" she asked, attempting a cool-headed response, in spite of the flutter rippling beneath her chest.

He arched his dark eyebrows, stepping back to examine the contents of her cart. After a fleeting glance at Emily, who by now had quieted and was all about investigating the stranger, he pinned her with his chocolate eyes. "Picking some food for the family, I see. Have you and your husband lived in the apartments long?" While she pondered how to reply, he gave her a pointed look. "I mean, I assume you're married."

Impatient with idleness, Emily kicked and whined. In Callie's opinion, her timing was perfect. She started inching the cart forward. "Sorry, I don't have time for chit-chat."

"No problem." He started to step back, then snagged hold of the front of her cart, stopping her. "I guess I made a pretty bad impression earlier today. Since we're going to be neighbors, I wouldn't want you thinking I'm always that rude."

What do you know? He does have a conscience, she thought. At the risk of caving in, though, she kept her back stiff and a smile from creeping to the surface. "It's fine, and now I—I better see if I can find someone to clean up this mess. Excuse me." She rested her gaze on his hand, still holding her cart.

"Oh, sure thing." He released his grip and moved aside, then quickly turned on his heel and snatched a jar of salad dressing from the top shelf, dropping it into her cart. "That was what you were reaching for, right? Johnson's Creamy French?" He tipped up the corners of his mouth to reveal straight teeth that had no doubt seen braces.

She sighed and allowed the tiniest smile of appreciation. "Thanks."

Fighting down frayed nerves, she scurried away, found a stock boy, to whom she reported the accident, then hurriedly finished shopping.

At the checkout counter, she unloaded her items while a young girl began the process of scanning and a young man took up the task of placing things in plastic bags. Every so often, the clerk would glance up and smile at Emily.

"She's cute," she remarked.

"Thank you." Callie smoothed down a portion of Emily's flyaway hair.

"What's her name?" the girl asked.

"Emily."

"Emily. That's nice," she replied, eyes darting from her task to the baby. "How old is she?"

"Just turned eight months."

Beside Callie, a man began placing his items on the counter prematurely, the moving belt meshing his items with hers and creating havoc for the young clerk, who automatically started scanning items from his order. Annoyed, Callie turned to face the culprit and sighed in exasperation to discover *him* again.

"These aren't mine," Callie told the girl, pointing out a razor, some blades, and a can of shaving cream that had already passed over the scanner. Fast coming up on those items were his bread and milk.

The girl took in a quick, sharp breath and stopped the moving belt. "What? They aren't? Oh, I thought you two..."

"No!" Callie exclaimed.

"Oh, dear."

"What's the problem?" Callie leaned into the counter, alarmed by the girl's panicked tone.

"I don't know if I—how to..."

"What? It's a simple error. Can't you delete the items you just scanned and then resume scanning my order?"

"I'm not....You see, I'm new here."

"Yes? Well, can you call your supervisor?"

"Oh no, I—well, I've already pushed him to his limits, I'm afraid." The poor girl looked near tears, and if Callie hadn't felt so annoyed with the guy beside her, she might well have been more sympathetic.

"Can't you call someone to help you, someone other than your boss?" she asked.

The teenager worried her lower lip and scrunched her face. "Do you think you could just pay for his stuff and let him pay you back?"

"You are asking me to pay for another customer's merchandise?" *Preposterous.*

"That sounds reasonable," her neighbor had the gall to say. "You pay the total bill and we'll settle up afterward. Outside. Seems simple enough." His mouth twitched with amusement.

The girl's brow shot up in a hopeful tilt. "Yes?" she said, looking to Callie for permission to proceed.

"Oh, all right. I guess I could do that, but don't let any more of his items pass through. My purchases stop here," she instructed, drawing an imaginary line across the counter, then straightening her shoulders to accentuate her point.

"No problem. You will pay her back, won't you?" the girl asked, hesitating at the register while she studied the man.

"Of course." He granted the girl a sparkling smile. "You can trust me."

Disgruntled, Callie started digging for her wallet.

"That will be eighty-six dollars and ninety-eight cents, please."

A sharp gasp whistled past her lips. "Are you sure? That seems excessive."

"Uh, my razor." The man's resonant voice echoed past her ear, breathy and close. "They're not as cheap as they used to be."

She tried to ignore the chill that ran the length of her spine, gave an impatient shrug, and paid the girl with five twenty-dollar bills.

"I'm sorry for the mix-up," the teenager said, handing over her change and offering a sheepish smile. It took great effort for Callie to return a pleasant look.

She stood on the sidelines while the young lady finished her neighbor's order. "You waiting for me?" he asked, feigning innocence when he glanced at her. *Oh, please.* Stuffing his receipt and change into his back pocket, he gave the young clerk a cursory nod, then snatched up his bags and sauntered straight past Callie and Emily.

"Excuse me. You owe me money," she called. Like a kid trying to keep up with her father's longer strides, she pushed her cart after him, angered when he headed out the automatic door ahead of her. A waning sun had dropped behind the trees, but the heat of the day still lingered. Callie panted in her attempt to keep up. Emily giggled with excitement.

"Let me see the receipt," he said, coming to an abrupt halt on the sidewalk, her cart nearly ramming him.

She fished the receipt from her purse and did a hasty calculation. "You owe me…"

He seized it before she finished figuring and studied it for himself. Inside she seethed.

"Looks like twelve bucks should do it."

She snatched it back, did her own mental computation, and came up with eleven dollars and some odd cents. "Twelve will do nicely," she said, extending her palm. "Pay up."

Dark eyes revealed a glint of humor. "I never had you figured for being so sassy."

"Just pay me what you owe."

Adjusting the handles of the plastic sacks on one arm, he withdrew a wallet from his back pocket. "So your daughter's name is Emily?" he asked, counting out a ten-dollar bill and two ones.

Apparently, he'd been eavesdropping. She took the bills he offered and dropped them into her purse. "Yes."

Bending at the waist, he came within inches of Emily's face. "Hi there, punkin. You're a cute one."

After tweaking her nose, he straightened. "It's nice that you can stay home to take care of her."

"I'm a teacher," Callie clarified. "I have my summers off." Immediately she wanted to recall her words. The less he knew about her, the better.

"Oh, yeah?" He quirked his mouth at the corners. "What does your husband do?"

She leveled him with a piercing glare. She did not

have time for this, nor did she wish to reveal the fact she was no longer married. Frankly, it was none of his business. "My ice cream will melt if I stand around and talk."

Lifting one dark eyebrow, he smiled and gave a ruminative nod. "Another time, then."

Fat chance.

"Good-bye, Emily," he called to her back when she whirled the cart and headed for her car.

"Baah!" was Emily's reply call, her arms waving crazily.

"Shh, Emily. Don't talk to that man," Callie hissed under her breath.

In response, Emily gave a whoop of delight and hugged her tattered doll to her soiled shirtfront.

Dan rolled out of bed on Monday morning with a headache. Any other time, he might have lingered a while until the ache subsided, but he was meeting his new boss and old friend, Greg Freeman, at his office, so there was nothing to be done but to pop a few aspirin tablets.

In the bathroom, he leaned into the mirror to study his reflection and mumbled a mild curse. He looked like the back end of a gutted truck. After rubbing a hand over his weekend-old beard, he grabbed his new razor, the one *she'd* paid for. Removing the wrapper, he felt his mouth spread into a lazy grin, then, just as quickly, dissipate. What was *she* doing at the forefront of his mind, anyway? Yeah, she was a cute little blonde, but apparently a married one—she had a wedding ring to prove it. *But she evaded my questions about her husband....*

He frowned and set about readying himself for his morning appointment.

At eight on the dot, Dan walked through the doors of Freeman Construction Company. It was a small office, not much more than a square cubicle with three desks. Greg sat behind a desk at the back of the room, so engrossed in a pile of blueprints that he failed to hear Dan's entrance. Two women occupied the other desks, both facing mounds of paperwork. The one who appeared to be the receptionist flashed him a toothy smile.

"May I help you?" she asked, batting her mascara-slathered eyelashes at him.

"Thanks. I think I've spotted him," Dan announced.

Just then, Greg looked up, pushed his chair back with a grating squeak, and leaped to his feet. "Dan, you old rascal," he cried, extending a hand on his approach. "Great to see you."

"Good to see you, too," Dan returned, laughing when Greg nearly wrenched off his hand with his hearty handshake.

"Look at you," Greg exclaimed, giving him a top-to-bottom assessment. "You been working out? You used to be a scrawny kid."

Dan laughed. "I could say the same for you. How have you been?" His friend hadn't aged a bit; he still had thick, blond hair, fair skin, and a friendly smile. His gut had grown a bit of a paunch, however.

"Great, just great. Come and sit down. I'll show you around later."

They moved to the back of the office, and Greg tossed a couple of construction magazines off the chair and onto the floor to give Dan a place to sit. Greg reclined in his own chair and propped his booted feet atop his marred desk.

"I was a happy man when you took me up on the job offer. You always were good with your hands, better than I was when it came to the detailed stuff. I'm hoping we'll get a kick out of working together again," Greg said.

"Yeah. Thanks to your dad, I got my start in construction and discovered I loved it. Kind of gave it up, though, when I…" He let the sentence fall, unfinished.

Thankfully, Greg picked up the slack. "Dad always did say you had talent."

"Does he still own that construction business?"

"Nah, he sold out. Actually gave me a good share of the profits so I could start my company down here. The folks moved to Florida. Karen's from around here, you know. It's a nice area." Dan nodded and Greg continued. "You been staying out of trouble?"

"I've been trying," he answered, going along with the spirit of the questioning.

"Never will forget some of those wild times we had as teenagers."

"We had some times, all right."

"Gave our parents some fits, especially that time you were driving a gang of us home from Sharon Wiley's football party, and you got pulled over. Remember that?"

How could he forget? He'd been the closest one to sober that night and gotten behind the wheel of his friend's car. His swerving over the center lane was what had caught the officer's attention.

"I remember all right. They hauled us to the station, where we sat in a cell for six hours while our parents tried to decide whether to make us spend the night. Nearly scared the pants off us, as I recall."

Greg chuckled. "Quickest way I know of to sober up." He shook his head. "Glad those days are behind me." He fiddled with a pencil, tapping the eraser end on a stack of papers. "Well, hey, how's your family?"

Dan swallowed a jagged breath and gave a jolt. "My..."

Greg pushed forward in his chair, face pinched and flushed. "Shoot, man, I'm sorry. By family I meant, you know, your folks and—Samantha and Ken."

Dan gave a fast nod. "Yeah, I know. Ken's great. He's still working at Sutter and Sutter Law Firm. They have twin boys. And Sam. Well, she hasn't changed much. Still tries to run my life. She and John have one little guy. Robbie. She still plays the flute and recently joined a city orchestra near her home."

"She's talented, could have traveled the world. A musical genius is what she is."

That much was true. His sister had won a merit scholarship to Juilliard school in Manhattan. After obtaining her degree, she'd earned a spot in the New York Philharmonic. But after only two years, she came home to marry her high school sweetheart, the pair deciding they could no longer endure a long-distance relationship. Within the year, she was pregnant with her first child.

"She's pretty happy being a wife and mother."

"Yeah, that's how Karen is. Loves staying home with the kids." As if he realized the discussion about marriage and family might make Dan uneasy, Greg changed the subject. "Hey, you want to have a look around?"

When Dan gave an eager nod, they both pushed back in their chairs and stood. "I'll take you out to some of our building sites. I'm probably going to start you out at my project on Oakwood Square. We've been working on this new housing development since early spring. It's coming along—you'll see. Houses around here sell fast. The local market is surprisingly good right now."

The two men walked outside and jumped in Greg's truck. As Greg pulled out of the parking lot and headed down the road, they talked about the job, some of the expectations Greg had for his company, the successes he'd already enjoyed, and some of his current ventures.

"So, you left your preaching job," Greg said, braking and taking the corner into a subdivision of upscale houses.

"Yeah, it was—necessary," Dan answered, bracing himself for more questions.

"Sometimes when tragedy strikes, it's good to take a different path, at least until you can figure out where you want to go."

The words struck him as ordinary but wise. Even his parents hadn't seen things quite in that light. He'd worried that everyone thought he was running away. Even he sometimes questioned his motives.

"At any rate, I'm glad you're here," his friend added, giving him a good-natured slap on the shoulder. "I sure can use the extra help. You've got a job with me for as long as you need it."

"I appreciate that." Greg's generous offer stirred up a whole bundle of unnamed emotions, so much so that Dan had to swallow down a hard lump.

"This is one of my subdivisions," Greg said, turning down a newly paved road dotted with For Sale signs at the front of empty lots, newly built homes with just-planted sod and shrubs, and some houses in their early stages of construction.

They spent the remainder of the morning driving from one location to the next, looking over Greg's projects and meeting the crew members. Greg employed eight to ten full-time men and several part-timers. They did the framing, flooring, cabinetry, tiling, siding, and roofing. Everything else—the excavating, dry walling, plumbing, and electrical—was subcontracted. It appeared there were four to five developments going at once, providing plenty of work to keep everyone busy. *Good,* Dan thought. He figured the more hours he filled with work, the less time there would be for mulling over his own problems.

After lunch, they went back to the office and talked

more business. Greg showed Dan plans for some future undertakings, some new building designs an architect had just dropped off that morning, and a scale model of a new shopping plaza he'd been given a proposal on. He claimed no interest in commercial building but said he wouldn't mind teaming up with another company down the road—if only to get his feet wet. Dan was impressed, if not pleasantly surprised, by the size of Greg's business and the fine reputation he had established.

Later, while the two of them headed for Dan's little Ford Mustang, Greg threw an arm around Dan's shoulder and said, "We usually start our work day at seven sharp. You up for that?"

"Does that mean I'm hired?" Dan gave his friend a sideways glance.

"You bet you're hired—if you'll have us. I know you're skilled. I saw that cabinet you built your mother a few years back. You've got the gift. You could probably go into business for yourself one day just building furniture."

Dan always had a knack for working with his hands. It was a passion he'd acquired as a young boy, watching his father in the garage, handing him tools while his dad taught him the fine art of woodworking. He'd built his own wedding bed with his father's guidance, somehow managing to keep the project a secret until just before the wedding. Later, he'd built the accompanying dresser, chest of drawers, and armoire.

He still remembered the tears of joy Andrea had shed when he presented her with each piece.

"Well, then, I'd be honored. Looks like you have a sound business going. You've come a long way, man." He punched him in the arm in a playful manner.

"Not all on my own. Like I said, I'll have you start out at Oakwood Square. I'll probably put you there for the next several weeks. I have those two houses going up, and I could use your expertise about now, especially with that oversized brick ranch I showed you this morning. Got a lot of detail work coming up with cabinetry, shelving, some built-ins. One thing I've lacked so far is a detail man, so I'm glad you're coming on board."

"Thanks, Greg." He paused slightly, his hand on the car door. "I want to thank you for something. I noticed that you hardly brought up the matter of my past. I appreciate that. I was wondering, do the other guys know about, you know, that I was a pastor?"

Greg looked Dan squarely in the eye then shook his head. "I didn't think it was necessary to let anyone in on your private affairs. I figure you have some things to work out in your life, and when you feel like talking, you will."

"I appreciate that—probably more than you know." Dan opened his door and prepared to climb inside, but Greg touched his shoulder before he had the chance.

"Let me just say, strictly as a friend, God loves you, Dan, and He's pretty patient about these kinds of things. I know I don't have to remind a preacher about God's love, but on the chance you're having a few doubts right now, well, just hang in there. He waited around a good long time for me. I lived a wild life in high school and college. Then God caught hold of me, thanks to my wife's Christian example. At least you didn't waste your college years as I did.

"I can only imagine what you're going through right now. I won't try to guess it or pry it out of you, but if you ever need to talk, you know where to find me." He smiled at Dan, dropped his hand, then turned and walked back to his office.

Dan stood watching his friend from his car, stunned by his words. For some reason he had figured Greg Freeman to be the last person on earth to turn to God. Wonder of wonders. Maybe God did still work the occasional miracle.

Callie worked on routine tasks all day Monday. Laundry, vacuuming, and dusting took up the bulk of her day. Then, while Emily slept, she wiped down cupboards, scoured out sinks, and cleaned the bathrooms.

A middle school English teacher, she cherished her summers, those months that allowed her to stay ahead of the game where housework was concerned, not to mention the treasured extra time with Emily. She loved her career, but summers and holiday vacations were a definite bonus.

She'd been living in this apartment for almost four years now, ever since she and Thomas had signed the lease together, and might have considered moving after their separation and divorce, but good apartments were hard to come by these days.

This particular apartment complex was situated adjacent to a development of nice homes, the neighborhood quiet and secluded. It was also conveniently located near shopping plazas and grocery stores, so finding anything comparable would have been nearly impossible.

At first, it'd been fun decorating the apartment with her husband, but it wasn't long before his enthusiasm petered out. His tastes were extravagant, probably a retaliation against his meager upbringing, so his mood soured when she wouldn't allow their budget to be stretched. Right from the beginning, money was a sore spot, even though Callie made every effort to comply with his wishes. She'd had to learn the hard way what it cost to disregard them.

He'd been an attentive husband in those early months, but his attention span never extended much beyond his self-absorbed concerns; when things didn't go his way, he often protested in the cruelest manner. In retrospect, Callie should have seen the end coming. To anyone else it must have been as clear as red paint on a white wall, but Callie had kept up her front, always hopeful and optimistic that things would one day turn around.

She reached across the kitchen countertop where she wiped down the final remnants of bread crumbs left over from a late lunch and switched on the radio, turning to a Christian station and catching the tail end of one of her favorite talk shows, this particular segment covering the aspects of single parenting.

Lisa's words of God's love rang loudly in her memory. If only she'd taken a different road right from the start—with God at the center—perhaps she wouldn't be in this predicament, almost twenty-nine, divorced, struggling to pay her debts, and raising an eight-month-old baby by herself.

"Try letting go of your struggles and watch God step in," Pastor Tim had said in his Sunday morning sermon.

Let go and let God....Let go and let God....

The words replayed in her head, seeming to gnaw a hole through the center of her heart, sneaking past the hardened parts and sinking in where she felt most open and vulnerable. What would it mean to surrender everything to God?

Late afternoon sun shone bright, its golden rays casting a rainbow of color through the living room window. When Callie walked across the room to slant the blinds, she looked down and spotted her new neighbor crawling out of his little black car, his muscular frame unfolding lazily like a bear too big for its own cage. She didn't care for the man. In fact, memories of their last encounter still rankled. That explained her humiliation when he looked up and caught her watching him. In less than a second, she closed the blinds altogether.

At four-thirty, Emily awoke from her afternoon nap. Since the sky was cloudless and Callie's work was done, she decided on a trip to the pool. Emily would love it. She always giggled with glee at her first glimpse of the water.

As expected, the pool was wonderful, crystal clear and warm as bath water. Four teenage girls swam enthusiastically, bantering back and forth about boys, fashion, and the latest movies. They smiled cordially when she and Emily entered the pool, one girl offering a friendly greeting. "Your daughter is a doll."

"Thank you," Callie said. "I'll soon be in the market for babysitters. Do you girls live in these apartments?"

"Oh, we don't all live here," the girl responded. "These are my friends from another neighborhood. But I live in Building C. Where do you live?"

"In this building," Callie answered, pointing to the one closest to the pool.

The girls nodded, then went back into their huddle, talking quietly before beginning a game of Marco Polo. They seemed to be having fun, and Emily, in a world all her own, enjoyed experiencing the water at her own pace, her mother's safe hold on her all the while, little giggles and squeals of delight erupting every few moments.

"Enjoying the water?" The low, gravelly voice

came from behind. She turned to find her neighbor approaching the pool, tall and handsome in his swimming trunks. A sigh slipped past her mouth, but she determined not to let poor manners give way to annoyance. Had he seen them swimming from his deck and intentionally come down to taunt her?

"It's lovely, thank you," she replied, nice as could be, but taking care not to acknowledge him with a smile.

"Still no husband?" He stood at the entrance to the pool then threw a towel to the nearest chair.

She stiffened and threw back her shoulders, dipping Emily down lower and then back up again. The child expressed her joy by way of splashing her hands on the water and smiling from ear to ear.

"He's—unavailable." That much was true.

"He must work second shift, huh? Haven't seen him around yet."

He threw her a crooked grin, accompanied by a cocky expression. She grimaced and turned away, trying to give Emily her undivided attention as she twirled her around in the shallow water.

"Hello, ladies." Every girl in the pool appeared to have lost her ability to talk, all staring wide-eyed as the newcomer lowered himself into the pool, his tanned, muscled frame making ripples on the water's surface.

Finally, one screwed up the courage to speak. "Are you that new guy that moved into *her* building?" She glanced at Callie and then turned her full attention back to him. Callie moved to the other side of the pool, feigning ignorance.

"I wasn't aware it was *hers*," he answered.

"Well, you know what I mean." The teen giggled self-consciously, pumping her arms idly in the water and making little waves.

"Well, then I guess I'm the man. Nice day, huh?" His tone was pleasant enough, and the girls were amply entertained. They nodded, gushed with smiles and more giggles, and eyed him as they might some teen idol.

Callie tried to think of an inconspicuous way to exit the pool, then rethought her position. After all, she'd arrived first. She told herself she could simply ignore him.

"Hello, Emily," he said, wading over to them. Then again, maybe she couldn't ignore him altogether. The baby gave him a curious stare, apparently unsure of the wary stranger, but not putting up a fuss either. "You don't remember me, do you? Just as well." He laughed lightly, the sound a low rumble coming from his chest. She noticed he looked Emily in the eye, but thankfully kept his distance. "She truly is a cute kid," he remarked.

"Thank you."

"Looks like her mom." He grinned and took off to the deep end, his strokes smooth, his face dipping in and then coming up for air with every other upward sweep of the arm. At the other end he poked his head under the water, gave a quick kick of his foot, and set off toward the end of the pool again, repeating the process several times until Callie wondered how he had the strength to continue. He didn't speak a word for the next twenty minutes, his concentration on swimming laps becoming his entire focus. Even the girls tired of watching him after a while, and once they climbed the stairs to leave, Callie quickly followed suit, never once acknowledging her departure. If he noticed, he did not attempt to say good-bye.

The following summer days were anything but lazy. On Tuesday, Callie took a trip to the Department of Motor Vehicles to renew her driver's license, her twenty-ninth birthday a mere two weeks away. She'd been a Fourth of July baby, her father always teasing her right from the start about being his "little firecracker." Because Callie was an only child, her parents cherished and coddled her to extremes. Her mother, recently retired from her secretarial duties at a local elementary school, willingly babysat Emily while Callie renewed her license and then invited them to stay for supper.

She used Wednesday for going through file cabinets, which turned out to be an all-day job. She'd discovered some delinquent bills Thomas had tucked away in a drawer, which explained why bill collectors had hounded her just months ago. She'd claimed to have never received the bills but wound up paying them anyway when they reissued new statements. One was a late payment for Thomas's motorcycle, another was an overdue rent statement for his bike shop, along with a nasty threat of eviction, and still another was an overdue credit card statement. What had he done with all the cash she'd handed him to deposit in the bank?

An unmarked manila folder was tucked at the back of a drawer, and inside, Callie found a blank envelope. Shaking fingers folded back the creased flap and yanked out a perfumed missive. What she discovered generated new waves of regret.

Dear Tom, it read, *I miss you more than you will ever know. When can we see each other again? Please tell me you meant every word you said to me the other night. I will die if I discover that you….*

The letter continued, but the first few lines were all Callie needed to read before she ripped it up and threw it into the nearest trash container.

How many women had her husband strung along while they were married?

She'd taken Emily to the pool twice more that week, successfully evading the new neighbor both times. She had strategically planned out her times, making a point to go when his car was nowhere in sight. Frankly, she wasn't sure what he did with his time, nor did she care. She didn't even know his first name, although the mailbox downstairs said D. Mattson. It could be David, Derek, Dirk, or Doug, but she'd given up guessing.

On Friday afternoon, after laundering and putting away Emily's blankets then ironing a couple of shirts, she decided on another trip to the pool. The child had smeared her lunch all over herself, and so the pool seemed a likely place to clean her up.

"Want to go to the pool, kiddo?"

"Maaa-aaaa!" Emily had taken to squealing her mother's name with delight whenever she heard the word "pool." Her arms and legs flailed in anticipation as soon as Callie released her from the highchair, her loud yipping noises enough to deafen her momentarily.

"Pool?"

"Maaa-aaaa!" More squealing.

"All right, I get the message. That pool seems to be your favorite place."

"Maaa-aaaa!"

Minutes later, Callie was fumbling with a diaper bag, a beach towel, a rubber ducky, Emily's favorite doll, and her apartment key.

The door across the hall opened at the same moment that Emily grabbed the doll from her mother's grasp and tossed it to the floor.

"Emily!" Callie scolded, bending to retrieve the doll. But a large capable hand beat her to the task, tucking the doll under Callie's chin, which was the only available place, given the rest of her paraphernalia. Emily quickly grabbed the doll and held it to her tiny chest.

"Want me to lock the door for you?" There stood her tall, strapping neighbor, donned in workout gear, his deep brown eyes penetrating her blue ones.

Callie stretched her short frame, stuck out her

chin, and slid her shoulders back. "I can manage, thank you."

"No, you can't."

"Yes, I..." He snatched the key from her hand, locked the door, and dropped it back into her open beach bag.

"There. Was that so bad?"

"Thanks," she said weakly.

Emily's doll lay nestled close to her, but she surprisingly gave it up for his inspection. He chuckled to himself after flipping it over. "Either she actually likes this, or you can't afford a new one." Both eyebrows scrunched, and a grin found its way to the corners of his mouth, creating deep creases on either side that might have been classified as dimples, had they been closer to the centers of his cheeks.

She laughed lightly, still facing him. "Amazing, isn't it? You spend money on a new toy, and they prefer old junk. I should have thrown this doll away long ago."

"But she might never forgive you if you did." He gingerly placed it back in Emily's outstretched hands. She quickly hugged it again, keeping a wary eye on the stranger.

Callie headed down the stairs and noticed he came alongside her, reaching the door at the landing ahead of her and pulling it open. She walked past him, giving him a polite nod.

"Heading for the pool, I see."

"Yes."

"So your husband works while you girls have all the fun, eh?" The glint in his eye put her senses on immediate alert. Why did he insist on questioning her about her private life? She could do the same for him. Not once had she seen a woman come or go from his apartment. Was he, too, divorced—or simply never married? And the notion that the question even crossed her mind rankled plenty.

"My husband is…" But she found herself unable to finish the lie.

"Never mind. I shouldn't be asking why he lets two such pretty ladies out of his sight on a regular basis. Matter of fact, I've never even run across the man." His gaze focused on the simple gold band on her left hand.

On instinct, she shifted her hand, making viewing the ring impossible. One would think its presence would send a clear message to any interested male it wasn't "hunting season." That was, after all, her primary reason for wearing it.

"Excuse me, Mr. Mattson."

"Oh, I see you've checked out my mailbox." He chuckled, clearly an attempt to goad her.

She turned on her heel, mortified that she'd let the name slip past her lips.

"Have fun at the pool, *Mrs.* May," he called. "I checked yours, too."

She kept her pace steady, taking care not to look back.

That weekend, Dan sorted through paperwork, organized files, drawers, and cabinets, and arranged his den exactly the way he wanted it. He'd decided to convert what would have been a guest bedroom into a private office. In the event that a family member ever decided to visit, he could always invest in a futon. However, the likelihood of that happening seemed remote, at best. Right now, he felt at odds with his family, his leaving the ministry and pulling out of Michigan a mystery to them all.

He hung a golf picture on one wall, stuck a vase of flowers on a flat stack of books, and carefully arranged some old softball trophies on a shelf of the oak bookcase he'd brought. He'd also dug an earthy looking rag rug out of one of the trunks he'd packed and thrown it across the hardwood floor, pleased with the masculine look it afforded.

After giving the place an admiring glance, Dan headed to the kitchen to make a pot of coffee. He was filling the carafe with water when the phone rang. There were four phone jacks scattered about, but so far, he'd only hooked up two phones, one in the bedroom and one in the kitchen. The office was a definite must, he told himself, yanking up the phone on the third ring.

"Dan Mattson, here," he said, clearing his throat.

"Hi, honey. It's Mom. How are you doing?"

"Hi, Mom."

It was the first they'd talked since he'd arrived in Oakdale last Saturday. He'd felt like a teenager checking in from college, but she'd insisted he call just as soon as he settled in, and he'd complied with her to appease her. "I'm fine. How are you and Dad?"

"Good. We're doing just fine. Are you enjoying your new apartment?"

He wouldn't have put it exactly that way. "Sure, it's fine. How are Sam and John?" Better to change the subject altogether. His little sister Samantha always made for great conversation.

"Oh, they're just fine. Sam's up for a flute solo in the city orchestra. Did I tell you that?"

"Really? That's great to hear. She'll be a hit."

"The concert's this Saturday night at Cochran Hall. Last I heard there were only a few seats remaining."

He knew what she was doing. "Mom, I can't come."

"Well, I thought you might like…"

"Another time, maybe."

"It'd be nice to show your support."

"Sam knows I'm proud of her. I'll send her an e-mail."

A brief pause ensued. He figured his mother needed a moment or two to pout. "How has that—construction job been going?" she finally asked.

"I like it fine," he said. "Greg's a great guy." So far, he'd enjoyed his work, the labor intensive enough to tire him out at the end of the day.

With the phone to his ear, his eyes drifted to a framed photo of Andrea and Chelsea. Absently, he picked up the photo, studying it while his mother droned on about his nephew Joshua's little league game and twin brother Justin's soccer tournament. Dan's mom and dad had attended both games, Josh's team winning, Justin's losing by three points. The twins belonged to his brother, Ken, whose entire family was big on sports of every kind. A part of him missed the excitement of cheering on his nephews. Under normal circumstances, he and Andrea wouldn't have missed a chance to watch the boys.

However, things were anything but normal these days, and he'd wallowed in solitude and self-pity. No more airs to put on, no more false pretenses. In the end, he'd gotten too tired of playing the game, pretending he was fine when on the inside he was dying. To preserve his sanity he'd had to pull away from it all.

"How is that boy, by the way? You two used to be quite inseparable."

"Greg? He's great."

"He was a polite young man—at least in my presence."

He couldn't help but chuckle at her add-on. "Yeah, he had a real gift for making good impressions."

Carefully, he placed the dusted photograph back in its proper place, then took the can of coffee out of the cupboard and flipped off the plastic lid. A nearby spoon served as a coffee scoop. He dipped it into the can, tossed some grounds into the filter, and hit the "on" switch. Within seconds, the coffee began dripping slowly into the carafe. And still his mother talked.

"Dad and I used to worry about you two. Gregory got you into more than one scrape."

"I hate to tell you this, Mom, but it wasn't all Greg." He heard the soft rumble of laughter on the other end and leaned into the sound. "In fact, he reminded me about that jail incident we got involved in. I was driving that night, if you'll recall."

"Oh, my word! I thought your father was going to strangle your neck that night. I had to do a lot of fast-talking on the way to the station."

"Did I ever thank you for saving my life?"

"Not in so many words."

"Well then, thanks." There'd been other narrow escapes with the law that his parents knew nothing about. He and Greg had made many a pact to keep their mouths shut.

"Has that boy settled down any? Or do I have cause for more worry?"

He grinned at her tone. "Mom, I'm thirty-one years old. You can quit with the worrying."

"Are you kidding? A mother's worries only grow with her children."

Another time he might have preached an entire message about laying one's worries and concerns at the foot of the cross, but he figured a rather backslidden pastor had few rights to preach to his mother—or to anyone, for that matter.

"And you didn't answer my question. Has that boy reformed—or is he still a wild child?"

"I couldn't tell you for sure. We didn't get into a lot of personal talk." He wasn't about to mention he was fairly certain Greg Freeman was a transformed man.

"Oh, you men are all alike. What does he have you doing, anyway?"

"At the moment I'm installing cabinets and building shelves. Some of the work is tedious, but I like it."

"You'll have to fill us in when you come home," she said.

Home? He wasn't even sure where home was anymore. When he failed to respond, his mother filled the awkward moment with questions about his apartment, to which he gave short answers.

He asked about his father, a public accountant; she said he was keeping busy. "When's he going to retire?"

"Not soon enough. He loves that office. If he'd retire, he could spend more time on his woodworking hobby. Heaven knows I keep telling him I want a new armoire, like the one you built Andrea. I suppose if I stop nagging...."

She chuckled lightly, skimming over the mention of Andrea's name. Most everyone tiptoed around her memory. Sudden irritation rose up inside Dan. He grabbed a nearby dishcloth and wiped a few crumbs to the floor, something Andrea would have chided him for doing.

After another lull, he had to strain to hear her next words. "I'm praying for you, sweetie. Maybe the ministry wasn't for you. Maybe we pushed you in the direction of ministry—Grandma Mattson, especially."

For the most part, Dan had enjoyed the profession, but even as a senior pastor, he often questioned if he was there because of God's call on his life or because his grandma had insisted that the Mattsons needed a minister in the family. He remembered well the day he'd accepted Christ into his life. It was at Renewal, the weeklong series of meetings at the Christian college he'd attended in Michigan, midway through his sophomore year.

When he'd called his grandmother to affirm his decision, she'd exclaimed, "Well, glory be! Now we know why God sent you to that school. You'll be a minister of the Word. I always knew it, son. Ever since you were a little boy."

"You're not turning your back on God, are you?" his mother asked, interrupting his thoughts.

His spine straightened, as a chill ran up its length. "Mom, I really have to go now. I have a slew of things to do. Tell Dad hey for me. Love you both."

After a few closing words, they bid each other an awkward goodbye. He suspected his mother knew she'd pushed the envelope.

The evening air matched his mood. Steamy. He ran until sweat poured like water down his arms and legs, his forehead dripping like a leaky faucet, blinding his vision, so that he had to keep swiping his eyes with the little towel he'd stuffed into his belt loop. Head down, he counted cracks in the sidewalk, evading walkers and bicyclists, keeping a fast, relentless pace, his running shoes pounding out a steady rhythm on the dry, hot pavement.

Up ahead, he glimpsed a woman pushing her child in a stroller. He moved aside before he recognized the lady. It was *Mrs.* May. He told himself to keep on running, to pretend he didn't see her.

Nevertheless, he slowed. "Hi," he said, gasping for breath, yet trying to sound in command of his body. He yanked the towel from his belt loop and swiped his face again.

She looked him up and down, taking in his sweat-soaked appearance. "Do you always run at that pace when it's ninety degrees out?"

"It's not that hot."

"It feels it."

"Yeah, I do," he said. "Rain or shine."

"You'll suffer from heatstroke."

"Nah." While he fought to snag an even breath, he watched her. Her demeanor hadn't changed. She still showed signs of insecurity. Did her husband, if there was one, contribute to that?

Her own face glowed with traces of perspiration. He wouldn't call her beautiful, but her wispy blonde hair, sharp little nose, plump lips, and attractive figure conjured Andrea's beauty—and caused him to want to prolong his admiring gaze.

It was definitely time for a change of thought, so he squatted down and rested one arm across his bent knee, coming face-to-face with Emily. "Hello there, jellybean," he said.

Her light blonde hair, swept back with an array of silver barrettes, blew in the gentle breeze. She studied him carefully, clutching tightly to her doll as if her life depended on it, and for the first time, Dan noticed that it was missing an eye. Her unusual attachment to the ratty thing was almost comical. He tried to recall if Chelsea had had a favorite toy, and when he couldn't remember, a sort of dull pain rose up in his chest.

A string of baby words spewed from Emily's mouth, after which she charmed him with a smile. He nabbed her bare toes and gently squeezed, then stood up, fastening his eyes on her mother. "What a little doll." *And you're not so bad yourself,* he couldn't help adding silently.

As if she'd read his thoughts, Callie shifted on her sandaled feet and gave a tentative smile, inching the stroller forward. "Well—don't keel over with heat exhaustion."

"You're not worried, are you?" He was curious if the pink in her cheeks would change a deeper shade, but she started walking before he had a chance to judge.

"No more than I would be for anyone else crazy enough to run in this heat," she shot back without so much as a glance his way.

He laughed outright. "See you around, Mrs. May."

She ignored the remark and kept walking, spine straight as a pin, shoulders back.

He stared at her until she disappeared around a corner. Good grief, what was he doing? The woman wore a wedding ring, for Pete's sake!

He gulped down a heavy dose of hot air and hit the pavement again, this time picking up his pace, determined to wipe both little blondes from his mind for the last time.

That night, Dan dove into a novel he'd been putting off. A political thriller by one of his favorite authors, it was mixed with international intrigue and plenty of action. He should have enjoyed the opportunity to unwind with a good book after the busy week he'd just put in, but somehow he'd lost the ability to relax; his mind kept trailing off to faraway places and fleeting glimpses of the past.

These days, it didn't take much to stir up old memories. Sometimes a simple smell like fried eggs in the morning or a song on the radio triggered some stored recollection. How long before he could think about his girls without that sorrowful pang stinging his heart?

A baby's cry had his thoughts running in another direction. *Emily.* He glanced at his digital watch, which read 10:30 p.m. *Shouldn't the kid be sleeping?* Maybe this was her fussy period.

He remembered them well, those nights when neither he nor Andrea could do anything right. If Chelsea had a mind to fuss, they'd figured they might as well learn to live with it. Sometimes it resulted from a sore stomach, sore gums, or just a sore attitude. Who could know?

He waited for more squeals from across the hall, but if any came, he couldn't hear them. Her mother had probably settled her down, he decided—or maybe her dad—even though he had yet to see one.

Annoyed with himself, he flung the book to the coffee table and headed for bed.

Saturday morning arrived with clouds and the threat of thunderstorms. True, they needed rain, but Callie was hoping it would hold off at least until she had finished running errands. Getting Emily in and out of her car seat was no fun in a downpour. On her agenda were trips to the post office, bank, nearest gas station, and food mart. Each stop required a good deal of maneuvering—climbing in and climbing out, fastening and unfastening.

Fortunately, Emily was good-natured—as long as it

wasn't her nap time. Even more reason for Callie to get a jump-start on the day.

If Emily's mood held out, Callie also wanted to make a stop at the local library. Lately, her Bible reading had inspired her in ways she'd not imagined possible, the book of Philippians especially encouraging her heart and mind. Paul, the apostle responsible for authoring the book, daily challenged her to rejoice and thank God in the midst of trials and heartache. This man was able to do it from a prison cell while chained to a post for days on end. Shouldn't she be able to do it from an isolated apartment where she lived with her beautiful daughter?

But where would one find the strength and courage to trust God as deeply as Paul did? Was his faith some kind of supernatural gift, or was it available to her, as well?

Today she would look for a book about this man, Paul. Maybe her searching would lead her to some answers for her own set of problems.

"Rejoice in the Lord always. I will say it again: Rejoice! Let your gentleness be evident to all. The Lord is near. Do not be anxious about anything, but in everything, by prayer and petition, with thanksgiving, present your requests to God. And the peace of God, which transcends all understanding, will guard your hearts and your minds in Christ Jesus."

She'd copied a passage of verses from Philippians that had both encouraged and challenged her, and she taped it to her bathroom mirror as a constant reminder.

How wonderful it would be if I could truly claim that passage—Philippians 4:4–7—*as mine,* she thought. *And how wonderful to be able to do what it commands!*

The phone rang just as she turned the knob to head out the door with Emily. She turned around and snatched up the receiver. It was Lisa. "Hi! I hope you remembered our date tonight," she said.

"Are you kidding?" asked Callie. "I've been looking forward to it all week!" She adjusted the baby on her hip, then decided to place her on the floor with one of her toys, keeping one eye on her as she talked. "What time are you coming?"

"What time did you tell your babysitter to come?" Lisa asked.

"Six—unless she hears differently."

"Perfect! I'll be there at six o'clock on the dot!" Callie laughed to herself. It was common knowledge—and a long-standing joke—that Lisa would never be there "on the dot." She was dependably late to almost everything.

They chatted a few more minutes before hanging up, Callie thinking as she scooped up Emily how excited she was about the prospect of going out with her friend.

The hot air was unusually moist and heavy. With Emily in her arms, Callie made the jaunt to her rusty car then promptly stopped in her tracks. Why did it always seem Mr. Mattson had the uncanny ability to appear from nowhere?

He leaned idly against his late model black Mustang and intently watched her approach. *Too intently.* With muscular arms crossed casually and one ankle resting atop the other, his self-satisfied expression made her otherwise cheerful mood take a nosedive.

Well, she wasn't about to let him ruffle her this time. She resumed her stride, talking quietly to Emily as if she hadn't a care in the world.

With keys out and ready, she planned to unlock Emily's side first to avoid any confrontation. *As if that would happen,* she mulled silently, particularly because his car sat next to hers.

"Looks like rain." If that was his way of saying hello, she figured she could safely ignore him. It wasn't as if he'd greeted her. She unlocked the front passenger door, reached inside, and quickly flipped the button to unlock the back door, which she opened, and bent to put Emily in the backseat.

"There you go, sweetheart," she said, securing the seat buckle. She stood up, only to collide with the man's broad chest. It couldn't have felt more like a brick wall if it had actually been one. "Excuse me," she mumbled, rattled by his nearness.

"You sure that car seat would pass legal inspection?" he asked, steadying her with both hands while ignoring the apology. She stepped away from his disconcerting touch and considered Emily's car seat.

"Granted, it's an older model, but it serves its purpose."

He raised one brow. "You buy it at an antique sale or something?"

"A garage sale, thank you. Not that it is any of your business." She chided herself for blurting information so freely. The terms of the divorce settlement meant money was tight, but divulging hints of financial hardship to a stranger went against her grain.

When she moved to the driver's side, she was dismayed to discover she'd left her keys sprawled on the front seat. *Great.* Of course, he was right behind her. "Excuse me," she said, turning.

"Never mind. I'll get 'em for you," he offered, jogging to the other side, opening the passenger door, and reaching across to unlock her door. "There you go."

"Thanks," she mumbled, crawling inside her less than immaculate car, embarrassed to realize he'd probably spotted the soiled napkins, empty baby bottles, and numerous toys on the floor.

She reached for the door handle, but he quickly blocked it. She heaved a sigh and glared at him. "Do you mind?" she asked.

He folded his arms across his massive chest. Bottomless, deep brown eyes seemed to look into her soul. "The husband must have left extra early, huh? He work on Saturdays, too?"

"Mr. Mattson, I wish you'd quit mentioning my—husband."

"Dan—you can call me Dan. What should I call you?"

"Mrs. May."

One of his dark eyebrows arched higher than the other. "So you *are* married." He pulled back slightly but kept his hold on the door.

Rather than answer, Callie merely clutched the steering wheel with both hands, wishing she could disappear.

"Why is it I've never run into the guy?" The question came out sounding husky.

"Mr. Mattson…"

"Dan."

"Mr. Mattson to me. I'd rather not discuss my husband. Now, please release my door."

He leaned closer. "Because there isn't one to discuss?"

She bristled, drew back her shoulders, and narrowed her eyes to mere slits, staring straight ahead. Would he never let up?

Finally, she drew up the courage to ask, "Why can't you leave me alone?" She heard the clog of her own voice and was embarrassed for having revealed her delicate emotions.

"I don't know." At least he was honest. "I'm not trying to bother you, but it's just that you seem rather skittish about this subject. Where is Mr. May?" he asked more gently, dipping his head closer to hers. "Where's Emily's father?"

"It's really none of your business, you know," she said, fingers tapping nervously on the steering wheel.

"I know that." His voice had lowered to a mere whisper by this time. "But I still want to know."

She heaved a sigh of resignation. "All right, if you must know—he left us, okay?"

"He left you? As in, he skipped town?"

"Basically," she answered matter-of-factly.

"So, you're divorced?"

"Yes. Are you happy now?"

He stood up and held the door with one hand, the other hand splayed on the roof of her car. "Not really. Divorce is a sad thing. Why do you still wear your wedding ring?"

"To advertise to men like you that I'm off-limits," she said with a dose of sarcasm.

"Off-limits? You think I...?"

"Never mind what I think. Would you please let go of my door?"

"Does he live nearby? Ever see his daughter?"

"No, he's in Florida."

"Florida?" His brow wrinkled, as dark, searing eyes showed disbelief. "Whew! Florida's a long way from here."

She made a clicking noise with her tongue and the roof of her mouth. "Were you always so good in geography?"

He flashed her one of his grins. "You're getting sassier, you know that?"

She laughed in spite of herself. "And you're nosy, so we're even."

He gave her a sidelong glance. "I like inquisitive better than nosy. Sounds nicer."

She shook her head. "Doesn't suit you quite as well."

He laughed. "What's your first name, Mrs. May?"

She went for the ignition. "I'll tell you on one condition, and that is that you unhand my door."

"Deal. You first." He seemed very pleased with himself.

"My full name is McCallister, and don't laugh."

"Why would I laugh? It's a nice name."

She relaxed some. "It's an old family name," she explained. "On my grandfather's side. My friends call me Callie, though—never McCallister. Ugh."

"Your friends, huh?"

"That's right, my friends."

His grin angled with mischief. "Does that mean you're still *Mrs.* May to me?" He stepped back, finally releasing her door.

"Absolutely."

She started the engine, after which he released her door. Shutting it, she backed out, and quickly moved forward, taking loose gravel with her. At the parking lot exit, she glanced in her rearview mirror.

He was still standing where she'd left him, arms folded, watching as she drove away.

Dust gradually settled where the wheels of her car had only moments ago kicked up gravel and debris. Dan watched until the rattletrap vehicle disappeared from view and then turned away.

He was beginning to hate the person he'd become—wearing down this woman with his questions, forcing her to tell him things he had no business knowing. She was right to call him nosy. Whether or not she was married should have made no difference to him—and yet somehow it did.

His gaze followed a trail to a party store across the way. In big neon letters, the word LIQUOR flashed in the store's front window. Since his parents never stocked alcohol, in his younger days, he'd used a fake ID card to purchase it, sneaked it from friends' refrigerators, or paid older kids extra money to buy it legally. Everyone did it, they'd all reasoned, and the wild parties were downright fun. If his parents questioned his whereabouts the next day, he'd say he fell asleep on Greg's sofa watching videos. Most times, they swallowed his lies—or so he thought.

Even after high school, when his parents insisted he attend a Christian college in their hopes of reforming him, he'd given the dean of students a run for his money. Known for pushing his professors, guidance counselors, and residence advisors to their limits, he had been issued more than one warning regarding his rebellious behavior. He'd somehow managed to hide the drinking from them, but his failure to abide by the campus rules made for a "bad boy" reputation. For that reason, his conversion at the Renewal conference in his sophomore year created a tremendous impact around campus. He was a natural leader, and his transformed life had spurred others into making the same decision.

Now look at me, he thought. He was ogling the party store across the way and longing for a drink, something he'd given up long ago, knowing the unhealthy hold it'd had on his life. Addiction ran deep in his family line—a couple of uncles on both sides of the family and some of his cousins had fallen prey to alcoholism. A great-grandfather had even died of some liver ailment, which most now attributed to his strong bent for alcohol.

"My Lord, what's become of me?" He muttered a desperate prayer and sauntered back to his apartment, his original plan to wash his car abandoned with the first drops of rain.

൞

Callie checked Emily's Winnie the Pooh clock. She still had five minutes before Lisa's proposed arrival time. She'd be late, of course. As sure as it had rained all day, soaking Emily and Callie both while they ran their errands, Lisa would be late. Callie smiled to herself as she stacked one more diaper on the neat pile beside Emily's crib, set the baby powder on the dresser where the sitter would find it, and folded several freshly laundered sleep sets before tucking them away in a drawer.

Satisfied, she moved to the kitchen, noting Emily on the floor, surrounded on all sides by toys and plastic books. Scurrying about, Callie wiped the countertop one last time, straightened a few items, checked the refrigerator for snacks, and rinsed a few dishes before putting them in the dishwasher.

When the doorbell buzzed, she expected to see the babysitter. She hurried to the door and flung it wide open, surprised to find Dan Mattson towering over her instead. The tiniest spark of pleasure ignited within her chest, but she mentally extinguished it.

His left eyebrow rose a fraction. "Did you even take the time to look through that peephole before you opened your door?"

"Excuse me?"

"You can't be too trusting these days," he drawled, pushing his hands into the pockets of his cargo shorts. Her eyes froze on his powerful frame. From top to bottom, he was certainly handsome—and she could have kicked herself for noticing. "You should be using your dead bolt, too," he added.

"I was expecting someone, and it certainly wasn't you."

Unfazed, Dan continued, "Well, whether you're expecting someone or not, you should at least ask who it is before you open the door."

"I wish I had," she muttered. He looked casually amused. She rested her head against the door, her hand clutching the doorknob. "Is there something I can do for you, or are you just here to lecture me about safety precautions?"

A flash of humor splashed across his face. "Actually, I came over to apologize." Now she was interested. "You were right to call me nosy earlier today. I had no business prying into your life, and if I offended you with my questions, well, I'm sorry."

"Oh—well, okay." Strangely disarmed, she put her hands on her hips and tried to focus on just why the man had irritated her so. "Apology accepted."

"Friends?" Lo and behold, he extended a hand with his one-word request, and since she couldn't rally quick enough to protest taking it, she placed her hand in his and felt it curl warmly around hers. There was barely a shake to accompany it, however, so she quickly withdrew, feeling strangely giddy.

"That should authorize me to call you Callie, I would think." He dipped his head slightly, gifting her with a warm smile.

Taking a moment to study him, she realized she still knew next to nothing about her neighbor, other than the fact he'd had a quick temper upon their first meeting. Granted, he was easy on the eyes, but aside from his good looks, common sense told her to stay clear of him. Thanks to her ex-husband, she'd learned a thing or two about men; number one, think twice before trusting another one; number two, if you think you're letting down your guard, run away as fast as you can and reconstruct it.

"As long as you realize I'm allowing it only because we're neighbors and nothing more," she relented.

He gave a matter-of-fact nod, his smile still firmly pasted in place. "Fair enough."

The door downstairs swung open as the babysitter walked in. "Come on up, Lori," Callie called down to her. "I'm still waiting for my friend, but she should be here soon."

Lori smiled, mouth shiny with braces, and gave a timid nod, then climbed the stairs and slipped past Dan without acknowledging him.

Callie moistened her lips, and looked at him. "Well, thanks for stopping by," she said, hoping he'd take the statement as a dismissal.

When he didn't budge, only peeked past her where Emily still contented herself on the floor with her toys, she shifted from one foot to the other, waiting for his next move. Just who was this Daniel Mattson—and why was he so inquisitive? Fleetingly, she wondered if he had children of his own. Was he divorced, never married, or simply detached?

"She sure is a sweet little kid," he remarked.

"Thanks. She keeps me busy." He seemed to comment about Emily every time they had a chance encounter. He seemed to like children, at least.

Callie looked around to see Lori kneeling on the floor beside Emily. The door downstairs opened again, and this time, Lisa appeared.

Callie braced herself, knowing Lisa would be full of questions about the handsome stranger in the hallway. "Hi, Lisa. Come on up. You're almost on time," she said with a chuckle.

Her friend ignored the mock insult, taking to the stairs like a puppy sniffing out a juicy bone. All smiles and warmth, she kept her eyes on Dan Mattson. "Hello," she greeted him, hand extended before she even reached the top step. "I'm Lisa Roberts. And you are…?"

Unleashed laughter rolled off his tongue like water off a duck's back as he took the hand offered him. "Dan Mattson. Nice to meet you, Lisa."

Tall and big-boned, Lisa was attractive and spry, always giving her husband, Jack, a run for his money. They'd been high school sweethearts and now, married almost ten years, were more in love than ever. Callie turned away to look at Lori and Emily. They were still entertaining one another.

"And where do you live?" Lisa was asking.

Dan poked a thumb backward.

Lisa's mouth dropped a notch as she looked from Callie to Dan. "Oh, my stars! Cal's neighbor? Callie, you didn't tell me you had a new neighbor—and so charming." She flashed Callie a chastising look, and if Callie had dared, she might well have given her friend a swift kick in the behind for her candor.

But Dan didn't act as if her forward behavior ruffled him. "Well, I doubt she's out there broadcasting the news."

Self-conscious, Callie shifted her gaze to Lisa. "We'd better get going, don't you think?"

"Well, you ladies have a good night," Dan said, stepping back.

"Thank you. I'm sure we will," Lisa answered, entering the apartment to stand beside Callie and watch him leave, jabbing her in the side as she did so. Callie ignored the nudge, smiling weakly when he chanced one final look at her before entering his apartment.

Once he'd shut his apartment door, Lisa exclaimed in wonder, "Oh, sweet land of liberty, that man is almost as good-looking as my Jack."

Callie laughed. "The way you were acting, he probably thought you were starved for male attention. Shame on you!"

"I flashed my wedding ring right in his face. Didn't you notice?"

"No, I didn't."

Lisa scowled. "Speaking of rings, when's yours coming off?"

The question stung. Callie twisted the plain gold band absently with her thumb. "Come on, Lisa. Don't start on me again."

"I'm just saying, you need to put things behind you. Maybe taking off that ring would be a good start."

"I'm thinking about it."

"Sweetie, he left you in the dust before Emily was even born. Don't you think it's time?"

She bristled at the truth. "I'll think about it. Don't rush me, okay?"

Lisa smiled. "Me?"

Later that night, Callie lay in bed, exhausted but emotionally replenished. Lisa's company had been good medicine, providing plenty of laughs, good conversation, and pure entertainment. After a hearty dinner, they'd taken in a chick flick, and then followed it up with dessert at a twenty-four-hour diner. Both girls joked about their full stomachs, saying they could never eat again—until breakfast.

Besides giving her a downright good time, being with Lisa had also afforded Callie the opportunity to talk about her lingering confusion, sadness, and sense of abandonment after the divorce. Added to these feelings was a sense of overwhelming guilt—didn't God condemn divorce in the Bible? Callie never thought she'd stray so far from His commands.

"Divorce is wrong, I'll give you that," Lisa had said. "God warns us about it in His Word. But you have to remember that He loves and forgives, Callie. And He never intended for you to endure such abuse. Nothing we do or say can possibly separate us from His love. Have you talked to God about your heartache?"

The question struck Callie as strange. Did God truly want to hear from her? Surely, her shortcomings disappointed Him. She had nothing to offer but brokenness, and she didn't want to be like all those others who went crying to God when they were in the throes of trouble, but then left Him as soon as everything started running smoothly again.

When Callie hesitated to respond, Lisa had reached her hand across the diner table and squeezed her arm. "You can't be responsible for Thomas's poor choices, Cal. God put within us all the will to make our own decisions. The question, is where will you go from here, and how will you respond to God's love and forgiveness?"

Callie shifted under her covers while her mind raced with uncertainty. "God," she finally whispered into the dark, pulling the warm comforter up snugly under her chin and staring up at the ceiling. "If You're listening to me, would You please show me the way back to You? And will You give me assurance that I'm forgiven for breaking our marriage covenant?"

In that moment, some kind of inexplicable peace blanketed her spirit, settling around her like a gentle breeze and calming her frayed nerves. Out of nowhere, Dan Mattson's face came to mind. Was he also seeking a place of safety and contentment, or was he one of those self-sufficient types who claimed he didn't need God?

Though she didn't see herself giving into the impulse to care the slightest bit, a tiny part of her yearned to know more about him. She squelched the feeling as soon as it surfaced.

The last thing she needed now was another man in her life.

∾

Across the hall, Dan lay in bed with a pounding headache and an embittered soul. The rancorous taste of alcohol still lingered in his throat, souring his stomach. He'd given in to temptation and walked across the highway to the liquor store he'd spotted earlier from the parking lot. Now he was paying for his spree by way of a splitting headache. He wasn't sure what had possessed him, other than that familiar desire to run from his pain. Holy smokes! He wasn't a kid anymore. On the other hand, maybe he was. *Maybe I'm just a big kid with a preacher's license.* He scoffed at his own depiction.

He'd thought apologizing to the woman next door might ease the turmoil thrashing in his gut, but it hadn't worked. If anything, seeing Callie earlier that evening only complicated matters, made him think things he had no business thinking—like what it might be like to kiss those pretty lips or hold her in his arms.

Andrea, how can I even have such thoughts when I still love you so much?

He rolled over and punched his pillow. "I don't have time for this," he groused, even as he pictured how Callie had looked in those baby blue shorts and shirt, freshly painted toes sticking out the ends of her strappy sandals, blonde hair tumbling loosely around her heart-shaped face. "Don't have time for soothing her fears." It didn't take a genius to figure out she didn't trust him. And who could blame her? Emily's father had abandoned them. Why should she trust another man?

*Andrea....Chelsea....*The two names meshed as one, wrapping around his head. *I couldn't protect them.*

He cursed into his pillow.

"I'm not drunk," he murmured while tugging the sheet over his shoulder. "Just a little tipsy, that's all."

And it was well into the night before Dan Mattson finally slept—tossing and turning, fighting hideous demons in his own strength, and forgetting what it was to call on God.

℘

The place was dark, hot, and sticky, the air thick with the stench of death.

Someone wailed in pain, but he couldn't find the source, couldn't make out the voice.

Clambering to reach it, he pushed past thorny bushes that snagged his clothing and cut his skin until his legs gave way and he fell in an exhausted heap.

Murky images had him struggling to his feet again, but knees too weak to keep him upright collapsed once more.

"Daniel, I need you. Please help me," a voice implored.

He knew that voice.

"Da-da." He knew that voice, as well.

Now he clawed the earth in search of something to grasp. Spiny roots jutted out. He clutched them in his fists, but they broke apart, blocking his path.

"I'm coming," he managed. "Hold on." With every ounce of strength he could muster, he dragged himself up, but the soggy ground and thick sheets of fog slowed his progress.

Extending his hand into the haze, he ordered, "Take my hand!"

"Daniel? Is it you?"

A scream ripped through the black veil of ambiguity while a baby's frantic cry sliced the night silence. "Andrea! Chelsea! I'm here."

He tried to put one foot in front of the other, but it was useless. Rain fell in torrents, drenching every inch of his being.

"God, why is this happening? Help us!"

Distant sirens reached his ears.

"Here!" he yelled. But no one came. "Here!"

Again, he tried to move, but sticky mire held him captive, and when he looked down to assess the problem, he was horrified, for thick, dark blood collected around his feet, covering his ankles, creeping ever higher.

"God!" he screamed.

"Take My hand," a gentle voice pleaded.

He looked around for someone to match the voice.

Confused, so confused.

"Take it," the voice ordered, gentle, yet firm.

How could he? There was no hand to grasp. If he reached out, it would have to be on sheer faith alone. How ridiculous to reach for an invisible hand.

"I—can't—see you."

"I am here, My child. Let Me help you."

Sweat now beaded his forehead, trailing down his body, mingling with the blood.

Sirens. Too loud for his ears to handle.

He reached out a hand and grasped a solid object, squeezed with all his might.

꩜

Suddenly, his eyes flew open to a blaring sound.

In his hand, he held his clock, its shrill alarm shattering the stillness.

Baffled, he looked around the room. Everything was as it was before—socks hanging over an open dresser drawer, a pair of running shoes in the middle of the floor, an assortment of magazines and books cluttering his bedside table. Sweat-soaked sheets were his only covering.

Fool! He hit the button on the back of the clock, tossed it to the floor with the rest of the muddle, and dropped back down on the bed.

Another nightmare. Would they never stop?

He clawed his fingers through his hair and then checked for blood. It'd been so real. All the voices, the crying, the darkness, the feeling of utter helplessness—it had all been so real.

For what felt like the hundredth time, he chastised himself for not going with his wife and daughter to visit her parents in Lansing that Saturday in late April. Andrea should have spent the night rather than drive back in that unforgiving rainstorm. Yet he remembered as clear as day how he'd asked her to return for Sunday morning services. It was an important Sunday. Several new couples were joining the church. A potluck luncheon would follow. It seemed imperative that the pastor's wife be present for the celebration.

Imperative to *him,* anyway.

Which made everything his fault. All of it.

"Let Me help you."

The mysterious voice of his dream found a pathway back to his mind. *God?*

Not ready to listen, he quickly ushered it back out. It would take more than some inexplicable voice in his head to convince him God still gave a rip.

He tossed the damp sheets off his body and hauled himself out of bed.

Chapter 7

Hazy days followed, one after another, the heat index climbing steadily along with the humidity. All across the state of Illinois, energy consumption increased as air conditioning units maximized their output. Little rain fell over the coming days, upping the threat of drought and forcing officials to declare a ban on excessive water use. Grass along the roadsides, not normally tended to, turned brown and straw-like, while wild flowers and other vegetation wilted away.

Callie and Emily spent more time at the pool, always waiting to go there until the sun began to set, so that the worst of the dangerous rays would have burned off earlier in the day. Sounds of splashing, laughing, and pleasant conversation filled the air every minute that the pool was open, as people dashed for its cool, refreshing waters.

It had been days since Callie had seen Dan Mattson; his apology was the last thing he'd said to her. It wasn't that she missed seeing him, but she had to admit that she was curious as to his whereabouts. From time to time, she heard his television or stereo; their incessant blaring made her question what it was he might be trying to drown out.

She knew he left early for work, because she'd once caught a glimpse of him walking to his car at six-thirty a.m. when she was up with Emily. He'd been dressed in worn-looking jeans, work boots, and a simple T-shirt. He was carrying a small sack, probably his lunch. Fleetingly, she'd wondered what he packed. Was it something homemade or prepackaged bachelor's fare?

She also knew he came home late and jogged most every night. Despite the heat wave that swept the state and parts of the nation and the dangers that went with it of possible heat exhaustion, the man was die-hard when it came to exercise. One night, she'd guiltily watched through the peephole in her door as he left and came back. The peephole he'd warned her to start using. He'd looked no worse for the wear on his return trip thirty minutes later, despite the sweat that poured down his tanned, muscled body. She guiltily jumped back when she thought he'd detected her watching, although it was a silly reaction. There was no way he could have spotted her from the hallway.

As the weeks passed, Emily advanced in leaps and bounds. She grasped hold of toys, picked up finger foods from her highchair tray, pulled herself up to walk around furniture, and laughed when she discovered how balls bounce. With every small victory, including new teeth, new words, or new sounds and silly antics, Callie's heart swelled with pride.

One afternoon while Emily napped, someone gave a quiet knock at the door. Forgetting to check the peephole in the door, Callie swung it wide and felt a surge of surprised pleasure at the sight of one of her coworkers.

"Amy Preston, what are you doing here?"

The young teacher gave a meek smile and offered up a floral gift bag, its handles tied together with a white ribbon, pink and yellow tissue paper bellowing out the top. "A few of us decided to put together a little care package," she said. "I'm the appointed bearer of gifts."

"What? You didn't have to…"

"We know."

Touched by the act of compassion, Callie's eyes misted over as she took the bag from Amy's hand. "Come in. Please."

Amy stepped inside and closed the door then followed Callie to the kitchen.

Callie peeked in the bag. "Open it," Amy urged.

With a flurry of excitement, she placed the bag on the counter, unloosed the ribbon to push past all the tissue, and hauled out a white basket housing several goodies, a home and garden magazine, a bottle of bath oil, some lotion, two scented candles, and a gourmet chocolate candy bar.

She smelled the candles first, then screwed the cap off the lotion for a whiff of its flowery scent. "Mmm," she murmured, looking heavenward. Next came the candy bar. "This is wonderful. Thank you so much."

Amy tipped her face so that her auburn-tinted hair brushed her shoulder, her smile eager and friendly. "I'm glad you like it. We've all been worried about you, wondering what we could do to make things a little better for you. Karen thought a bag of feminine things might lift your spirits." Karen Swanson was the history teacher whose classroom was across the hall from Callie's.

"She was right," Callie said, setting all the items on the countertop and preparing to fold up the bag when a card fell out and fluttered to the floor. "Oops—pardon my faux pas!" she said, stooping to retrieve it. "My mom used to have to remind me every year at my birthday to read my cards slowly before opening my presents, but I've never been good at that. When I see a present, my instinct is to rip into it."

Amy giggled. "Christmas is the worst."

Callie slipped a finger under the seal and opened the envelope, perusing the Hallmark card that contained a message of encouragement and the signatures of several female colleagues, all teachers she'd come to know well over the past six years. "Thank you," she said, swallowing hard to fend off the tears. "I never expected…"

"It was nothing. Now, come here." Amy extended her arms and pulled Callie into a warm embrace.

The women sipped on coffee and talked for the next half hour, Amy going into detail about a recent family vacation, the yard work that consumed her mornings, and the list of household jobs she'd promised herself she would accomplish before summer's end. Callie spoke mostly about Emily and the "joys" of single parenting.

"You amaze me. I can't imagine raising my two little squirts on my own," Amy said when Callie talked about the "busy stage" Emily had entered. "John is such a help to me and the boys."

Callie couldn't imagine that Thomas had a nurturing bone in his body. In fact, after only a year of marriage, his love for her had dwindled to mere stagnation. She saw the way he looked at other women, ogling them when they passed him on the sidewalk or in a store or restaurant. Once, he'd gone so far as to whistle at a leggy woman crossing in front of them while they sat waiting for the traffic light to change. She'd burned with inner rage, but didn't let on. In those days she'd still had hope for their marriage, thinking his flirting was a phase that would pass.

But she'd been wrong, of course, for in the second year of marriage he had an affair, something she'd learned about quite by accident. While at the dentist's office, she'd run into Carole Barton, an old high school friend, someone she and Lisa had once been close with, but with whom they'd lost contact during college. She had been thumbing through magazines in the waiting room, and the two struck up a conversation. During the course of their visit, Carole revealed she'd witnessed Thomas coming and going from her neighbor's house, a recently divorced woman with a young child, and wondered if he did odd jobs for people.

That night, Callie had broached the subject with him and, of course, he denied it. But a few days later, after looking up Carole Barton's address and driving past her house at one in the morning, she'd spotted his motorcycle sitting in the neighbor's driveway. And didn't she see the two of them entangled in a tight embrace in front of the well-lit window!

She might have figured then that the marriage was over or had little hope for reconciliation, but his convincing promise two days later never to see the woman again compelled Callie to give him a second chance.

Thus began the string of other women who came and went from his life and the string of second chances—and third, fourth, and so fourth—she doled out for the next two years.

"How do you manage things on your own?" Amy asked.

"Thomas left home shortly after I got pregnant, so even though the divorce took a bit of time, I've been managing on my own for quite a while."

Amy took a quick sip of coffee, swallowed, and then angled Callie with a gentle glance. "Does he—visit his daughter?"

Callie scoffed and shook her head. "When he found out I was pregnant, he couldn't leave town fast enough. No, Thomas and commitment are fast enemies. Too bad I didn't realize that before I married him." She took a few hot sips. "You don't know how many times I've kicked myself over that one. He was such a charmer when we dated, so smooth, so attentive and caring, but, well, let's just say things aren't always as they seem. I think he mostly wanted me for my steady income, what with his floundering motorcycle shop." She clicked her tongue. "I'm still paying off some of his delinquent bills—on my little teacher's salary."

Amy laid her empty coffee mug on the counter and folded her hands. "You've had a rough road."

Suddenly sorry for having burdened Amy with her sad tale, Callie flicked her wrist. "Oh, we're getting by. My parents have been wonderful—and of course, my friend, Lisa. I just take each day as it comes."

"Can I ask you a question? Are you a Christian? Have you asked God to help you?"

She laughed lightly. "You sound like Lisa. She just recently preached me a little sermon."

Amy tossed back her head and laughed along with Callie. "I think I like her."

"You'd probably be great friends. Lisa loves everybody. But to answer your question, not long ago I did pray a sort of feeble prayer. I asked God to set me on the right path. Whether He heard me is another story."

"Of course He heard you. God is our ever-present help in trouble. He longs for us to call on His name, particularly when we feel like we have nowhere else to turn. Have you ever invited Him to take charge of your life?"

The question sent a jolt through Callie's body and set her to thinking.

"When I was just a kid at summer camp, I asked Him into my heart." She shrugged. "But I think I've—what's the word? Strayed?" She couldn't help the tiny bit of sarcasm that filtered through her tone. "I've been reading my Bible again, though, searching for some answers."

"You're looking in the right place," Amy said with warmth. Then, reaching into her purse, she brought out a small book. "I'd like to give you this little book of daily devotionals. Each day includes a Bible verse and a brief commentary about how God loves us individually and wants to give us abundant life through His Son, Jesus." When Callie hesitated, Amy placed it on the kitchen counter. "I bought it especially for you."

Warmed by her kindness, Callie fought the moistness behind her eyes. "Well, then, thank you. I'll be sure to read it faithfully."

Amy stood up. "And on that note, I'd better get going. John's taking me and the boys to McDonald's for hamburgers. Not my choice, but when you have two growing boys on your hands, it's the easiest solution to a depleting checkbook."

Callie leaped to her feet and ushered Amy to the door. "Thanks for stopping by. It was so nice to see you."

They briefly hugged. In the open doorway, Amy turned. "I'll pray for you, Callie. God has something special for you, a good and perfect plan. Believe it."

After closing the door, she put her back against it to

mull over Amy's parting words. God still had a plan for her life? Even though she'd completely botched it?

Dan's days were filled with work, exercise, and eating. In the evening hours, if sleep refused to come, a good, strong drink helped remedy the problem. And since taking up the nasty habit that had once engulfed him as a young adult, his life had slipped into a downward spiral.

If there was one bright spot, it was that he enjoyed his job. He loved hanging out at the building sites and putting final touches to the jobs after the rest of the crew went home. He loved running his hands over a finely sanded cabinet or beveled banister, lived for the smells of wood shavings and plaster, the sights of freshly painted walls or newly tiled floors. Long ago, this business had gotten into his blood, and until now, he'd forgotten how passionate he was about it.

Greg moved periodically from site to site depending on the project. His outfit was growing almost faster than he could keep up with it, his frustration mounting simultaneously. Thus, he'd approached Dan about the possibility of taking on more responsibility. What he really needed, he'd said, was a job supervisor for the Oakwood development. If Dan were to take on the responsibility as supervisor, it would free up Greg for other, more pressing projects. In short, his faith in Dan's ability had grown significantly in the brief time he'd been with him, and Greg was convinced that Dan could do the job.

Dan balked, hesitant because of his lack of prolonged professional training, but Greg argued that he was better suited for the job than most. His former experience in leadership, his college degree, not to mention his uncanny talent, gave him an edge.

"Pastoring a flock of people in the ways of the Lord is a trifle different from giving orders at a work site," Dan had said.

"If you can get a congregation of people to listen to your sermons, you can get a few guys to follow your orders," Greg retorted with a grin.

Dan shrugged. "I guess I could give it a whirl. But don't hesitate to demote me if you find me lacking. And don't say I didn't warn you," he added.

So that settled it. Dan would assume the task as supervisor. He hoped he had what it took to do the job. At present, he didn't believe in himself half as much as Greg Freeman apparently did.

By design, he'd seen Callie May only twice since the night he'd apologized to her—once when he'd glanced down at the pool and seen her playing with Emily, and again from the top of the stairs when he'd caught her struggling to get the stroller out the front door, Emily draped over one arm, the stroller on the other. She never knew he watched or that he'd almost bounded down the stairs ahead of her to lend a hand.

He had problems enough as it was, he'd told himself, without involving himself in some needy woman's life. The more distance he kept between them, the better off they'd all be.

"I will continue to rejoice, for I know that through your prayers and the help given by the Spirit of Jesus Christ, what has happened to me will turn out for my deliverance. I eagerly expect and hope that I will in no way be ashamed, but will have sufficient courage so that now as always Christ will be exalted in my body, whether by life or by death. For to me, to live is Christ and to die is gain."

Callie read the words of Philippians 1:18–21 with interest. Did this mean she needed to rejoice in her loneliness and solitude because God was going to one day deliver her out of her despair if she trusted Him? It seemed an unusual course to take—to rejoice in hard times. But in the apostle Paul's case, to live was Christ; to die was gain. A little suffering here on earth was nothing to him. *Another unusual concept,* she thought to herself.

She'd been digging into her Bible more and more, and the discoveries brought revelations of God's love and faithfulness. She'd read with interest about the calling of the first disciples, the miracles of Jesus, Christ's Sermon on the Mount, and His many teaching parables, some with hidden meanings that required serious study and contemplation. But it was His message to believers to love their enemies that affected her most. In the Sermon on the Mount, Jesus said, *"Love your enemies and pray for those who persecute you, that you may be sons of your Father in heaven."* When Callie read the words of Matthew 5:44–45, her immediate reaction was to close the book and put it on a high shelf, for the verse implied forgiveness. But instead, the verse called out to her, challenging her in ways she'd not imagined possible.

It was Saturday morning, the Fourth of July and her twenty-ninth birthday. For some reason, she felt old beyond her years, but today should be a pleasant diversion, she decided. She was joining her parents, aunt, and uncle for a family picnic, a joint holiday and birthday celebration. *Ironic that the holiday we are coming together to celebrate is Independence Day,* she pondered.

A crystal-clear day greeted her when she looked outside, sunlight already streaming through the shiny glass panes of her large living room window. Since her parents didn't expect her until early afternoon, there was plenty of time to take Emily to the pool.

Though she was eager to see her mother's sister, Sharon, and her Uncle Bud, she didn't relish the sympathy that was sure to come her way because of her recent divorce. Her childless aunt and uncle had always doted on her, treating her as their own, showering her with gifts and unconditional love. The divorce was certain to stir up feelings of compassion on her aunt's part. And Callie didn't do well when people made a fuss over her. Emotions ran too deep right now.

Ten minutes later, phone rang before she and Emily made it out the door. To her utter surprise, the clear-sounding voice identified itself as Jerry Watson, a male teacher she'd befriended last year but certainly not encouraged. "Callie, it's nice to hear your voice," he said, throat cracking midway through. He was a nice enough guy, even good-looking by anyone's standards, but not necessarily her type. Friendly and outgoing, not to mention markedly available, he'd been divorced himself for a couple of years. She guessed him to be in his early thirties with no children, as far as she knew.

"It's—nice to hear yours," she said, doing her best to hide her surprise. "How are you, Jerry? And is your summer going well?"

"It's great. How have you been? I mean—since..." He left the question unfinished and her mind scrambling for a way to respond. Apparently, he'd heard through the infamous grapevine about her singleness.

"I'm doing just—okay." Why lie? "Are you staying out of trouble?" She aimed for a cheerful tone, but realized it didn't come easy. What prompted Jerry Watson to call her? A heavy rock-like knot formed in her chest.

"Me? I have to work at it." He laughed at his own joke. "I just returned from a trip out west. Tried my hand at surfing for the first time and loved it. You ought to try it. There's nothing like the high you get from riding those waves. Of course, I spent more time under my board than on it."

She forced a genial laugh but couldn't generate a response.

An awkward pause of several seconds followed. "Hey, you must be wondering why I'm calling."

"Well, I..."

"I'll just come right out with it then. How about going out tonight?"

"What? Um, it—it's the Fourth of July," she stammered.

"Exactly. I thought we could enjoy a nice dinner, have some drinks, maybe go see some fireworks."

"It's just—I..." Emily squirmed, then made a babbling sound into the phone.

"What's that noise?"

"Noise? Oh, my baby."

His voice stilled. Had he forgotten about Emily? "Oh, yeah. How is he? Or should I say she?"

"My daughter is wonderful," she answered. Premature relief flooded her chest. Most men weren't interested in a woman with a child. Emily was her drawing card right now, her safe parachute to a manless world.

"So, what do you say?"

Her breathing stopped. "I'm sorry, I can't. I'm going to my parents' house for a picnic, then afterwards to see the fireworks. It's sort of a family tradition." It was also her birthday, but that was the last thing she'd confess.

"Sure, I understand." Had she bruised his ego?

"But thank you anyway," she added in haste.

"How about Monday night, then? I was thinking we could do dinner, maybe see a movie afterward."

"Monday night?" She couldn't think of a single reason to decline—other than plain lack of interest—and she felt her shoulders slump in resignation. "I guess—that would be fine." She mentally kicked herself square in the shins.

A heavy sigh whistled through the phone lines. "How about I pick you up around seven?"

"Uh, I guess seven works."

Exactly one more minute of conversation ensued before they said good-bye. Her mind went numb when she placed the phone back in its cradle.

"What just happened here?" she asked Emily, who was busy fingering her mother's blonde hair and kicking with impatience. The child watched her with anxious eyes, a dumbfounded expression filling her countenance. Her swimsuit was on, after all. It must have made no sense to her why her mother would have stopped to talk in that silly machine when they could have been wading in that wonderfully warm water instead.

~

Dan woke up late, another headache pounding into his temples like some drummer banging on a set of bongos. His eyes fluttered open, and his gaze trailed off to the window. Clear skies. It was the Fourth of July, but certainly no holiday in his mind. In fact, he'd likely go out to Oakwood Square and take a look at what needed to be finished. He'd left all his tools sitting beside a cherry cabinet, his current work in progress. *Good day to work in solitude,* he thought. *Just me and the radio.*

He dragged himself out of bed, ran calloused fingers through dark strands of thick hair, and sat for a moment, orienting himself. The clock registered close to ten. He was normally an early riser, and the late hour made him cranky. *I should have been out at the site by now,* he grumbled.

Wearing only his boxers, he scuffled into the kitchen and faced a heap of dirty dishes, a collection of empty soda cans and beer bottles on the kitchen counter, a couple of unread newspapers scattered on the floor, and an empty cereal box discarded in the corner. *Disgusting.* Clumsily, he pried open a trash bag and shoved the junk inside. Next, he took a stale, damp cloth and swiped at dried bread crumbs, aiming for the sink, but mostly missing and hitting the tile floor instead.

The coffee can sat next to the coffee pot where it'd been all week. He pried it open and measured out a scoop. Filling the carafe with water, he poured it into the coffee maker, flipped the switch, and walked away, thinking a shower would restore his energy.

Midway to the shower, he decided on a trip to the pool instead. What he needed was a few hard laps to clear his head. He'd grab some breakfast afterward, then head for work.

To his relief, the pool was quiet. *Good.* Solitude was what he needed most right now. He tossed his towel on a nearby chair and dove in without first testing the water. It was refreshing, immediately waking his placid nerve endings.

As soon as he came up for air and ran a hand over his unshaven face, he saw *her.* She'd been sitting on a chair with her daughter at the other end of the pool. Funny he hadn't noticed them when he'd entered the fenced-in area. Probably the tilting umbrella under which they sat had blocked his view of them from the entrance.

"Hi," he said. "Nice morning."

She gave a polite nod, then fumbled around for something in her beach bag.

"You been down here long?"

"We just got here."

"I didn't see you when I came in."

No response.

"Sun's bright today."

Still nothing.

She removed Emily's shirt and began the job of smoothing sun block over her body. He couldn't take his eyes off the task, mother attending to child. Curious as to what went on inside her charming little head, he swam to the edge of the pool where she sat and draped an arm over the side.

"It doesn't bother you, does it? My coming to the pool. I'm just gonna swim some laps."

A few wisps of blonde hair wrapped around her face, temporarily obscuring her vision when she raised her head to look at him. She reached up and brushed them aside, pushing her chin up just a notch when she said, "It doesn't bother me in the least, so feel free to get on with it." He hadn't thought much about it before, but now he knew it with certainty. His presence filled her with uneasiness. Her sassy abruptness was nothing but a cover-up.

Just what had her husband done to her? Had he abused her in some form—physical or otherwise? The thought made him churn with fury. But the notion that he cared an ounce about her irked him even more.

She continued smoothing the lotion onto Emily's back and shoulders; he looked on in silence. Finally, he asked, "She afraid of the water at all?"

"Not a bit. She loves it. In fact, she goes a little crazy if I so much as mention the word 'pool.'" A breeze ruffled a few of Emily's short hairs, and Callie smoothed them down. The baby didn't have much on her downy head, but what she did have was blonde as the day was light.

"She's smart, then, if she recognizes the word."

A glint of pride skipped across Callie's countenance. "Her grandpa thinks she's a genius."

A low chuckle bubbled up from Dan's chest. Relaxed, he propped another elbow on the edge of the pool. "My dad is pretty much the same way about his own grandchildren. Even at their worst, he thinks they're perfect."

A slow smile crept into view, as if she might be weighing what he'd just revealed. It was the first time he'd ever touched on his family, and immediate regret swallowed him up. He wasn't ready for any questions.

"Maaa-aaaa!" Emily suddenly squealed, rearing her head back and kicking impatiently, successfully changing the tone.

"I think she wants to swim," he remarked, pushing away from the side of the pool.

Hoisting the baby in her arms, Callie stood, tossing the towel that had been covering her legs on a nearby chair. With a pang of guilt, Dan scanned her figure, admiring her sculpted legs and thin waist.

Okay, so he found her attractive. *It's nothing more than that,* he mulled. He could deal with this. He'd ignored her for the past several days; surely he could continue to do so in the months to come.

Annoyed with himself, he gave the lady and her baby a cursory nod and turned away. It was high time he swam off some of this building tension in his chest. *Fifty or so laps ought to do it.*

When Callie arrived at her childhood home, her parents, Ralph and Elizabeth Jacobs, along with her

Uncle Bud and Aunt Sharon Wiley, were in the backyard. Ralph and Bud were tending the grill; Elizabeth and Sharon were talking over tall glasses of iced tea. Summer breezes ruffled the corners of the colorful tablecloth adorning the large wooden picnic table, but the heavy ceramic plates, mugs, and silverware served as excellent weights. Aunt Sharon was the first to spot Callie and Emily when they arrived.

"Oh, Bud, look what the wind blew in," she teased, running to her niece's side to plant a kiss on her cheek and offer to take Emily. "It's our two babies."

Callie's aunt, attractive for her fifty-five years, could still run circles around her. She'd always been fun-loving and active during Callie's growing up years, taking her places and buying her gifts her own parents couldn't afford. She remembered well the scowling looks her mother gave her sister. "You are going to spoil our daughter to pieces, Sharon," she would say in jest. "She won't want to live with us anymore if you keep that up." Sharon would dismiss her remarks with a laugh.

Callie had learned early on that her aunt could never bear children due to a hysterectomy she'd had as a young woman. She'd always figured her mother expressed unspoken sympathy to her sister by allowing her to spoil her niece. Somehow, the vicarious parenting must have worked as a salve to help ease Sharon's emotional wounds.

"Hi, Aunt Sharon and Uncle Bud." Callie spoke for

Emily, who went gladly into her great-aunt's arms; even though she didn't know her well, the woman's warm-hearted demeanor was a definite draw.

"Happy birthday, darling. I can't believe you're so grown up."

"Oh, here we go again," Callie groaned. "Every year it's the same old thing: 'Where have the years gone? Wasn't it only yesterday I bounced you on my knee?'"

"Oh, stop it," Sharon said, slapping her playfully. "You don't know how old you make me feel." She kissed her lightly on the cheek. "How are you, honey?" Her aunt snuggled Emily close but rested her eyes on Callie, whispering her concern and condolences.

"I'm okay," Callie insisted.

"You sure? You know you can't fool me." It was true; her aunt knew her well. Lying would be like trying to cover up an elephant with a handkerchief.

She smiled. "I'm okay," she repeated, leaning into her aunt's embrace, feeling a little like the child again instead of Emily's mother.

"We'll talk more later," her aunt assured her, "when things quiet down."

"Don't hog my nieces, Sharon," Bud called from across the yard, his booming baritone voice filling the air. "Especially the birthday girl. Come over here, kiddo."

Callie laughed and approached her uncle for his usual bear hug. Her father stood on the sidelines turning steaks, a quiet smile on his lips.

"Hi, Daddy," she whispered into his ear once her uncle released his hold and moved off to see Emily.

"Happy birthday, honey. How's my sugar?" he asked, his face somewhat drawn and worn-looking. He leaned over and kissed her cheek.

"I'm perfectly fine, but how are you?" He'd had a heart attack five years ago, and since that day, Callie never ceased to be concerned about him.

"I can't complain," he said, pasting on a hurried smile. "I'm just concerned about you and Emily."

"We're going to be okay," she promised. "You look a little pale today." At sixty years old, he should have been more youthful, but the heart attack had drained much of his energy.

He turned over a piece of meat on the grill and studied it for doneness. "I'm fine. How about seeing what you can do to help your mother?" He always did that—pushed her away when the attention turned toward him. If he were ailing, she'd be the last to hear about it. Even her mother seemed to shield her from the truth. She studied him a few seconds more, but when it was clear he wouldn't elaborate on the subject, she turned on her heel and made for the house.

Her mother was in the kitchen, monitoring a steaming kettle of sweet corn. A large lid in one hand and a big spoon in the other, she spun around as soon as she heard the screen door squeak open. "Hi, sweetheart. Happy birthday. We'll do presents right after we eat. That okay with you? Aunt Sharon still have Emily?"

"Yeah. Mom, Dad doesn't look good today. How is he?"

Her mother's brow crimped uneasily, and she turned back to the kettle to roll an ear of corn over with the wooden spoon, a sober look crossing her face.

"He's been extra tired, but I don't want you worrying over him. Right now, you have enough to deal with, given your recent divorce, your finances being what they are...everything." She shook her head and sighed. "Your dad's concerned, that's all, and it tends to slow him down." She chuckled softly. "He never has been good at hiding things from either of us."

"Mom, Em and I are going to make it. It's Dad who has me worried. What did the doctor say when you took him in last week? You never did mention it, and, quite selfishly, I forgot to ask."

Elizabeth bent to retrieve a colorful platter from the cupboard. "Oh, pooh, Callie, you haven't a selfish bone in your body! Think of how generous you were to that pathetic husband of yours, giving into his every whim, letting him buy that motorcycle of all things, paying his rent payments at that shop he owned with that—that no-good..."

"Mom, I don't want to talk about—that man. I asked you about Dad."

Frown lines etched themselves into her mom's forehead. "Honey, I'm sorry. I didn't mean to bring up a topic that might spoil your birthday. We'll talk about Dad later, okay? Besides, it's all in God's hands." She bent at the waist and kissed Callie on the cheek. "Now, it's almost time to eat. Take the corn out to the picnic table, would you? I'll grab the potato salad from the fridge."

Obeying, Callie took the platter of corn, then turned toward the screen door, pushing it open with her hip.

So that was all she'd be getting by way of information. Well, she'd pick Aunt Sharon's brain later. Maybe she'd be able to enlighten her.

But there wasn't much time for talking later. After the meal was eaten and the gifts had been opened, Uncle Bud announced that he was surprising his wife with a trip to the Bahamas. Sharon gasped with delight, and the two left soon afterward to go home and pack. They were world travelers, having visited nearly every country on the globe, Callie figured. She'd often wondered if their lack of children drove them to keep busy. They never stayed in one place for very long, yet they always seemed immensely happy together.

On the positive side, neither one of her parents was eager to see the fireworks, particularly since Bud and Sharon left early. Callie lingered at her parents' house till evening, and when they hinted about a desire to go to bed early, she gathered up Emily and went home.

Chapter 8

The remainder of the week breezed by without incident. Callie saw nothing more of Dan Mattson, and that suited her just fine. He seemed harmless enough, but she didn't trust him entirely, and the fact that he brought out her vulnerable side made her want to avoid him all the more. Of course, she had Thomas to thank for that, memories of his abusive nature coming back to haunt her thoughts and dreams.

"What's he done this time?" her father asked, pulling her through the front door, face awash with concern.

"Locked me out of the house. You have my spare key." She wouldn't tell him about the pain in her side from Thomas's flinging her forcefully against the kitchen counter before shoving her out the back door and locking it, and all because his dinner wasn't on the table. Never mind that blinding snow and downed power lines had blocked traffic, slowing her progress home after a long day at work.

"What on earth? Why would he do that? We're in the

middle of a snowstorm," her father said, clearly peeved at Thomas for his apparent thoughtlessness.

"I'm sure it wasn't intentional," she lied.

Callie's mother rushed to the front room, wringing her hands, her own face a portrait of worry. "Well, you can't go back home until this storm ends."

And so she'd stayed the night, venturing back home the next day and taking care to prepare an extra special meal for Thomas, relieved to find him mellow, sober, and contrite.

Callie jerked back to reality, surprised to discover she'd been dozing on the sofa, Emily asleep in the circle of her arms, the recollection of the episode with Thomas still painfully fresh in her head. She checked her watch and discovered she had exactly thirty minutes before her date with Jerry Watson. "Ugh," she moaned. Her stomach churned merely at the thought of dating again—particularly someone like Jerry, divorced himself—making her wish she could somehow beg off the date. Jerry was nice enough, she supposed, but he wasn't the kind of guy she imagined herself with. She'd always thought of the divorced man as a party animal, an apple-polishing ladies' man.

Suddenly, she wanted nothing more than to fast-forward through the movie, the date—the entire night.

Pulling herself upright, she skimmed a hand over Emily's soft cheeks in hopes of waking her. It was then her eyes fixed on the simple wedding band she still wore. Knowing she could hardly wear it on a date, she twisted the thing off and dropped it on the coffee table, reveling in the odd surge of relief that followed.

Lori arrived on time and was busy playing with Emily when the doorbell sounded. "I'll get it," Lori called.

"Thank you," Callie called from the kitchen, her stomach a knot of tension. "Please tell him I'll be right there." Mindlessly, she ran her fingers through her hair and pinched her freshly tinted lips together. She wore a pair of beige linen Capri pants with a matching sleeveless shirt. Doing a quick self-survey in the mirror, she ruled it was just dressy enough for a casual night on the town. Straightening her shoulders, she prepared to greet the first man she'd dated since Thomas.

But it wasn't Jerry's voice she heard when Lori opened the door. "Would you mind giving this to her?" asked the deep voice.

A strange thrill ran up her spine. What was Dan Mattson doing at her door?

"Thank you," Lori was saying. "I'll give it to her."

"Tell her I found it in the parking lot next to her car. I just assumed it was hers, but maybe..."

Unable to resist, Callie peeked around the corner and spotted the object of their discussion—her purse. What on earth? "You found my purse?" she exclaimed, coming into view.

Dan towered in the doorway, a crooked smile

accompanying his casual stance. She didn't miss his hasty scan of her as he extended the handbag. "Here you go. Found it on the ground."

Flabbergasted, she took the small leather bag, and their hands brushed in the exchange. A sort of odd warmth crept up her arm. "I never even missed it. I must have laid it down when I was lifting Emily from her seat and forgot to pick it back up. Thank you so much."

"You're welcome." Both eyebrows arched as his gaze dropped and a smile tickled the corners of his mouth. "I see you're all dressed up. Got another hot date with Lisa?"

"Lisa? No, actually I…" But before the words came out, Jerry Watson opened the entrance door below, hesitating only briefly at the bottom of the stairs. When he spotted her in her doorway, he gave a broad smile.

"Ah, this is the right building. I was beginning to think I'd gone to the wrong one." He swept a hand through his sandy-colored hair and mounted the stairs, eyes only on her. "How are you, Callie? You look wonderful." He looked pretty good himself, but he was no match for the taller, sturdier looking Dan Mattson.

Callie felt awkward, and an uneven laugh bubbled forth. "Hello, Jerry. Good to see you."

A moment of clumsy silence engulfed the three adults. Finally, Callie gathered her wits. "Oh, forgive me. Jerry Watson, meet Dan Mattson," she said, gesturing to Dan. "My neighbor."

They shook hands, Jerry forcing a smile, Dan not going quite so far.

"Well, shall we go?" Jerry asked, voice on the edge of impatience.

"Of course. Just let me get my sweater." She quickly grabbed it off the back of a chair, and when she did, Emily let out a yelp, startling them all. Apparently, the baby had been pulling herself to a standing position when the toy box lid dropped on her, just missing her head—but not her finger. More startled than sore, Emily continued squealing until her mother dropped everything to pick her up. Callie rocked her back and forth, soothing her with her touches, and then glanced up to find the two men in her doorway wearing entirely different expressions—Jerry's face showed blatant irritation, Dan's genuine concern.

"Is she okay?" Dan asked first, looking as though he were ready to bolt through the door, invited or not.

"She's fine," Callie said, inspecting the finger for a red mark but finding none.

"It probably scared her more than anything," Dan offered.

"I'm sure you're right." She rocked her daughter gently a few more seconds before setting her back down on the floor next to Lori.

But then the sobs resumed.

Jerry shifted his weight and looked at his watch.

Suddenly, Dan strode in, bent over, and lifted the screaming baby into his arms.

To Callie's amazement, Emily went still, cutting loose a couple more sobs as she rested her head against Dan's broad chest, then curled into that space between his neck and shoulder.

"You look like you've done that before," Callie commented, watching as he soothed her baby with a gentle back rub.

His gaze trailed over Emily's head and met up with Callie's. "I just have the magic touch, that's all," he said softly with a tiny smile. "I'll stay with her for just a bit. When she settles down, Lori can take over."

"I can't expect you to…"

"I insist," he argued, giving her his back, as if that should settle the matter.

Jerry stood waiting; his impatient gaze alternated between Callie and his watch.

"Are you sure?" she asked.

Dan turned and issued them both a rather firm look. "Go. Everything will be fine." Jerry took his cue and gently nudged Callie out ahead of him with his hand on the center of her back.

"I shouldn't be too late, Lori," she said. The poor girl looked ready to bolt herself, probably wondering what to do with the man who now stood in the center of the living room doing the job she'd been hired to do.

Unfortunately, Callie didn't know what else to say to her.

∽

Dan paced the floor of his apartment. The baby was crying again, this time in loud pleas of desperation. She'd been quiet for the last hour, but now she was going strong. *It's none of my business,* he kept telling himself. But believing it was another story. The kid had sucked him in. He might just as well admit it. Her mother—well now, that was another story—one he'd just as soon let simmer on the back burner. Perhaps if he just ignored the feelings, they would evaporate on their own.

The mantle clock registered ten o'clock, well past any baby's bedtime. Lori was probably having trouble putting her down, her inexperience no doubt rubbing off in the form of insecurity, something Emily had detected.

Dan had stayed with Emily and Lori until he was sure Emily had ceased her initial sobs, but her fussing had continued in periodic spurts throughout the evening, making it progressively more difficult for him to resist intervening. Lori would be exhausted about now. He flipped on the TV as he'd done half a dozen other times tonight, anything to drown out the squeals and obliterate any sense of responsibility he might be tempted to feel, then flipped it back off, unable to concentrate. He didn't usually hear her cries unless they were persistent, as they had been tonight.

The phone rang and he tossed down the golf magazine he'd just picked up.

"Daniel Mattson, just how long were you planning

on putting off calling your dear, sweet sister? It was your turn to call, you know."

"Hi, Sam. I figured I'd give it another couple months." His sister's voice sounded clear and warm, just the diversion he needed. Maybe now he could block out Emily's cries.

"Oh, you." Her soft laughter cheered his spirits. "How are you getting on, Danny? Are you settled into your new place?"

"Yeah, it's not bad."

Sam was the only one who still insisted on using the childish nickname he'd grown out of with everyone else who had used it when he was a kid. Always forthright about her opinions, she'd also once confided that she'd always thought it was his Grandma Mattson rather than the Holy Spirit that was the driving force that had put him behind the pulpit.

He'd laughed at the plainspoken remark but now tended to agree with her. As long as Dan could remember, his grandma had harped about needing a minister in the family tree, her gaze always falling to him rather than his older brother, Ken. "You will make a fine preacher, dear," she'd announced one Sunday afternoon when he was a mere teen, the entire family listening in.

After her persistence, Dan had finally set out to obey "the call," thinking that perhaps God had chosen Grandma Mattson as a mouthpiece for dispersing His divine will.

However, after finding himself in the throes of bitterness and loss, Dan had begun to question his faith, as well as his life's vocation. Had he sought his grandmother's approval and gone into the ministry for all the wrong reasons?

God help him if he had.

"I can't wait to see your apartment," Sam said, breaking into his thoughts. "I'm going to come visit one of these days, you know."

"Warn me first, would you? I don't want to shock you with my lack of housekeeping skills. I think I need a maid."

"You need more than that," she challenged with a giggle. "Now, tell me about this job with Greg Freeman."

The baby's cries across the hall ceased for the moment, and so he felt freer to talk, even enjoying the opportunity. Of all his family members, Sam was the most easygoing, despite her meddlesome traits. Not much slipped past her, and if it did, she made sure she caught up in due time.

"My job is going fine. I'm afraid it wouldn't interest you that much. Mom told me you performed with the city orchestra not long ago. I'm glad you're not letting your talent go to waste."

The flip in subjects seemed like a good idea. She told him about the concert, her husband John and their six-year-old son, Robbie, then their parents, and finished with an update about the congregation he'd left behind just months ago. "We have a good lead on a new pastor. He's from Dallas."

"Really? What's his name?"

"Winters, I think. He preached last Sunday, but I couldn't bring myself to go listen. You understand. But I heard he was a very good speaker."

"Sam..."

"Well, it's not the same without you. John and I have been looking for a different church."

"Be sure your reasons are the right ones."

"Like you should talk."

"Don't preach to me, Samantha."

"I wouldn't dream of it," she said with a hint of friendly sarcasm.

"Right. They should have put you behind the pulpit. God knows you have what it takes to preach up a storm. You've been telling things like they are since the day you spoke your first words."

"That's not fair. I'm merely concerned for you, that's all."

"I know," he conceded.

"Have you asked God for direction in your life, Danny?"

Dan laughed. "Sam, you don't have a shy bone in your body, do you?"

"I've been told it's my downfall," she said. "Seriously, do you blame God? Mom is worried you've turned your back on Him for good." He could tell by the nervous chuckle that she shared their mother's worry.

"Like I said, don't preach to me."

"Oh, listen to you. I've had to endure your sermons over the past few years; shouldn't you have to listen to just one of mine?"

Suddenly, Emily's crying cut loose, this time in the form of a blood-curdling scream. He heard the door across the hall open and a knock at his own. "Sorry to cut your sermon short, Sam, but someone's at my door. I'll call you soon."

"Thank you for everything, Jerry. It was a nice evening." Callie's hand was on the passenger door handle.

"I'll walk you up."

"That's really not necessary."

"Don't be silly. Stay put; I'll get your door."

The date hadn't been a complete disaster, but it came close to qualifying as one. Callie had worried about Emily most of the night, excusing herself twice to call Lori, both times hearing her baby's cries in the background. Jerry seemed annoyed by the interruptions, but he'd held his tongue.

They tried for a quiet dinner, but wound up sitting next to a rowdy party of eight who enjoyed drinking their booze and telling lewd jokes.

Finally, Jerry requested a different table, but there wasn't one available. The place seemed filled to capacity with riotous diners, people who had come into town for a rock concert festival, a five-day event beginning Tuesday.

The movie he'd chosen wasn't much better than the dinner they had to endure—it was rife with crude language and partial nudity, despite the PG-13 rating. Had she known Jerry better, she might have insisted that they leave early, but it was difficult to read him. Half the time he looked like he was enjoying himself. When he placed his arm across the back of her chair to pull her closer, her automatic response to pull away must have nettled him, for he withdrew and sulked. She wouldn't have predicted that kind of reaction from a grown man. What had he expected on their first date?

She climbed out of his car when he opened her door and allowed him to take her arm and guide her up the lamp-lit sidewalk. The hallway to the apartment building was peaceful, and she breathed a sigh of relief.

At the top of the stairs, she turned. "Thank you again, Jerry," she said, grabbing her apartment key from her purse.

"No problem. We'll have to try again sometime. Next time I'll be sure to select a quieter restaurant."

"Oh, don't worry yourself over that. The dinner was fine. Really."

"So you wouldn't mind going out with me another time?"

She hadn't meant to lead him to the wrong conclusion. In her mind, there'd been no chemistry. "We'll see."

"We'll see?" he questioned, stealing the apartment key from her hand and turning her to face him. "I think we deserve another chance, don't you?" He tipped her chin up with his thumb, and the simple touch sent shock waves through her body, dredged up hideous memories of Thomas. "How about a little kiss to remember me by?"

"What? No!" she answered, trying to take back her key. His behavior made her nervous.

"Come on, just one?" he coaxed, tugging her close.

Something in his eyes made her cringe, the way they glittered with wanton lust. When he lowered his face and came close, she angled hers away, her spine stiff with resistance.

"Don't!" she said, squirming in his clutches, pressing her lips together in anger, even as his fingers clenched her forearms and hauled her closer yet, pinching, stinging. When she raised her hand between them and pressed hard against his chest, he had the nerve to laugh.

"What's the matter?" he asked, his voice a husky whisper.

"Don't, please," she said, catching her breath. But he took advantage of the moment and pressed his mouth to hers, temporarily quelling her ability to talk, pressing her lips with force.

It seemed an eternity that he ground his mouth into hers, pushing and prying, his hot breath repulsing her senses.

"Stop it!" she spat out, finally succeeding in setting him back from her.

Confusion furrowed his face. "I didn't have you figured for an iceberg, Callie." Fraught with determination, he seized her arms and hauled her against him again. "You're divorced, remember? Come on, invite me inside."

Just then, her apartment door swung open, and in its wake stood Daniel Mattson, his commanding appearance a welcome relief to her pounding heart. The question of why he stood there never even entered her mind.

"Get your hands off her." Dan's voice was steady, his tone as cold as a spring hailstorm.

Had she not been so upset, Callie might have laughed at Jerry's stunned look—the way he hurriedly stumbled backward, then shifted to one side. "No harm intended," he declared with upheld hands. "Just trying to end the night on a sweet note."

"Stop talking and get out of here," Dan issued through clenched teeth, his tone unchanged from his earlier demand. The way Jerry backed away indicated Dan had his attention.

"Sure, no problem." Sneering, he tossed Callie's apartment key in the air. Dan reached out and seized it in one quick motion. "You didn't tell me you had a bodyguard, Callie."

Dan's jaw flicked, dark eyes brimmed with anger.

Jerry seemed to sense he'd crossed the line. "Hey,

we were done anyway, right, Callie?" he said with a shrug. "Sorry if I assumed too much."

If he'd intended his final remark as an apology, it was lame. He sprang down the stairs and out the door without so much as a backward look. Callie stood mute, staring at the closed door, feeling somehow numb and humiliated. She had no idea how long she might have stood there, either, had it not been for Dan's grip on her arm and the gentle way he guided her inside.

"That guy's a jerk," he was saying, closing her door and turning her to face him. "Are you okay?" The way he studied her face made her want to retreat. Not that she felt threatened, especially when compared to Jerry Watson. No, if anything, she was mortified that he'd had to rescue her.

Callie rubbed her forehead. "I'm fine."

"Where'd you find *him*?"

She sucked in a slow breath and exhaled. "We work together. He's a history teacher and he—coaches football. He—heard about my divorce."

"Phff," Dan scoffed. "No point in wasting any time jumping back into the fish pond, huh? At least, do your homework next time, teacher. Obviously, you don't know this guy as well as you thought you did—coworker or not."

Not ready for a lecture, she raised her defenses. She wrangled free of his clasp and walked to a chair, plopping into it with a heavy breath. "What are you doing here, anyway?" she asked, nerves still taut as a drum. She laid her sweater on the armrest beside her and looked around. "Where's Lori?"

"I sent her home."

The taste of unexplained anger pooled in her throat. "Why would you do that?"

A muscle flicked in his jaw. "You need to find an older, more experienced person to watch your daughter."

"I've used her before without a problem."

"Yeah? Well, she came knocking at my door an hour or so ago with big tears in her eyes. She didn't have a clue how to soothe Emily's cries."

"And you did?"

Dark brows slanted upward. "Do you hear her crying now?"

It was difficult to argue point-blank truth.

He glanced at his watch. "It's late. I'll be going now." He put his hand to the doorknob. "I paid the girl for her time."

For some reason, his curtness riled her. First, he waltzes into her apartment, takes over a job she's hired someone else to do, then pays the girl for her trouble? *Talk about nerve.*

"I wish you hadn't done that. I can manage my own affairs, thank you very much."

Dark eyes, snapping with sarcasm, looked straight at her and carefully narrowed. "Oh? Like the way you were managing Lover Boy a while ago? Seems to me you could use a lesson or two in the tricks men play."

She gripped both arms of the chair and gritted her teeth. "Believe me, I don't need any lessons. I learned a world of knowledge from my former husband." As soon as she made the remark, she wanted to call it back. Why should this man be privy to her private life? "You don't even know me, *Mr.* Mattson."

He chuckled. "Oh, so we're back to the formal stuff? Calm down, okay?" He turned his body full around and leaned against the door, folding his brawny arms across his chest. "I didn't mean anything by the comment, unless it was to say that I think you're a little naïve. I bet when you fall for a man, you fall hard, regardless of the circumstances—and you fight to the finish to hold things together. Was that how it was in your marriage? You didn't realize what a loser he was until it was too late…maybe even in spite of mistreatment….Callie, did your husband mistreat you? Physically, I mean?"

She hated that he'd pegged her. *How did he know?* To hide her dismay, she lifted her chin in nonchalance and folded her hands in her lap. "That is none of your business."

Invisible sparks ignited between them, but he just grinned. "No, I'm sure it's not."

Wanting to put in a few digs of her own, she asked, "What makes you the authority on babies, anyway? Do you have progeny of your own somewhere? Or everywhere?"

"I'm no authority," he said, ignoring her second question. He pushed off from the door and strode to the kitchen, snatched a paper cup from the counter and stuck it under the cold faucet. His back to her, he gulped the liquid down then tossed the cup into the wastebasket under her sink. Apparently he'd familiarized himself with her kitchen while she was away.

"You seem to understand Emily's needs, as if you've had practice," she pushed.

He sauntered back to the door. "Have you replaced that antique car seat yet?"

She didn't miss the evasion. She straightened. "As soon as I've saved the money I intend to buy a new one." In fact, she'd made room for it in next week's paycheck. But, again, that was none of his business.

He nodded, reached for the doorknob, and turned his body slightly. "You don't plan to go out with that Watson character again, I hope."

She gave a dry laugh. "Not on your life."

He chuckled. "Good." Then opening the door, he turned the lock button and gave her one final backward glance. "And, Callie?"

"Yes?"

"Keep your door locked."

"I will."

It wasn't until he closed the door behind him that she realized she'd forgotten to repay him the money he'd given Lori for babysitting.

The month of July marked its end with a raging thunderstorm. Streaks of lightning pierced the night sky, followed by loud bursts of thunder and drenching rain. It was seven-thirty, a good night for reading, popping corn and watching a movie, or simply listening to quiet, inspirational music. Lisa had promised to stop by later and show Callie some pictures she'd taken on a recent family vacation. She looked forward to their visit—adult conversation was always a welcome treat after a day of baby talk with Emily.

Callie had seen Dan Mattson twice in the last two weeks. The day after the babysitting incident, she'd come home from visiting her parents and found a brand new car seat propped in front of her door. Without hesitating, she'd knocked on his apartment door, instinctively knowing him to be the source. She said that she couldn't accept the gift, but he'd replied that the gift wasn't for her; it was for Emily. And she couldn't very well speak for someone else. She'd tried to argue the point, but he wouldn't hear it, claiming he was fond of Emily and wanted to ensure her safety.

"You don't think I'm capable?" she'd asked.

"I think you take offense too quickly. Loosen up," he'd said. "It's not that big a deal."

"Well then—thank you. Are you sure I can't pay you for it?"

"If you do, then it won't be much of a gift, will it?" He'd been leaning in the doorway, shirt untucked, feet bare, and sporting paint-stained shorts. His mussed black hair hung over his forehead, nearly reaching his dark eyes, lending to his devilishly handsome demeanor.

A few days later, she'd dropped off a large platter of cookies and brownies on a brand new pewter tray she'd told him to keep, as well as a check written for the amount he'd paid Lori. He'd met her on the run, which was a good thing—she didn't want to loiter. This time, he wore his running shorts and a muscle shirt, and she was careful to keep her eyes focused on the clock just above his head on the wall behind him.

She couldn't help being curious as she looked past him and into his sparsely decorated apartment. Across the room, she saw a photo frame resting on the fireplace mantel. From where she stood, it looked like it depicted a woman and child, but she couldn't be sure. Dan had moved slightly, blocking her vision, perhaps on purpose. "Sorry I can't invite you in," he'd said. "My apartment isn't exactly visitor-friendly."

"Oh, goodness, I wouldn't expect you to," Callie said. "I just wanted to drop these off and thank you again for the lovely car seat. Emily thanks you, too." Dan looked beyond her. "She's sleeping," she'd added.

He'd taken the tray of baked goods and lifted a corner of the fresh towel she'd draped across them. "Mmm, they smell wonderful. Do you like to bake?"

"I do, but I don't do it very often. I've been known to eat an entire batch of brownies if they're sitting in front of me."

His eyes swept the length of her. "You don't look any worse for it." Most of his smiles amounted to crooked grins, but now he'd given her the real thing, straight teeth and all, and she'd had to remind herself she didn't trust him—or any man.

When the phone rang later, she'd assumed it was Lisa begging off coming over because of the storm. "I'll understand if you can't come," was her glib greeting upon picking up the phone.

"Callie? That you?" responded a male voice she didn't recognize right off.

"This is Callie. Who's calling?" For the umpteenth time she scolded herself for not adding caller ID to her monthly service.

"Don't you recognize my voice, darlin'?"

Alarm as pointed as the streaks of lightning outside her window pierced her insides. *Thomas?* She moved to the sofa and sat down, suddenly overcome.

"Wh-what do you want?"

"S-sweetheart, is that any way to talk to your h-husband?" He slurred his words. *Drunk.*

"You're not my husband."

"'Course I am. That will n-never change," he said, accentuating the statement with a hiccup.

"Where are you calling from?" she asked, pressing her palm against her forehead, as the ripples of fear intensified.

"Where do you think?" His low-sounding laugh chilled her to the bone. *God, please don't let him be back in Illinois.*

"I can't talk now," she exclaimed.

"I need money, Callie."

Now she clutched the pulsing knot at the center of her chest. "I don't have any money to give you."

"Come on, Cal. I'm broke."

"How could you be broke, Thomas? Are you throwing everything away on liquor?"

"What's to throw away? I told you, I'm broke. My shop's goin' under." A violent curse traveled the airwaves, and she put the receiver away from her.

Glancing at Emily, who was playing happily in the middle of the living room, Callie whispered an urgent prayer for help. She could only trust that God heard it.

"Where are you?" she probed, determined to get that out of the way before she said anything further. If he were back in Oakdale, she would need to be extra cautious.

"Why? Ya need some lovin'?"

A bitter taste gathered in her throat. "I just want to know where you are."

He mumbled something indecipherable, following it up with another curse. "Are ya goin' to loan me money or not?" he pushed, unwilling to answer her question.

"You're drunk. Why should I give you a cent knowing you would waste it on more booze? Besides, I don't have anything extra. And what I do have goes to support our child."

Raucous laughter and some kind of twangy country music played in the background. A live band, maybe? "Why'd ya have to go and divorce me? We could've w-worked things out."

It was an outlandish statement, almost funny enough to make her laugh. Once, when she'd suggested counseling, he'd literally spat in her face.

"Wanta get married again?" he asked, trailing the question with a round of crude laughter. "You, me, and the kid, the all-American f-family." He laughed at his own joke, then topped it off with another hiccup.

"I'm hanging up now, Thomas. Don't call here again."

"Why shouldn't I? I've a right to know what my wife's up to. You ain't gettin' it on with some dude, are you? I'll kill him."

"I'm warning you, leave me alone—or I'll..."

"What—call the police? You think they're gonna come chasing all the way down here? Cops don't cross state lines, honey."

So he was still in Florida. Relief flowed like rain. "Good-bye, Thomas."

She slammed the receiver down just as the doorbell sounded.

Lisa greeted her with a full smile but quickly sobered. "What's wrong?"

The simple question was all it took to make Callie collapse into her friend's welcoming arms.

The summer storm raged. Dan lay sprawled on his sofa, mindlessly flipping through TV channels, bummed that he couldn't get in his nightly jog. Not that a little rain bothered him, but lightning, now, that was another story. Propping his bare feet atop the coffee table, he paused his channel surfing at some religious station and listened while the guy preached about God's sustaining grace through hard times.

"God never promised us a life void of pain and sorrow," the TV preacher was saying, "but He does promise to be with us, and for that we should rejoice. James chapter one, verses two and three, tell us to  *'Consider it pure joy, my brothers, whenever you face trails of many kinds, because you know that the testing of your faith develops perseverance.'*"

Dan blinked at the TV screen, his mind a mass of muddy reflections. He knew the verse well, had based a sermon or two on that very passage. Something inside him churned with uneasiness.

"Do you blame God?" His sister's words echoed in

his head. *"Mom is worried that you've given up on Him completely."*

A streak of lightning pierced the skies, cutting short his train of thought. *It's just as well,* he mused, quickly switching off the television in favor of reading. Thunder ripped the silence in two, suiting him just fine. What he needed was a good diversion. He pulled himself off the sofa and headed for the kitchen to retrieve the novel he'd started a couple of days ago.

Spotting it on the counter, he snatched up the book and turned around, but then his eyes caught sight of the platter of goodies Callie had dropped off a couple of days ago. He'd been nibbling from it ever since. It was a thank offering for the car seat, she'd said. He smiled to himself. She'd wanted to reimburse him for the seat, but since he wouldn't hear of it, she'd presented him with a platter of baked goods instead.

Now that was his idea of fair compensation.

Although he wasn't especially hungry, he lifted one corner of the aluminum foil cover and seized a big, frosted brownie between thumb and index finger, popping the entire concoction into his mouth and licking his lips to savor any stray icing. That woman could certainly bake!

What else lay buried beneath that self-sufficient exterior, that cloak of independence she so carefully wrapped about herself? Did she worry about such things as comforting her daughter in a thunderstorm or fixing broken pipes or paying her bills or raising Emily alone? Single parenting wasn't an easy job. He'd counseled one or two single parents in the past. Out came that old protective nature, that side of him that sought to lend a hand, soothe away worries.

Why had he really bought her that car seat? The question nettled. *"A gift for the baby,"* he'd said. *Right.* She'd admitted to having tight finances, so it was probably because he wanted to lighten her budget burdens. Had her husband drained her monetarily?

Not for the first time, he contemplated what he'd like to do to the fellow if he ever laid eyes on him—tear him apart, limb from limb. And it wasn't any different for that Jerry Watson character.

Dear God, what's happening to me? It was a feeble start to a prayer, but the closest he'd come to the real thing in a very long time.

Callie and Emily spent part of the next morning at the pool, then grocery shopped, ran errands, and wound up at the Jacobs' house, where they shared conversation and a meal. She was careful to keep the news of Thomas's phone call to herself, not wishing to upset her father. His peaked color and unusual fatigue bothered her, but when Callie mentioned it later to her mother in the kitchen, Liz Jacobs denied any changes in his appearance or health. She claimed Callie was imagining things and needed to stop her incessant worrying.

But Callie couldn't help it. Her father's health was declining before her eyes, and there didn't seem to be anything she could do about it.

"Have you insisted he see a doctor, Mom?"

"He wouldn't go. You know your father. Unless he's bleeding to death, he won't set foot inside..."

"But he had a heart attack a few years ago. Aren't you worried? When was the last time he had a checkup? You should be insisting..."

"Callie, haven't you learned by now what a stubborn man he is? When he sees a doctor, it'll be his idea, not mine."

"Well, that's just plain ridiculous."

Liz Jacobs nodded her head. "I couldn't agree more. If we hadn't been at Bud and Sharon's five years ago when he had his heart attack, he would be dead by now. Bud practically carried him to the hospital that day." Liz frowned at the memory and slung a kitchen towel over a hook under the sink.

"Well, can't you make a subtle suggestion? He doesn't look good, Mom."

Liz placed her hand on Callie's arm and rubbed lightly. "I'll do my best, sweetheart. In the meantime, try to think about other things. You've been through so much yourself. I don't want you spending all your time fretting over your father when he's probably just tired."

"Mom, sometimes I think you're in as much denial as Daddy."

Liz stepped back and turned so she could gaze out the window over the sink. "You may be right, sweetie. Perhaps I don't want to know the truth. It can be a painful thing to deal with."

~

Mid-August brought milder temperatures than those typical for that time of year, a welcome relief from the hot and sticky weather Oakdale had been experiencing lately. As the summer wound down, so did Callie's enthusiasm for returning to work. She loved her job, but spending time with her daughter far outweighed any desire to return to the workplace. The question of what to do with Emily while she worked weighed heavily on her mind—until her mother volunteered to watch her.

"That's too much for you," Callie had argued. "Em's a handful." But her mother, who'd recently retired from her job as a receptionist, would have none of it. "What else am I going to do with my extra time?" she'd reasoned. "We love our granddaughter, and having her here will brighten my day—and Daddy's, too." Once Callie acquiesced, Liz started to stockpile baby essentials, as if her house wasn't already crammed full of ample necessities for Emily's periodic visits.

Still, Callie worried about the implications of the extra responsibility on her father's health. Lately, just walking from room to room seemed to zap his strength.

"I wish you'd see a doctor, Dad," Callie suggested one night over dinner.

"Why would I want to do that? They'd just run more tests and tell me what I already know: I'm getting old."

"Sixty-two is not old," Callie protested.

"It is when you're in this body," he answered with a grin. On the weighty side, he'd always had a sweet tooth and a proclivity for fattening foods. Callie worried that his cholesterol levels were dangerously high. "I'll be fine, honey," he added when she'd slumped back into her chair, tired of the fight.

One bright Saturday morning, Callie planned a special outing—a trip to Oakdale's own zoo. Theirs was nothing like Chicago's two big parks, but it boasted a couple of tigers, a bear, a monkey exhibit, a bird sanctuary, and a reptile house. At first, Lisa had welcomed the invitation to tag along, saying Jeffrey would love it, but later had to decline when a migraine struck unexpectedly. Disappointed but determined, Callie made the decision to go without her.

Music played in the background while she readied Emily and herself for the day, a praise and worship CD she'd bought in the church bookstore just last Sunday. Wrapped up in the lyrics, she moved rhythmically about her apartment, Emily in tow. "Open the eyes of my heart, Lord," the singer challenged. "Open the eyes of my heart—I want to see You."

Last Sunday's message had been a simple one:

"Faith Is the Key!" Callie had listened with rapt interest as the pastor spoke about the dangers of harboring resentment and withholding forgiveness. "A growing number of believers are peeved at God," he'd said. "They may not admit it, but deep inside they hold some kind of grudge against Him because they believe He doesn't care about their problems. They say, 'Show me and I'll believe,' but God says, 'Believe Me, and I'll show you.'"

Did God care about her personal struggles? She wanted to believe He did.

The parking lot was sparse, midmorning shoppers already out and about. Callie opened the car door and bent to buckle Emily's new seat into place, then went around to her own side. The baby babbled happily, always excited by the prospect of going somewhere. Her own seat belt buckled, Callie adjusted the rearview mirror, then turned the key in the ignition, fully expecting to hear the grinding of the motor.

Silence.

Leaning forward, she put more energy into turning the key, pumping the gas pedal simultaneously.

Still nothing—unless she counted the awful gas fumes that rose up around her.

A rap on the window made her turn her head. Dan Mattson stood on the other side of the door, dressed in worn jeans and a single pocketed white T-shirt. He gave her that familiar jagged grin and leaned over.

She rolled down her window and greeted him with a frustrated frown.

"I doubt you're going anywhere with a dead battery," he said, crouching down so that their eyes met straight on.

"Do you think that's all it is?"

"I'm no mechanic, but that's what it sounds like. The engine's not turning over. Could be a faulty ignition switch, too." She wrinkled her nose. "Or maybe a bad fuel pump, although I wouldn't suspect that, since your engine wasn't making any attempts to start."

"Please stop. I think I prefer the dead battery. It sounds cheaper to fix."

He tilted back on his haunches and swept a gaze over the old car's exterior. "She looks a little worn. Could be just about anything."

Callie felt her face crumple into an even bigger scowl. "Don't tell me that."

"Your ex couldn't afford to leave you with the better car, huh?"

She paused, squinted at the sun, and blurted, "He drives a brand-new motorcycle."

He bowed his head and murmured something. Then quickly raising it again, he gave her his full attention. "Where were you headed?"

"I was taking Emily to the zoo today, but it can wait."

Leaning forward, he peered at Emily, then asked, "How about I drive you over to the nearest automotive supply, help you pick out a battery, then take you to the zoo myself?"

To say she wasn't tempted would be lying. "I couldn't..."

"Why? Got a better idea for getting yourself a battery?" He had a point there. She could always call on her father, but with his health as it was....

There was also Jack, but she hated to bother him since Lisa was sick with a migraine.

"I wouldn't want to put you out."

He leaped to his feet and opened his arms. "Do I look put out?"

Dark hair, gleaming in the sunlight, fell in its usual haphazard fashion. Had he even run a comb through it yet? Touches of humor around his mouth and eyes had her scrambling for excuses.

"I don't know. I should probably..."

He opened her car door and gave her his hand. "Come on, I have no other plans."

"I thought you worked on Saturdays," she said, allowing him to pull her up and out.

"Been keeping tabs on me?" he asked with raised brows. She ducked her head, embarrassed. He laughed. "Granted, sometimes I work on Saturdays, but today—ah, today I woke up and said to myself, "Self, what a great day for the zoo!"

She smiled, charmed. "No, you didn't."

"I swear." His hand on his heart made hers take a dangerous dive. And when he tipped his face in close, she felt a shiver of delight run the length of her. "What do you say?" he asked. "You game?"

And because she couldn't think of a single excuse, she gave a nod of surrender.

They purchased a new battery within the hour, then headed for the zoo, Emily's backseat banter continuing with Dan as her new audience. She seemed to appreciate his attention, and to show her appreciation, kicked her legs and waved her arms with enthusiasm.

His late model Ford Mustang was small and sporty, just the vehicle she would have pictured him in. They rode in companionable silence, every so often commenting about the nice day, various sites along the way, Callie pointing him in the direction of the zoo since he was still unfamiliar with the area. A local soft rock music station played in the background.

The lot was nearly empty. Dan found a parking space close to the gate and killed the engine. "Here we are." It took a while to get Emily situated in her stroller, but when they did, he assumed the job of pushing, and together they approached the ticket counter—like a family.

Dan brought out his wallet before she could protest and paid the small entrance fees.

"Thank you." She wasn't accustomed to someone else paying. Thomas had always expected her to whip out her wallet wherever they went.

"I always loved the zoo as a kid," he said on their way to the first exhibit. They sauntered along, every so often brushing elbows. She sidestepped to avoid his touch.

"We rarely went. Maybe if I'd had siblings…."

"You're an only child, then?"

"Yes. You?"

"I have an older brother and a younger sister. Ken and Samantha." A smile crossed his face and he glanced her way. "Ken is five years older than me and much wiser."

"I doubt that, the wiser part. What about your sister?"

"She's two years younger, twenty-eight." *So he's thirty himself.* She had wondered. "Sam's extremely gifted musically. And a live wire. She'll tell you what's on her mind." His eyes gleamed like glass. "Sometimes you remind me of her." For some odd reason the comment touched a tender chord.

Balmy air kept whipping up a few strands of hair that Callie continually tucked behind her ear.

"I always wanted a brother or a sister, but my mother—had difficulties." Now, why had she told him that? Never mind that it was true. Like her aunt Sharon, her mom had had a hysterectomy just months after Callie was born.

"Does your family live around here?" His voice showed interest.

"Yes. My parents live just outside of Oakdale. I grew up here."

"Oakdale's a nice community. Close enough to Chicago to be convenient, but pleasantly isolated." Dan followed the arrow to the bears. She enjoyed that he took the lead. "Look there." He pointed a long index finger straight ahead. A black bear sat on a slab of cement, munching a snack. "Emily, can you see him?" he asked, hunching over to release the strap around Emily so he could hold her up for a closer look. The baby was instantly elated about the prospect of being carried. Dan lifted her effortlessly, and her fingers curled around the nape of his broad neck to hang on.

"See?" he said softly, the warmth of his smile echoing in his voice. He was a natural.

When Emily spotted the big, black, hairy creature, her round eyes brightened with glee, her mouth formed an "O," and she giggled. Dan and Callie exchanged smiles.

Callie took over pushing the stroller, relieved to have something to do with her hands. They continued on their way, visiting one exhibit after another, Dan giving Emily his attention, occasionally throwing shadowy glances at Callie, the baby's ceaseless banter working as a buffer.

When it was time for lunch, they found an unoccupied picnic table. Callie spread out the checkered cloth she'd brought along and set out items of fruit, cheese, sandwich fixings, drinks, and paper products. They worked side-by-side, laughing and joking with ease, then ate heartily, enjoying quiet, easy conversation.

Callie spoon-fed Emily a jar of baby food, and, for a treat, a few bites of pudding. The baby scarfed them down, kicking her legs appreciatively and dribbling drool onto her bib. Dan laughed, picking up a nearby napkin to wipe her sticky chin.

Callie turned her body around on the bench and stared out at the park. "You have a way with her," she remarked. A gentle breeze tickled her bare arms.

Dan shrugged. "She's a cutie."

She glanced at him. "So you've said." Then sticking her hands between her closed knees, she looked at her toes peeking out the ends of her sandals and asked the question that had been eating at her almost from the very beginning. "Do you have any kids of your own?"

"No." There wasn't a moment's hesitation between question and answer.

His curtness set off some kind of internal warning signal, but she plunged ahead. "You could have fooled me. It seems like you might have a family out there somewhere."

As soon as the words were out, she regretted them, for his brow furrowed in anger. "Sheesh, Callie, what do you take me for? Would I be spending the day with you if I were married?"

"I'm sorry. I—I just....Were you ever married? Are you divorced, too?"

A dark, distant expression spread over his countenance. "I'm neither married nor divorced."

Startled by her own relief, she took a moment to gather her thoughts. *So he'd never married.* She still had questions, but wanting to get on safer ground with him, sought a more comfortable arena. "Where are you from?"

"Michigan."

"Really? My aunt and uncle live in Michigan—the west side. They have a beautiful place on the Lake Michigan shoreline."

"I grew up in the Lansing area." He relaxed, returning to his former mood. "I like the west side. The beaches are beautiful."

"Yes, they are. Where do you work?"

"I'm in construction."

"Really? Have you always done that?"

"You're full of questions, aren't you?" He smiled, balled up a napkin and tossed it into the nearest waste container, hitting the mark like a pro. He glanced at Emily as if she were his charge. "Look, she's getting droopy-eyed." The child was slumped in her stroller, head falling sideways. "She'll be out soon."

Callie smiled. "It's been a busy day. It's past her nap time."

Snatching a peek at her watch, she noted it was well past two. Bending forward, she tucked a light blanket around Emily's body, taking care not to disturb her slumbering frame.

"I'm glad I caught you when I did. When we get back, I'll put the battery in your car for you." Apparently, he didn't plan to answer her last question. She noticed he was quite skilled at darting around those areas he considered none of her business.

"You don't have to do that. You've already done more than was necessary."

"You skilled at installing batteries?"

"Not really." She laughed. "But I could ask Lisa's husband."

"Ah, the infamous Lisa. So your friend is married."

"Yes. In fact, she was planning to come with me today but got a migraine at the last minute."

"I'd say I'm sorry, but it'd be a lie."

Callie giggled. She had to admit she'd been somewhat glad herself with the turn of events.

He swiveled around on the picnic table so that they faced the same direction, shoulders touching, and spread his legs straight out, crossing them at the ankles, his thigh connecting with hers, causing her to readjust her seating. With a lazy yawn, he glanced up at the trees, wove the long fingers of both his hands together and put them behind his head as a kind of neck rest.

"You're very different from my first impression of you."

Anxious jitters tickled her stomach. "In what way?"

He tipped his head in her direction, then back at the trees. "You're pretty tough for a woman, probably more so than you realize. It can't be easy raising a child alone. I admire your strength." He paused, as if measuring his thoughts. "You're not exactly hard to look at, either," he teased, his elbow coming down to poke her playfully on the head, his languorous gaze resting on her face.

"Thanks—I think," she said, laughing at his antics. She didn't know about the tough part. At the moment, she felt pretty vulnerable, especially since he appeared to be flirting.

Eyes narrowed, he leaned back and studied his crossed ankles. "You're a little skittish, too, as if you're worried what might be around the next bend." Wind rustled the leaves overhead, scattering a flock of birds in varying directions. "Can I ask what ended your marriage?" he suddenly asked. "Besides the fact you married a jerk," he added, as if to assure her that he was on her side.

A wry smile creased her lips at the bitter truth. "That pretty much sums it up."

"How long were you married?" he pushed.

The question set her off-balance, made the muscles in her neck go taut. *He refuses my personal questions but expects me to answer his?* Still, she figured if she responded with openness, he might reciprocate. *Not that I'm all that interested,* she mulled.

"About a year. I knew him in high school, but we didn't really date until after I got my teaching job, and then we only dated a short time." She chuckled to herself. "We fell in love pretty quick. Unfortunately, we didn't talk much about the important stuff—like how many kids we wanted. Found out after the fact he wasn't too excited about having kids, period. In fact, he was downright mad when I got pregnant, accused me of tricking him. I did forget to take the pill a couple of times, but I didn't intentionally—you know—make the choice to have a baby.

"Things just went downhill after that." She kicked at a stray pebble and watched a low cloud of dust gather near her foot. "I never should have married him in the first place. He wasn't—good for me." Or *to* me, she might have added.

He glanced at the sleeping child. "Tell me he at least pays child support."

Now she did laugh. "You're kidding, right? When Thomas left, it was with the understanding that he wanted nothing to do with our daughter. He has no legal claim to her. And he likes it that way."

Thomas. At least now Dan had a name to go with the heartless jerk. He shook his head and muttered something under his breath. "He is a loser. You think he'll ever have any regrets—about Emily, I mean?"

Deep sadness settled around Callie's heart. "He's too self-centered for that." Recalling the recent phone call made her shudder. She could only pray he would heed her warning not to call again. But something told her she'd not heard the last of him.

Dan unfolded his big frame and stared at her. "You okay? You're shivering."

Words seemed to wedge in her throat.

"Callie?" His hand rested on her shoulder then and, innocent as it was, she instinctively jolted. Quickly, she centered her gaze on a passing bicyclist, watched him pedal past at breakneck speed, tried to ignore Dan's sizzling touch. "Something wrong?" he asked, his voice a mere whisper. Without warning, a tiny tear trickled down her cheek. She was losing it—right in front of him—and the rawness of the moment made her quiver the harder.

When he leaned into her to swipe at the tear with the pad of his thumb, his breath fanning her face, she sucked in a lung full of air and forgot to exhale. Her thundering heart told her to breathe, but the shock of his nearness made it difficult to think, let alone breathe.

Another shudder passed through her. He put a finger to her chin and turned it so that their eyes met. Dark, penetrating, guileless eyes meeting up with her blue ones. "What did he do to you, Callie?" he asked.

"Nothing," she answered, breathless and flustered, turning her face away, too ashamed to have him see her like this.

"I don't believe it." Slowly, his calloused hand went from her face to her shoulder then down her arm, brushing at the tiny hairs that stood on end.

"Don't," she snapped, withdrawing her arm and slanting away from him.

"What are you afraid of?" he persisted while making an attempt to pull her close, not in a forceful manner, but with a certain sense of purpose.

Fear mingled with awareness. "Don't—touch—me," she ordered, quickly wrangling out of reach by sliding to the other end of the picnic bench, her arms flailing pointlessly.

He raised both hands in a show of surrender. "I won't—I promise. Calm down, okay?" She relaxed. "Good grief, what happened to you?"

His question sent her emotions toppling in different directions, as more tears threatened at the surface. "I don't want to talk about it."

It appeared they both had secrets—secrets neither was ready to divulge.

The ride home hardly mirrored the pleasant morning drive. Emily continued napping. Dan had turned off the radio, adding to the awkward silence. She longed to explain her strange behavior, but how could she when she didn't understand it herself? How could she admit his presence frightened her, made her feel things she didn't want to feel? How could she tell him that his touch, while lovely and innocent, had set off a string of bad memories?

Back at the apartment complex, he shut down the engine. Staring straight ahead, he clasped the steering wheel with both hands. "Sorry about what happened back there. I didn't mean to scare you."

"No, no, you've nothing to apologize for," she assured. "It was—just—nothing really." She forced a smile. Perhaps someday she'd talk about her abusive ex-husband, but not today. Swinging her head around to get a look at her sleeping child, she said, "Well, thank you for a wonderful day. Oh, and for helping with the battery. I—um—thanks." *Best to keep things light,* she told herself.

When she went for the door, he reached across the front of her to stop her progress.

"I'm not the ogre you probably take me for. Okay, I have a few secrets of my own, but I don't want you thinking I'd ever harm you." Her breath halted in her throat, while his floated weightlessly across her face and neck, his dark eyes connecting with hers. "You believe in God?"

"What?" It was about the last question she'd have expected, but at least it was an easy one. "Of course. Don't you?"

He released her door handle and leaned back in his seat, giving a casual shrug, allowing seconds to pass before he opened his mouth to reply. "I've been on a sort of search for truth." Head resting on the neck rest, he shot her a withering glance and winked. "That's part of my mystery," he said with a chuckle. Nodding, she felt her body relax. "I ask myself—is God truly personal, or is He just some abstract, mystical higher power? And if He's personal, why doesn't He care more about His children's pain? Take yours, for instance. Beautiful baby, absent father. That's got to hurt. Don't you ever want to shake your fist at God? Or wonder why He seems to abandon us?"

Callie bit her lip, searching for the right words. "I think He does care, but we have to open our hearts and minds to His truths, accept the things that happen to us as a part of His bigger plan and purpose for our lives. Accept that He loves us even when life throws junk at us. It's a matter of faith." Portions of last Sunday's sermon replayed in her mind.

He eyed her with suspicion. "You go to church, then?" he asked.

"All my life—off and on. More so since my divorce. I find I need something to hang onto, something strong and stable. Maybe you should give God half a chance," she suggested.

He shifted in his seat, removed the key, and clenched it in his fist. "I'll think about it."

Chapter 10

Dad finally agreed to see the doctor," Liz Jacobs told Callie during a phone conversation a few days later. "Dr. Bronson says his heart is failing."

Callie felt her own heart clench painfully. Because she was in the middle of feeding Emily, the child kicked and screamed when her mother stopped to answer the phone. "I can barely hear you," she said over all the racket.

"We'll talk about it later, sweetie. I can tell you're busy with the baby right now."

"Mom, wait, tell me what else the doctor said," she insisted, Emily's cries drowning out all hope of a decent conversation.

"There's not much to tell. He ordered several tests. Seems Dad's heart has deteriorated since the heart attack."

"What do they plan—to do about it?" A clogged throat made her voice break mid-sentence.

"The doctor changed his medication, hoping to thin the blood a little so his heart won't have to work as hard at pumping."

"I don't see how that…"

"He also prescribed something for his angina. And something new for his high blood pressure. It was alarmingly high."

"He should have gone sooner," Callie said, cradling the phone under her chin while she handed Emily a cracker to tide her over. Immediately, she put it to her mouth, her big eyes pooled with tears.

"I know you're right, but your dad is a stubborn man."

"Is he going to be all right?" Callie asked, fear eating at the edges of her chest. "Did the doctor say if… what…?"

"He's in God's hands, Callie. All we can do is trust Him."

๑

Sunday morning sunlight glimmered like glass on the tile entryway. Ready for the morning service, Callie yanked her purse off the hook beside the door and draped it over her shoulder. Then, slinging Emily's diaper bag over the other, she scooped Emily up into her arms and made for the door, locking it behind her.

"Your car running all right these days?"

She turned around to see Dan locking his own door. Lately they'd established a kind of safe friendship. They might go days without running into each other, but when they did, a friendly chat usually transpired.

His actions were pleasant but distant; courteous, but wary. She couldn't fault him for it. Anything more would have been too risky. They both had secrets too painful to uncover.

He was dressed in workout clothing, gym shorts, worn T-shirt with the sleeves ripped off, and running shoes. His muscular calves flexed as he took the stairs beside her.

"It's working great, thanks to you." The "Little Red Rust Bunny," as Lisa so affectionately called it, got her where she needed to go—never mind the fact that it looked as if it were on its last legs.

He opened the door at the bottom of the stairs, and she walked out ahead of him. "All I did was install a new battery. Can't take credit for more than that."

Side by side, they walked to the parking lot. "You don't look dressed for church," Callie jested, hoisting Emily higher.

A light snicker tumbled out. "Very observant of you."

He stopped at her car and watched as she searched for her keys. When she finally pulled out the jangling mass, Dan grabbed them from her and unlocked her door, then jogged to the other side to unlock Emily's door. Callie followed after. "Here, give me the baby," he ordered, taking Emily before she could argue.

"Hi, cute stuff," he said, rubbing noses with the child to her delight and giving her a little squeeze. Bending over, he fastened her into her seat, Emily babbling the entire time, a noisy rattle in her fist lending to the clamor.

"What church do you attend?" Dan asked, closing Emily's door and heading back around to Callie's side. Callie opened her own door and climbed inside.

"Fellowship Chapel," she answered, closing it and rolling down the window. It was a beautiful summer morning, quiet save the twittering birds and a distant siren. "It's a wonderful place to worship. Terrific music, great biblical teaching, friendly people. You should check it out sometime." She peered up at him, his bulky frame outlined by the sun's rays. "It wouldn't be too painful, you know." She turned the ignition, and her motor came to life.

He took a step back, folded his massive arms. "Maybe I will—visit sometime."

With a smile and a wave, she set the gearshift in reverse and backed out.

A quick glance in her rearview mirror showed him jogging down the path toward town.

The sermon touched her in places cold and dark, quenching thirsty corners of her mind. After absorbing it, she was convinced more than ever that she needed a closer walk with God. It wasn't some kind of revelation based on emotion; rather, it was an uncovering of truth, a reality that gnawed at her heart. Still, something kept her from jumping in headfirst and giving herself completely to Him.

She spent the afternoon with her parents, enjoying

quiet conversation over a home-cooked meal. After dinner, she went to her old room. Emily's crib was set up in the center, her old twin canopy still made up with the same bedding she'd had in high school. She smoothed out a wrinkle in the comforter and moved about, fingering one shelf for dust and finding none. Her mother was the Queen of Clean.

Callie's high school senior picture, encased in a gold frame, sat atop the antique oak dresser. Surrounding it were various keepsakes she'd collected over the years. She would probably never reclaim some of the items; they were just a part of the old room. To remove them would have been to steal a piece of history. She smiled when she picked up her old yearbook and began leafing through its pages. *Talk about history....*

Instinctively, she thumbed through the pages until she reached Thomas's class picture. He'd been handsome back then, perhaps even charming. Unfortunately, she'd not known the *real* Thomas until after marriage, when he adopted an abusive nature. Or maybe his abusive nature was latent; maybe it took an institution such as marriage, the success of which depends on two people's mutual sacrifice of self-will, to unleash it. Would she have married him otherwise?

"Recalling the good old days?"

She turned at the sound of her father's voice. "Daddy, you should be resting." He wore a haggard look.

"I'd rather stay awake while my girls are here."

"I'm planning to put Emily down for her nap soon. We'll be here a while. Why don't you go watch sports on the couch?" Her mother was in the kitchen feeding Emily.

Ignoring her suggestion, he nodded at the yearbook open to Thomas's picture. "You're better off without him, you know."

Plopping onto her bed, she patted the spot beside her. Ralph Jacobs accepted the silent invitation to sit. Callie felt her shoulders slump. Silently, she thumbed the page featuring Thomas's face. "If only I'd known him better before I married him."

She thought about the phone call. Tempted to discuss it with her father, she quickly thought better of it. Why add more stress to her parents' lives? It should be enough that Lisa knew.

"It's not worth worrying over." He rested a hand on her shoulder. Callie leaned into him, as if to absorb some of his quiet strength.

"Do you ever pray for him?" she asked. If ever there was a saint, it was Ralph Jacobs.

"Now that is a very good question. I suppose I have prayed for him, but more so before your divorce, and then I prayed more for your safety, though I'm sure you would have told me if I'd had true cause for concern."

She cowered under his words, feeling a tad guilty for having kept the entire truth from her parents. They'd known about Thomas's temper, his verbal outbursts, but not about the physical episodes that often resulted. And what was the point of talking about it now that it was all history?

"I don't hate the young man," he went on, "and you shouldn't, either. Besides being Emily's father, he's still a child of God. He may have failed as a husband, but we have to remember the Lord still loves him. Perhaps one day he'll see the error of his ways and give his life to Christ. It's never too late for that."

Rising, Callie walked to the window to stare up the street, hugging the closed yearbook to her chest. Most of the original families from the old neighborhood had moved out, making way for younger ones. Two of the driveways across the road were peppered with tricycles and wagons. The sight brought a sense of nostalgia.

She swiveled on her heels to face her father. "I know you're right, Daddy. Today's sermon drove home that point. In fact—I think it's past time I recommitted my life to God."

Ralph's brows flickered as his mouth curved with tenderness. "You can do that right now if you like," he said, his voice low and steady. "God will meet you wherever and whenever. He's not fussy about the time or place. Would you like me to pray with you?"

The question both surprised and pleased her. "Yes, I think I would."

And so, in the quiet comfort of her childhood bedroom, Callie prayed, with her father as her witness, to invite God to be the Lord of her life and to take full possession of her heart.

൭൯

Dan had thought a great deal about Callie's suggestion to visit Fellowship Chapel. Curious, he'd even driven by the place later in the day. It was a modern, brick structure, large and commanding, situated in a neighborhood of nice homes. He noted the many different service times, even Saturday night worship. He liked a forward-thinking church.

But after mulling it over, he decided he was in no shape to darken any church door. He'd been drinking a lot lately, using foul language, and generally setting a bad example. Even Greg Freeman had grimaced a time or two. "Hey, Dan, watch your language when you're on the job."

Shamed, he'd nodded, but later scoffed at the rebuke. He wasn't the only crass guy in the company; virtually all of them, save Greg, were hard-nosed, unrefined characters. You almost *had* to be like them in order to fit in. Of course, that was something else on which he'd based many a sermon—maintaining one's witness in a spiritually dead environment.

It seemed the Reverend Daniel Mattson had fallen far in a very short time.

Throughout the day, Callie's face flashed across his mind, but he kept pushing it back, reminding himself he hadn't sufficiently grieved the loss of his wife and daughter, never mind that it'd been well over a year since the accident. He wondered how long was long enough, then finally concluded there were no pat answers.

ღ

A ringing phone tore Callie away from her blissful slumber. Not in a long while had she slept so peacefully.

"Hello?" was her groggy greeting.

"Honey, it's me. Mom."

In seconds, her sheets fell away from her. "Mom! What's wrong? It's two-thirty in the morning!"

"Callie," Liz's voice cracked. "I'm at the hospital. Your dad…"

An eternity passed before someone, a male voice she didn't recognize, took over. "Callie, this is Pastor Tim. Your mom called me from her house a while ago. She had to have an ambulance bring your dad in. I think, well, you better come to Mercy Hospital." His voice assumed a solemn quality.

Tightness kept her throat from working properly. "I'll get there as quickly as I can."

Tim Strickland, an associate pastor at Fellowship Chapel, was relatively new to the staff. The only thing she knew about him was that he was married and had two small children.

After she replaced the phone, she jumped from the

bed then quickly sat back down, overwhelming weakness consuming her.

Dear God, please help me do this.

Taking a couple of calming breaths, she tried again. *I need to have faith, trust the Lord for strength,* she told herself. Rising, she moved across the room, took off her nightgown, then slipped into the same pair of Capri pants she'd worn the day before, thankful she'd been remiss about putting them away.

Once dressed, she headed for the bathroom, dragged a comb through her mass of tangled blonde waves, and glanced at her sleep-lined face. *I need to be strong for Mom,* she silently reminded herself before hurrying to the living room in search of her sandals. Finding them under the coffee table, she slipped into them.

Now—what to do about Emily? she mulled. Moments later, she had her answer.

~

Dan padded across the room in nothing but his boxers, Callie's pounding on the door and hollering enough to wake the dead. Confusion and concern mingled when he threw wide the door and got his first glimpse of her.

"What's wrong?" He dragged her inside. "Where's Emily?"

"She's sleeping. Can you come over and watch

her? I have to go to the hospital. My dad…something's happened."

He could see tears welling up in the corners of her eyes. "Of course, no problem, but what's going on?" Unable to resist, he brushed his fingers down her bare arms, felt her fear as if it were his own. "Do you have any idea…?"

"It's his heart." Dread, dark and vivid, glittered in her sapphire eyes, as more tears pooled around the edges. "I don't know how long I'll be. I don't—know what to expect."

Wanting to reassure her, but knowing there was little he could say or do that would ease her mind, he simply gave her arm a gentle squeeze. "You go ahead." He looked across the hall and saw that she'd left her apartment door open.

She lingered in the doorway. "The nursery is just down the hall," she said, pointing back with hooked thumb. "There are diapers under the changing table. You'll find a bottle in the fridge, top shelf. You'll need to warm it just slightly." He gave a slow nod. "You shouldn't have to feed her, though—that is, if she sleeps until morning. I would hope I'd be back before then. But just in case…"

He put a hand to her shoulder to still her chatter. "Callie, we'll be fine. Just go."

Looking like she didn't believe him, she granted him a weak smile, turned, hesitated, then skittered down the stairs and out the door.

Grabbing a shirt and a pair of jeans to throw on, and thanking God that he hadn't had more than two beers before bed, Dan snatched his keys off the kitchen counter and headed across the hall.

When Callie entered Mercy Hospital, she was out of breath from running. Approaching the front desk, she sought directions from a middle-aged woman.

"My father was brought into the ER..." she started to explain.

"Callie?"

Spinning around, she recognized Pastor Tim. He'd apparently been waiting for her. Tall and brawny with short, curly, brown hair, he had the look of an oversized teddy bear. A cautious smile lined his thin lips. "Pastor Tim," she greeted.

"Your mother is upstairs."

"Upstairs?"

"Yes." His smile waned ever so slightly. "Come. I'll take you."

A sense of foreboding caved in on her. "My dad, is he...?" The words stuck in her throat like peanut butter.

Rather than answer, he took her by the elbow and led her to the elevators. Zombie-like, she followed. When the elevator door opened a couple of nurses emerged, nodded politely, and slid past. Pastor Tim nudged her inside, pushed the button that would take them to the fourth floor, then folded his hands in front of him. Unsure what to say, Callie merely stared at the closed doors and prayed for strength.

"I'm sorry to have to tell you this, Callie," he said, quelling the silence, his voice little more than a low murmur, "but I think you should know." Her head shot up, dreading the words. He put a hand to her arm. "They are sustaining your father with life support until you arrive. I don't think there is much they can do."

A strange, prickly sensation swept over her body, starting at the top of her head and moving slowly down to the tips of her toes. *Dizzy, so dizzy.* Clammy fingers swiped at her sticky brow, as she slumped weakly against the wall of the elevator, her own abilities slowly evaporating.

"You can do all things through Christ," came the whispered truth. *"Trust in Me."*

A persistent ring shook Dan awake. Disoriented, it took a moment to register his whereabouts, but when he did, he yanked the phone piece, which was sitting next to the sofa, off its cradle. "Hello?" he said, dragging himself into a sitting position and raking a hand through his thick head of hair.

Upon first arriving at Callie's apartment, he'd checked in on Emily and found her sleeping soundly.

Satisfied, he'd wandered back through the apartment, familiarized himself with where things were, then switched on the TV set and settled into her sofa. Within the hour, he'd drifted back to sleep, his ear subconsciously awaiting the first sign of whimpers coming from the nursery.

Callie's voice, soft and unsure, murmured a greeting.

His back went straight as a fence post as reality set in. "How's your dad?"

A mile-wide pause had him holding his breath. "He's gone," she finally replied, her voice a mere whisper.

Gone? As in, he left the hospital—or, worse—was deceased? Since he didn't want to push for clarification, he closed his eyes and waited, hoping she'd expound.

"They were keeping him alive until I could arrive." Just like that, he had his answer.

"I'm sorry," he replied past the lump of emotion sitting in his own throat. A river of longing washed over him. If only he knew what to say to make the pain go away. Unfortunately, he was all too familiar with how it felt—the anguish, the misery, the uncanny sense that everything and everyone is moving on without you. "What can I do for you?"

"Could you—would you mind staying with Emily a bit longer? I'll need to drive my mother home. She rode over in the ambulance. There are phone calls I need to make. Pastor Tim is here with us now...."

Pastor Tim?

"Callie, you do whatever it is that you need to do. I'm in no rush," he assured her.

"But you'll need to head for work soon," she was saying, "and I'm not sure how long…"

"I'll give my boss a call. No big deal. Really." He sat back again, his eyes coming to rest on a floral painting above the fireplace. On either side of the painting was a set of pewter candleholders, and on the far side of the mantel, a small bouquet of flowers that matched those in the picture.

"But Emily…"

"…is still sleeping," he finished. "When she wakes, I'll handle it. Try not to worry." He couldn't believe his own sense of calm. It'd been a while since he'd had full responsibility for a baby unless he counted the night he'd helped Lori with the babysitting. It'd also been a while since he'd opened his heart wide enough to feel another's pain.

"Can you change a diaper?"

He swept a rough hand down his face and willed himself not to think about Chelsea. "I think I can manage. Trust me, okay?"

He heard her heave a sigh, and in his mind's eye, he envisioned drooping shoulders. "I guess I don't have much choice."

Since there was little point in trying to reassure her further, they said their good-byes.

Dan sat for a moment, digesting all that Callie

had just imparted to him. A lone light over the oven gave him a shadowy glimpse of her tidy little kitchen, poles apart from his own, which even now was cluttered with beer and soda cans and several days' worth of dirty dishes.

His stomach growled, and the refrigerator, bedecked with photos and a small, magnetic white board, seemed to call to him. He stood up and strolled across the room, and, on a whim, threw open the door, bending at the waist to have a look inside, one hand looped over the door. *No beer or booze for this little lady,* he noted. *Good thing.*

Instead, he found a large supply of baby bottles, a half-gallon of milk, a quart of juice, bread, some plastic containers, lettuce, tomatoes, eggs, and a variety of other healthy-looking stuff. Again, quite a contrast to his half-used package of lunchmeat, large hunk of cheese, half loaf of bread, and peanut butter and jelly, not to mention his favorite brand of beer. He shut the door, scoffing at his nosiness.

In lieu of eating anything, he settled for a tall glass of water from the spigot.

Sauntering down the hall with the intention of checking on Emily, he paused to study several framed pictures hanging on the wall, noting one of Callie and Emily standing alongside an older couple. *Her parents, perhaps?*

Emily's door stood open, an angel night-light glowing in the corner. He lingered for a while in the doorway, reassuring himself that he heard the baby's steady, quiet breathing. While her blanket lay in a ball at one end of the crib, she wore a one-piece, flannel gown that sufficiently covered her, with her little backside pointing to the sky. His heart clenched at the sight and he gave a mental shake, tearing himself away.

He figured Callie's room was the one next to Emily's. Tempted to check it out, he resisted and headed back to the living room. It wouldn't be long before Emily stirred.

Flopping back into the sofa, he propped both bare feet on the coffee table. Next to his feet lay a leather-bound, maroon-colored book—her Bible. Curious, he leaned forward and snatched it off the table. The front page bore the words "To Our Darling Daughter with Love." Inside were several underlined passages. He thumbed through the feathery pages, carefully reading each highlighted verse until a hard knob at the back of his throat made swallowing difficult. Quickly, he snapped the book shut and placed it back where it belonged—this time further from his reach.

When six-thirty rolled around, he called Greg Freeman to explain the situation. As he'd figured, Greg was more than understanding, even going so far as to commend Dan for his willingness to help. "Hey, don't go giving me any undue credit, man," Dan said. "All I'm doing is sitting with my neighbor's kid till she comes home."

"I'm sure it's a little more than that," Greg countered.

"If you need to stay longer, feel free. Sounds like the lady could use some help."

"I think she's had some tough breaks."

"Yeah? I wonder if she has a church affiliation," Greg remarked.

"She told me she attends Fellowship Chapel. She mentioned a Pastor Tim."

"Oh, sure—he's a good guy."

"You know him?"

"Sure, Karen and I go there as well. Tim is an assistant pastor. I might even know your neighbor."

"Her name is Callie May," Dan said.

"Don't know her well. Karen might. Pretty little thing. From what I hear, her husband was an ungrateful jerk. Left her while she was pregnant. Don't know much beyond that. I only know that much because Karen's mother is a good friend of Callie's mom."

"Small world."

The conversation ended abruptly when Dan heard Emily's first little squeals. Greg chuckled when Dan said, "Wish me luck."

"You don't need luck, man," he assured. "It'll all come back to you; you'll see."

"It'll all come back to you." The words echoed in the chambers of his mind as he made a beeline for Emily's room.

Outside her door, he paused. What if she screamed in fright at the first glimpse of him? Surely his unkempt appearance would frighten the daylights out of anyone, particularly a baby. He finger-combed his hair, then frowned when he brushed a palm over his day-old beard. Strange how he felt like a teenager about to embark on his first date. What if she couldn't accept that he was here? After all, she was used to being greeted by her mother every morning, not some dark-eyed, dark-haired, burly monster.

Slowly, he stepped inside, caught sight of little hands batting at a hanging mobile. "G'mornin,' Em," he greeted her softly.

The child stilled, craned her neck to the side until she saw from whence the voice came. A look of shock washed over her as did a little tremor. He held his breath, waiting for an explosion of emotion.

"Hi, baby," he repeated. "Your mommy's not here right now, but I promise you she will be," he crooned. "You want to come see me?"

He reached out his hands, inviting her into them. Rather than accept the offer, she stuck a couple of fingers into her mouth and studied him. After a minute, she pulled herself into a sitting position, using the rungs of her crib, big round eyes sweeping over him all the while.

When he determined she wasn't quite ready to be held, he crouched down. "Shall we talk a bit first?" Surprisingly, she picked up a toy and shoved it between the bars. *A peace offering?* Smiling, he took the plush animal.

Thumb in mouth, she settled back, and for the

next few moments, they simply played a quiet game of "stare." Nerves on edge, he gingerly offered up his arms once more.

This time, she complied.

The drive back to the Jacobs residence was mournful at best. Neither mother nor daughter had much to say, their minds still trying to process the shock of the morning's events.

Early morning clouds blocked the first rays of sunlight, reinforcing the dark waves of grief washing over Callie's soul.

"I can't believe he's gone," she finally said, lifting the silent blanket that lay between them.

Callie pulled into her parents' paved drive. Her father's car was parked in the place he'd left it yesterday, under the rusted basketball hoop.

"I know, honey," was all her mother could manage. Ralph Jacobs had suffered a massive heart attack—one the doctors claimed had done irreversible damage. What were they going to do without him? He'd been their rock for so long.

Liz sat motionless, eyes still swollen from earlier tears. There were sure to be more, but for now, both women's emotional wells seemed to have run dry.

Callie cut the engine, dread of entering the empty

house keeping her glued to her seat. "I recommitted my life to the Lord yesterday."

"Callie."

"Daddy prayed with me in my bedroom." The memory of that precious father/daughter moment replayed itself.

"I didn't know. Perhaps God was waiting for that to happen before…"

"Maybe so."

Climbing out of the car, they took to the sidewalk leading to the front porch. The screen door groaned open. "Your dad was going to oil that today. I heard him mention it last night."

"We'll find someone to fix it," Callie replied, closing the door behind her mother. Looking around the barren house, she swallowed a sob and straightened weary shoulders. Then walking her mother to the couch, she sat her down. "I'm going to make some phone calls while you rest. I'll call Aunt Sharon first. I know she and Bud will want to come right away."

Liz, usually strong and self-sufficient, acquiesced, her eyes clouded over with unshed tears.

~

Emily spent the morning riding on Dan's hip. She'd not been interested in playing with her toys, nor did she relish being left alone. So far, they'd had breakfast together, played pat-a-cake until his palms went numb, read five animal books, and then settled down to watch portions of *The Today Show, Exercise for Health, Cooking with Martha,* and the local news and weather.

He'd explained the details of the weather map to her, including the heat index, the long-range forecast, what the weatherman meant by high and low air pressure, and the reason for the heat wave in Texas, pointing out that it was closer to the equator than Chicago. She seemed to grab onto that concept with enthusiasm.

By mid-morning, it was time for another diaper change, his nose making the determination. He hauled her back to the nursery, found the diapers, wet-wipes, and powder, and went about the task, turning up his nose at the smell, even as Emily kicked her feet and jabbered nonstop. Her constant babble had him laughing in spite of himself.

After snapping the one-piece outfit in place, he drew her up into his arms again. "Shall we put some clothes on you, jellybean?" he asked.

"Gaaah," was her apt reply.

"I thought you'd agree."

He opened a couple of drawers and pawed through them single-handedly until he located a pair of pants and a frilly little summer shirt. Whether they were meant to match remained a mystery.

"These should do," he muttered, setting Emily on the changing table. Managing her flailing arms and kicking legs was a chore, but finally, the job accomplished, he snatched up a pink blanket and the bottle she'd started earlier and headed for the rocking chair.

In less than ten minutes, she'd drained the final few ounces of her milk—and her energy.

While she slept, he watched in rapt wonder. Could it be? Had the little stinker completely captured his heart?

Callie fumbled with the doorknob and found it unlocked. Proceeding through the door, she took a hasty breath, her heart and lungs heavy with emotion. She'd just put in a long morning on the phone with friends and family, tending to her mother's needs, and wondering how to handle her own.

The first thing she spotted was Dan slumped in the sofa, eyes closed, brawny, bare legs propped on the coffee table. Thick, black hair lay tumbled across his forehead, his wrinkled, short-sleeved shirt an indication that Emily had spent a good share of the morning nestled against his broad chest. Had the man slept at all, or had her baby kept him pacing? Some kind of unidentifiable emotion skittered past her heart. Just who was this guy—stranger one minute, friendly neighbor the next? Latching the door as soundlessly as possible, she set her purse on the floor and tiptoed past him to head toward the nursery.

Spare diapers lay stacked on the changing table,

powder and baby wipes in plain view, an array of toys strewn about on the floor, indicating he had opened the toy box. Emily slept soundly, her expression soft and serene, a light blanket covering her body. It appeared Daniel Mattson had done a good job of caring for her baby.

"Callie." A husky voice ruptured the silence. She turned in haste and found him looming in the doorway. "I must have dozed a minute. How are you doing?" He stepped all the way into the room, finger combing his hair, his muscled frame stretching the fabric of his shirt. Raven eyes studied her with particular care.

She shivered with chill and fatigue and forced a weak smile, running a hand up and down her arm. "I'm okay," she managed.

He must have recognized her exaggeration. He advanced slowly, drawing her into his arms, whispering condolences over the top of her head. The heat of his breath created more shivers. One big hand was splayed at the center of her back; the other cradled her shoulder, her own arms encircling his solid frame. Although part of her wanted to resist the embrace, another part couldn't let go, and so they stayed like that for several moments, his gentle swaying movements lending comfort, even as her quiet tears drizzled downward.

When it seemed the tears had slowed, he took her by the hand and led her to the living room, pointing her toward the sofa. Giving her shoulders a gentle push, he sat her down, then settled in beside her. She hesitated, then came closer, resting her head on his shoulder. "Get some rest," he ordered, his tone firm but gentle. "We'll talk later."

Willingly, she closed her eyes.

~

An hour later, Dan was cursing the blaring phone. Callie's head, which had started on his shoulder, now rested comfortably on a pillow in his lap. Slow, steady breathing indicated she'd fallen into sound slumber. Trying his best to maneuver himself without disturbing her, he reached for the phone but she sat bolt upright.

"Hello?" he mumbled.

A slight pause ensued. "Is—is Callie available?"

"May I tell her who's calling?" he inquired of the female voice.

"It's Lisa."

"Oh, hi, Lisa. Yeah, she's right here." He handed over the phone. Callie's gaunt expression unveiled volumes about her inner feelings, but she pulled herself together with determined fortitude.

Her voice cracked when she spoke, as did Dan's tightly clamped heart. What was happening to him? He refused to surrender to the thoughts the question stirred in him.

"That was Dan, my neighbor," Callie was saying, sending him a fleeting look. "Yes." Another pause. "My aunt and uncle are with her now....Em and I will spend the next several days over there….What? The funeral is tomorrow….Three o'clock….I know. I appreciate that. Yeah, that'll be fine….Okay. Thanks for calling. G'bye."

The entire conversation lasted less than two minutes. He took the phone back. "You okay?" he asked after placing it in its cradle. "You were sleeping pretty good there."

She swept a hand through her tousled blonde hair and slid a couple of inches away, as if she'd only just noticed his close proximity. Several tresses fell back where they'd been, and he fought the urge to flick them behind her ear. A flustered look skipped across her face.

"I'm fine, thanks."

He wrinkled up his brow and narrowed his gaze on her, resting his arm along the top of the sofa, his fingers just centimeters from her bare shoulder. "You're not fine," he asserted. "You've been through a lot in the past few hours. I know what it's like to lose…" he started, instantly regretting those last words and mentally calling them back.

Her gaze, focused on her lap, suddenly snapped to attention. For just a moment, their gazes locked, and he knew she wanted him to finish the statement. Instead, he asked, "How about I get you some tea—or coffee maybe?"

She fixed him with a curious stare, then shook her head. "I'll get something at my mom's house later." She took in a long breath that ended with a deep sigh. "I don't know how to thank you for everything you've done."

He pushed himself forward, preparing to stand. "There is absolutely no need."

"I could, I don't know…make dinner for you sometime."

The gesture, while generous and appreciated, seemed unnecessary, especially in light of her circumstances. He'd only done what any good neighbor would do, and since when did that require compensation? Besides, he wasn't sure he could trust himself to be alone with her again. Even now, the temptation to touch her was more than he could handle, forget that he'd already discovered her softness while she'd slept cozily beside him.

"Thanks, but you don't have to do that." *I might be tempted to do more than hold you in my arms next time.*

"I make a mean pork tenderloin," she declared, hands clasped tightly.

He thought about his last home-cooked meal, Sunday dinner at his parents' home, a sort of farewell to him, although no one dared referred to it as such. Since then, his meals had consisted of canned spaghetti and meatballs, macaroni and cheese, or, if he felt especially energetic, his very own hamburger casserole.

The thought of juicy pork falling off the bone made his taste buds spring to life. "Do you now? You're tempting me." *In more ways than one.*

A pinkish flush settled in and around her cheeks,

giving him the strongest urge to kiss them, discover their softness.

"It's a recipe I acquired from my Grandma Jacobs," she said, roping in his thoughts.

Behind him, the clock on the wall ticked a steady cadence. "Tell you what. You let me know when things settle down for you, and then we'll talk dinner." He would just take special care to keep his growing feelings under wraps. How hard could it be? "In the meantime," he said, straightening his shoulders as he stood, "let me know if there's anything I can do for you."

She waved him off, her jagged emotions clearly in check. "Oh, no, you've done enough. I'll be fine and—thanks again."

Now she was walking him toward the door, so he took that as a definite cue to leave. He had the distinct feeling she would be fine. It would take time, yes, but she would make it.

She was soft and fragile around the edges, but tough as nails where it really mattered. Was that the way she'd learned to survive the desertion of Emily's father?

Not for the first time, he wanted to know this guy, wanted to eyeball him one-on-one, wanted to ask him how in the world he could possibly have left this beautiful woman and her precious daughter.

The following weeks went by in a blur of activities. Not only was it necessary for Callie to spend time with her mother sorting through her father's clothing and other items, making financial decisions, visiting lawyers, bankers, and accountants regarding his assets, but she found herself back in her classroom preparing for the beginning of the school year. There were bulletin boards to decorate, posters and notices to hang, desks and chairs to arrange, student letters to mail, and class lists to finalize. She'd actually found comfort in her busyness, enjoying the distraction from the otherwise morose atmosphere.

To add to her turmoil, she was bothered yet again by Thomas May. He phoned just ten days after her father's passing. At first, she thought he'd called to offer his condolences. What a pipe dream that had been! His manner of lending sympathy was far different from that of others. Instead, he simply acknowledged his former father-in-law's passing, then had the gall to accuse the man of always hating him.

"He never hated you, Thomas," she said in her

father's defense. "He just didn't approve of the way you treated me."

He swore. "I treated you darn well, woman. When did I ever mistreat you? If I did, it was deserved."

She wanted to jog his memory, but the whole thing seemed useless. Besides, Thomas would not have considered pushing her around synonymous with maltreatment. Rather, he thought it his duty to keep her "in line." If she wasn't performing her wifely duties, as he'd often referred to them, supplying him with plenty of beer, keeping the house neat, providing his meals in a timely fashion, and offering her body at the drop of a hat, then a good "reminder" was sure to follow. Sadly, she'd come to expect his ranting, often belittling and blaming herself for not measuring up to his standards.

"It's not important," she finally answered.

After a time, he mentioned the aspect of his bleak financial picture. This was, of course, his reason for calling; he even tried to hold her partially responsible for his financial woes, claiming that if she hadn't wanted the divorce, he would have saved a lot of money. Trying to reason with the man in his present state was futile, so the argument that she hadn't been the one to instigate the divorce certainly held no water in his mind. He only argued that she should have stopped the proceedings. In the end, she allowed his angry fallout until it petered out and his tone softened. "Can't you send me a little extra cash, Cal? I won't bother you again. I promise."

"I can't, Thomas," she said. "I have nothing extra to send. All my money goes into supporting my child." Why even acknowledge that the child also belonged to him?

"That idiotic kid," he blurted, letting go a trail of curses.

"Thomas!" She wanted to hang up on him, but somehow, he still held claim to her attentions. Not that she carried any feelings of affection for the man, but he still posed a threat—even with the hundreds of miles that lay between them. Plainly put, maintaining peaceful relations seemed paramount.

"You'll regret this," he warned. "One of these days, I'll show up on your doorstep." That said, he slammed down the receiver, leaving her shaken and frenzied for hours afterward.

~

Ever since her disastrous date with Jerry Watson, she'd been dreading their first encounter, which, after all, was inevitable what with the startup of the school year. There'd be after-school staff meetings, teacher conferences, breaks in the day, and brushes in the hallways. She couldn't just ignore his existence, although she would have liked nothing better. It was late one afternoon, a week before the first day of school, when he showed up at her classroom door, one hand shoved in his pocket.

"Hey, Callie," he said. She'd been mindlessly attaching address labels to some envelopes. His unexpected company gave her a jolt.

"Hello," she replied, laying down the labels and folding her hands in front of her. She forced a weak smile, hoping he would say his piece and leave her be. She prayed quickly for a sense of calm.

"How are you? I heard about your dad. Sorry." At least his offer of sympathy beat out Thomas's crass words. Several of her colleagues had also expressed their condolences, some even sending flowers and cards. It was nice to know folks cared.

"Thank you. I'm doing—fine."

He glanced around the room then stepped inside, uninvited. "Your room looks great," he commented. "I see you're ready for the start of another year." He advanced on her, coming to stand in front of her desk. No matter how hard she tried, she would never be able to look at him as a casual friend again—not after the stunt he'd pulled in July. She bit back the urge to tell him so.

"Yes. You?" Pulling open her desk drawer, she made a great show of looking for something.

"As ready as I'll ever be," he muttered. "Summers just go too fast."

"That's the truth." Actually, she'd been happy to see this one go. Too many memories lay buried in the season. If she had any regrets about returning to work, they were wrapped around leaving Emily. Her mother still insisted on babysitting, and Callie couldn't help but believe it would do her good.

When she failed to look him in the eye, he walked to the window and gazed out. "Nice day today, eh?"

Since the small talk bored her, she took up with her address labels again, hoping he'd recognize her busyness and excuse himself.

Suddenly, he turned his body toward her. "You wouldn't want to go out for coffee sometime, would you?"

What? If nothing else, she had to admire his nerve. She shot him an incredulous look.

Jerry raised both hands innocently. "This time, I promise—everything will be on the up and up—hands to myself, no funny stuff."

Slowly and solemnly, she shook her head. Of all the reactions Jerry might have chosen, he decided to laugh. "You can't blame me for trying," he stated in a matter-of-fact fashion and with a sort of helpless shrug. Then, "Can we at least be friends?"

He asked the question as if she ought to be able to dismiss what happened between them with little more than a nod. She eyed a large pair of scissors in her opened desk drawer. It would be so easy to propel them across the room. And she knew exactly where she'd aim them! "Things could get a little awkward around here otherwise," he added.

She thought to tell him that was his problem, but, newly recommitted Christian that she was, she thought of forgiveness and goodwill, and held her tongue. "I think you should leave now," she said.

"No problem." He headed for the door, then paused. "By the way, how's that guy next door to you—the bodyguard character? He seemed pretty interested in you."

It took awhile for the question to register. *Dan Mattson?* "Of course not," she replied curtly, irritated that he would voice such an observation. In fact, their paths hadn't crossed since the night her father passed, her promise of a home-cooked dinner still unfulfilled.

Jerry's eyes flashed with suspicion. "Figured he'd have nabbed you by now."

Ridiculous. "Good-bye, Jerry. I'll see you at next week's staff meeting."

He grinned, apparently unmoved by her impatience. "Yep. See you next week," he answered, disappearing around the corner, whistling a tune as he headed down the hall. Callie shook her head in disbelief. Not only was the man a jerk—he was a *dense* jerk.

Later, still stewing over her annoying encounter with Jerry, she picked Emily up at her mother's house, stopped by the drugstore for a few necessities, and then set off for her apartment. Climbing the stairs precariously while hauling a sack full of items in one arm and Emily in the other, she somehow managed to unlock her apartment door and push her way inside.

"How are things going?" Dan's mellow voice halted her steps, forcing an about-turn. A niggling knot of excitement centered itself squarely in the middle of her chest at the first sight of him lurking in the hallway, wearing khaki dress pants, a silk shirt, and Docker slip-on loafers, his tanned muscles standing out against the pale yellow of his shirt.

"Oh, pretty well, thank you," she replied, setting her diaper bag and purse on the floor to rearrange Emily in her arms.

He stepped forward to give Emily's cheek a playful pinch. She wiggled with glee and rewarded him with a smile. Dan tore his eyes from her to center them on Callie. "And how about your mother? How is she handling things since losing your dad?"

Emily was growing heavy in her arms, so she set her on the floor, then turned her gaze upward. Dan's handsome, well-groomed appearance set off a string of questions she dared not voice. Did he have a date? And how would she feel about that if he did? Since meeting him, she'd never spotted him with a woman. As a matter of fact, no one else but the cable guy had ever set foot in his apartment, as far as she knew. Plainly put, the man was a mystery.

"My mom is doing remarkably well. She's been sorting through my dad's belongings, carting some items off to charity, cleaning out the garage, even attempting a few repairs around the house. My mom works circles around me. She's a strong woman, and I don't mean just in a physical sense."

Dan grinned. "I would like to meet her someday."

"Maybe you will."

Had the room shifted, or was that pulsing knot within her screwing up her equilibrium?

"It sounds like she's finding ways to stay busy," he remarked, casually sticking a hand in his pocket to jangle his keys. "That's good. Hey, I noticed you're driving a different car. Did that Buick belong to your dad?"

"Yeah, his pride and joy," she answered. "My mother insisted I take it."

At first, Callie had refused the car when Liz Jacobs offered it to her. It seemed so extravagant. But when her mother explained she had no need for two vehicles, and that Callie should think of it as one final gift from her father, she'd relented. Put that way, how could she refuse it? Since then, she'd been enjoying the automatic windows, keyless entry, and air conditioning that actually served its purpose!

A thoughtful smile curved his mouth. "I think it's a good thing you accepted the car. Not sure how much longer the Little Red Rust Bunny—as your friend used to call it—would have lasted." This he said with a low chuckle, the sound of which made her senses spin.

She giggled in response. "Are you implying that she was less than reliable?"

Twinkling eyes sparked with humor. "I'd never say that about Lisa."

"I'm referring to my car!" she said with a laugh.

When he tilted his head, a beam of afternoon sunlight shot through the windows, glancing off his dark eyes and making an impressive silhouette. Downstairs, someone in another apartment was cooking up something, its delectable smells carrying through the walls.

"Ah, the car. Well then, if you'll recall, *she* failed you on your way to the zoo. And if it hadn't been for my heroic rescue, you might still be out there attempting to get the old girl in motion."

An unexpected wave of laughter erupted, and she placed a hand over her heart. "Okay, I confess—you're my hero."

The playful exchange continued, a sort of flirtatious banter, until Emily interrupted their wordplay with a high-pitched squeal. Spinning on her heel, Callie's eyes went wide. "Emily!" she clucked. "What did you do?"

Sometime between Callie's update about her mother's well-being and her declaration that Dan was her hero, Emily had discovered the milk chocolate candy bar she'd opened in the car and partially consumed. Never expecting her nine-month-old to go snooping, Callie had slipped it into the side pocket of the diaper bag.

Now, sitting beside the bag, guilty as a puppy in a mud puddle, the little girl smiled mischievously. Chocolate was covering her arms and the front of her shirt—not to mention splashed across her cheeks and over her eyebrows.

Callie dashed over and prepared to shuttle Emily to the kitchen sink, but she wasn't exactly sure where to grab hold. Her reaction to the situation must have amused Dan, who released a riotous fit of laughter.

Turning, she placed her hands on her hips and scowled at the man in mock indignation, which was answered only with more deafening cackles.

It was in that moment that something warm and enchanting rose up from deep inside her. Maybe it was that since her father's death she'd seen little humor in life, Thomas's persistence in contacting her only adding to her troubles. Or maybe it was that placid look on Emily's face, that "I've-just-discovered-something-better-than-the-Hope-Diamond,-and-its-name-is-chocolate" look that made her double over, sent her into a half-laughing, half-crying fit of mirth, blending with Dan's choking chuckles. Whatever, the two joined in laughter for the sheer joy of it.

Later, Callie was thanking Dan for his assistance in turning Emily back to human when the notion that she hadn't yet made good on her offer for a home cooked meal crossed her mind.

Suddenly, a safe and simple solution occurred to her. "Would you like to join my mother and me for dinner this week? At my apartment?"

Emily, still propped on the kitchen counter in front of them, had a couple of Dan's fingers in a tight grasp. Dan turned his attentions away from the child, cocked his head at Callie and flashed her a smile, revealing straight teeth. "Hmm, I was beginning to think I'd imagined that promise you made to me awhile back."

His cologne, subtle yet sensual, had been lulling

her like a drug ever since he'd come to stand alongside her at the sink. "I didn't forget. Would Thursday night work for you?"

"My social calendar is pretty open," he said with a laugh.

"Good. How does seven o'clock sound?"

"It sounds like a date," he replied, nudging her side. Warmth settled in her cheeks. "And speaking of date, I better get a move on," he suddenly announced, pulling away from Emily's tight hold to peek at his watch. Heading for the door, he halted. "I'll look forward to meeting your mom. She sounds like a great lady."

She watched him disappear through the door. *Date? So he* was *dressed for a woman.*

And a beautiful one, no doubt. She shook off the niggling thought and hauled Emily off the counter. Then moving to the window, she pulled back a single slat in the blinds and, together, they watched Dan Mattson climb into his Mustang.

So she'd invited him to dinner after all—along with her mother, which was just as well—hadn't he said he would like to meet her sometime? Her mother would serve as buffer—help to keep his growing attraction in check. Callie would use her for security, of course, someone to fall back on in the event that conversation lagged or, worse, if he touched an emotional chord that disturbed her fragile control.

What was happening to him that something as simple as shared laughter could wrap him in a blanket of euphoria, change his mood from sullen to buoyant? Until catching sight of her, he'd been less than enthusiastic about joining Greg's family for a summer barbecue. Now, the prospect seemed less threatening.

Distracted, he picked up the map and made his way to Greg's house.

"Pass the mustard!"

"*Please.*"

"Please."

"Here."

"Mom, this potato salad is good."

"Been fishing lately?"

"Not since I caught that eight-pounder."

"My napkin fell!"

"Thank you, dear. It's an old recipe. I'll give it to you."

"I'll get you a new napkin."

"Can I have my dessert now?"

"You haven't finished the main course yet."

Conversation topics at the picnic table ran the gamut. Dan joined in when the occasion called for it, but he mostly found himself enjoying listening. It'd been a while since he'd attended a family outing such as this one. He observed his friends, Greg and Karen; the interaction between father and son, Karen and her mother-in-law, and the two younger children was a remarkable sight. Anyone not belonging to such a tight-knit circle might have felt like an outsider, but this family bent over backwards to make Dan feel welcome. He appreciated their warmth and hospitality.

"How are your brother and sister, Dan? And what were their names again?" It was the older Mrs. Freeman who asked the question.

"Samantha is my baby sister by two years, and my brother Ken is five years my senior. They're both doing very well, thanks," Dan replied, wiping his napkin across his lower lip and taking a quick sip of iced tea with lemon. The meal had been delicious, the conversation light and easy.

"Samantha is a musician, you remember, don't you, Mom?" Greg inquired. The two families had raised their children in the same town in central Michigan, but after Greg graduated from college, his parents retired to Florida. Once Greg and Karen had married, they decided to settle near her parents, Greg's construction company taking off almost right from the start with his dad's financial support, professional input, and personal expertise. It'd been a good move all around.

"Yes, I seem to recall her graduating with honors and winning various scholarships. Is she still putting her talents to use?"

"She does occasional concerts with a local symphony but is mostly busy raising her son and keeping her husband happy," he said with a grin.

Conversation continued on various topics until the two women stood and began to clear the table. Greg's two children, a boy of five and a girl of seven, had skipped off to the jungle gym at the far end of Greg's property. "Greg tells me your neighbor is Callie May," Karen offered unexpectedly.

Overhead, a band of blue jays squawked at a pesky squirrel then rustled the leaves and flew off. "Yes," Dan replied, handing her his soiled dish when she couldn't quite reach it from across the table.

"She's a sweet girl. My mother and hers are good friends."

"So Greg informed me."

"Do you know her well?"

"Not really."

"Poor thing has been dealt a bad hand. Her husband was a no-good…"

"Karen…," Greg interrupted, his eyes scolding.

"Well, it's true," she argued, reaching for an empty water glass and balancing it atop several plates.

"Where is he now?" Dan asked, his curiosity to know more about this fellow suddenly peaking.

"Florida, I hear."

He knew that much, but something inside him longed for more details. "What does he do?"

"Not sure. He tried to run a motorcycle shop

here, but it failed miserably. I hear he wiped Callie out financially."

"Karen, you're repeating gossip." Greg's warning tone should have halted her, but apparently, she was accustomed to ignoring her husband's scolding.

"That's not gossip. Everyone knows his shop went under." Greg rolled his eyes and shot a glance in Dan's direction.

"My mom thinks he mistreated her," she said, throwing another soiled napkin to the mile-high pile of dishes.

"How do you mean?" Dan sat up straighter, chasing down a chill that went up his spine.

"Callie never confessed to anything, but the signs were all there. I think her parents were in denial."

"Really? Why do you think that?"

"My mom volunteers in a woman's shelter and is well aware of the signs of abuse. She said Callie used to wear turtlenecks and long sleeves on the hottest days of summer. Mom thinks she was covering bruises. But when Mom confronted Liz about it, she blew her off, saying Callie's air-conditioning was always set so high in order to please Thomas."

"Karen, for Pete's sake," Greg chortled.

"Okay, I'll stop." She gathered up a couple spoons and dropped them on a plate, then glanced down at Dan. "She's a very sweet woman who deserves a break." He thought for sure he'd glimpsed a ray of interest in Karen's eye. "If I'd thought about it earlier, I would have invited her along. The two of you just might hit it off."

"Karen Freeman, stop trying to use your match-making skills on my poor old friend. My wife is always up to something, Dan. Don't mind her." Karen passed behind her husband and flicked him playfully on the shoulder while balancing the soiled dishes with her other hand.

"Well, you can't blame me for trying," she said, flashing Dan a smile on her way into the house.

Dan laughed off the comment.

"Sorry about that, Dan. It seems my wife is a bit of a romantic," Greg said once he heard the screen door close with a thump.

"Don't worry about it. I'll admit I'm a bit curious about the lady next door."

One tawny eyebrow shot up. "No kidding? Well, I'm sure if you want to know more, Karen will gladly dig up any and all information needed."

Dan laughed. "I think I'd just as soon leave the matter untouched."

"Smart move, my friend."

The ride home was uneventful, if not contemplative. The evening ended on a spiritual note, the family discussing church related affairs and inviting Dan to attend next Sunday's service.

Who could know that, as he walked to his car, Dan would give serious thought to that very idea?

Dan wiped his sweat-soaked brow during a quick break on the job.

"It's hotter 'n blazes today," Jack Turner shouted from the rafters overhead.

"You ain't kiddin'," Bill Rood hollered in return before starting up with his nail gun. Everyone had been complaining about the unusual heat and high humidity. T-shirts had been tossed aside, but even without them, perspiration flowed amply down the fronts and backs of the hardworking crew of men.

"Must be nearin' the hundred degree mark," someone else said. "Too bad we can't fire up the air conditioner."

"We would if the fool thing was hooked up," said Dan, standing back and tossing a crumpled Coke can on the floor beside him. "We've got deadlines to meet, guys. Let's get back to work."

"Hey, we weren't the ones slouching on the job," someone teased sarcastically. Ever since Dan had assumed the position as supervisor at Oakwood Square, there'd been camaraderie of sorts—a quiet understanding that Dan had authority, and what he said went. Some had initially turned up their noses when the "new kid on the block" was put in charge, but it wasn't long before his ability to lead and delegate became clear to everyone. But there were still those days when Dan felt less than adequate, especially when his mind was still fuzzy from imbibing the night before. Amazingly, the workers seemed to pick up the slack, something he had yet to thank them for. Maybe he was too embarrassed.

"Okay, I deserved that," Dan said with a chuckle, stuffing a hammer and some miscellaneous tools back into his belt before taking to the ladder. "I think a storm is brewing," he added. "Those clouds moving in from the west look heavy with rain."

"We could use it," Bill said while reaching into his pocket for more nails.

"I'm just warning you, if it starts raining, I'm gonna stand in the middle of it and get this sweat off me," said Jim Harper.

The afternoon of teasing and working side-by-side ended about the same time the first loud clap of thunder erupted. "Quitting time," Dan issued. "See you guys tomorrow."

"Right," Jim said, tossing his belt aside and reaching for his lunch box. He waved on his way out. One by one, men called it a day, making comments of farewell to one another, everyone glad to see an end to the hot workday.

Actually, it was on days like this that Dan felt most satisfied. He liked going home in the evening feeling exhausted and spent. It usually meant for a better night's sleep. And any night that he could claim a good five to six hours of uninterrupted sleep was better than average. He had been drinking himself to sleep when troubling thoughts threatened to keep him awake, but more recently, he'd been trying to lay off the booze, so falling asleep remained a challenge.

With the men all gone, the place was quiet, aside from the occasional passing car and the sound of the impending storm. Every so often, another clap of thunder shook the walls.

About the time Dan was putting away the last of his tools, the door opened and in walked Greg Freeman. "Just came to check things out." He stomped his muddy feet at the door. The guy was dressed for something fancy.

"Where are you headed, all gussied up?"

"Taking Karen to a concert tonight. She called me three times today to remind me not to be late. I went home an hour ago to change clothes, and then remembered I had to swing by the office for a couple of things. Thought I'd see how everything is going over here on my way back home. The place is shaping up nicely."

"Yeah, it is. Hey, I wanted to thank you again for dinner last night. I appreciated the invite. Your family is really nice."

"We enjoyed having you. Glad it worked out for

you. And I meant what I said about church this Sunday. We'd like to have you come with us." Greg perused the large room with the eye of a professional. The rafters were still in plain view, studs in place, plumbing functional, electrical wires exposed but installed, windows and doors positioned to secure the house and protect it from the elements.

"Once we get the drywall underway, we should be able to start digging the next site on River Drive," Dan said, attempting to change the direction the conversation headed. "Bill and Jeb can stay here most days and tie up any loose ends."

"Good." Greg kicked a stray screw with the toe of his shoe and stuffed his hands into his pocket.

"What's on your mind?" Dan asked, tossing off his belt and laying it on a nearby workbench. He knew Greg Freeman well enough to sense when his visits had another purpose besides examining the day's accomplishments. Besides, he'd already been out earlier that day to tend to matters. It was rare for Dan to see his friend more than once a day unless he was planning to devote a good share of his time to a particular project. He had so many irons in the fire the guy could use a clone.

"Just curious, I guess."

"About?" Dan braced himself.

"About how you're doing—really doing, I mean. You adjusting okay?"

"I'm fine." Dan shifted his weight. Up until now,

Greg had made no move to prod him about his personal life.

"You're doing an excellent job, Dan. I've no concerns there. The guys admire you..."

"But...?"

"The thing is, Dan, I've detected alcohol on your breath a couple of times. In the morning, no less. Some of the guys have mentioned it."

"I'm cutting back on the stuff."

"That's a good thing. That's real good. You need some help, man?"

"Absolutely not!" came the hurried response.

Greg kicked at something else on the floor. "Sometimes the one who needs the help is the last one to see it."

"You don't think I know that? I'm the pro here, remember?"

Greg's eyebrow arched curiously. "Are you now? Care to tell me what's eating at you, *Mr. Professional*?" He grinned. "Strictly as friends, of course."

Dan sneered. "Not really."

He stalled. "You need to move on, my friend. It's been well over a year. Shouldn't you...?"

Dan shook his head. "You haven't got the slightest idea how long it takes to get on with life, Greg."

Greg's hands went up in a show of surrender. "I didn't mean it the way it came out. You're right, of course. I don't have the faintest clue."

Dan nodded and gave a glum smile.

His friend shrugged his shoulders. "One thing I know is that alcohol is not a problem-solver." Dan couldn't argue with him on that point. He'd counseled many people on the verge of alcoholism about the dangers of turning to drink to try to soothe away one's troubles. It was hard to believe he now fit into the same category with many of them. Trouble was, it hadn't taken him long at all to get to this point. Where would he be one year from now if he didn't get a grip on himself? The question scared the daylights out of him.

"Don't you think I know that?"

"Dan, alcohol and construction don't mix. I'm sure you're aware of the dangerous implications..."

"How dumb do you think I am?" He cursed under his breath, making Greg wince. "Of course I know they don't mix. I've been careful." If Greg wasn't such a good friend, he might not have been half as riled.

"The fact you're on edge is pretty good indication to me you have a problem."

"No, it's indication you're butting in where you don't belong. Are you firing me?"

Greg's eyes went wide with disbelief, then narrowed into beady little marbles, his forehead furrowing. "No! Sheesh, don't be so defensive, Dan. I just came to talk, nothing more."

"Yeah? Well, I'm done talking."

Dan brushed passed Greg, knocking him temporarily off-kilter.

"God has a better plan for you, man," Greg said quietly.

Dan stopped short before reaching the door. "I know about God's plan."

"Do you? Why don't you tell me about it?"

"He took my wife and precious daughter before it was time. Some plan that was. We didn't even have the chance to grow old together. I made vows to Andrea that I thought would take us into our golden years. I made those vows before God. What kind of plan is that? Sometimes it feels like nothing but a dirty trick."

"I can see why you'd think that, but God doesn't make mistakes, and His timing is perfect. He knows what He's doing, and nothing that happens in life takes Him by surprise, no matter how grim the circumstances. You just need to give Him a chance to prove Himself. But why am I telling you this? You're the preacher."

"Yeah, I'm the preacher. I should have all the answers." Dan practically laughed.

"I didn't mean it like that. I meant that you've no doubt preached a sermon or two about trusting God when the going gets tough, when you can't see much beyond your own nose. Sure, life is hard, but God hasn't moved. In your gut, I know you believe that." Greg paused, his gaze speculative. "Think about it, okay?"

"Yeah." Turning the doorknob, Dan stepped into the rain. He'd think about it all right—over a six-pack.

Still stewing later that night, Dan picked up the phone to call his mother. It'd been weeks since he'd taken the initiative to do the simple task. For some reason, even at thirty years of age, he needed to hear her voice. She answered on the third ring.

"Daniel, I'm so glad you called. I was just thinking about you."

"You were?" A smile crept in. She'd always had the ability to work magic on his sullen moods.

"Yes. I was just talking to old Mrs. Boone in the grocery store tonight, and she reminded me of the neighborhood pranks you and Greg Freeman used to play. Do you remember her?"

Dan chuckled. "Of course. She lived four or five houses down from us. Nice lady."

"Three. That white two-story with the picket fence out front." He remembered. "We got to laughing about the time you two sprayed shaving cream in Mr. Morton's rose bushes and he thought it had snowed. Remember that? You set your alarm clocks so you could get up and watch him walk out to the street for his morning paper."

Dan laughed outright. "What in the world made you think of that, Mom?"

"I don't know. Maybe seeing Mrs. Boone triggered the memory. She called me that very morning to tell me how flabbergasted Charlie Morton was by the snow on his rose bushes. He couldn't believe his yard was the only place the snow had hit. 'My poor rosebushes,' he'd groaned. Of course, Mrs. Boone always knew when you boys were up to something."

"Mom, that man was always a tool short of a perfect set."

She cackled. "I think we all knew it. Poor man; rest his soul. He used to waddle around in his garden with his undershorts on and those high rubber boots. Oh, dear."

"You watched him?"

"Of course. His garden was right outside our kitchen window. Your father watched, as well. He used to say someone ought to report him for his senile behavior. He was just a little eccentric, that's all."

"More than a little."

"Mrs. Boone asked about you, by the way."

"Really?"

"I suppose that's how we got on the subject of you boys. She mentioned again how sorry she was to hear about—the accident. Of course, she mentions it every time I run into her. Everyone is so sorry about it, Daniel. We all miss you a great deal, too."

"I miss you, too, Mom." *Tonight especially.* But he wouldn't add that bit of truth.

"Why don't you come home for a visit?"

"I'll be home at Thanksgiving."

"Thanksgiving? That's so far away, Danny."

The old nickname warmed a cold spot in his heart. "Mom, I'm a thirty-one-year-old man."

"And you think age means anything to a mother?" Sally Mattson chortled into the phone, bringing another smile to his face. She was a tough one.

"No, I guess not."

"Have you found a church you like yet?"

"And I suppose you'd say being a mother gives you the right to be nosy as well," he said lightly.

"Naturally. Well, have you?"

"I'm still looking." Truth be told, he hadn't spent one single moment looking unless he counted the time he'd driven past Fellowship Chapel.

"Sometimes I think..."

He sighed. "What, Mom?"

"Well, I wonder if maybe you're blaming yourself for the accident—at least in part. Do you?" *Do I?* "It just seems to me you haven't quite come to terms with it all."

"I don't know. How do you come to terms with the death of your wife and baby? I haven't figured that one out yet. Have you?"

There was a long pause. "Not really, honey. But I do know that God wants you to trust Him—all of Him with all of you. Maybe that's part of it."

He figured he knew what she was getting at, but going into it with her was the last thing he wanted right now. He'd called her for some diversion. If he'd wanted to be preached at, he could have continued his earlier discussion with Greg Freeman or turned to the religious channel on TV.

"There's a battle raging within you, Daniel. Until you give God full reign of your life, it's going to continue."

"I can manage, Mom."

"Would you listen to yourself—*Pastor* Mattson? You can *manage*?" She sounded dismayed.

"Don't call me that."

"Why not? You haven't lost your credentials."

No, just my faith....

"You're going through a rocky time, but I know God's not anywhere near done with you."

"Mom, you're preaching at me."

"You'll see. He loves you too much to let you stay the way you are. Something is going to shake the very foundation upon which you're standing. I feel it."

"I don't think I like the sounds of that," he said in jest, fighting down the chill that raced up his spine.

"Well, enough of my preaching, as you say. Samantha says she's going to come visit you one day soon," she offered unexpectedly.

"Really? I haven't invited her," he gibed.

"You think your sister needs an invitation?"

He laughed for the second time. "You're right. What was I thinking? Well, thanks for the warning. How about giving me a call the minute she starts out? That way I can get out my ammunition."

"Not a chance," she said, her tone considerably lighter now.

They chatted on for several more minutes, her telling him about his father's latest projects, their grandchildren's silly antics, and more about Mrs. Boone—until at last they'd both run out of conversation topics.

"Give Dad my best, Mom," he said.

"I will," she promised.

And they wished each other good night.

౿

By Thursday afternoon, Callie, exhausted from her day of scurrying, was deeply regretting having invited Dan to share a meal with her little family. She swiped her damp brow and scolded herself. *This is just a one-time deal,* she mused, *a simple means for saying thanks for coming to my aid more than once.* After it was over, she could breathe a sigh of relief. No point in getting so worked up over nothing.

And no need to bowl him over with her culinary skills, either.

So why, then, was she taking great pains to produce the tastiest salad, the creamiest potatoes, the most tender pork loin this side of Chicago, and the best-ever chocolate mousse dessert? She wasn't even sure Dan was a meat-and-potatoes man. *Although what all-American male isn't?* she reasoned.

And he was definitely that. An all-American male.

She gave her blonde head a mournful shake. What was she doing? She'd been telling herself for weeks (was it now months?) that she needed to beware of this man. He posed too many questions in her mind, called up a legion of doubts. And yet, here she was preparing a meal fit for a king.

Of course, her mother would be present, she reasoned—and Emily. That should settle her qualms.

Liz Jacobs arrived just after six. "Tell me again about this man who's joining us," Liz said, her body barely through the door before she made the inquiry.

"He's just my neighbor. He was helpful and kind enough to watch over Emily the night that Daddy—died."

She still had difficulty with the word, but she noticed her mother didn't even flinch. The woman had been a tower of strength.

"*Just* the neighbor?" Liz bent to sweep Emily up into her arms. Emily clung to her neck as if she hadn't seen the woman in decades, never mind that she'd spent the day with her so that Callie could work in her classroom, then run to the grocery store afterward.

Callie smiled and turned back to the stove. "Yes, mother, just the neighbor. Now, don't go embarrassing me while he's here."

"Me? I wouldn't think of it." Her knowing tone of voice almost made Callie regret inviting her. "Well, I think it's wonderful you've included him. I'll try not to interfere, honey. However, if he appears especially nice..."

Callie cast Liz a warning look. "Don't you dare."

Liz propped Emily on her hip and removed a kettle lid to snoop inside, stepping back when steam roiled from the boiling potatoes. She popped the lid back on tight and sniffed. "He's not married?"

"Mother! For heaven's sake, wouldn't I have invited his wife over, too?"

"Well, I thought perhaps he was going through a divorce."

"Even so, I wouldn't have...oh, never mind." She almost laughed in spite of herself, and might have if it weren't for her own misgivings. "He's never been married," she added.

"Well, that's good. Divorced people tend to carry baggage."

Callie frowned. "Thanks a bunch."

"You know what I mean. Is there anything you'd like me to do?" Liz asked, quickly changing topics. Emily rested her head in the crook of her grandma's neck.

"I think I have everything under control." Callie swept a critical eye over her apartment, then poked a fork into the potatoes she would soon be mashing.

"Are you ready for school to start?" Liz asked, turning with Emily and heading for one of the living room chairs. Classes were set to start the following Monday.

"About as ready as any teacher mourning the end of summer can be," she answered. "Actually, I'm looking forward to focusing on someone other than myself. Does that make sense?"

"It makes a world of sense. Why do you think I'm volunteering my time at the church office? Pastor Bobby said he's considering hiring me on a part-time basis."

"Don't take on more than you can handle, Mom."

"Now, listen to yourself, young lady. I'm not some old fuddy-duddy who's planning to spend the remainder of her years feeling sorry for herself. Yes, the Lord took my wonderful husband, too early I might add, but God's been faithful to me, showing me His presence in wonderful ways, revealing His love to me by way of my dear friends and family. If I can give back just a fraction, it will help ease my loss." Her mother was a wonder. "Well, perhaps those are things you discover with age," she tacked on.

"Age? You're not old, Mom."

Liz grinned. "It's the mind that counts anyway, right? When that goes, then I'll start worrying about my age."

"No, you won't. At that point you won't care anymore."

Their laughter mingled, easing Callie's tense muscles. When the doorbell rang, though, they went taut again. She touched her hair and smoothed out a wrinkle in her shirt on her way to the door.

He was here, and it was essential that she keep her heart inside her chest where it belonged, not out on her sleeve for all to see.

൫

She looked wonderful.

Blast! He didn't want to feel anything for this woman when she opened her door. He'd wanted to look at her as he would any other woman he might meet on the street; wanted to glance at her and be unmoved. But there it was—that ache in the pit of his stomach at the first glimpse of her tentative smile, her guarded look.

She wore a pale green, cotton shirt, sleeveless and dipped in the front, revealing just the slightest swell. His throat went suddenly dry. "Hi," he offered, waiting. She wiped her hands on her shorts, and his eyes traveled down her shapely legs to her freshly painted toes peeking out of her bone-colored sandals. Everything about the woman exuded feminine beauty. Andrea had always expressed her femininity, no question about it, but he couldn't recall ever having been this aware of it.

Just what was he doing? His life was a shambles right now, certainly too messed up to consider some woman's feminine wiles. Shoot! Greg Freeman had half accused him of having a drinking problem. What made him think Callie May would even be interested? Even now, her eyes glittered with apprehension. He could barely handle his own list of uncertainties without delving into hers.

"Hello," she said, stepping back to allow his passage. Smiling down at her, he handed her a small bouquet of flowers, stepped past and promptly laid eyes on the woman who must surely be Callie's mother. She sat in a chair across the room, cuddling Emily. Her features were much like her daughter's—lively blue eyes, blonde hair, though not as light, (probably recently doctored up at a salon, he figured), small frame, slender and soft-looking. The main difference he could see was in the woman's manner. Where Callie held back, this woman wore a relaxed, friendly smile, entirely warm and inviting. He liked her on the spot. Another troublesome admission, he deduced.

"You must be Mrs. Jacobs," he said, approaching her. She put out her hand, preparing to stand with Emily. "No, stay put," he ordered, taking her hand in his and giving it a light, friendly squeeze. "I'm Dan."

She smiled bigger now. "Oh, my," she muttered, withdrawing her hand to put it briefly to her throat. "Please, call me Liz. The other sounds much too formal. Callie's told me all about you, Dan."

Behind him, Callie busied herself with a vase, carefully arranging the flowers, and no doubt listening to their exchange.

He raised his eyebrows at the older woman. "Has she now?"

"Mother, no, I haven't."

"Well, she told me how kind you've been, and helpful. Yes, helpful. I want to personally thank you for the part you played in coming to her rescue the night her father passed on. It was difficult enough without her having to worry about Emily's welfare. But you were certainly there for her, and I want you to know we both appreciate your kindness."

"Well, it wasn't much." He glanced at Callie, now busy filling the vase with water. Slowly, his eyes drifted back to Liz. "By the way, I'm sorry for your loss."

It felt awkward being on the other side of compassion for a change. Normally, he was the recipient of the sorrowful looks and spoken condolences.

"Thank you." Liz flattened out a couple of stray hairs on Emily's head. "It was a blow, but I think I'm slowly coming to terms with it. We had been married thirty-one years, you know."

"Wow, that's a long time," Dan acknowledged, thinking how he and Andrea had been married fewer than four, and yet how deeply he still felt his loss.

She heaved a sigh. "Yes, but listen, enough about me. Callie tells me you've never been married."

"Mother!" Callie had been placing the vase of flowers in the center of the table when she literally froze in thin air.

An abashed look washed over Liz's face. "What? Was that rude? I'm sorry. I do have a way of speaking my mind. My husband used to warn me about being too curious. Or maybe 'nosy' is a better word. With him gone, there's no one to keep me in line." Her smile was impish.

Dan might have laughed if he hadn't been so busy trying to come up with a suitable response. His pretty little neighbor had no inkling of the secrets he carried around with him. Maybe he would enlighten her later—just not now. "Marriage is—just—not—in the cards, I guess," he replied, completely evading the truth of the matter. *"Not in the cards"? Dumb!*

Liz made a clucking sound. In the kitchen, the

oven timer went off. Callie rushed to turn it off, clearly flustered. "Pity," Liz bemoaned. "You certainly are one handsome young man. My goodness, if I were younger..."

"Mother!"

"Oh, there I go again," Liz cried, giving herself a good bonk in the forehead.

This time, Dan did laugh. "No problem," he said between chuckles.

The room went silent until the baby whimpered from boredom. "Say, why don't you and Callie visit while I mash the potatoes?" Not giving either of them a chance to respond, Liz stood and handed a very willing Emily over into his care. The child's hands went possessively around his neck. "Look at that!" Liz exclaimed, hand to her mouth. "She's very attached to you."

Dan hugged the child close. "I'd say it's mutual."

"Go ahead, have a seat," Liz ordered. Dan lowered himself into the nearest chair, situating Emily on his lap. "Callie, come sit down," Liz said, and her tone meant business.

Callie gave a shrug of resignation and walked across the room.

The meal was delicious: pork tenderloin to die for, broiled to perfection; creamy mashed potatoes and gravy; sweet corn, homemade rolls, and a delectable chocolate mousse completed the menu. Dan couldn't remember when he'd last eaten so well, unless he counted the picnic he'd enjoyed at the Freemans' place.

But even that didn't compare. To top matters off, he'd thoroughly enjoyed himself.

Liz Jacobs proved excellent company, not to mention an interesting conversationalist. She spoke freely about her deceased husband, related stories of Callie's upbringing and the house she'd grown up in, talked about her sister, Sharon, and brother-in-law, Bud, and how they doted on Callie and Emily, then interspersed questions for Dan regarding his own family history. He'd been vague when it came to his college days and after, not wishing to delve into the more sensitive issues, but talked a great deal about his parents and his brother and sister. Thankfully, she didn't inquire beyond what he was willing to offer. She had asked him how he'd come to work for Freeman Construction, though, commenting on her friendship with Karen Freeman's mother, and to that he'd simply said he'd been made an offer he couldn't refuse. Miraculously, she hadn't asked him what he'd done before the construction job surfaced. He might well have had to lie if she had.

Callie had remained reserved but attentive through most of the meal, stealing an occasional glance at Dan and interspersing shy smiles, then tending quietly to Emily who sat in her highchair tossing food to the floor and every so often nibbling on little tidbits. Dan always returned the smile, surmising she was happy to let her mother carry the bulk of the conversation. Frankly, he hadn't minded. He'd been interested in hearing about Callie's background, though he noticed the subject of her former marriage had been left untouched. There were many questions he could have asked but figured that if he got a response, he'd be expected to reciprocate.

At the conclusion of the meal, Liz pushed her chair back and prepared to clear the table.

"Mom, I'll do it later."

"Let me," Dan offered, surprising both women when he pushed his chair back and stood. "What? Did I say something wrong?" Laughing to himself, he began picking up plates.

"Not at all. I think you just said something right," Liz said laughing, reaching for Emily, whose sticky hands stretched to her grandma. Dan continued with the job of hauling dirty dishes to the sink and rinsing them while Callie followed suit. In time, Liz headed for the nursery, Emily in tow, while the two of them worked side by side in uncomfortable silence.

Dan spoke first. "Your mom is great."

That brought a smile. "Yes, she's pretty amazing. Her heart is broken by my dad's absence, but you'd never know it. She's taking it far better than I am."

Had he given into the urge, he might have stretched an arm across her shoulder, but he doubted she'd appreciate it. She'd been taking great pains to avoid not only his glances, but also any physical contact.

Not that he blamed her. He'd not allowed her access to see inside him. Why should she trust him to touch her? Still, he had to admit the temptation to lay a kiss on her plump, inviting lips was becoming almost more than he could handle. He had half a mind to surprise her with one tonight just to see whether the chemistry between them truly flowed, or whether it was pure imagination on his part.

But finding out the truth might be more than he bargained for. Might just give him reason to run the other way.

⁓

His presence unnerved her, as together, they rinsed off the last of the supper dishes. Surely, he wasn't any more interested in pursuing a relationship with her than she was with him. And she *wasn't* interested, she thought, working hard to convince herself even as she drove down the bolt of excitement that rushed through her body when his arm accidentally brushed against her side. She'd just gotten out from under a difficult marriage to Thomas. She neither wanted nor needed the complications of another troublesome relationship. For all she knew he could be a carbon copy of Thomas—smooth-talking, charming, and handsome to boot.

A con artist, that's what he was.

Worst of all, he carried secrets.

As sure as the sun would shine tomorrow, he kept them under lock and key. Why else would he refuse to talk about his life after college? He thought it went unnoticed, the way he so aptly wove in and out of topics, redirected the conversation when the questions grew too personal. Well, maybe he'd fooled her mother with his charms, but not her. No sir. More likely than not, he led a double life, perhaps had a wife stashed away in some godforsaken place. And kids. Maybe even…

"I think that's that," Dan said, his voice colliding with her thoughts. He folded the washcloth and tossed it across the bar between the two sinks, smiling down on her. She wanted to tell him to leave, to go call his *wife,* for Pete's sake. But what would he do if he knew he'd been found out?

"Well, it's been wonderful getting to know you, Dan," Liz said from behind. "You should come along the next time Callie joins me for dinner at my place." She'd entered the kitchen minus Emily, meaning she'd put the child down for the night.

Callie nearly choked at her mother's suggestion. She knew even less about Dan than Callie did, and that wasn't saying much. "Mom, I don't…"

"I think it's a wonderful idea, Liz," he cut in. "I'll gladly take you up on that. I don't have the knack for cooking myself."

No, but you have a knack for smooth talk.

"Well, we'll arrange something soon then," Liz said with a wink.

Callie narrowed her gaze at her mother. Tomorrow she would give her a tongue-lashing.

"Perhaps I'll see you in church Sunday?" Liz asked Dan, snatching up her sweater.

"You might. I've been thinking about visiting." That was news to Callie.

"Wonderful. I'll look for you." Then to Callie, "Good night, dear."

"You're leaving? So soon? But…" Panic rose to the surface when her mother moved toward the door.

"Yes, I have several e-mails to respond to. You two enjoy the rest of your evening."

And when the door closed behind her mother, Callie had to force her mouth to close, as well.

Emily was sleeping soundly. At least, that's what Dan figured when Callie came back a few moments later after checking on her. She'd kicked off her sandals sometime during the evening, the innocent gesture only adding to her sweet appeal. He wanted to knock some quick sense into his head before he did something he'd regret. Leaving would be a good start, he ruled. However, something kept him fastened to the sofa while he watched her move about her kitchen, perhaps simple fascination.

"Why don't you sit down?" he asked, both arms stretched across the sofa back, legs stretched out in front of him. You'd have thought he'd suggested she take a vacation to the moon the way she gawked at him. "Come on, let's talk for awhile." He patted the space next to him. Would she take the bait?

She pressed out an invisible wrinkle in the front of her shorts before walking to the chair situated on the other side of the room from him. Not tonight, she wouldn't. Sitting, she checked her watch, then wrapped protective arms about herself.

No question about it, the woman was scared witless. He silently cursed the dimwit she'd been married to, ruling him the ultimate cause for her insecurities.

"I think your mom had a good time. I'm glad you invited her," he offered to start a conversation.

One bare foot tucked beneath her, hands loosely clasped, she made a visible show of trying to relax. "You mentioned that you wanted to meet her sometime, so I figured this was as good a time as ever. I hope she didn't talk your ears off."

"You kidding? She's a great conversationalist. But now I'd like to have a conversation with you. You don't mind, do you?"

With a quick shrug of the shoulders, she swept her tongue across her top lip. "No, I—guess not. What'd you have in mind?" He could see she was trying her best to appear aloof, but he wasn't fooled.

"For starters, what scares you about me?"

"What?" Obviously taken aback, she cleared her throat and stirred uneasily in her chair, frowning. "You don't scare me."

"Liar," he answered, noting her sudden flush. "Do you think you can hide your fidgeting fingers and those blushing cheeks?"

Her gaze swept upward, as a look of annoyance suddenly flared. "I thought you wanted to have a conversation."

"We are. Why are you nervous? Is it because of what he did to you?"

She flicked at an invisible crumb in her lap. "Let's talk about something else."

"I'd rather talk about this," he pushed.

Some kind of inner torment shone through her eyes just before she lowered her lashes. "My husband was not a nice man, okay? End of story. Look," she flung her left hand outward and flashed him with a fiery glance. "I don't even wear my ring anymore."

He smiled. "I noticed that a while back. That night you went out with that Watson character. You must have figured the wedding band wasn't fitting for a first date. So anyway—you divorced the cad because he didn't treat you right?"

"*He* divorced *me*," she clarified, sitting straighter. "In spite of everything, I wanted to work on saving the marriage. I thought that we'd be defying God's laws about marriage—vows we had made before Him. But Thomas refused—he laughed at the very notion of counseling." She studied her lap. "My husband always wanted things his way. Counseling would have pointed out a need for change, and Thomas was not about changing anything—except maybe the wedding vows he made to me. Those put a definite crimp in his style."

"So you're saying he played around?"

Cold laughter whistled past her throat. "More than once." Pulling her chin upward, she regarded Dan with a hint of censure. "Divorce tends to make a person wary around others. Of course, *you* wouldn't know about that, since you've never been divorced—or married, for that matter." Her words touched on sarcasm, but could he blame her? He wanted to know all her secrets, but wouldn't reveal his own. Best to ignore the remark altogether.

"What does he do now?"

She gave an exasperated sigh. "He tries to sell motorcycles, but he's not very good at it. Most of the money he makes goes into booze and women."

Disgusted, he shook his head, then cautiously asked, "Did he ever hurt you—physically, I mean?"

As if she'd been sitting on a beehive, she shot right out of her chair. "Okay, I thought we were going to have a regular conversation, but since that's not about to happen I'm thinking maybe you should leave."

"Huh?" Rising just as quickly, he strode across the room, stopping within inches of her. "Was it such a hard question? Did the guy lay his hands on you? Did he hurt you, Callie?" Since a few strands of hair had fallen across one eye, he tucked them carefully behind her ear. His senses wavered when her soft fragrance floated past.

Dropping her gaze, she swallowed hard. "It was—I don't like thinking about the past. It happened. It's over."

Moved by compassion, he cupped her soft cheek in his rough and calloused palm, savoring the feel of skin on skin. Slowly, she turned into it.

A mild curse fell from his mouth. "He can't hurt you anymore, Callie," he whispered. Tenderness bumped against his otherwise tough exterior, seeking entrance. When he detected gathering moisture around her eyelids, he moved his hands to the small of her back and drew her close.

"Aw, honey, you're crying. I shouldn't have pushed you." His throat went dry like parched desert sand, the vertex of his feelings suddenly crashing in on him. "I'm sorry, okay?"

Her heavy sigh rattled his senses. "Callie, sweet Callie…"

A shuddering sound spilled out of her, and Dan wanted to kick himself for unraveling her memories. "Sometimes I felt like—it was my fault, you know?" She sniffed into his shirt and hot, moist breath penetrated the fabric. "If I could have just worked a little harder, been a little prettier, spoken a little softer—maybe we could have worked things out."

A moan of empathy escaped his throat. "Aw, Callie, listen to me." He gently set her back from him, but kept his hands on her slender shoulders. "No man ever has the right to push a woman around. Nothing on earth justifies it, not your actions, not anything. And you have to quit making excuses for the sick fool." He bit back a couple hundred bad words. "Did you ever press charges against him?"

"I threatened to call the police."

"But you never actually followed through?"

"I tried, but he tore the phone connection out of the wall and turned the threat on me, saying he'd kill me if I ever tried to pull that stunt again. There were times he really scared me, but I don't know—maybe it wasn't as bad as I'm making it sound."

"Do you hear yourself? You're making excuses for him when there are none to be had. The guy doesn't deserve to breathe the same air as you. He should be locked up somewhere." Fury almost choked him. "What did your parents think—about the abuse?"

"I mostly tried to shield them from the whole truth. They knew about his verbal abuse, but the rest I kept hidden." She shuddered. "Thomas was careful to hurt me in places that wouldn't leave telltale signs, like my stomach and chest, sometimes my arms, which I could always cover with long sleeves."

He recalled Karen Freeman's report of Callie wearing long sleeves and turtlenecks even in the middle of summer. Something like a low growl escaped the deepest part of his chest. "You never told *anyone*?"

She chewed her lower lip. "Lisa knew, but I spared even her most of the details."

He drew her close again, this time feeling the full impact of her words, hating the man who'd touched her in any way but tender. She was a sweet, special woman who deserved special treatment. What would possess a man to lay a finger on her—or any woman, for that matter?

Dear God… The start of a prayer formed on his lips but went nowhere. *Dear God, I'm feeling something here,* he attempted again.

Some unnamed emotion settled around his heart and he allowed it.

Bending, he kissed the top of her head, her soft, sweet-smelling hair mingling with his lips. Slowly but surely his mouth dropped to kiss the indentation of her left temple. Inwardly celebrating the fact that she didn't shove him away, he tentatively trailed minute kisses to her earlobe, lingering there to test her acquiescence should he decide to kiss her lips. Would she resist? He decided then and there he wouldn't force her if she did. To do so would be akin to pushing a child into the middle of a busy street.

Amazingly, it was Callie who made the next move. Her head slowly angled upward, making her face more accessible. He took advantage of the silent invitation and moved in closer, his mouth journeying from earlobe to cheek—slowly, patiently, tenderly. Finally, the moment spiked with pleasure when his lips touched hers, melding gently and cautiously at first, then building with confidence as the kiss grew in depth and intensity. It took him by surprise, this fierceness with which he felt. It seemed in one fell sweep of the second hand, his heart had gone from black to white, from hard to soft, from buried to risen.

But just as quickly as the moment capped, she stepped backward, pulling from his embrace.

"What is it?" he asked. His arms, now hanging at his sides, felt suddenly lost.

"I..." Her gaze went to her toes.

"Don't be afraid," he coaxed, lifting her chin with his fingertip. "I would never try to hurt you."

Her blue eyes locked with his brown. "It's just that, well, I know next to nothing about you. Don't you think you should tell me more about yourself?"

It was only fair, and yet to do so might jeopardize what little progress he'd made with her. "Callie, I'd never lay a hand on you. Isn't that enough for now?"

Her head shook back and forth. "I want to know what you're running from. I know it's something. Are you in some sort of trouble with the law? Are the police looking for you?"

"What?" His eyes must have grown the size of boulders the way he gaped at her. "Holy cow, you're not watching for me on *Unsolved Mysteries,* are you?" He couldn't suppress the chuckle that suddenly welled up.

Obvious frustration soured her expression. "No, of course not." Her eyes fastened on his top button. "Why won't you talk about your past? Are you ashamed of something you did?"

The question thudded against his chest. "Not really." *Unless, you count my guilt for insisting Andrea come home in that driving storm.*

"Are you married, then?"

It wasn't the first time she'd asked the question, and it probably wouldn't be her last. "Believe me, if I was, I wouldn't be here." Inhaling deeply, he swiveled his body just a fraction, so that he didn't have to look her straight in the eye. "Okay, I was married once, yes." He hadn't wanted to go this far, but here he was, putting it on the table.

"But you said..."

"I never really said I wasn't married before; I merely said I wasn't divorced. You misunderstood, took that to mean I'd never married."

"I don't understand."

"Callie, think about it." Her face remained expressionless. "My wife died."

She gasped. "Oh no! I'm so sorry. How—when?"

"Car accident. It happened about a year ago."

Her hand covered her mouth. "Was she driving?" she asked through her thin, muffled voice.

"Yes....Do we have to talk about this now?" Unexpected edginess crept into his tone.

"No. It's just that..."

"What?"

"Nothing. Never mind," she said, shaking her head with fervor. "You don't owe me an explanation. In fact, neither of us owes the other anything, right?" He could see what she was getting at. Best to keep things neat and simple between them.

And maybe she was right.

After all, what could she possibly see in a foul-up flunky like him? He was a pastor dodging his obligations. She was a woman betrayed, bruised, and battered. She needed someone who could help heal her wounds, someone strong and worthy.

And what of his loss of faith? She seemed to be a woman in touch with God. He was nothing short of depraved, certainly no example for a woman of her high caliber.

A woman like her deserved better.

He reached up and removed a strand of hair that blocked her vision. "Callie,..."

"It's okay," she cut in. "Don't say anything more. Please." She took a step backward.

"Y-you want me to go?" he stammered stupidly.

"I think it's best." The certainty in her statement made him ache to stay, but then he questioned his motives.

He never should have kissed her. He was in rotten form for commitment. With nothing to offer her, he'd made a huge mistake in even touching her. And then to have led her on with his lies—because that's what they were. He'd told himself that evading the whole truth was different from lying. Now he knew there was little distinction between the two.

"Thank you for the dinner. It was..."

"It was nothing," she said, extinguishing his next words.

Why was he so tongue-tied, so incapable of reassurance? Was it really so difficult?

Guiltily, he realized he'd still failed to mention Chelsea. *Precious Chelsea....*

"I'll see you around, then."

Idiot! Coward! Fool! He cursed himself with every

name he could think of then silently acknowledged her with a nod before heading out her door and across the hall to his own private, dismal domain.

Callie turned over in bed on Sunday morning and moaned with a headache. She'd put in two rough nights in a row, her thoughts mostly of Dan Mattson, the memory of his kiss a constant prompt that she was falling for a man she still barely knew. She did know one thing; he'd been married before, and the woman he loved had been killed in a car accident. What other tragedies surrounded him?

Most of the bedding fell in a disheveled heap that she had to climb over on her way to the bathroom. She raked her fingers through her blonde head and then accidentally tripped over a shoe. Another moan slipped past her lips.

A glance out the doorway and down the hall revealed straight beams of sunlight stretching across the hardwood. It appeared the final days of August would not be a disappointment to sunbathers, boaters, and gardeners.

Many would head for the nearest beaches today—some before church and others afterward—anything to beat the relentless heat. As for her, she always preferred taking Emily to the pool once the sun's peak intensity gave way to afternoon shadows.

The phone rang as she was settling down at the table with her Bible, a cup of tea, and two aspirin tablets. She resented the interruption but recovered when she heard Lisa's voice, even though it had the timbre of an excited child on Christmas morning.

"Hey, Cal, what are you doing?"

"Fighting off a splitting headache. You?"

"Fighting off a husband," Lisa said jokingly. In the background, she detected some sort of horseplay going on between them. "I'm sorry about your head. Anything I can do?"

"I'm afraid not. I was about to down some drugs with my tea. Want to join me?" she asked sarcastically.

"Hmm, sounds tempting, but I think I'll pass. Stop it!" Lisa grunted in lower tones now, soon giving way to muffled giggles. "You want to do lunch today?" she asked Callie. "Jack's taking Jeffrey to the children's museum after church. You know, one of those male bonding activities. I'm not invited." More shenanigans were heard in the background, followed by spurts of intermittent laughter.

Something close to envy welled up inside—not for her friend's happiness (she'd never wish that away from her), but for her own sense of loss. *God, forgive me,* she prayed instinctively. *I don't need a man to find true fulfillment and purpose.* No sooner had her prayer been issued when Lisa gave way to more riotous giggles. This time

Callie managed a smile. *Marriage has its advantages,* she reminded herself. Lisa proved them personally, and she was happy for her friend.

In the beginning, she and Thomas had been happy, too. But his tenderness was short lived, lasting only as long as it served his purposes. She would have enjoyed a little innocent, flirtatious sparring with her husband, but that had never been Thomas's style.

Oddly, thoughts drifted to the man across the hall. Was he trained or experienced in the art of wooing women?

"What do you say, girl? I bet I could do wonders for your headache."

Callie laughed. "Oh, I've no doubt about what you'll do for my headache. The possibilities are endless."

"Good, then it's settled. Shall I pick up you and Emily around two?"

"I'll pick you up. It's my turn to drive, remember?"

"Whoo-hoo! A ride in the new Blue Bullet! How's she been running?"

Callie grinned at the nickname given her blue Buick. "Great! No more dead battery."

"Hey, what do you see of your neighbor—the one who came to your rescue that day?"

"Uh, we run into each other occasionally." She choked on her answer, then quickly took a sip of hot tea to quell the cough, jolting when she burned her tongue.

"Is something going on that you're not telling me?"

The woman was a wonder at detecting secrets, always had been.

"No. Nothing," she lied. Before the day was out, Lisa would have wheedled everything out of her, including all the details of the amazing kiss.

"Oh yeah? I recognize a cover-up in the making."

"There is no cover-up, silly. I'll see you at two."

ൟ

The church was packed. Dan slipped into the back pew, taking care to keep his face buried in the church bulletin, intent on reading the thing from front to back until the service began. He didn't want to run into Callie, her mother, or the Freemans.

"Good morning," a deep voice resonated above his shoulder. A big hand, outstretched in front of the bulletin and blocking his view, gave him little choice but to look up. The voice belonged to a man whose face beamed with kindness. He waited patiently for Dan to take his hand. "Good to have you here this morning," he said as Dan stood to his feet and accepted the friendly handshake. "I don't believe we've ever met."

"Dan Mattson," he offered. So much for sneaking in undetected. And his plan to hide in the back row's obscurity had backfired. *The greeters must be trained to start at the back,* Dan mused.

"Richard Borgman," he said, the handshake continuing. "Call me Rich. Great to have you. You live nearby?"

"I'm staying in the Oakwood Apartment complex—temporarily." Why he'd fastened the last word to the sentence, he didn't know.

The man's eyebrows arched, and still the hearty handshake went on. "Looking to build like so many others? It's a good market right now, they say."

"Hmm," he murmured.

"What's your line?"

"I'm sorry?"

"Of work. What do you do?"

"Oh. Construction."

The man looked abashed, finally letting loose of Dan's hand. "Ah, I should have known," he laughed, flexing his muscles. "You got the build for it." Thumping him on the shoulder, he smiled. "Great talking to you, young man. Hope to see you again real soon. I best mingle a bit more before the service starts. God bless you." A friendly smile washed across his face before he moved along to some folks a few pews ahead. The entire pew stood to greet the man, as if they were about to speak to the president himself. He was certainly a friendly sort, the kind of person every church needed to make newcomers feel welcomed.

The congregational singing was lively with the worship band, choir, and song leaders. Dan was familiar with some of the choruses and hymns, but most were new to him. He supposed that's what he got for being out of the loop for so many months. Regardless, he found himself joining in, mechanically at first, but then with heart and soul.

When the congregation stood, he scanned the audience, telling himself he was seeking out the Freemans' pew when, in reality, he was looking for a petite woman with blonde hair, fair-skinned with just a hint of a summer tan, large blue eyes, and a tiny dimple in her right cheek. So far, no sign of her.

Thoughts trailed back to that shared kiss. It'd been the most tender kind, one that left him wanting more. Had she felt it, too? It was cowardly of him to walk out the way he had, so many unspoken truths still wedged stubbornly between them. If he ever hoped for a relationship with her, he'd need to remove them all—by spilling it all.

Surprise met him head-on when the senior pastor—who turned out to be Rich Borgman—delivered the sermon. No wonder the people in the pew ahead of him had greeted the guy with such enthusiasm.

His trained ear listened with interest as Rich discussed the Scriptures, taking a passage from Isaiah to speak about God's strength and dominion. Dan recalled a sermon he himself had once delivered on a similar passage. But those were far different times. He'd had a wife then, a beautiful daughter, a lovely home....People listened to him, respected him, trusted that he knew what he was talking about.

What would those same people think now if they could see him now, huddled in the back pew of an unfamiliar church, trying desperately to sink into a place of hiding? Would they shake their heads in disbelief at how drastically he'd changed? He used to preach hope versus despair, used to walk the path of optimism and encourage those who found little reason for rejoicing. Simply put, he'd fallen very far.

At least this morning he was thinking clearly, and that was something. Some mornings his thinking was fuzzy, still clouded over from a night of drinking into oblivion. *That has to stop,* he determined. It wasn't safe. What if he caused a traffic accident on his way to work? Most days he didn't regain a sense of normalcy till close to ten in the morning after he'd downed half a dozen cups of coffee.

Slowly but surely, his mind turned back to the sermon. "How quick we are to run to God in times of trouble," Rich was saying. "Like the Jews of old we struggle for freedom—freedom from depression, from worry, from debt, from despair. Ever been there?" he inquired. "Well, let me just say that when you have a right-standing relationship with God, you have a life of freedom. You are not lost to God, my friends. There is always hope."

Not lost to God? Is it true? Dan wondered. Or was he the exception to the rule?

~

Callie returned home after church with a song in her heart. Pastor Rich's sermon had been just the ticket for easing the tension behind her temples. Add to that the fact she'd spotted Dan at the back of the church, an answer to her prayer, and her heart nearly exploded. Of course, afterward, he'd headed out the door like a man on fire. He was probably afraid of crossing paths with her.

Moments later, Emily under one arm, purse over her shoulder, she headed up the path to the apartment entrance, the hot August sun seeping through her scoop-necked sundress. That was when she spotted a beautiful young woman sitting on the step, blocking her entrance. Raven hair cascaded around her shoulders and scintillated in the sunlight, while blue, saucer-like eyes surveyed Callie's approach.

"Hello," the woman greeted, rising gracefully in her petite pantsuit to allow Callie to pass. "Beautiful day, isn't it?"

"Hi. Yes, very," Callie said, sneaking a quick peek at the high-cheek-boned woman with the creamy complexion, a stark contrast to her otherwise darker-than-usual skin tone. She deduced that looking at her might equate to watching a lovely sunset, so perfect were her features.

"You don't happen to know Danny Mattson, do you?" the woman asked.

She'd been about to walk past her when the question drew her up short. "Danny?"

"Well, he's Danny to me. Always has been. I thought he told me he lived in building C—um, Apartment 2C. But there's no one up there. I expected him to be home, so perhaps I have the wrong apartment." Her pretty brow furrowed ever so slightly.

"There is a Dan Mattson, yes. He lives across the hall from me—upstairs," Callie answered.

Her throat caught as she studied the dark-haired beauty. *Was Dan dating her?* Funny, she'd had him pictured earlier with just such a woman. Someone perfect in every way.

Callie must have been kidding herself to think he'd be interested in her.

The kiss had been nothing more than a fluke. She'd seen the immediate regret that followed, particularly once she'd grilled him about his past, discovered he had indeed been married.

"Great! I'll just stay here and wait then. I drove a long way to see that man, and I don't intend to leave until I have." Of course, her radiant smile revealed perfect teeth.

Rather than pining over the matter, Callie sought to accept the truth. This woman was far better suited for someone as handsome as Daniel Mattson. She probably had her life together, likely knew all his secrets, undoubtedly knew about his dead wife, had even soothed his broken heart.

Emily's weight was growing heavy on her hip, so she shifted her to the other arm, all the while fastening her gaze on the woman. Awkward and inept, that's what Callie was—especially compared to this ravishing beauty.

"Your baby is very sweet," the woman said, bending to get a better view of her. "She looks like you."

"Thank you."

The sound of an approaching car turned both their heads.

"Is that…? Oh, it is, it's Danny!" the girl cried, dancing prettily down the steps and along the walk toward the parking lot. "Danny!" she squealed, waving a slender arm.

Callie watched with curiosity as the young woman raced to Dan's car, threw wide his door, and manually hauled him out of his seat, first, placing a big kiss on his cheek, then, wrapping tight arms around his middle.

Callie wondered why she hadn't kissed his lips, but then let the notion fall by the wayside. It was obvious she loved him, and by the pleased look on his face and the way he wrapped his arms possessively about her, the feelings were mutual.

His eyes connected with Callie's over the woman's head, but Callie quickly headed inside without looking back.

And when she shut the door to her apartment, she made a point to close the door of her heart, as well.

"Danny, this apartment needs a woman's touch," Samantha said later without forethought, then just as quickly added, "Oh, sorry. That was thoughtless." She had shed her leather sandals at the door and spread out on his sofa, not wasting any time in making herself feel right at home.

Dan gave a light laugh as he filled the carafe with water to make coffee. "Actually, I couldn't agree more. Got any decorating tips?"

She laid a finger on her cheek, looked thoughtful. "Have you got the money for my extravagant taste?"

He laughed again. "I received a good settlement from Andrea's life insurance, but I'm not rich. So, on second thought, I'll make do with my sparsely decorated bachelor pad. It's not really so bad, is it?"

She allowed her eyes one good sweep across the room. "You need to hang a few pictures, put some things on the shelves, get some flowers, add some color, buy a few rugs. I could help you with that much. I was only kidding about my expensive taste. You already have everything we need to make this place a home. Did you leave it all back in storage?"

"Most of it."

It was true. When he'd meant to start over, he meant to start over. Most of what he dragged along with him in terms of his past were photos of Andrea and Chelsea, a couple of paintings, his favorite furniture pieces, kitchen and bath necessities, and a few lamps. Otherwise, he'd left it all behind. Everything else had

Andrea's name written all over it. He'd not been sure he could live in a place so filled with memories.

She studied him with care, eyes drilling deep. "How are you, brother of mine? Tell me the truth." Tucking her pretty feet under her, she settled in more comfortably.

"I'm fine."

"The truth."

"Most days, I am fine," he amended.

"Most days? And on the days you're not?"

"Then—I'm not." It would be a cold day in a hot place before he confided his drinking problem—if it was a problem.

She heaved a sigh. "I miss you, you know. Everyone does."

"I miss you, too, but it was time I moved on."

Dark, finely sculpted eyebrows shot up. "You mean, ran?" she asked. Only Sam could get away with being so blunt.

"Okay, ran," he admitted. "Was I even cut out for the ministry, Sam? I mean, even you once said that it was probably more Grandma Mattson's voice I heard than God's. I've thought a lot about that."

A soft snicker fluttered from her lips. "Grandma did have a way of talking us into doing most anything. Remember the time she took us kids to the barn and told us to count all the boards in the ceiling? She said Grandpa needed to replace the roof but had no idea how many shingles to buy. Why would we need to count the boards for that? It took me a few years, but I finally figured out she was just trying to get us all out of her hair for an hour or so. She was the only person I knew who could have talked a goat into sitting gracefully at the dinner table."

He threw back his head and laughed. "You describe her to a tee."

She stretched her arms out lazily on the back of the sofa. "So tell me, do you feel *called* to construction?"

Her question struck him as odd. *Called?* "Not really, but I'm good at what I do, if that's what you're wondering. Maybe someday I'd like to open my own business, build furniture. I like to work with my hands."

"And you're good at it; no question. If you feel God leading you in that area, then you should do it. But you shouldn't do it if you're merely looking for escape. If it's peace you're seeking, you'll only find that once you stop running."

"Sam, my darling sister," he said, starting the coffee maker and going for a bag of cookies in the cupboard. He hadn't planned on a guest for dinner, so he had little else to offer her. "I think Grandma missed her mark with me. You're the real preacher in the family."

Amused, she cut loose a giggle, then jumped up and walked to the sliding door. Pulling it open, she stepped out onto the deck overlooking the pool. "This is nice," she remarked, hanging her head over the railing to get a better view. Sounds of splashing water and squealing kids carried upward.

Popping a cookie into his mouth, he joined her, bent at the waist, and propped his elbows on the railing. "Did you tell Mom you were coming?" he asked between chews.

"Yeah, why?"

He smirked. "She was supposed to warn me."

Sam's blue eyes sparked with mischief. "Ah, you wanted time to plan your defense?"

"Not exactly. But I might have at least prepared a meal or something."

"I'll do you one better. I'll treat you to lunch, how's that? Somehow, the idea of cookies for lunch doesn't set well with me."

"Really?" He studied the bag of chocolate chip cookies he'd brought with him, then retrieved another. After swallowing down the dry morsel, he nodded. "You're right. A juicy steak would be much better."

Their laughter penetrated the walls, drawing Callie to the door where she peered sheepishly out the hole to watch them descend the stairs. Once Dan and his pretty companion reached the stoop, she made a beeline for the window. He opened her door like the gentleman that he was. *Smooth-talking gentleman,* she amended bitterly.

To think she'd allowed him to kiss her so passionately just two nights ago, and now here he was entertaining another woman—a beautiful one, at that. She called herself every kind of fool she could think of, scolding herself for coming so close to trusting another man. "Never again! I've learned my lesson," she muttered, turning away from the window and throwing a glance toward Emily, who eyed her mother with seeming concern. "Take it from your mommy, Em: men will bring you untold heartache. It's best you learn this at a young age."

She walked over to the child and plopped down on the floor beside her, taking up a red block and poking it through the square shape it was intended for. Emily clapped her hands with glee at her mother's accomplishment and one-by-one, started handing her other shapes, yellow, blue, and orange, as if to test her brightness with all the rest of the puzzle pieces.

"Now don't get any ideas about doing this all afternoon. We're picking up Aunt Lisa for lunch soon." Another block fell into her hands. "Then maybe we'll stop at the store to buy you a toy. Would you like that? And how about we buy Mommy something for her first day at work tomorrow? Doesn't that sound like fun? We deserve something new, right?"

A blue triangle fell into her hands this time. "Oh, now, let me see. This one is hard. Where does it go?" Wonder of wonders, Emily pointed to the triangular hole. And together they celebrated when it fit perfectly.

Monday morning arrived too soon, the blaring alarm a spiteful reminder that this was to be her new routine. This morning marked the screeching halt of her summer vacation. She moaned when she rolled over to shut the thing off and realized she'd set it a full hour ahead by mistake. "Five o'clock? What was I thinking?"

She quickly reset it, but by the time she settled back under the covers, her body was fully awake, wide eyes studying the ceiling, mind a whirl of thoughts about the first week back to school—lesson plans to review, new names to learn, books and essays to assign.

She downed a hurried breakfast, enjoyed some quiet time with God, and then dragged Emily from her crib. "Sorry, Em," she crooned softly, "Mommy has to take you to Grandma's house so she can head for work."

The first thing she noticed upon stepping outside was how quiet the parking lot was, except for the songs of waking birds intent on announcing the dawning of a new day. Glorious sunlight peeked through the eastern clouds, its orange brightness promising mid-day scorching temperatures.

"Heading out already?"

Jolted by the all too familiar male voice, she swallowed down her excitement and slowed her steps to the car when she saw Dan approaching up the walk, his fine-tuned, sweaty body indicating he was finishing his morning jog. The sight of him set her back a bit, although she tried her best not to show the effects his masculine attraction had on her.

"It's my first day back to school," she declared, pointing her remote at the Blue Bullet to unlock the doors. Still catching his breath, Dan jogged ahead of her and opened the back door, taking Emily without so much as a how-do-you-do and buckling her in place. Emily's eyes flashed with interest when Dan bent over her, all the while talking gibberish to him, her favorite doll tucked under her arm.

When he stood, he swept the back of his hand across his brow then pushed back a few strands of thick hair. The simple maneuver did nothing to settle her frayed nerves. Dark eyes gave her a quick once-over. "Ah, first day, huh? Little nervous about that?"

His keen eye amazed her—or was it that she was just too transparent?

"You never know quite what to expect, I guess. Every year is a little different."

"How many years have you been at this?"

"This will be my sixth." She ambled to her side of the car, and again, he made it there ahead of her, but rather than open her door, he anchored himself in front of it, legs set apart, making it impossible to get past.

"Callie, about the other night…"

"No need to bring that up," she said, eyes trained on her door handle.

"Yes, there is. I've thought about it a lot—the kiss."

"Well, you shouldn't have. It was a mistake. Would

you excuse me?" She went for her door, but as predicted, he didn't budge.

The rest of him ramrod straight, he tipped his head downward, and she dared to meet his gaze before watching a river of sweat course down his straight nose and drop off the end. "Let me clarify something," he said between hurried breaths. "It was no mistake."

"Yes. It was."

Seemingly unmoved, he went on. "Maybe that's the way you see it—because of the things I haven't told you about myself. I guess I can't blame you for being a trifle shy around me. But that kiss—it was meant to happen, Callie."

She gave her watch a hurried glance. "Sorry, I don't have time to discuss this."

Rearranging his stance, he asked, "What about tonight, then?"

"Tonight?"

"Yes. Would you allow me to take you to supper?"

Chin raised a notch, she answered, "That's not a good idea. I'll be—tired tonight." *And you are dating a beautiful woman. I saw you kiss her.*

"All the more reason. A nice relaxing dinner should ease tired muscles and a cluttered mind." She focused all her attention on the early morning traffic heading down the main drag until both his hands settled on her shoulders.

Suddenly, all she could think about was the way his splayed fingers jangled her resolve. "It doesn't have to be a late night," he said softly. "In fact, bring Emily. We won't even call it a date."

"We won't?"

He shook his head. She couldn't believe she was considering it. Hadn't she vowed never to trust another man? Especially when he already had a girlfriend.

"There're a few things I'd like to tell you—about me." His voice went suddenly gravelly, and she nearly caved.

"I—don't know."

His body sagged with his release of a deep sigh. "Look, you had a bad experience with your ex-husband. But *I'm not him*." He took great care in emphasizing each word. "If you go out with me tonight, I promise not to touch you. How's that sound?" He bent to her level so that their eyes met, his hands still planted squarely on both shoulders.

Suddenly, her mind's eye caught the picture of him holding that woman in his arms yesterday, and her anger resumed its rightful place.

"I don't think so." Her chin jutted upward while she drew in a breath. "Besides, your girlfriend might object."

Muscles taut, he dropped both arms to his sides and stared point-blank at her, his brow wrinkled, one corner of his mouth slightly tilted upward. "What was that about a girlfriend?"

"You heard me." Reaching around him, she went for the door handle, but his hand on her wrist blocked the attempt. Looking at him was out of the question, so she found something to center her gaze on over his right shoulder. "I saw you cozying up to her just yesterday. And don't think I didn't notice. I even talked to her on the front steps before you got home. She wanted to know if I knew where *'Danny'* lived.

"Oh, and to think I actually allowed you to kiss me like—like—*that!*" If she'd been a child, she might have stomped her foot. The urge was certainly there.

Clearly amused, he tipped his head at the sky and laughed, which only nettled her the more. "Girlfriend?" His laughter rose in decibels now, creating in her the strongest urge to kick him in the shins.

"I saw you hug and kiss her," she said, refusing to allow his laughter to push her to the limits. "I even heard you laughing in the hallway."

"Because I enjoy being with her."

"There, you see? Now, would you please move out of my way?" She pulled her hand free of his grasp and again, reached around his large frame in her twelfth attempt to open her door. She shouldn't have been surprised when he blocked her attempt.

"Callie." The tenor of his voice was low but intense. "That woman I was with—I'll admit I love her."

Something like a rock slid down the back of her throat. She pulled back her shoulders and willed herself to breathe. "Well, at least it's out on the table. Now if you'll please move…"

"She's my sister."

"I need to…get to…huh? Your sister?" Her words petered out as the shock of his statement found a place to settle in her head. *His sister?* It did make sense, now that she thought about it. Same dark hair and olive skin, same clear-cut nose and sensitive mouth, same brilliant smile. Even their eyes, hers blue and his, the darkest shade of brown, shared a similar shape and sparkle.

Dan's hands clutched the upper part of her arms as he bent at the waist just so. "Yes," he stated, his eyes even now sparkling with humor. "My sister. She paid me a surprise visit. And for your information, I don't make a habit of dealing with more than one woman at a time." His voice, smooth as honey, tickled her senses, melted down the last of her stubbornness. "Actually, you're the first one I've even looked at or talked to since my wife died."

All of a sudden, she felt about two inches tall. "Really?"

"Really. So, back to my earlier question. Will you have dinner with me tonight if I promise to be good?"

"Were you serious about me bringing Emily?"

"Absolutely."

Reflected light from the early morning sun glimmered over his handsome face, as a few of her previous fears slowly fell away. "In that case, we accept."

He dropped his arms to his sides, leaving her lonely for his touch. He turned and opened her door. "I'll pick you up at seven."

She scooted inside and buckled up. When he would

have closed the door, he draped an arm over the top of it and grinned down at her. "My, my," he said, shaking his head. "The first day of school would have been plain enjoyable for me if I'd had a teacher as pretty as you."

Flustered, Callie felt her cheek color deepen. "I'd have to put you in the corner then," she chided quietly.

With a chuckle, he took a step back and winked at her. "Have a good day, teacher," he said, closing her door. She started the engine, somehow proud that it purred in his midst.

"Lord, help me," she muttered, glancing in her rearview mirror and putting the car in reverse. "I've fallen in love."

Behind her, Emily chattered with delight. "Da-da-da-da-da!" she chimed all the way out of the parking lot.

Dan worked steadily, albeit distractedly, that entire day. Now and then, he found himself grinning for no particular reason and surmised it had to be the memory of Callie's sweet face that did it to him. She'd been relentless in her attempt to keep distance between them, going out of her way to avoid a confrontation, scrounging for every excuse she could come up with not to accept his dinner invitation. And the visible anger he'd spotted on her rose hued cheeks only served to make her more appealing.

Satisfaction burned deep within him. If he'd not been such a dumb fool, he might have imagined she was starting to care for him. And it hadn't hurt that he'd insisted she bring Emily along. The child would make a nice safety net if his closeness hemmed her in.

It had been four nights since that amazing kiss, and all the memory did was make him want to taste more of her sweetness. "God Almighty…" The pathetic prayer attempt fell like a paper airplane gone bad.

"You say somethin', boss?" Pete England called from another area of the roof where both men worked, fastening shingles to the final two peaks before calling it quits for the day.

Dan felt his face go red, glad he could blame it on the heat of the day. "I might have been muttering to myself."

"Thought I heard you use the Lord's name. Havin' troubles over there?"

There was a time not so long ago that no one would have accused him of such a thing, not Pastor Mattson. However, these men still didn't know who he was. "Everything's fine. I'm just about done here. You?"

"A couple more pieces to go. That should do me on this side."

Why hadn't he set the man straight, told him his words had actually been a futile attempt at prayer? But what would be the point to that? Pete England would never understand. When it came right down to it, very few would.

"Anxious to see how my little girl did at school today," Pete suddenly offered, a lilt to his voice.

"Oh yeah?"

"Yeah. It's her first day of kindergarten," Pete said, squatting down over a shingle to put it in its proper place before nailing it into position. "The wife said she shed a few tears."

"Who? Your daughter or the wife?"

Pete chortled. "Now that you mention it, I'm not quite sure. Probably both of 'em."

Talk of school only had Dan thinking about Callie

again, wondering how she'd handled her first day. More likely than not, the halls were filled with riotous laughter and unruly teenagers, girls flaunting their fleshly wares, and guys trying to impress. He wondered how a little slip of a woman like Callie May managed to govern a classroom of hormonal teenagers, especially those who didn't give a poor man's penny for going to school, even less for completing reading assignments, diagramming sentences, and memorizing grammar rules. Somehow, he figured she did okay for herself.

He couldn't help but wonder what it would be like to sit in one of her classes. No doubt he'd be gaping with the best of them, lazing back in a chair too small for his long legs, pencil tapping, as he waited for her fiery eyes to meet his gaze, her stern voice suggesting he stop his annoying behavior before she notified the principal. There'd be a glint in her eye and a tiny hint of a smile, but her stance would be no-nonsense, and everyone would know she meant business. *Blast!* He'd probably sit up straighter than a pin if she ever yelled at him.

"Sure is a hot one," Pete said, shaking Dan out of his daydream.

"Sure is." One more shingle and he'd be off this hot skillet. He stopped a trickle of sweat making a trail down his nose. "We could use a few cool days—can't wait for fall."

"They'll be here soon enough, boss. No point in wishin' 'em here before their time."

The men had taken to referring to him as "boss" ever since Greg had signed on for a huge mall project on the other side of town, making his appearances on the home front scarce and increasing Dan's responsibilities as supervisor. He enjoyed the extra duties, even thrived on them. Even though Greg had had to speak to him about his drinking, he'd still been confident enough in his abilities to trust him with the extra duties. For the most part, Dan had flourished under it, even needed it to give him purpose and meaning. And he prided himself on the fact he'd not had a drop of drink in four long days.

"You're right about that," Dan mused in agreement. "The month will soon come when we'll miss this warm weather." He raised his free hand swiped his sopping brow. "Come to think of it, I much prefer the sun beating down on me to sleet and hail."

Pete grunted in response, his way of saying he couldn't argue.

Moments passed in silence while the two finished off their peaks; the only sounds passing between them were the rustling of leaves overhead, an occasional scolding squirrel, the chatter of birds and other critters, and the nail gun's swooshing sound as each shingle was fastened meticulously in place.

Dan shifted his body to reach one last shingle, the final one of the day, and quicker than a flash, lost his footing, the beating sun undoubtedly lending a slickness to the hot tar beneath the fresh laid pieces, though it was only a theory. The toe of his boot, which normally held fast to the makeshift 'brake' on the steep incline, slipped from position, throwing him off balance at the same instant that he lost his grip on the nail gun.

That move sent him reeling further down the roof, clawing instinctively—and futilely—at the smooth surface. When this effort failed, he began to slide, slowly at first, but then gaining momentum as sheer gravity pulled him down the dizzying two-story slope. In the back of his mind he thought he heard Pete swear, then saw him make a dive to catch him, failing. Fingernails dug deeply into fresh laid shingles, only sending him spiraling further downward.

In anticipation of completing the job, he'd prematurely freed himself of the safety harness. Now he would pay dearly for such a blunder in judgment.

If Dan could have had the time to prepare for what came next, things might have been different. He might have been able to stop their progression, might have been more intent on staying focused. But that wasn't the case. Instead, the seconds that followed went beyond his worst imaginings.

"Dan!" Pete's voice croaked out on the wings of panic. "Hang on!"

And he made every attempt to, but the closer he got to the overhang, the more futile his attempts. He was on the steep roof of a second story structure and the only thing that could save him now was good old-fashioned, supernatural intervention. "Dear God, save me," he uttered, the prayer falling out of his mouth as instinctively as a baby's first cry, even as he spiraled downward, tumbling and rolling, and groping for something to slow his descent. Then, as if practicing the maneuver a hundred times, just before going over the edge, he balled up his body, tucked his head under his arms, pulled his knees up close to his belly, and prepared for impact.

It would seem the decision proved wise, though it certainly hadn't lessened the pain any when he hit, his lungs heaving and gasping for air, his ribs afire, his shoulder throbbing, and his leg twisted oddly beneath him.

When he was sure he was still alive, he opened one eye, almost fearful of what he'd find. To his surprise, he was lying on a mountain of debris atop the dumpster into which the crew had been tossing useless materials. Pieces of boards, rags, bags of sawdust, odd pieces of cedar siding, and leftover shingles were now his bed. His other eye opened just as slowly, shock setting in along with intense pain. "Thank you, Lord," he mumbled. "I'm alive…I think."

"Dan!" Pete's shrill voice carried to his ears, breathless and frenzied.

"I'm…all right."

"I'm calling 9-1-1. Stay put."

"You think I'm…going…anywhere?" Dan managed to ask between jagged breaths, wondering warily what, if anything, was broken, afraid to straighten for fear of discovering the worst. Pete must have disappeared for he made no response to the muddled remark.

"Dan! What in the…?" This came from Phil Meyer, a new fellow Greg had hired just days ago. He'd been installing tubing in the basement in preparation for the plumber's arrival. Others of the crew were three lots down, laying footings on a new structure. "Hang tight, man," he added helplessly. "Everything's gonna be fine. I'm praying for you."

Phil's words came as a comfort and a surprise. Until now, he'd not known Phil to be a Christian. Could God have put the man here for the express purpose of reminding Dan of who he was in Christ?

"Thanks," he murmured. "I…think…I can use it about now." Wincing, he readjusted his mangled body.

"Don't move, man. Wait till help comes. Something might be broken."

Unprecedented pain forced him to lie there, quickly squashing any argument he might have had about moving. Suddenly, a sound from behind alerted him the more, and he felt a hand on his shoulder. Phil had climbed into the dumpster. The next thing he knew, the man was praying quietly at his side, his soothing words seeming to melt his bones, lending much needed solace.

And as the words floated past his ears, he closed his eyes and fell into a blackened state.

It was quarter past seven and Dan was exactly forty-five minutes late. As far as Callie knew, he hadn't even come home from work. His usual parking space remained unoccupied. He must have been tied up at work, she decided ruefully, unless perchance he'd forgotten altogether about his invitation to take her to dinner.

She glanced at Emily, playing quietly on the floor with her toys. She was contented now, but give her another hour or so and she'd be entering her cranky, restless stage. Oh, what had she been thinking by accepting a dinner invitation?

The overstuffed sofa seemed to beckon, so she dropped into its softness and stretched out her feet, kicking off her sandals and wiggling her painted toes, lying down to mull over Dan's lateness. Heaven knew she'd been put on the back burner enough times where Thomas was concerned. Was it happening all over again?

The first day of classes had gone as smoothly as any she'd known. Already, she had a positive feeling about many of her students. An unusual number of them seemed eager to learn, especially those in her Advanced English class.

Having taught eighth-grade English, composition, and literature classes in the past, she was excited about the prospect of teaching a more challenging course for gifted learners. When her principal had approached her in the spring about the opportunity, she'd at first balked, overwhelmed by the thought of planning an entire year's curriculum for the new course. But Blanche Austin, the middle school principal, was convinced she could do it, given Callie's own writing portfolio and track record from college.

Just as she was about to close her eyes, the phone rang, calling her back to the present. *Dan.* He was probably calling to explain his lateness. Car trouble, perhaps? Emily still played quietly but took the time to watch her mother strain to reach the phone.

"Hello, Callie." Her heart sank in despair. *Thomas.*

"What do you want?" Leaning forward, she planted both feet squarely on the floor, drawing back her shoulders.

"What? No greeting? No 'hello, darling'? Callie, sweetheart, you've got to learn to be more polite when talking to your husband."

"My *former* husband," she reminded him. "I've asked you not to keep calling me."

"I miss you. Can't a guy miss his wife?" His voice seeped with sarcasm.

I don't miss you. She whispered a quick prayer for guidance, fighting down a swirl of panic.

How was it that the man still held such power over her mental state? Even with the miles that separated them, she still shuddered at the sound of his voice. She knew what he was capable of and feared the manner in which he regarded human life.

His was a slanted view, biased by his angle on life.

Thomas May's perspective was not in harmony with the majority of the human race, though he had a masterful way of covering up that aspect of himself. When Thomas saw something he wanted, he'd stop at nothing to obtain it—even if it meant stealing, wounding, entrapping, or tricking. He always seemed to play his hand correctly, soon rendering others helpless or obligating them to give in. Callie had seen it work a thousand times for him if she'd seen it once. The man was a master at manipulation. That was how he landed jobs, made what money he had, won over countless women, even entrapped her in a loveless union of abuse.

Well, not anymore. She was done with him.

"I need money, Callie," he was saying.

"I…I've told you before, I don't have any to give you."

"Of course you have money, honey,'" he said with forced sweetness. "You got a raise, didn't you?"

"Certainly not enough to make any difference. I'm supporting my daughter, remember?"

"You mean *our* daughter," he corrected.

A hasty breath whistled through her lungs. "You wrote her off, Thomas."

"How about I reclaim her then? I bet she misses her daddy. Put her on the phone so I can say hi to the kid."

Galled that he should think he had the right to make such an outlandish request, Callie mentally counted to ten before responding. "I have to go now, Thomas."

"You hang up on me, and I'll make you sorrier than

you've ever been before. Understand?" he growled. "I'll be on your doorstep faster than you can count to three, and don't think I won't." Frozen in place, Callie closed her eyes and prayed for strength, tried to corral a fresh batch of shivers scampering up her spine. "Yeah, you guessed it, beautiful, I'm at my dad's place," he said, bringing his voice back under control. "Been stayin' here for a couple of days."

He was back in Oakdale? But how could that be? He'd barely given Florida a fighting chance. As if reading her thoughts, he said, "Business wasn't all that great in Florida. But don't you worry," he hastened, "I have some good leads up here. I might even partner up with Billy Ray Berger. You remember him, don't you? Owns Berger Ford." And from what she'd read, the high school dropout was undergoing some kind of investigation with regard to embezzlement. Just the sort of person Thomas enjoyed connecting with. "Still got my bike, though," he went on. "Not ready to part with her, not even if Berger offers me a car. They do that, you know—give their salesmen free wheels."

While he rambled, fear, stark and vivid, coursed madly through her veins. "I missed you something awful while I was down there," he was saying. "Bet you're chompin' at the bit for a glimpse of me, huh?"

Quivering from trying to assimilate the nonstop prattle, Callie jumped up and started pacing, barely digesting what came next. "A few hundred should tide me over, Cal. At least till I find a job."

"What?" He couldn't be serious. Mindlessly, she walked to the window and peeked through the blinds. A woman and her child were climbing the stairs in the apartment building across from hers. There was still no sign of Dan Mattson. "Thomas, I..."

"The way I see it, I can come over there and get it, or you can put it in an envelope and stick it in my old man's mailbox tomorrow when you get out of school."

Dizzying panic spun around her head like a menacing bee. No way did she want to give Thomas May a single cent, but if she ignored his pleas, wouldn't he continue hounding her? On the other hand, were she to give him so much as a dollar, wouldn't she be setting herself up for blackmail?

And what about Emily's safety? She wouldn't put it past Thomas to make some irrational threats regarding their innocent daughter.

Oh, dear God, please help me.

"I'll need to think about this, Thomas," she hemmed. "I'm not sure if tomorrow..."

"Tomorrow, Cal." His unyielding tone thundered past her ears. "I'll be waiting."

ൟ

"You ready to go home?" Greg Freeman stood over Dan, helping him to a sitting position. The last few hours in the emergency room had been harried, but eye-opening, bringing Dan to his senses more than anything else he could name.

"Is snow white?" he joked.

Greg swept Dan with a narrow gaze and frowned. "You okay, Dan? You seem...," he tipped his head first one way, then another, "...I don't know. Different."

"I am that," Dan admitted, grinning like a fool at his friend.

Pain still wracked every muscle, but miraculously he'd come out in one piece—no broken bones, but plenty of bruises. Doctors shook their heads when Phil and Pete explained the height from which he'd fallen, surmising that the pile of sawdust bags and roofing shingles into which he'd fallen had saved his life. Of course, Dan knew his life had been spared, and not by fate or a fluke.

God had intervened, plain and simple.

In fact, he'd heard His voice while lying on top of the rubble. Maybe not audibly, but he'd heard it nonetheless. And now that he was back among the living, he was anxious to tell the story of the vivid dream he'd had.

As a young boy, he'd often visited his great-grandpa and great-grandma Mattson, their massive home and surrounding wooded property a definite draw to any young boy. The century-old edifice boasted a huge wraparound porch, gaping windows decked with frilly curtains, a friendly porch swing, and welcoming front door. Porch steps leading up to the front entrance were wide and steeper than most, adorned on either side with glorious rose bushes, daisies, and day lilies.

Many were the times that Dan would race to the top of the porch, climb over the high railing, balancing himself on the other side, and challenge his grandpa to catch him midair. The robust man, elderly though he was, would spread his giant arms out like an eagle, capable and strong, ever young in the boy's eyes.

Yet despite his overwhelming amount of trust and confidence, there always remained that particle of fear that chased around inside his stomach, that tiny piece of doubt that nagged like an ornery hornet. What if Grandpa misjudged the distance between them? What if his weight was more than the man could handle, strong and mighty as he appeared? What if when he landed in his arms, it was just enough to send them both reeling to the hard earth below? What then? "I'll catch you, my boy. Trust me," he'd say, his ancient voice a mixture of warmth and conviction.

"I do, Grandpa. But now all a'sudden I'm scared."

"Here, look. My arms are big. See my muscles?"

Invariably, he'd raise his shirtsleeves, dirty and torn from working in the barn, and flex his arms. To his wide, alert eyes, those arms were a mile in circumference.

"Don't you know I love you, boy? If we fall, you'll fall on top of me. So what have you got to lose?" He'd chuckle then, amused by his own words, probably picturing the scene were it to happen.

"Here I come, then," Dan would warn playfully, still pausing to count, his heart racing against the wind, his stomach churning fast enough to make butter. It couldn't have been more than a five-foot drop, but to his six- or seven-year-old mind, it looked more like ten.

"Come on, then," Grandpa Mattson would urge, feigning impatience. "I haven't got all day."

With one giant breath, he'd leap through the air like a baby bird in flight, afraid of losing his nerve if he waited any longer. And sure enough, responsive, thickset arms caught hold, wrapping securely around his small frame, sweeping him up and spinning him round and round, the older man's jovial laughter filling his senses with unspeakable pleasure.

"Didn't I tell you I'd catch you?" he'd whisper in his ear, his voice so low he could barely hear it. "When are you gonna start believin' me?" Then he'd place him securely on the ground, pat his behind, and nudge him along toward the barn to help with the farm chores.

"I believe you, Grandpa, I believe you," he'd whisper back, placing his small hand inside the oversized, callused palm, its roughness a reminder of his strength and greatness.

☙

"I believe you," Dan muttered, having roused later with a sense of wholeness, the doctors and nurses surrounding him in the ER barely fazing his brand new state of mind.

"How are you feeling?" a young man had asked, concern etched across his face. He wore a doctor's coat two sizes too big, and the picture reminded Dan of his younger days when he played doctor, as every kid does, with Ken and Samantha. Someone older and wiser-looking had stood beside the young man, putting Dan's mind at ease.

"Like I've been sleeping on a bed of nails."

The older man chuckled. "You've had a close call, but I believe you're going to be fine with a few days' rest. You suffered some bruises, so you'll probably be sore for a while." He'd then assessed a cut on the side of his face, up near the eyebrow, proceeded to press on his rib cage and stomach, then examined the neck and back area. Dan winced under his perusal.

The older man shook his head in wonder, muttering to himself. "That fall you took should've produced a lot more than just bruises and cuts. You're a lucky man." He'd patted him on the shoulder and grinned.

"What would you say if I told you God had His hand on me today, that He had plans for my life, and a fatal injury wasn't one of them?"

"I'd probably say that I'm pretty sure *someone* had his hand on you. If not God Himself, then at least your guardian angel."

The doctor jotted something on a chart, then hung the clipboard on a hook over the foot of his bed. "You can gather your things and leave after the nurse gives you some final instructions. Get some rest, young man."

"I'll see that he does," Greg said, speaking for the first time, having been the silent observer on the other side of the examining room. "Thanks for everything."

"Can't say I did much," he said, standing at the door, shaking his head. "Pretty amazing, if you ask me." With that, he and the younger doctor headed out the door.

Greg moved across the room, picking up Dan's shirt from the back of a chair and handing it to him. Dan was more than a little antsy to go home. The clock on the wall registered a quarter past seven. He'd missed his dinner with Callie. He could only hope she'd open her door and give him a chance to explain himself.

On the drive back—Greg at the wheel, Phil following behind in Dan's Mustang—Dan shifted in his seat and gazed out the window. Never had the trees looked better. Even the weeds along the side of the road, which blossomed purple flowers, had an unparalleled beauty all their own.

"You okay?" Greg asked again, negotiating his car down the road Dan lived on. Dusk was just beginning to settle on the town of Oakdale.

"Oh yeah." He grinned. "You should've let me drive home."

"You fell off a roof, dingbat," Greg gibed. "The least I can do is drive you home."

Dan shrugged. "You heard the doctor. I'm fine."

"He also said to get a few days' rest. You got banged up pretty good, which is why I don't expect to see you for the rest of the week."

Dan shot his friend a surprised expression. "You're kidding, right? What am I supposed to do? Sit on my fanny?"

"Maybe drive up to Michigan? See your family?"

He let the notion settle for a bit. It wasn't a bad idea. "I might do that."

"Good. Now tell me what's different about you," Greg encouraged, pulling the car into the apartment parking lot, Phil following in the Mustang. He parked and cut the engine.

"It was the weirdest thing," Dan said, "but while they were working on me in the hospital I had a dream about my Grandpa Mattson."

Hands on the steering wheel, Greg angled his face at Dan. "I'm listening."

Dan filled him in on the details. "Interesting," Greg commented thoughtfully.

"I've been walking around with a mask on my face. Nobody really knows who I am. Shoot, there have been times when even *I* didn't recognize myself. I pastored a growing church, Greg. But who would believe that now? I'm ashamed for the way I've turned my back on God."

"And you think it was this dream that triggered your change in attitude?"

"It played a huge part. I remember thinking for

a second while rolling down that roof that if I died, I might not be worthy of heaven."

"Nobody is."

"I know that, but lately I've questioned my own salvation. I've been madder than a hornet at God for so long, Greg, that I'd almost forgotten what it was to be a Christian. But when I saw my grandpa standing there with open arms, inviting me to jump into his embrace, I knew it was really God's voice I heard.

"I can't change what happened to my wife and daughter, but I can change the way I react to each day." He shook his head. "Man, I've made a mess of things. You were right, Greg. I was drinking too much. That stuff is going down the drain before I put my head to the pillow."

"You going back to pastoring?"

The question dropped like a boulder in front of him.

"Whoa! I believe God has a purpose for me, but I'm going to be good and patient about waiting on Him to see what it is."

"Smart move." Greg reached across and put a hand on Dan's shoulder. "I always knew you'd come back. Sorry you had to fall off a roof to have some sense knocked into you."

Dan winced. "Some of us are thicker than others." He opened his door but took his sweet time about moving. "Thanks—for everything."

"You bet. Get some rest, friend."

"I plan to do just that."

But first, I plan to ring the doorbell of one Callie May and introduce myself to her.

Chapter 17

"Honey, I'm so relieved you decided to stay here for a couple of days."

Callie was curled up on the sofa, her mother reclining in the overstuffed chair across the room. Both watched Emily while she sat in her highchair, sucking on soda crackers, smearing a good bit of them into the tray and squealing with delight at her own antics.

"I just couldn't be alone, especially tonight. I figured you could use the company as much as I could."

Her mother smiled and flattened out invisible wrinkles from the lap of her pants. "I just can't believe that—man—would call and threaten you like that. What are you going to do?"

"I don't know. I didn't want to worry you, that's for sure. You've already got plenty on your mind."

"Oh, piddle! I don't have *enough* on my mind. It's high time I started focusing more on you and Emily."

"Mom, you are the least selfish person I know."

Her mother flicked a hand at her as if to dismiss her statement. "God knows I spend more than my fair share of time feeling sorry for myself."

"You lost your mate, for goodness' sake."

Both women reposed in momentary silence.

"I miss Daddy." Callie tugged a cotton afghan over her body.

"He'd have a fit about now if he knew Thomas was asking for money. You know what he'd say, don't you? He'd warn you not to give him a penny. It'll never end if you give in."

"I know," Callie said, glancing down at her fidgeting fingers. "But what else can I do? The police as much as told me there's nothing they can do until he hurts me."

"That's ridiculous! Can't you file a restraining order?"

"He hasn't truly 'threatened my life,' in the words of the officer, or been a consistent enough nuisance. Three phone calls hardly constitute a restraining order. Most divorced people don't want their spouses coming within one hundred miles of them. If the police filed restraining orders on everybody's ex, the paperwork would be astronomical."

"Most divorced women don't have psychotic ex-husbands, and now—he's back in town." Liz's face pulled into a worried frown. "Callie, he was violent with you before, wasn't he? Dad and I had our suspicions."

"A couple of times, but it's over now."

Liz rose and came to sit beside her daughter. "Oh, Callie. You should have told us."

"Daddy's health wasn't good. Telling him might have sent him to his grave even sooner."

"Well, no more secrets. Understood?" Liz warned.

Her grin was sheepish. "Understood."

Dan rang Callie's doorbell only moments after unlocking his own apartment, shuffling inside to drop off a few items, then slowly, painfully, making the trek back across the hall.

He inclined his ear to the door, awaiting the sound of approaching footsteps. Nothing. Either she was back in her bedroom watching TV or she wasn't home. There was also the chance she didn't want to see him. He had, after all, stood her up.

He glanced at his watch, which had miraculously made it through the fall in one piece, save the scratch across the middle of the face. It was just after eight. Highly doubtful she'd already gone to bed.

"Callie? Are you in there?" He felt foolish talking to a door. "I'm sorry about tonight, but I had a little run-in with a dumpster." Nothing.

Something pestered his thinking. It didn't seem likely she'd go out on a school night with Emily. Earlier she'd hesitated to accept his dinner invitation for that very reason. Yes, he was bothered, but unfortunately, he could do little about it aside from scrawling a quick note to her and shoving it under her door.

Besides, his headache was beating out a rhythm to match bongo drums.

Callie was lying in bed, wide-eyed, counting cracks in the ceiling. Her childhood bedroom was mostly uninhabited, save for the few overnight guests her parents had occasionally hosted. That would explain why the drywall was in dire need of repair. She was certain her father would have had it on his "to do" list, come fall and winter. He'd always taken pride in the little Cape Cod she'd grown up in, usually seeing to repairs as often as needed. But the house was old, and, though sturdy and well-built, required frequent maintenance. In later years, as his health deteriorated, so apparently did his motivation for fixing every little thing. The notion saddened her, adding to her already sullen mood.

Across the room, Emily snored softly from her crib, while at the lone window a gentle breeze stirred up the frilly white curtains. Turning over, she put her face to the wall and tugged the blanket over her shoulder, shivering. What were Thomas's intentions? Should she take his threats seriously? She'd seen him at the height of anger, experienced his physical blows, and not for a minute did she doubt his ability to come after her again.

Thoughts drifted to Daniel Mattson. Why had he failed to show up for their supper date? He'd seemed so eager that morning. Had something more pressing come up, something more demanding of his time? Was he apt to place more importance on his job than on people? Although she had little to go on, that notion didn't seem to fit.

An odd feeling of insecurity seeped through her pores.

"Dear God, please give me peace for my soul and the wisdom and courage I need to face the coming days."

"Be still and know that I am God," He seemed to whisper in return.

At the sound of the bell, students filtered through Callie's classroom door, a mixture of sleepyheads who'd still need several more weeks to adjust to the early wake-up hour and those who wore untempered eagerness on their faces. Some carried nothing but a pencil, certain that their teachers held a bounty of supplies, while others arrived armed in heavy backpacks, looking ready to climb Mount Everest. There were scruffy ones and tidy ones, smiling faces and grim faces, those who looked anxious to please, and those who didn't. The contrast was striking, and before the first month of school was up, Callie would know which students would be her true writers, which ones the plagiarists; who would eat up the classics and who would make a mad dash to the nearest bookstore for CliffsNotes. Advanced English was designed for students who were especially skilled and studious, and could keep up with a lengthy reading list and frequent writing assignments, but even the slouches could make it this far. Only time would tell if the slouches would rise to the occasion.

"Hi, Mrs. May."

"Good morning, Kaley. Did you have a nice summer break?" The pretty eighth-grader fairly flitted past her desk where Callie stood propped against the front of it, legs crossed at the ankles, hands placed on either side of her, gripping tightly. Determined to appear composed, she wore a ready smile, forced as it was.

"I had an awesome summer. Did you? Oh, man, forget I asked that." She temporarily covered her mouth. "I was sorry to hear about your divorce." Then, looking more serious, she added, "Should we call you 'Miss,' or 'Mrs.'?"

Surrounding students quieted, waiting for their teacher's answer. Callie cleared her throat. "'Mrs. May' is fine."

"I remember when you were Miss Jacobs," Curt Martin called from the back of the room, accidentally dropping a book and several papers when he took his seat.

A hundred years ago, Callie said to herself.

"Klutz," jabbed someone she wasn't yet acquainted with, his full head of dyed blond hair coming close to his shoulders, several earring studs lining his left lobe.

When he bent to take his seat, his face disappeared behind his locks. Callie swallowed a hard lump but managed to keep her smile for the continuing trail of students.

"Yeah, a lot of guys had wild crushes on her back then," said Curt with a mischievous grin. "Then she up and married that motorcycle guy."

How this particular topic had managed to make it into her classroom at the speed of light was a mystery, but there it was.

"It's true that I recently got a divorce," she said, folding her arms in front of her. "And the only thing I'll say on the subject is that you should never go into marriage blindly, particularly if you're not certain you want to spend the rest of your life with that person. I made the mistake of rushing in with my head screwed on crooked."

Most sat in rapt attention, so she continued. "I don't mean to stand on a soapbox, but I hope there will be those who will learn from my mistakes before making their own."

"You sound like my mom," said Kaley, rolling her eyes.

Callie laughed, unfolded her arms, and rubbed her hands together. "Enough about that. This is Advanced English, not Marriage 101."

The majority of the class went back to their usual learning positions: boys slumped down and stretched out, girls straight backed and cross-legged. And with that, Mrs. Callie May set about to keep some semblance of order amid the chaos that normally filters through with the start of any school year.

൳

All day, Dan shuffled and limped about his apartment, determined not to waste any part of it feeling sorry for himself or fretting over where Callie had spent the night. Several times, he'd taken the stairs to check for her car and figured she was gone for the night. The notion that she'd stayed away purposely to avoid facing him chewed a hole through his already wounded skin.

To make matters worse, he ached from head to toe, the gash on the side of his face, where he must have collided with a board, seemed to have doubled in size while he slept, and the side where he'd taken the brunt of the fall was one big bruise. Although he'd sworn off the hard stuff, he forced himself to down his pain medication every four to five hours.

While milling about his apartment, he managed to mail a few bills, answer some e-mails, watch the sports channel, and read his Bible. He'd had to find it first, of course, but as he skimmed its silken pages, reread familiar passages, his heart and soul feasted on the knowledge that his journey back to God had started.

"What should I do with my life, Lord?" he asked in the quietness of mid-afternoon. "Go back to the ministry, enter counseling, or continue at the 'mission field' I'm already working on?" Most of the men Dan worked with, except Greg and Phil, were unbelievers. Surely they could benefit from learning about God's forgiveness and cleansing power. Who was to say his ministry couldn't continue from a pulpit made of bricks and mortar, tar paper and shingles?

"Lord, make me the man You intended me to be on this job. Let my witness of Your grace be evident." He whispered this heartfelt prayer on the wings of yet another. "And, Lord, that woman and child across the hall invade my thinking more often than I care to admit. I wouldn't mind if You'd reserve a spot for them in my future."

Driven by a sense of responsibility and a basic need to talk to family, he phoned his sister to explain what had happened. She reacted just as he'd suspected—with a gasp of shock, and then a mile-long string of questions that required his dispensing every detail—and none was insignificant. He spent the first few minutes convincing her he was nowhere near death's door. Next, he moved onto a more personal level, retelling his dream experience, the manner in which he heard God speaking to him, and finally, the sense of peace and renewal he felt throughout the day.

"I'm so thrilled to hear you're getting back on track. Have you called Mom and Dad yet?" she asked.

"No, I thought I'd leave that to you. You know how hysterical Mom gets about accidents."

"I'll let them know you're fine, but promise me you'll call them soon."

"I promise, Sam."

"Want me to come help out? I could use a couple days away from the kids," she teased.

"I'll be fine," he assured. "Got some business I need to tend to, but I'm going to try to make it home by the weekend. I want to visit the church."

"I think folks would love to see you."

"I'm not so sure about that. But it's something I need to do."

"People understand why you left."

"Maybe. Not sure about Sister Cratchet, though."

"Oh, well, Sister Cratchet may be another story," she said with a giggle. The older woman had always been a thorn in Dan's side, always unhappy about something in the church—and never failing to make a point to inform him about it after his weekly sermons. "She would be unhappy if she planted her good-sized behind on a hundred dollar bill. Probably complain that it hadn't been a thousand."

"Sam! Shame on you." Much as he knew he shouldn't laugh, she'd hit upon a chord of truth.

"What kind of business do you need to see to?"

He'd thought the word "business" would have deterred her from asking any questions. Not so with Sam.

"Oh, just some personal stuff," he tried.

"Too personal to share with your favorite sis?"

"Sam…"

"You're not seeing someone, are you?" The question shot out from nowhere, catching him completely off guard. How did she do it?

"No, I am not seeing anyone," he answered truthfully.

"You know, it'd be all right by me if you started dating again."

"Thanks for giving me permission, kiddo." He laughed in spite of himself. "And now I'm heading back to bed. Another king-sized headache is on the horizon."

"You sure you don't need me?"

As much as he loved his sister, he could only take so much of her doting. "I'm very sure. I'll talk to you soon."

Later, thinking to graze the fridge for some nourishment, he heard a puzzling commotion in the hallway.

"Open the door, Callie!" yelled a gruff voice. "I know you're in there." Dan looked through his peephole to see a burly guy on the other side, the thumb of one hand hooked in a belt loop while he pounded on her door with the other hand.

"Open up!" he shouted again. *Could this be Thomas?*

Dan studied his physique. He was big and brawny, but not well-defined—still, he wasn't someone you would want to mess with. He might even qualify as halfway decent-looking with a shower and a shave, but right now, "disheveled" was about the only word that came to mind.

"Open this door, woman!" He let go a string of curses that could shatter glass. Dan winced and opened his door.

"She's not home," he said to the stranger. Dan leaned into the door frame, more for strength than anything. Though he'd done nothing physical all day, he was whipped, so it went without saying a tussle with this character would be ugly. Instinctively he prayed for wisdom.

"Now, what's it to you?" the creep drawled.

Dan shrugged. "Thought I'd save you the trouble of waitin' around. Haven't seen her since yesterday," he answered, forcing an unbiased tone.

"You haven't been watching for her…?"

"Not particularly," he fibbed. "You want me to give her a message?"

"Where is she? School was out long ago."

It was all Dan could do to restrain himself. "Don't ask me. She doesn't keep me informed of her whereabouts."

As if the guy was seeing him for the first time, he asked, "What happened to you?"

"This?" He pointed to the gash and grunted. "Fell off a roof yesterday."

A hint of a smile played around the fellow's unshaven face. "No kidding. That had to hurt."

"You could say that." Pausing in the doorway, he

made a quick trip over the guy's body with his eyes. "Like I said, I'll be glad to give her a message."

"Not necessary. I'll be back later. The little missy owes me money." His voice was rough with contempt.

Dan's hair stood on end. He wondered how he was doing at covering his rage. "You a friend of hers?"

Laughter, cold and bitter, spewed out. "I'm her husband." The laughter continued as he took to the stairs. "She'll be thrilled to see me."

"Husband? Humph, I didn't know she was married."

The man swiveled his bulky frame at the bottom step and looked up at Dan. "We're not actually married anymore, but I still control things."

He turned with a half-wave and exited the building.

Callie's stomach felt twisted beyond repair, her nerves were shot, and worry mingled with fear as she drove slowly past Herb May's mailbox. No one stirred in the yard, and the ramshackle house where her former father-in-law lived appeared dark and closed up. The place looked condemned. Garbage strewn about and a broken window with a curtain hanging out lent to its trashy appearance.

She carried an envelope that held one hundred dollars. It was all she could spare, and she hoped it would suffice. She fingered it nervously; the way the name "Thomas" had been scrawled unevenly across the envelope was evidence of her jitters. What if she caught a glimpse of him just as she slipped the money into the rusty mailbox? Worse, what if he came bolting out of the house and grabbed her? She never wanted to see him again.

She hadn't told her mother she was partially giving in to Thomas's demands. After all, he'd asked for a few hundred dollars, and she was only doling out a portion of that. Still, her mother would have a fit if she discovered her plans involved more than just running back to her apartment to pick up a few necessities.

"Heavenly Father," she prayed audibly, "please keep me safe and somehow prevent me from doing this if it's wrong." She pulled the car to a stop across the road, putting the gearshift into the park position. Swallowing a mouthful of bitterness, she went for the door handle, her heart pounding so hard she swore she could hear it.

"Here goes." But just as the whispered words escaped her mouth and she'd opened the door a crack, she was met with a vicious, snarling sound—one that caught her off guard and triggered her instinct to slam the door shut. Horror swept through her veins when she came eye to eye with a big, mangy, black dog that stood on his hind legs and propped his paws menacingly on her car door, his drooling mouth making a wet stream down her window.

Her blood ran hot and cold. *A stray?* He was skinny and rabid looking, his frantic, venomous eyes haunting her to the core. Where had he come from? Hadn't she scanned the run-down neighborhood carefully before preparing to make her swift exit? His bark persisted, evolving into a low, savage growl, as if to warn her of her fate if she so much as stepped one foot out of her car.

"Somehow, prevent me from doing this if it's wrong." Her prayer replayed itself in her mind. In the next instant, she was setting the gearshift into drive and

racing away from Herb May's house, away from her former life. And, with God's help, away from Thomas May, once and for all.

Ever since Liz Jacobs called to tell him that Callie was on her way to her apartment, Dan had been pacing and praying. "I'll be on the lookout for her," he'd promised, knowing Thomas could return at any time. Right now, he didn't trust the brute as far as he could throw him.

"I feel better knowing you live across the hall from her," Liz had said. "Maybe you can convince her not to let that man badger her into giving him money. He's a dangerous character, and I hate to think what he's capable of doing."

Dan saw no point in telling her he'd already met the detestable Thomas May. She had enough on her mind. "Don't worry, Liz. I'll take care of Callie," he'd assured her.

And if it was the last thing he did, he meant to keep his word.

Just as the evening news was coming on, he heard the door at the foot of the stairs open. Praying it wouldn't be May come to show his ugly face again, he walked to his door to glance downstairs and swallowed relief when he saw Callie. She stopped in her tracks at the first glimpse of him.

"Oh, my goodness, what happened to you?"

"I had a little accident," he answered, meeting her at the top of the stairs and pulling her into his apartment, kicking the door shut behind him.

"What are you doing?" she shrieked, pulling out of his grasp.

"It's okay. I just want to talk."

Staunch shoulders drooped in obvious weariness. "In your apartment?"

He shoved his hands into his pockets. "Yeah, come and sit down."

Wary-eyed, she stepped fully inside then turned and gave his face the once-over. "What—kind of accident did you have?"

"I fell off a roof yesterday. Sorry I missed our date."

She appeared not to have heard his apology. "You fell off a roof?" she exclaimed. "But that's terrible. Are you all right?"

Her genuine look of concern pleased him no end. "I'm fine, but right now we need to talk about something altogether different."

There was a pensive shimmer in the back of her eyes. "What?"

He led her to the sofa and pulled her down beside him. "I know about Thomas bothering you. I talked to your mom."

Hands folded, she chewed on her bottom lip. "My mother shouldn't have burdened you with that."

He ignored her. "I met the guy a while ago—outside your door."

She gasped, sputtered something indiscernible. Instant fire rose in her cheeks. Without thinking, he attempted to lend comfort by drawing her close, but she quickly extracted herself from him, inching forward on the couch.

"He was here?" she asked, eyes bulging. "You met him? What did he want? What did you say to him?"

"It's okay," he said, resting a hand on her arm. "We only exchanged a couple of sentences. He insisted he needed to see you, said something about you owing him money. I convinced him you weren't home, so he left."

She shook her head in disbelief, eyes clouded with pooling tears. "I'll never be done with him," she muttered.

He slid forward on the couch and pulled her into an embrace, determined not to let her escape this time, consumed by an overwhelming need to protect her. When she smothered a sob against his shoulder, he tried to soothe her with shushing sounds, kissing the top of her head.

Minutes passed before she finally calmed down enough for him to set her back from him.

"Have you eaten?" he asked.

She gave a slow shake of the head and wiped her still damp cheek.

"Then I have just the ticket for you."

After filling her up with a cup of hot tea, a chicken sandwich, and a small salad, he called Liz Jacobs. "Wanted to let you know your daughter's fine," he told her. Callie, reclining on the sofa, had tucked her feet beneath her, at last seemingly relaxed. "I'll follow her back to your home in my car later," he told Liz. To that, Callie sat forward and shook her head, but he ignored her attempts to counter his plan.

They spent the next hour listening to quiet music and talking, Dan apologizing again for missing their date and Callie assuring him she understood. She'd wanted to know all about the accident, just as Samantha had, so he'd appeased her by filling her in on the details, including the enlightening dream. She'd listened intently, stopping him every so often with a question or a request to clarify some minor aspect of the story.

When the conversation finally slackened up, Callie rose and walked the perimeter of Dan's living room. He watched her scan pictures on the wall, study various trinkets along the way, and pause to peruse a photo on the curio cabinet. "Is this—your wife?" she asked.

A knot rolled around in his gut. The time had come for more truths. "Yes."

"She was beautiful."

"Yeah, she was. Even won a couple of beauty pageants."

"I can see why." Her back was to him as she fingered the silver frame.

"She gave it up after we married—the pageants."

She nodded, moved along, eyes trailing to a couple of miniature sports cars on the coffee table. "Do you collect these?" she asked, pointing.

"Nah. I did as a kid, but most of them are packed away in a box somewhere."

Again, a slow nod gave way to further meandering. She slid her hands along the top edge of a standing bookcase. He figured she'd find plenty of dust if she checked her fingertips. At the fireplace, she paused to study another photo. "Is this your family?" she asked. "I seem to recognize your sister from that day she was here." She picked up the frame for a closer look.

"Yep. My mom and dad, older brother Ken, Sam, and myself. Somebody shot that at a reunion about five years ago. As you can see, I've changed a bit."

She made no comment; just replaced it and, as he'd supposed she would, stopped at the next photo. It was one of Andrea and Chelsea. "You lost a child, too," she said with hushed reverence.

"Yes," he said, breath catching. "That's something I failed to tell you earlier. It's not an easy thing to talk about."

Both hands holding protectively to the heavy pewter frame, she whispered, "I'm sorry for your loss, Dan. Your little girl—she looks like a sweetheart."

With care, she set the picture in its original location and turned to face him, hands clasped behind her. "I'm not surprised, you know, that you had a daughter. You've always been so good with Emily."

"Emily is an easy child to love," he said, meaning it. "On top of that, she's a pretty little thing—just like her mother," he tacked on, taking a chance.

A clear blush broke through her already pink cheeks. As if feeling the need to escape, she moved to the sliding door overlooking the pool. "You have a nicer view than I do."

"Yes, my view is very nice." He chuckled to himself, wondering if she caught the double meaning of his words. Looking at her now in her belted khaki pants and sea foam-colored cotton pullover, blonde hair slightly mussed, made him want to walk across the room and claim her with a kiss.

She wrapped her arms about herself and asked, "Do you think I should give Thomas money? I mean, would he leave me alone if I did? He claims he needs a few hundred dollars."

That brought him to his feet. "You're kidding, right?" he said, walking across the room. It hadn't occurred to him she might consider giving in to her ex-husband's demands.

Resting a hand on her shoulder, he turned her toward him. "Giving him money won't solve a thing. If anything, he'll expect more."

A wooden nod followed the assertion. "Those were my mom's words."

She pushed a golden strand of hair out of her face and quirked an eyebrow. "The strangest thing happened, Daniel," she started, her expression somber. "I drove to his dad's place today after school, fully intending to place an envelope of money in the mailbox."

"What?" Dan bellowed. "You shouldn't have..."

"I know." She shushed him with a hand to his mouth. "I didn't go through with it, and I'll tell you why. Just as I was about to open my door, a huge, mangy, foamy-mouthed, black dog approached my car and nearly chewed my head off. Eww!" She visibly shivered. "I've never been so scared by a dog! It was strange, too, because I scoped out the area beforehand, and there was no dog. After I drove away, I remembered asking God to intervene if giving Thomas money wasn't in line with His will. Do you think...?"

But she left the question unfinished.

A smattering of chills rose on Dan's arm when he thought about it. Would God have used a scary-looking mutt to deter Callie from exiting her car? "Yeah, it's possible," he admitted. "Even probable. You did the right thing by driving away. No telling what might have happened otherwise. Promise me you won't try that again."

When she gave him a nod and smiled, he pulled her close.

෴

Dan's arms around Callie were a stable force in the midst of upheaval. While knowing in her heart that God was her ultimate source of strength, this man lent tangible comfort, even sparked the silly notion that maybe, just maybe, he was the real deal. Still, his presence unnerved her, the idea of caring for him a frightening proposition at best. How could she give her heart to him when another man still held her in his manipulative clutches? Besides, there was still so much she didn't know about Daniel Mattson.

Dear God, help me....

When Dan drew close enough to kiss her, Callie jolted back, assailed by her own uncertainty. His hands shot up in a show of surrender. "Didn't mean to spook you, Callie. It's just that—I'm feeling things here."

Chin quivering, she moved to the safety of a chair and sat. She started to speak, but had to clear her throat and begin again. "I still know so little about you." And she had to know every detail if she was ever going to lose her heart to him.

Her quiet announcement seemed to have knocked the air out of him, for he stood stock-still for at least a full minute before finally dropping into the chair opposite hers. Leaning both elbows on his spread knees, he stared at the floor, the dark crescents of his brows furrowed.

At last, he looked at her. "I'll be glad to tell you whatever you want to know. I'll warn you, though, you may not like what you hear."

She held her breath, fearing his answer, yet needing to purge her soul of all worry. Had he committed some unforgivable wrong in his loathsome past? She forced a half-grin. "I'll try to keep an open mind," she assured him.

He plunged a hand through his thick hair and snagged a heavy breath. Solemn eyed, he said, "The night that my wife and daughter were killed, I was studying for my…"

Waiting, she raised encouraging eyebrows. "Yes?"

"I was studying for my Sunday morning sermon."

The words sat there between them like a brand new book just crying for its rich leather-bound cover to be opened. Still stunned by his words, she wasn't quite sure how to proceed. She thought she knew what he was saying, but her next words would be of great importance, her reaction significant.

"And so—your *crime*—is that you—are a minister of God's Word?" she asked, trying for all she was worth to suppress a giggle of relief. She doubted it was the reaction he sought, but there it was, regardless. A smile she could no longer hold back burst forth.

"*Was.* I'm not anymore," he inserted, ignoring her smile.

"They revoked your license?" she asked, sobering.

"Not to my knowledge."

"Well, then?"

"Callie, I stepped out on them, my entire congregation. Left them in the dust."

"I'm sure it's not as bad as you think."

"My name is Mud in their eyes. I couldn't take the pressure any longer, don't you see? I walked out.

Actually, *ran away* best describes what I did. They were all there for me, trying to help me through the muddled mess of my life, many of them hurting almost as bad as me, but a lot of good I did anyone.

"I wasn't much of a man, Callie, and I'm not proud of myself for what I did. In many ways I was like a kid, even jumped back into the nasty drinking habits I'd acquired before I gave my heart to Christ."

He shook his head, hands clasped between his knees. "I think about the men I work with, what they must think of me. I've set a rotten example."

"You can change that," Callie inserted.

"Maybe. It'll take some work."

"I doubt they judge you half as much as you judge yourself," she attempted. "Tell me about the church you pastored," she suggested. "It might help to talk about it."

She hadn't expected he would take her up on the idea, but over the course of the next hour, he willingly and enthusiastically spilled out story after story about the little church he and his wife had shepherded. Callie drew on his every word, particularly those reports that involved his wife and the tremendous influence she must surely have held over the little congregation.

"I couldn't understand how God could take my beautiful Chelsea and a woman as vibrant and talented as Andrea was," he said midway through the conversation. "It made no sense to me, still doesn't really. But at least now I'm ready to start trusting God again. Okay,

I'll probably never understand why God allows tragedy, but I do know without it we'd have no reason to cling to Him."

He lifted his head and grinned at her, his hands still clasped loosely between his thick, spread legs. "And there you have it, Cal, all my well-kept secrets."

Later, Callie pulled into her mother's driveway, Dan following. "Let me escort you, madam," he offered, throwing open her door before she even had the chance to grab her belongings from the front seat. Before driving back to her mother's, she'd grabbed a few necessities—some extra diapers, additional baby formula, and a few sets of school clothes.

Laughing, she handed him the small suitcase, thankful that the atmosphere had lightened during the course of the evening. At the door, he gave her a gentle nudge, forcing her to look at him. "Thanks for tonight, Callie. You've been a great—friend."

She noticed how he paused at the word. Was there a reason for it?

Dear God, this man….

"You're welcome. But I think I'm the one to be giving the thanks. Trouble seems to follow me, and so far, you're my number one rescuer." That produced a giggle.

Suddenly, his rough hand went to the side of her face and cradled it with utmost care, his eyes seeming to create little pools of pleasure somewhere in the center of her heart while he moved his thumb ever so gently along the base of her chin. She stilled, waiting, her pulse pounding into her eardrum. For a moment he neither said nor did anything, just gazed down at her as if mystified, rocking his head slowly from side to side.

"What?" she couldn't help asking.

"I'm just amazed, is all," he said on a whisper, his voice husky.

"Amazed?"

"By your sweetness."

With that, he bent and touched his lips to her cheek. "Mind if I call you tomorrow?" he asked, his breath hot and moist on her ear.

She hesitated. Not because she was unsure what her answer should be, but because the fire on her cheek where his lips had just been had left an indelible mark on her heart as well.

"If you'd rather I didn't..."

"Actually, I would like that."

"I want to make sure you're okay. I don't want Thomas May coming around. I trust that guy about as much as I trust that rabid dog you saw earlier." He looked around the yard, studied his surroundings.

"We'll be fine."

He looked doubtful. "How long are you planning to stay here?"

"Maybe a couple of days. I know it's silly, but I feel safe with my mother."

He chuckled. "Maybe you should be doing this the other way around. Bring your mom to your place."

"We're not helpless," she chided.

"You'd be safer. Trust me, I met the infamous Thomas May, and I wasn't impressed."

She laughed. "You sound like my dad, you know that? He was always so protective of me." The words escaped without forethought, followed by instant regret and the fresh realization that the man she'd looked up to all her life wasn't coming back.

He tipped his face downward. "If it helps any, I wish I could have met him. He sounds like my kind of guy." Her gaze dropped to the sidewalk, something about his closeness making her all shivery despite September's balmy air. She rearranged her armload of belongings.

"I should be going, huh?" he said, probably waiting for a sign from her that he was welcome to stay longer. Instead, she nodded.

"Yes. You look like you need your rest," she said, resisting the urge to touch the gash beside his eyebrow. He was close enough that she could hear his breathing, catch its warmth as it drifted through the air.

"I'm not particularly tired."

"Oh."

"How about I check on your mom and Emily before I leave?"

"Oh, I…"

Moving past her to open the door, he pushed her inside and followed close behind. She smiled at his clever workings. It would seem that Daniel Mattson was back in full swing; never mind that he'd just fallen off a roof.

Chapter 19

Liz Jacobs reclined in a chair, eyes closed, open book resting under one hand, a cotton afghan draped haphazardly across her slim frame. Dan thought she slept, but as soon as Callie started to tiptoe past her, she roused and sat up, no doubt embarrassed that she'd been caught. "Don't get up, Mom," Callie whispered.

"Nonsense. I was just resting my eyes."

Callie glanced down the hallway. "Is Em sleeping?"

"Out like a light," Liz said, shaking off her sleep and standing, offering Dan a ready smile. "Thank you for seeing my girl back safely," she said, then looking closer, added, "Well, for mercy's sake, what happened to you?"

Dan chuckled at the horrified look on her face. "Oh, nothing much—just fell off a roof." His wounds, though still fresh and painful, were starting to heal. Of course, it didn't hurt that he'd recently popped a couple of strong painkillers.

She gasped. "Oh, my stars! You look like you've just been granted an honorable discharge."

He laughed outright this time. "Thank you, Liz. I hardly deserve a compliment for clumsiness, but I think I'll accept one anyway."

"I think you'll sit," she ordered briskly. "I'll bring you some tea." She turned on her heel, the mother in her rearing its dutiful head, any earlier fatigue evidently gone. "You do like tea, don't you?" she asked from the kitchen to the tune of running water and rattling dishes.

"Yes—that's—fine, I guess," he answered loud enough for her to hear, shrugging his shoulders helplessly at Callie while suppressing another chuckle and mouthing to her alone, "Do I have a choice?"

She shook her head and gave a meek smile, her expression more relaxed now that she was back in her mother's living room. "Watch out," she whispered in return. "She will mother you to death if you don't find a way to stop her."

He raised an eyebrow at her. "Maybe I wouldn't mind a little mothering."

He gave the house a quick scan. It was cozy if not slightly dated, the rust-colored carpet, beige walls and drapes, and dark fireplace all giveaways of a sixties-inspired décor. Still, it spoke of warmth and trust, stability and comfort, despite the recent losses these two women shared. That Thomas May could come at any moment and jerk away what little security they still had made Dan want to fight for their safety, even if that meant camping out on their doorstep to ensure the creep steered clear of them. Problem was, he couldn't promise their safety during every waking hour of the day. He had a body to heal. What made him think he was in any shape to defend anyone?

"For their Defender is strong; he will take up their case against you." The words from Proverbs 23:11 replayed in Dan's head, as if God Himself were sending a clear message that it wasn't entirely up to him alone to defend these women. How quickly Scripture sprang to mind now that he'd righted his relationship with the Father. Silently, he thanked Him for the gentle prompt.

"Is this your dad?" Dan asked, walking across the room to the fireplace where several photographs sat propped in various frames on the mantel.

Callie edged up beside him, her closeness creating in him a heady feeling that he might never get enough of her. "Yes, that's Dad and Mom on their wedding day," she said, pointing out the first picture. "Here's our first official family photo," she said with a little giggle. "I think I was a few days old."

Moving on down the row, she continued. "This is Aunt Sharon and Uncle Bud. They're so special to me." She tucked a few stray strands of hair behind her ear. He spotted another that could use rearranging but restrained himself. She was skittish. Best not to press his luck with her. What she needed most right now was gentle reasoning and understanding, not touching. Of course, what his head and heart told him were two entirely different things.

"And who is this?" he asked. "You or Emily?" The picture could easily have been either.

She looked closely. "That's me. I was just learning to walk. This is Emily," she pointed out, picking up another framed photo and handing it to him. Her sweet smile had him rethinking his reasons for not touching her. Thankfully, Liz's appearance put an end to that.

"I thought I told you to sit," she scolded, rounding the corner with a tray of cookies and a steaming teapot.

"Mother, don't be bossy," Callie said, turning away from the fireplace and Dan's searing gaze, her tone a blend of firmness and wit.

"Oh, pish-posh! You'll know when I'm getting bossy. What he needs is a cup of my spiced tea." Her straightforward prattle had Dan chuckling to himself. "Come on now, sit down, have some of my ginger cookies, and tell me all about this accident you had," she instructed.

Placing the picture of Emily back in its proper spot and moving to the sofa, he obeyed. Callie, to his chagrin, headed for a chair on the other side of the room.

"Callie, sit there next to Dan, please, so I don't have to crane my neck to see you both."

The woman was clever. Callie shrugged helplessly and came to sit beside him, taking great care to leave some space between them.

"That's better," she said, sitting down and taking a deep breath, as one who'd just accomplished a major task. "Now, while I'm pouring our tea, I want you to relate to me the entire episode."

Liz Jacobs had a masterful way of pulling information out of Dan. The way she leaned into his every word, listened with utter intentness, questioned him at just the right intervals, made Dan want to tell her every secret he'd ever held captive. Before he knew what was happening, he had revealed everything there was to tell about his past, perhaps even more than what he'd earlier told Callie, even including his excessive imbibing. Both women seemed captivated if not intrigued by the deceptive manner in which he'd been living for the past few months, covering up his former life as a husband, father, pastor.

"I'm not proud of myself," Dan said. He chuckled halfheartedly. "I also can't believe I've gone on as I have. I didn't intend to tell you my life story." He checked his watch, felt the effects of fatigue, and shifted uncomfortably, suddenly realizing neither woman had said much, except for the questions and sparse comments Liz had made throughout his long account.

Liz sniffled and dabbed at her eye. Had she actually been crying? "Well, I think it's a marvel when you think of God's grace," she said shakily. "To think He's had His hand on you this whole time. Yes, you had to suffer a great deal when you lost your family, but God never left you. Why, look how far He's brought you.

"It just goes to show that even when we fail Him, doubt Him, walk away from Him, He never ceases to love us. Even the roof accident was no surprise to Him. He knew what it would take to bring you back to Him. We all need wake-up calls from time to time."

Dan nodded, the truth of her words blanketing the newfound trust that connected the three of them. "Thanks for that, Liz," he said quietly. Callie had moved to the far end of the sofa, feet tucked under her. *What must she think,* he wondered, *now that I've exposed my very soul?* Did she trust him even less than before now that she'd learned he'd been living a lie?

He pushed himself up. "I should be going."

Everyone stood at once. He was grabbing his jacket from the back of the couch when the phone rang. Callie reached it on the second ring.

Her darkened expression was the first sign that something wasn't right. "What? No, you can not come over here." She gave Dan and Liz her back and lowered her voice, but it did no good. Dan heard every word. "I told you I didn't have it," she hissed.

Liz threw Dan a worried look. He patted her arm.

Seconds later, Callie slammed the receiver down and turned, face ashen. "That was Thomas," she whispered in a surprisingly calm voice.

"What did he say?" Liz asked.

"Did he threaten you?" Dan demanded to know, the room sparking with tension.

With a slight tremor, she replied, "Not really. I—I think he means to come over here, though. Or maybe he was just trying to scare me."

"I'm calling the police," Liz announced, marching to the phone.

"It won't do any good," Callie said, angling her head at Liz.

"Callie," Dan said quietly. "Tell me his exact words." He walked across the room and methodically removed the phone from Liz's hand. She blinked in surprise.

"Tell me what he said," he repeated.

She shot him a withering glance. "He said he was furious I hadn't dropped off the money and that he was coming to get it. He said he drove past and saw my car, so he knows I'm here."

Dan took up the receiver and dialed 9-1-1 for himself. It was all he needed to hear.

൴

Callie fairly trembled under the mountains of blankets her mother had heaped upon her. The house was quiet, except for the hall clock's ticking, an occasional passing car's engine, and Emily's gentle snoring. Dan, their knight in shining armor, was sprawled on the couch in the living room. He'd insisted his presence alone would be a deterrent should Thomas decide to show up after the police left.

The police had come as requested, scoped out the yard and surrounding neighborhood, even checked inside the house, their reason for that still unclear in Callie's mind. Had they expected to find him hiding out in some obscure closet? She'd half expected it herself, which only added to her current case of frazzled nerves.

In the end, her ex-husband hadn't made good on his threat. Had he merely called her bluff, meaning to scare her and nothing more? Had he perhaps driven by and spotted the police cars? To say she felt foolish was putting it mildly. What had the police thought? She'd already called to complain about her ex-husband's unfounded threats, and they had as much as said there was nothing they could do.

Dan had been angry. If ever she'd seen a case of righteous indignation, it was tonight. In as pointed a manner as possible, he'd said that if Thomas May ever so much as laid a finger on Callie, there would be no one to blame but Oakdale's ill-prepared, ham-fisted, incompetent police force, and that they had better think twice before ignoring the threats of Mr. May. He'd met the man firsthand, he'd said, and he didn't for a minute doubt what the fellow was capable of doing.

"He do that to you?" one officer asked, pointing to his wounds.

"No, I fell off a roof," he huffed.

"That's good," the officer replied, immediately realizing his blunder. "What I mean is…"

"Never mind," Dan muttered, giving his head a shake. "Just—stay alert, okay?"

Before leaving, they promised to pay Thomas a visit at his father's house—issue a warning, maybe scare him a little. Callie could only hope and pray it would make a difference.

Thirsty, she got out of bed and slipped into her robe, careful not to awaken Emily as she tiptoed out the door.

Dan was lying on the sofa, still as could be, one muscular leg protruding from under the bed sheet. He still wore his jeans, but it looked as though he'd tossed off his shirt, for it lay in a rumpled mass on the floor beside him. She turned her gaze away, a tiny smile tickling her lips. He'd been through a lot, this man, and yet, here he was asleep on her mother's sofa, playing the proud warrior.

Opening the refrigerator, she reached for the orange juice then quietly shut the door behind her. Taking a small glass from the cupboard, she proceeded to pour the cold liquid.

"Can't sleep?" Her nerves came undone like a ball of yarn, causing her to spill a portion of the juice. In a flash Dan was at her side, reaching for the roll of paper towel next to the stove, tearing off a section of it, and wiping away the sticky puddle.

After tossing the wet towel into the wastebasket, he put his hands on her shoulders. "I'm sorry. I should have known I'd startle you. Are you okay?"

A dim light in the hallway swathed his features and illuminated the puffy gash on his cheek. Instinctively, she brushed her fingertip over the abrasion and winced. "Does it hurt very much?" she asked.

His cool fingers closed around hers. "No, not really."

Their gazes locked, and for a moment, they stood in utter silence. Her pulse quickened. She shifted her gaze and his fingers tightened their hold, as if to show his reluctance to let her go.

A worried part of her insisted it was much too early to trust another man.

She swallowed down her panic.

He is nothing like Thomas May, she reasoned. She was safe with him.

He'd kept secrets from her all summer long, yes, but tonight the walls had crumbled and a glorious bond of friendship had been born.

Still, it was too early. There were too many unsettled issues regarding Thomas. She could not drag another man into the mess.

She pulled her fingers from his grasp and he released her.

Turning, she asked, "Would you like some juice?"

"No, thanks."

She gulped down several swallows, knowing he watched.

"Why did you marry him, Callie?" he asked on a hoarse whisper.

Although the question surprised her, it was a fair one, and since he had laid bare his soul, it seemed only right that she should bare hers. "I thought I loved him," she stated matter-of-factly, pouring the remaining liquid down the drain. She put the empty glass in the dishwasher, closed the door, and turned around to face him, leaning against the sink.

He leaned up beside her, crossing one bare ankle over the other. "Go on," he urged.

"Thomas can be charming when he puts his mind to it. I saw only the side I wanted to see. My parents never approved of him, but even their influence wasn't enough to deter me. Besides, I was in my twenties, a college graduate, and still unmarried. I think a part of me figured, 'Hey, if I don't marry this guy, what are my chances of meeting someone else?' Silly, huh? We dated in high school, not so much in college. When I came back to town and accepted a teaching job, Thomas was right there, ready to rekindle the relationship. Of course, back then it wouldn't have occurred to me to ask God for insight and wisdom."

Dan nodded. "When did you discover his abusive side?"

"Truthfully? Not till after we married. I saw his controlling side beforehand, and he was always jealous, but I figured that was because he loved me so much." It was embarrassing now to think about how naïve she'd been, worse to bring it out in the open. She laughed self-deprecatingly. "I thought it was sweet that he wanted me all to himself. Not till later did I realize he wanted several other women all to himself, too."

Dan let out a breath. "Guys like him don't generally reform simply because they've signed their names to a marriage certificate. Not only did he pride himself on keeping you under his thumb; he enjoyed the trail of women he had on the side. The guy's ego has to be the size of Texas."

They talked for several more minutes. He listened, asking questions now and again in his low voice, and before she knew it, half an hour had passed unnoticed. A yawn she'd been working to suppress finally escaped.

"It's late," he said quietly.

"Yes." When she would have headed back to her room, he stopped her with his hand. She glanced at him uncertainly. Turning her, he cupped the back of her head and pulled her close. Wordlessly, he put his mouth to hers, kissing her with deliberate skill, as if he was determined to soothe away her past.

When the kiss ended, she felt an overwhelming desire to continue, and he lingered, toying with her bottom lip before fully pulling back. Her heart was a tangled mess, and he must have sensed it.

He touched a finger to her chin and lifted her face up. "That was to prove to you that you're worthy, that you don't have to settle, that God has a better plan."

And the next thing he did pleasured her even more; he prayed a quiet prayer for protection, asking God to divert her thoughts, help her to trust in Him alone, and to fill her up with a sense of His sweet, abiding presence.

Once he said the final "Amen," he placed one last

fleeting kiss on the tip of her nose, pointed her in the direction of her bedroom, wished her good night, and ordered her not to waste another minute of her time worrying.

Oakdale Middle School was abuzz with chattering students, bells announcing the start of class, lockers slamming, and the occasional sound of teachers greeting students in the hallways. Callie's own classroom was filling up with her first-hour students, most only half awake. It was Friday morning, the final day of the first week of school, and she was more than ready for a weekend break. The first week of school was always stressful. Getting to know the students and gauging their levels of learning, planning lessons, and adapting to new schedules required extra time and energy. And as if that wasn't enough, Callie had her former husband's threats to contend with.

Although she'd not had an actual run-in with Thomas since his recent phone call, she found herself on edge most of the time. When would the next threat come? Or worse, when would he plant himself on her doorstep and demand entry to her apartment? Ever since going back home with Emily, she'd been fearful of the doorbell, even though it was usually a visit from Dan, her mother, or Lisa. She could only hope that the visit the police had paid Thomas would be enough to discourage him from making future threats, although something told her Thomas didn't scare that easily. He was a tyrant who refused to be bullied, even by the Oakdale Police Department. If anything, he was waiting until things settled down before making his next move.

While her students filed in, she thought about Dan. He'd been more than kind to her; perhaps protective and concerned best described his recent actions, a far cry from the Daniel Mattson she'd met just months ago. That one had been ill-tempered, rude, and irritable, her memory of their very first encounter in the apartment stairwell still vivid. This man was softer and genuinely considerate. It was like meeting someone for the first time, his renewed spiritual experience having made a drastic change in his overall temperament.

The notion that love could be brewing terrified her, her earlier claims that she wouldn't give her heart to another man still pounding away at her consciousness. Although she enjoyed drawing from his strength, she knew she must be realistic; he had lost a wife and daughter to death, she had lost a husband to divorce.

Well, no matter, he'd invited her out on a date tonight, and she'd accepted.

"Hey, Mrs. May, did you read the paper last night?" Rob Rankin, the middle school football team's quarterback and captain, broke into her thoughts.

Callie stepped behind her desk and fumbled

through her plan book, giving Rob only half her attention.

"No, I didn't have a chance to read it, Rob. Why?"

The rest of the class had just settled into their seats.

"There was something in there about your ex." Her interest spiked.

"Really? In reference to what?" She prayed it had nothing to do with his threatening phone call and the police being summoned to her mother's residence. The last thing she needed was a tainted reputation at the beginning of the school year. Her divorce was bad enough. Had the man mouthed off to the officers who'd paid him a visit on Tuesday night and consequently gotten himself arrested?

"I guess he got cited for a DUI. He showed up in the circuit court section last night."

Shaky fingers picked up a pen and tapped it lightly on her plan book while she took a seat behind her desk, still attempting to maintain a disinterested façade. "Well…that's interesting."

"Yeah. I always read that section of the paper. Never know when I might run across someone's name from Advanced English." He glanced good-humoredly at his peers while sprawling his large frame back into the undersized student chair. Several wails of protest rose up.

"Yeah, you'd be the first one to show up in black and white," hollered Josh Hansen, his humorous tone joining with Rob's to help set the tone for more senseless chatter.

"Settle down, guys," Callie urged.

"I thought your ex was in Florida," Rob continued.

Callie shifted nervously. How was it that these middle schoolers were more interested in her personal life than in learning English? Of course, she knew the answer to that; as bright as these young people were, most any topic unrelated to school would top their attention scale.

"Seems he's back—temporarily."

"You're not gonna—oh, never mind."

"No, I'm not," she finished, the hint of a smile showing up on her lips. These students, much as she loved them, were a bit too forward for her liking. Still, she thought it best to stifle any rumors of a reconciliation with Thomas May right from the start.

"Good, Mrs. May," Rob said, "because I think... well, everyone here thinks...that you can do a lot better." Several heads bobbed in agreement.

She pushed back a giggle. "Well, I thank you for your kind words. Now, may we once and for all get off the subject of my social life and get on with English?"

"Sure, but..." Kaley Robinson sat up, her short skirt barely covering the tops of her skinny thighs.

"Yes, Kaley?" Callie asked with a sigh.

"Do you have a boyfriend?"

"No!" And with that, she moved onto the "Three

A's of English": antecedents, appositives, and articles. Unfortunately, by the end of the class period, Rob Rankin's eyes were heavy, Josh Hansen had yawned all of twenty times, and Kaley Robinson had filled her notebook with words—words Callie was certain weren't lecture notes.

At the close of the day, Callie found herself walking down the long corridor toward the school parking lot with Anne Hardy at her side. The older teacher was just a year away from retirement. She'd been a special education teacher for as long as Callie could remember, and the students loved her.

"How was your first week back?" she asked. "Anybody give you trouble?"

Callie smiled, thinking about all the Rob Rankins, Josh Hansens, and Kaley Robinsons she'd encountered throughout the day.

Every class seemed to have those who spoke out at inappropriate times, acted crassly, or simply needed extra attention in some form or another. She couldn't deny there were times she was tempted to throw up her hands in dismay, but those times were few. "No one gave me any trouble, but a few gave me a run for my money," she teased.

Anne laughed. "Well, at least you've kept your sense of humor about you. Gotta hang onto that in this field."

"That's for sure."

"I was sorry to hear about your divorce, Callie,"

the older woman offered. "And then to lose your father on top of everything else." Her tone grew softer still.

"Thanks."

"I know God is watching out for you, especially in these hard times. You know that, don't you?"

"Yes, I've experienced His grace in numerous ways."

Anne stopped walking and touched Callie's arm, halting Callie's steps as well. She'd always been viewed as a saint, the kind of person you looked to for wisdom. She *had* to be a saint to have stayed in the special education department for as long as she had. Middle schoolers with emotional issues and learning disabilities were not an easy lot, but Anne's patience never wavered.

In fact, her strong Christian values had won the respect of students and colleagues alike. Though many didn't hold to her same principles, few would dispute her words. To be frank, Anne Hardy was one of the most esteemed, respected teachers in the district.

"Thomas was one of my students, did you know that?"

The disclosure surprised Callie. She shook her head.

They resumed their walk down the long corridor. "Believe me; I know how difficult that boy was to get along with. Frankly, I'm surprised you lasted as long as you did. In fact, I don't know why you married him in the first place."

Callie smiled and released a breath. "Well, for one thing, Anne, I didn't know the Lord as well as I do now. If I'd truly sought His will in the matter, I doubt I'd be in the mess I'm in now."

"Mess?"

Callie gulped, unsure how much more to say on the matter. In the end, she plunged ahead, certain she could use the woman's prayers. "Thomas has been coming around lately, asking for money—well, you could say *demanding* it."

"Don't give him a cent, understand?"

"I'm trying to be strong."

"Callie, giving into that man will only put him in a more domineering position. You need to stand your ground."

Reaching the door, Callie opened it first to let Anne pass. "I know you're right. But he can be so convincing."

"Has he threatened you?"

"You're very perceptive, Anne."

She smiled meekly. "Perhaps that's what comes from teaching special education students for so many years. I've learned to assess their mood swings, behavior patterns, determine why they react to situations as they do."

Another pause. "Well, has he? Threatened you, that is?"

This time they stopped in the middle of the sidewalk before parting ways.

Callie looked at the cloudless sky, breathed in the warm September air, felt the heat of the afternoon sun penetrate her sleeveless cotton shirt. In the distance, just a hint of red leaves tainted an otherwise green maple, tall and aged. She sighed. "He hasn't really threatened bodily harm—yet. But I don't trust him." It was true.

He'd said he was coming over to collect the money he'd demanded when she'd failed to put it in his father's mailbox. He'd placed a couple of menacing phone calls to her, had even visited her apartment when she wasn't around and then driven past her mother's house. Still, he hadn't actually threatened to harm her.

"Callie, I wouldn't trust that man, but I'm sure I don't need to tell you that. You be very careful. Is someone looking out for you?"

Dan. "I'm learning to trust God more and more."

"Sometimes God puts people in our lives to help do His work."

"Well, if you put it like that, I suppose I do have a guardian angel of sorts. The man next door. He's been very kind and protective, but I can't depend on him forever."

A smile crossed Anne's face. "Well, that's good then. And if you need anything at all, and I mean anything, you call me. All right?"

"I appreciate that."

Anne placed a warm hand on Callie's arm. "I'll be praying for you, honey. You just hang in there."

"Thank you, Anne."

Anne moved off the sidewalk and threw her a final wave.

Dan stepped out of the shower, threw a towel around his neck, and moved to the bathroom mirror. He leaned in close to peruse the gash above his eye. It was healing nicely, as was the rest of his body. Much as he hated to admit it, the week off had done him good. Even the aches and pains and bruised ribs were healing more quickly than expected, his doctor declaring that his already excellent health and strong physique helped. Dan flexed in front of the mirror, then frowned at his narcissistic behavior.

Dan thought about Callie while he readied for his date. She was as nervous as a puppy that had been kicked, afraid to trust again. It must be unnerving to think you were falling for a guy who had been less than honest from the start about his past.

Lately he'd been praying that she would be able to see beyond his initial deceit and into the real person of Dan Mattson. He had restitution to make, not only with Callie, but also with the little congregation at Bible Fellowship Church in southern Michigan. And if getting her to trust him meant a little bit of courting and wooing, he was more than up for the challenge.

He'd been glad to hear that Thomas had kept his distance. Maybe the warning the police had issued had been enough to jar some sense into him. But then when he'd read the article in the paper about his recent brush with the law, he worried that it would take a lot more than a visit from the Oakdale Police Department to scare him off. He wished to goodness the guy would have been tossed in jail for the misdemeanor, but according to what he'd read, a hefty fine and warning were all he had been cited with. Would he now come to Callie and expect her to pay that additional debt? No, Dan would stop Thomas May before that happened.

He pulled a pair of new khakis from his closet, threw them on the bed, then went in search of a proper golf shirt. Next, he grabbed a newer pair of slip-on loafers. While debating which socks and leather belt to wear, the phone rang. He flung himself at the foot of the bed to take the call.

"Danny, Mom told me you're coming home this weekend."

"Hello to you, too, Samantha," he answered with a grin.

"I'm so excited. We're having everyone over for dinner tomorrow. I've already done all the shopping. I'm making your favorite, Danny boy."

"A beef roast and potatoes?"

"You guessed it."

"Then I'll be sure to arrive on time."

"What prompted you to come home this weekend?"

"Would another weekend have worked better for

you?" he quizzed, enjoying the banter that usually evolved between his sister and him.

"No, silly. I was just wondering, that's all. Are you planning to go to church Sunday?"

"Yes, and I've asked the new pastor if I might have take a minute to address the congregation."

"You're kidding!"

"Don't sound so shocked. It's something I need to do, Sam."

"What if you're setting yourself up for more humiliation?"

"I think a little humiliation is what I deserve. I blew it big time with those great people. They were all counting on me to pull them through, to show them what trust and faith are all about, and I didn't have what it took. Plainly speaking, I jumped ship. If nothing else, the people of Bible Fellowship Church deserve an explanation."

"You sound so sure of yourself."

"I'm anything but that, Sam. But what I am sure of is who I am in Christ. He loves me, Sam, and He forgave me. Now, if I can just convince that church full of people to forgive me, I'll be all set."

"I'll be praying for you."

"Will you and John be there?"

"You bet. We'll be supporting you all the way."

"I figured I could count on you."

They talked a few more minutes. Then Sam announced she was receiving another call. Dan took that as his opportunity to bow out of the conversation. "I'll see you tomorrow, Danny."

The clock registered half past five. A bad case of nerves gnawed away at his confidence. It'd been years since his "first date." The day trip to Oakdale's zoo hadn't been a date, not with Emily there to furnish distractions, and neither had the dinner invitation with Callie and her mom. But this? This was a real date—something he'd spent precious time planning.

With a little luck and God's blessing, it might even end with a kiss.

~

The babysitter arrived on schedule. This girl appeared self-assured and friendly. She'd come highly recommended by Lori, who apparently wasn't quite ready to babysit again after her last experience. "Hello, Rachael," Callie greeted at the door. "I'm glad you could come tonight. This is Emily." She pointed to the baby who was busy crawling across the floor, making every attempt to pull herself up to the coffee table and take her first steps. Callie suspected that at the rate she was going, she would beat the odds for walking before her first birthday.

"Nice to meet you," the girl replied, immediately walking across the room to greet Emily.

Callie showed her around the apartment, took her into the nursery, instructed her as to bedtime, where the snacks were, and whom to call in case of an emergency. She didn't foresee anything happening but said that her mother would be on the alert, just in case. Rachael exuded confidence, assuring Callie that she had six brothers and sisters, so she knew what to do.

The doorbell sounded just before six. Nerves flapping foolishly, she flung wide the door. This time it was Dan. His wounds healing nicely, he was the picture of strength and confidence, not to mention utter masculinity. And the realization struck her with intensity. *Hang on to your heart, girl.*

"You didn't check your peephole," he scolded. No greeting, just a gruff reminder.

"I forgot. I knew it would be you," she said.

"No, you *assumed* it would be me," he warned. But then his tone softened when he gave her a sweeping once-over. "You look mighty fine, by the way." He smiled, then donned his scolding look again before coming within an inch of her face. "I could have been Thomas."

The notion gave her a chill. "I know. I'll try to be more careful."

"Please." He arched an eyebrow in his customary way, and her heart took an unexpected leap. "I would like to think you are using every precaution."

"I can't live my life as if there is danger lurking around every corner."

"Yes, you can, and you'd better," he said.

"But..."

He put a gentle finger to her lips to shush her and mouthed, "We'll talk later." Then moving into the room, he swept Emily up into his arms, and for the next several minutes, sounds of teasing and squeals of delight filled up the place, indicating that, at least in this apartment, everything was right in the world.

The evening turned out to be everything Callie had needed it to be after an unusually stressful week. Conversation was light but comfortable, Dan entertaining her with one story after another about his childhood, right down to the spats he'd had with his siblings. They shared plenty of laughs, and for the first time she discovered how animated he could be. Like a sparrow that's just learned to fly, he was all energy and spirit. And, of course, the fact that he'd recently recommitted his life to Christ made all the difference in the world.

He'd stayed clear of the topic of his marriage but later in the evening had shared freely about his daughter, what she had been like, the sound of her giggle, the things she'd loved. Callie had the distinct feeling she was one of the few with whom he'd felt free enough to share these memories.

She couldn't imagine life without Emily, didn't even want to consider what it would be like. How did a parent ever survive the loss of a child? And in those moments while sitting across from him at a candlelit table in a quiet restaurant, empty plates and half-full coffee cups before them, she began to understand why Daniel Mattson, minister, had felt the need to escape.

Balmy September breezes accompanied their after-dinner walk through the quaint streets of downtown Oakdale. The main square boasted a century-old courthouse building, an ancient Methodist Church crafted of stone, a sprawling bank with clock tower, and a two-story redbrick post office. The town was staid and dignified, yet still upheld that homespun feel. Old buildings with refurbished fronts and upstairs apartments with welcoming overhangs decorated the main street. It was a mixture of the old with the new, a comforting blend for a century-old town.

At the corner of Park and Michigan, Dan took hold of Callie's hand and led her across the street. Up until that moment, he'd kept his hands in his pants pockets. Hers had swung comfortably at her sides.

"Want to sit down?" he asked, leading her to a snug park situated on a vacant city block. Crosswalks shaded by ancient oaks, elms, and maples, and lined with rows and rows of petunias, welcomed visitors. They strolled toward the middle of the square and sat on a bench. Dan held Callie's hand on his knee.

Across the way, a middle-aged couple stopped to gaze down at a patch of flowers before resuming their leisurely walk. In another area of the park, a couple ambled along while their two children ran ahead.

"What a perfect night," Callie offered, settling back against the park bench, its chilled steel frame cooling her warm skin. She'd never felt more comfortable or safe.

But then that worried part of her sprang to mind again, braking against any hasty forward motion. *Don't give your heart away too quickly,* it warned.

"Yes it is, but I'd say you have the stars and moon beat by a long shot," Dan said, unexpectedly removing his hand from hers and placing it behind her shoulders to draw her closer, the simple act enough to steal away a piece of her comfort. She gulped down a bountiful supply of air to calm herself.

"Worried?" he whispered.

"A little," she admitted.

He chuckled deep in his throat. "Callie, I won't do more than rest my hand on your shoulder if that's what you want. You need to learn to trust me. I'm not going to hurt you, honey."

"Honey"? The sweet endearment made her skin tingle. "Oh, well, I know that." But did she really? Months of living with Thomas had taught her the dangers of placing too much trust in men. But she had to remind herself this man wasn't Thomas.

He looked out over the park as if to conjure up his next thought. "Thomas let you down in a big way, Callie; you trusted him with your whole heart, and he failed you miserably. It shouldn't have been that way. Husbands are supposed to love their wives just as God loves His church. Since he broke that commandment, I guess I can see why you'd be a little skittish."

He was drawing little circles on the rounded part of her shoulder. She glanced at him and what she saw in his eyes were the makings of a tender promise. Without hesitation, she leaned against his warmth, inhaled the musky scent of his aftershave, and pondered what it would be like to share the future with him.

She knew one thing. She liked being with him.

"You're a very nice man."

The vibrations of a low laugh rumbled in his chest. "Not as nice as you, I'm afraid."

She snuggled in a little closer. "Nor half as cute," he added.

Callie giggled. "I've enjoyed getting to know you this summer."

He rested his chin on her head. Her heart lurched at his nearness. "We got off to a shaky start, you and I. I was a bit of a screwball when we first met."

Overhead streetlights attracted swarms of nighttime insects. Their darting movements and Dan's gentle ministrations were a mesmerizing combination.

"And I was a bit of a snoot."

Dan smirked. "Wouldn't even pay for my razor at the grocery store checkout."

She smiled at the memory. "That girl had no business working a cash register."

"Did you ever see her in there again? I think they must have fired the poor thing."

"Oh!" A burst of laughter tumbled out of her.

He readjusted his chin then swallowed, and she felt the bob of his Adam's apple.

Several feet above them, bats dove for their dinner.

Callie watched in silence as they whizzed past the streetlight, lunging and darting with proficiency. Although she knew the creatures served their purpose, she still shivered at the sight.

As if sensing her uneasiness, Dan lifted his chin from her head and curled his arm more snugly around her shoulder. He brushed his lips against her neck. "They don't really get in your hair, you know." His whispered touch left her dizzy and somehow wanting.

"What?"

"Bats building a nest in your hair. It's an old wives' tale."

She sagged into him. "I know."

A full minute of easy silence passed between them. "Gotcha!" His hand swooped down and ruffled her hair, startling her into a tiny yelp. She laughed and threw him a playful punch in the arm.

Soft laughter mingled between them.

"Still worried?" Dan asked after a moment.

She shoved her freshly mussed hair out of her eyes and tilted her head back. "Not so much."

"That's good, because I'm about to tell you something."

Her mind fluttered in a million different directions. *Dear Father, could it be?*

Again, he nuzzled her neck and moved to her ear. "I love you, Callie." He reached up and ran the back of his knuckles along her cheek. And waited. She opened her mouth, then clamped it shut again. Although she ached to return the sentiment, she couldn't—not yet, anyway.

"I feel so—undeserving," she said instead. "I have nothing to give you right now, and my greatest fear is that God won't forgive me if I..." She searched for the words even as Dan's face clouded with confusion. "I'm divorced, Daniel. Wouldn't it be the same as adultery if...?"

His lips on her cheeks were warm and moist. "Callie, sweet Callie," he murmured. "The beauty of God's grace is that He allows for our mistakes, even forgives us of them entirely. Don't you believe that a gracious God would allow you to open your heart to love again?"

She pondered that before reflecting on another thought. "Suppose you get tired of me."

He tossed his head back and laughed. "Trust me; that could not happen. You're fresh and bright and funny. Besides, real love doesn't die, Callie. It stays, grows, blossoms, changes, and deepens. Believe me, I know...." His last words fell and faded into the night.

"I am nothing like she was," Callie said, suddenly recalling all his photos of Andrea. "I wouldn't want you to think that just because I have a daughter, we could serve as a substitute for Andrea and Chelsea."

He stiffened. "Is that what you think I'm looking for—someone to take their place in my heart, to fit their molds?"

"It's crossed my mind."

"Well, that's not the way it is for me. Besides," he said, bending to kiss her earlobe, the imprint of his lips leaving a moist, warm spot, "you're nothing like her. It would be hard for you to take her place, that being the case."

With his free hand, he brushed his knuckles against her cheek again, this time dipping his head close. "I love you for *you* and nothing else. And I love Emily; not because she's a sweet little girl, as my Chelsea was, but because she's a precious little creation, a miniature of you."

And as if to seal his words, he turned her to face him, cupped her face with both hands, and kissed her soundly.

On the drive home, Dan told her he was heading up to Michigan for the weekend. "I think it would be wise if you stayed at your mom's place, or have her come stay with you."

"We'll be fine, Emily and I. I can't live my life in fear," she said, exhibiting a bit of her old stubbornness.

"It's not about living in fear, sweetie; it's about living smartly."

"Think about it, Dan. What could my mother do to deter Thomas?"

"Sometimes there's safety in numbers," he argued.

"How about Emily and I stay holed up in my apartment all weekend?"

"Do you have all the supplies you'll need?"

"I just picked up a bunch of groceries and baby

things two days ago. I'll keep busy with laundry, cleaning, and organizing some closets, all stuff I need to do anyway. Now that I'm back to work, I need to stay caught up with things. We'll even have church with a TV pastor, how's that?"

He turned the car into the apartment parking lot and drove into his usual spot. After cutting the engine, he threw a doubtful gaze her way. "I'd still feel better if…"

She put a hand to his forearm. "We'll be fine."

Both hands gripping the steering wheel, he captured her with his gaze. "Promise me you'll keep your door locked at all times."

She cocked her head at him and saluted. "Yes, sir!"

Half-expecting him to scold her for her flippancy, she was surprised when he gave grinned instead. "You are fast becoming irresistible to me, did you know that? I just want to be sure that you'll be waiting for me when I get home Sunday night."

The last hint of light had faded from the sky, and the Milky Way was splattered over the inky blackness, a full moon reflecting off the hood of the car and casting a shadow over Dan's strong profile.

"I'll be here," she whispered.

They climbed out of the car and headed up the walk, hand in hand. In the air was the delicious scent of new beginnings.

Bible Fellowship Church seemed filled to capacity—whether because news had leaked out that former pastor Dan Mattson would be in attendance (and rumor was he would say a few words to the congregation), or simply because the church had grown in numbers, Dan couldn't be sure. All he knew was that it felt good to be back, despite the bundle of nerves rolling around inside his gut.

Several friends, acquaintances, and parish members greeted him, while others stayed noticeably on the sidelines, smiling only from a distance.

"Shall we move to the front?" Dan asked, Sam on his arm and John following close behind.

"If you want to," she said. "You lead the way, Danny."

Walking down the center aisle, he heard whispers aplenty, though it was unclear to his ears what all the comments were about. Once he thought he heard something uttered about Andrea's absence and how sad it all was. "She was such a lovely person," someone else whispered.

Dan wondered briefly what these people would think if they discovered he'd fallen in love all over again. But for now that bit of information would be kept private, he determined. Only Sam was aware of his recent love interest, and he'd only told her the bare minimum last night while sitting out on her front porch, just the two of them, the rest of the family still enjoying the last of Sam's delicious dessert while his mother cleaned up the kitchen. He figured she would indulge his mother in the news at her earliest convenience; probably today once he headed back for Illinois following the morning service and his quick trip out to the cemetery. His sister never had been one for keeping juicy secrets to herself.

Once Samantha had pieced together that Callie was the one she'd met out on the apartment steps that day she'd visited, she'd fairly whooped with joy. "She's so pretty, Danny. And I noticed her little girl, so sweet and cute. Oh, Danny...." With that, she'd flung herself into his arms, practically squeezing the next breath right out of him. He still felt bruised and a bit battered up from his fall of a week ago, but now his pain had diminished to faint jabs and usually only bothered him when people like Samantha went overboard with hugs.

A small worship band and a few singers led the morning service in much the way Dan remembered. Prayer and the offering followed. He thought the overall spirit of worship great, the only uneasiness he felt coming from his own stomach.

What would he say when finally called upon? He

thought he had it planned out pretty well—that is, until the doubts moved in, and then he questioned. He had spent time on his knees the night before at his parents' house, pouring his heart and soul out to God, pleading for just the right words that would ease the hurt he'd caused, narrow the gap he'd put between himself and these people.

The new pastor's name was Ryan Winters. He was young and enthusiastic by all that Dan could see, having taken hold of his hand and shaken it firmly when first they met in the church foyer. Sam and John had stood protectively at Dan's side, as if they expected the worst and were prepared to whisk him away at the slightest hint of trouble. Dan smiled inwardly even now at their prickly behavior, but he would thank them later for their love and concern.

Twenty minutes into the service, Pastor Winters stepped up to the pulpit, threw a glance in Dan's direction, and, after a two-minute introduction, welcomed him to the front.

There was no applause as he made his way forward, just the final squeeze of encouragement Sam gave. The people, however, looked receptive when he first scanned their faces, and that was a plus.

"Good morning," he started, clearing his throat after his feeble greeting. *Lord, give me the words to say,* he prayed inwardly.

"I am with you, My son. Just speak the truth."

In the moments that followed, he did just that, spoke

from his heart and to the people. And what started out to be an unrehearsed attempt at explaining himself evolved into a heartrending monologue that brought people to tears and hearts to a point of healing.

"After losing Andrea and Chelsea, I didn't know what to feel, how to act," he stated, five minutes into his talk. "I'd lived my life believing that a man's character is measured by his degree of strength in hard times, by how capable he is of holding himself together. So it was a bit of a shock to me when I saw myself beginning to crumble. It didn't dawn on me even as your pastor that I had been trying to stand on my own two feet, apart from God.

"Somehow, I had it figured that I should be able to handle this crisis. After all, I was the pastor, and people counted on me to be strong, to set an example. I wanted to; believe me, I did. I wanted you to look at me and say, 'My, look at Pastor Mattson. He is dealing with his loss so well. He is a man of God, a true saint. His faith surpasses all of ours.'" Dan chuckled, shifting his gaze so that it rested on Sam and John. He appreciated their support and prayers. Perhaps that was what kept him going.

"I suffered all the key components that accompany the grieving process: the shock, the devastating pain and sorrow, the guilt, and the anger, ah, the anger," he said, emphasizing the latter. "I suppose that was where I truly tripped up.

"For a time, I ignored the anger, supposing it would

go away. I didn't want to deal with it, so I tucked it away, choosing not to discuss it with anyone or to try to fix it; certainly not to talk to God about it. And because of that, my anger festered and grew in size. Like a cancerous tumor, it overtook me, became bigger than anything I'd ever encountered. And before I knew what had happened, it had all turned outward. Yes, where once I had blamed myself for this tragedy, I chose to blame God.

"My blame resulted in a multitude of things; first, I began to question the authenticity of His Word; second, His love and plan for my life; and third, His very existence. And that, my dear friends, was the beginning of Dan Mattson's downfall. I figured if God loved me so much, He would surely have chosen an entirely different road for me than this rugged path of grief He had put me on.

"In short, I couldn't feel His presence, so I assumed He wasn't there. My faith faltered miserably, and, in the process, so did my desire to be your pastor."

All around, Dan heard a rustling of sorts, as women went for tissues and men shuffled in their seats. The temptation to quit right there was great, but something urged him to press on.

"Before I tell you where my journey took me, may I just say that I'm sorry for deserting you? One Sunday morning, much like today, I simply stood behind this pulpit and announced that I was leaving. I failed to give you much explanation, just stated that I no longer had what it took to be your pastor. And in a sense, that was true. I was completely ineffective. In retrospect, I probably should have taken a leave of absence, but with the state I was in, I wasn't open to that. I simply wanted out; wanted an escape.

"And may I also thank those of you who came forward with words of encouragement and even asked me to stay? You had no idea of the condition of my soul, but you loved me anyway. I appreciate that more than you know."

In the moments that followed, he told them about his move to Oakdale, his job with Freeman Construction, and his flight from God. He confessed to hiding his true identity from everyone but Greg Freeman, living a reclusive, self-absorbed lifestyle, and failing miserably in his Christian witness.

From somewhere in the back came a woman's loud cough. In that moment, he nearly lost his nerve—until he caught a glimpse of Sam. She sat perched on the edge of her pew, encouraging him with her eyes and whole self.

Finally, he came to the moment when he told about his fall from the roof. "That was when I sensed God's presence, knew it had been there all along, but I'd simply missed it," he told them. "My faith had been too small, my eyes too fixed on myself and my problems that I couldn't see far enough past them to know that God was there."

He related the dream he'd had in the ambulance,

the sense of calm that had followed, and the silent recommitment he'd made to Christ in those moments. But even in the telling, he knew it was unfair to expect others to understand firsthand just how significant the whole experience had been for him. Perhaps it was enough that *he* knew.

In his final remarks, Dan thanked everyone for their kind attention, asked their forgiveness one last time, promised to pray for them and their new pastor, and without further ado, made his way back to his pew. On the way down the aisle, he heard the beginnings of faint clapping coming from the back. Another joined in, and then another, until the entire congregation filled the church with riotous applause and loud cheers.

Before he'd found his seat, the congregation was on its feet. Dan sat down, and for the first time in a very long while, he put his face in his hands and wept.

Later, on his drive back to Illinois, Dan found himself reflecting on the morning's events. Following the service, he was swarmed with well-wishers, those who claimed to have understood his pain and his reasons for fleeing and who wanted to offer their words of hope and encouragement. Sam and John, visibly relieved, laughed and conversed freely with some friends a few pews over.

"You gonna be a preacher again?" a young boy had asked him while standing in the middle of the huddle, his gaze firmly fixed on Dan's face. A hush fell over the gathering. At first, he hadn't recognized the boy, but soon recalled him as the youngest of three sons belonging to a new couple who'd started attending shortly after the accident. Because of his distraction, they'd barely gotten acquainted before his desertion.

"You know, that's a good question, young man," he said, leaning into him. "Unfortunately, I don't have the answer. I'm certainly willing, but right now I'm waiting to see how God leads." His response didn't appear to satisfy the boy completely, but he gave a slow nod and shrugged.

Off to one side Dan spotted a familiar figure, old Mrs. Cratchet, her face drawn and taut from all the years of frowning deeply. A marred cane helped to steady her as she made her way toward him.

Compelled to leave the circle of supporters, Dan approached her. "Sister Cratchet," he offered, giving her his best smile. Even on a good Sunday, she wasn't known for returning friendly greetings, but today she'd presented him with a sort of half grin.

"It was good to hear you admit to being human," she'd said with a little sniff. Dan took it as a compliment, coming from her.

"Why, thank you, uh, I think," he'd said, extending his hand. She took it. He found it surprisingly warm.

"I believe that was the best sermon you ever delivered. Yes sir, it truly was."

He tossed his head back and laughed. "If that was my best, perhaps it's a good thing that I've left the pulpit. For now, anyway."

"Yes, perhaps." She smiled, her ancient face a mass of wrinkles, but her deep-set eyes still held the hint of a twinkle. "You're a good preacher, Daniel Mattson. A little rough around the edges, maybe, but that's because you're young. I always thought you sounded a bit too polished before, like you sat up all night rehearsing. But today—well, today you showed us who you really are. Yes, you did. And frankly, I like you much better this way."

Dan accepted her subtle attempt at cordiality. "Why, Sister Cratchet," he'd said in jest, "I do believe that's one of the nicest things you've ever said to me."

"Humph—and maybe the nicest you'll ever hear," she'd replied, slapping him lightly on the cuff of his sleeve and grinning.

∾

Dan smiled at the recollection, his eyes trained on the road ahead, glancing every so often at the speedometer lest he break the law trying to make it back to Illinois in record time.

He stopped briefly at the cemetery on his way out of town. Someone had planted flowers in front of the gravestones. Probably Sam—or maybe his mom, he mused. A wave of guilt swept over him for not tending better to the sites, but visiting the place had never given him much comfort. His pain had driven itself so deep that standing next to mere graves had never appeased it. So rather than visit often, he'd avoided the place altogether. Today, however, his sorrow seemed more contained, more defined.

In his mind, he compartmentalized his feelings, sorted through them even while he allowed more tears to flow. Whether it made any sense or not, he stood before Andrea's grave and told her about Callie and Emily. "She hasn't said she loves me, Andrea, but I'm pretty sure she will. She finds it really hard to trust anyone right now. She's been hurt and needs time to heal. I know it's silly to say so, but I'm sure you'd like her, Andrea. And Emily. I know you'd love her. Your heart was always so big and accepting."

Next, he'd found himself kneeling at Chelsea's grave and fingering the lettering on her small granite marker. "God's Precious Angel," it read. "You came on angel's wings, a precious gem so rare. There never was, nor will there be, a match for one so fair."

"Oh, God," he'd prayed, "thank You for lending them to me—if only for a short time. And thank You for Your forgiveness and patience in dealing with my anger."

The tears fell harder then, as if a dam had finally broken loose to let go of the raging river. Though he was surprised by his sudden release of emotion, he actually welcomed it. It seemed the tough exterior of Dan Mattson had at last crumbled before his eyes.

Callie finished putting away the last of her laundry when the phone rang. She was just closing the lingerie drawer when she spotted Emily crawling past her bedroom, a roll of toilet paper dragging behind her diapered bottom. "You come back here, you little stinker," she called while snatching up the cordless phone. "Hello?" she said into the receiver. A trail of white led from the bathroom to the kitchen, the baby on a faster-than-usual-crawl, giggling at the prospect of a pursuit.

"Callie?"

"Dan!" It was difficult to contain her excitement. It was the third time he'd called that weekend, and she'd be lying to say it hadn't pleased her. "Where are you?"

"On the road," he answered. "I should be back by late afternoon. You sound out of breath."

She laughed. "It's not easy keeping up with a ten-month-old. Some days are harder than others. Right now I'm chasing after a half roll of toilet paper."

"A what?"

"Never mind," she answered, bending to snatch the roll from Emily's grasp. He chuckled knowingly, and the sound warmed her clear to her toes. "How did it go this morning?" she asked, still winded. Ever since their conversation last night, she'd wondered how his talk at his former church had gone. While she waited for his response, she began the task of rolling up the long strand of toilet paper.

"It was amazing, Callie. The people were so forgiving and open."

"I knew they would be."

"You did, huh?"

"Yes. I prayed for you," she admitted shyly.

"Thank you. I felt your prayers. I'm anxious to tell you about it, but more than that, I'm anxious to see you. I've missed you."

Her heart leaped. She wanted to tell him the same, but the words came hard. "How is your family?" she said instead.

He laughed quietly. "They're fine, same as last night when you asked."

"Oh."

"I want you and Emily to reserve tonight for me," he said, his voice containing a hint of authority.

"You do?"

"And I'll not take no for an answer."

"You won't?" His words made her tingle with giddiness.

"Nope. Plan on going out to eat."

"Emily, too?"

"I promised you and Emily dinner a week ago, remember? And I mean to follow through."

She couldn't keep from smiling into the phone. "What time?"

"Well, I plan to knock on your door the minute I enter the building, but we'll go for dinner more like five-thirty or six. How does that sound?"

"Which part?"

He laughed again. "Did you know that I've fallen in love?"

Now her heart fairly swelled to capacity. Backing up to the wall, she slid down to settle on the floor, legs crossed. "Anyone special?"

"Ah, yes, someone very special. I'll have to tell you about her sometime. In fact, how's tonight?"

She giggled with delight, enjoying the banter. "Tonight would be fine."

They talked for several more minutes, him telling her a bit about the church service and asking about the one she'd watched on TV from the privacy of her living room. She shared freely.

The afternoon dragged on. After putting Emily down for her nap, she sauntered into the den to check her e-mail. Finding nothing, she went to the living room to watch TV, sift through some magazines, and sip on a cup of hot tea.

The weekend had been long, particularly since promising both her mother and Dan that she wouldn't step foot outside her apartment the entire time. Oh, there'd been plenty to do to keep busy, and thankfully, Lisa had come over last night, but now she found herself growing more and more restless.

Dan had called again to inform her he'd be arriving in less than half an hour. So when the doorbell sounded it wasn't surprising that she had assumed he'd be there to greet her, which would explain why she'd thrown the door wide open without first looking through the peephole to see who it was.

"Callie." Thomas pushed his way inside and closed the door. Callie's heart stopped at the sight of him. His breath and clothes were strong with the stench of alcohol and cigarettes.

"What are you doing here?" she asked, trying to hide the tremor in her voice.

"What does it look like? Came to see my wife." He leaned down and, aiming for her mouth, grazed only her cheek with his lips when she angled her head away from him, his foul breath engulfing her senses.

"You're not welcome here," she murmured. "I want you to leave. *Now.*"

"Is that any way to treat your husband?" His words were cold and slurred. "I'm not goin' anywhere, girl, till I get what I came for."

"You are *not* my husband—and I'm not giving you anything."

He smirked and lifted her chin with a clammy finger. "You're mine, lady, always will be." Immediate fear stole her breath when his hand moved to her throat, encircling it. "You disappoint me, Callie. I expected to find money in my old man's mailbox. Wasn't I clear enough?"

His hold on her neck tightened ever so slightly. She remained motionless when instinct ordered her to kick him in the shins. "I told you I would come for it myself if you didn't cough up some cash."

"A vicious dog met me before I could even get out of my car, so I drove away."

He threw back his head and let go a peal of hollow laughter. "That's pathetic, princess. Ain't no vicious dogs in that neighborhood." He released her throat, and relief like water surged through her veins. She swallowed hard and took a step back.

I can't let him see my fear.

"I guess it's just as well," he continued, knocking into her on his way to the refrigerator. "I got to missing you." Throwing wide the door, he bent at the waist to check out the contents and something jutted from his side pocket. Her heart dropped to her toes.

A gun. What was Thomas doing with a gun?

Red-hot shivers skidded over her spine. *Oh, God. Oh, God....*

The temptation to bolt was strong but quite impossible with Emily asleep in her crib.

"What? No beer?" Frustration threaded through his voice as he pushed aside one container after another.

She swallowed and pulled back her shoulders, resolving not to surrender to his little game. "I don't keep beer in my house. Besides, you smell as if you've already had enough."

Hollow cackling followed her remark. "Well now, if I'd had enough, I wouldn't be looking in the fridge, would I? How about you run out and get me some?"

Day was when she would have pacified his foolish

demands just to keep the peace, but not today. Not while she had a daughter to consider.

As if reading her mind, he slammed shut the refrigerator and made a hasty study of the apartment. "You worried about leavin' the kid in my care? Where is she, anyway?"

When he looked down the hall, Callie raced ahead and blocked his passage. "She's sleeping. You can look at her later—when she wakes up." *If you're still here.* Her prayer was that he'd grow weary of pestering her, realize his need for more booze, and leave without incident. One thing was sure; she wanted him gone before Dan arrived.

He teetered, his shoulder thumping against the wall, and gave a half shrug. "F-fine. I'll look at her later then." To her great relief, he made an about turn and headed back down the hall. Callie followed on his heels. In the living room, he turned. "Let's get down to business, shall we, Cal? Where's the m-money you promised me?"

"I didn't—promise you any money, Thomas."

"You said yourself you came by, but—uh-hum—a vicious dog stopped you. Likely story, Callie, but anyway, that tells me you intended to cough up some cash. So just give me my hunk of change and I'll be out of your hair."

"I don't..."

"No excuses," he warned with a raspy chuckle. "See? I brought me a friend." He put a hand to the gun in his pocket, his eyes cold and proud. "'Course there'll be no need to introduce you if you do as I say."

Her senses screamed alarm. "Thomas, I..."

"Shut up!" he shrieked, bringing his hand up and cracking it hard across her face. Unspeakable pain exploded behind her eyes, and for a split second, confusion wound itself like a tight knot around her mind. When she might have toppled over from the blow, she quickly steadied herself against the back of the sofa and righted her stance, then checked for signs of blood with the back of her hand, surprised when all she found was a tender lump of already swollen flesh.

He cursed bitterly, then squeezed her jaw in a vise-like grip. "As usual, you try my patience," he snarled.

His hold tightening, Callie fought to stay alert. "My purse—it's over there," she mumbled through the stinging throb, angling her eyes at the wall hook beside the door. "You'll find an envelope with some cash inside. All I could come up with was a hundred bucks. I—I don't have anything else to give you, Thomas. See for yourself."

"You stupid..."

But the doorbell stopped him mid-sentence. "Who's that?" he hissed through rancid breath. Pushing her back, he stared at the closed door.

"I—I don't know," she answered, knowing what dangers awaited Dan if she opened the door. For it would be him.

"Don't answer it," he warned under his breath.

"I have to." Slipping away from him, she headed for the door, but he yanked her arm nearly out of its socket in his haste to stop her. "See this?" he asked, eyes glittering with contempt as he caressed the butt of his pistol, forcing her gaze downward. "Picked her up in Florida. Now, whoever that is at the door, you just send 'em on their way, you hear?"

She shot him a withering glance and walked the rest of the way to the door. Once there, she put her hand to the knob, but he jerked her around by the hair before she had a chance to turn it. Tugging her close, he put his mouth to her ear. "Do as I say, Callie, and everything will be fine. You understand me?" he snarled. She gave a slow nod. "Don't mess up."

Turning the knob, Callie pasted a smile on her face and opened the door a mere five inches, just enough to peer past the crack and see into Dan's dark chocolate eyes.

"Hi, Dan," she murmured.

The ready smile he'd had for her quickly turned to a frown. "You gonna let me in?" he asked. When she didn't respond, he pushed the door gently, but she resisted. "Callie..."

"I...I have a splitting headache. Sorry. I'm afraid you'll have to come back another time."

He quirked his brows in question. "Another time? Hey, what happened to your face?" He tried to reach through the opening but she held tight to the door, preventing it.

She rubbed her cheek. "This? It's nothing. Guess I laid on this side too long while I was napping and left a mark."

He watched her closely, searching her eyes as if trying to see into her soul. She noticed he'd stuck his foot in the door. "Everything all right?"

Instantly, Callie felt a sharp jab in her side and knew it to be the pistol. She drew in a jagged breath and tried to say with her eyes what Thomas wouldn't allow with words. "Everything is—fine. I better go now."

"Yeah, you have school tomorrow," he said with a nod. "Maybe you should turn in early." He looked at the floor as if preparing to turn, then raised his head again. "How's Emily?"

"Emily's—sleeping." Her voice wobbled. *Don't go!*

He seemed overly composed. "Maybe I'll see you tomorrow." He drew something out of his pocket and placed it in the doorjamb, holding her gaze for a solid five seconds before pulling the door shut of his own accord.

"Well, that was sweet," said Thomas. He stuck the gun back in his pocket. "He your new boyfriend?"

"He's a very good friend," she replied, praying Dan wouldn't try anything foolish. Who could compete with a gun?

"You sure it's nothing more than that? I'd hate to think of another man trying to steal you away from me." His hot breath sent a shudder down her back when he leaned forward to nibble at her ear.

She ducked away from him and walked to the kitchen. At the sink, she set to putting away a few clean dishes. Anything to stay busy. "Why don't you just take the money I offered you and leave me alone?"

"What? And spoil all the fun?" Thomas stepped up beside her and set to rubbing the pad of his thumb over her cheek. "Suddenly I want more than just that measly amount of money you offered me. I think I deserve something more, don't you?" he whispered.

What meager amount of confidence she may have held to fast started crumbling. She sidestepped in her attempt to avoid his touching her, then immediately flinched in pain when he yanked her to his side. Fear got a firm hold on her gut, and the need to scream nearly overtook her, but Emily's face in her mind's eye squelched it.

He bent to deliver a punishing kiss on her neck, then dropped several more sloppy kisses up and down her cheek, grazing her lips, his hands groping, his body shoving her hard against the counter. She twisted in his embrace, frantic to be free of him. "Thomas, don't..."

"I'll do as I please, and you'll like it, little lady."

At the sound of the door nearly coming off its hinges, Callie's eyes flew open. Snarling noises such as she'd never heard before coursed through the air as big hands settled on the back of Thomas's shirt, then lifted and hurled him across the room, as if he weighed little more than a rag doll.

The sudden seizure sent Callie grappling backward,

and it wasn't until she found herself plastered against the kitchen wall that she managed to look up. Hastily righting herself, she blinked hard and pressed her palm to her mouth. *Daniel!*

Like a mad dog, Thomas flung himself at Dan, and the gun left his pocket, landing on the floor. Dan met Thomas with equal amounts of ferocity, upending him with a fist to the chin. Stunned, Thomas fell backward, quickly rubbed the spot and checked for blood, then lunged forward again, this time throwing a punch of his own and managing to hit his mark: the wound on Dan's face that was only now beginning to heal. Helpless to do much else but watch, the sickening sound of fist beating against flesh moved Callie into action.

Racing to the phone, she quickly dialed 9-1-1, only to discover that officers were already en route. "Hurry!" she bellowed into the receiver, as if her frantic plea should make a difference.

After slamming the receiver back in place, she watched in horror as the combatants warred back and forth across the room, neither one able to land a sound blow on the other. Dan gave ground to Thomas, and then swiftly retook it, all the while searching for a foothold. At last, he found it.

Dan clenched his fist and with lightning speed sent it surging into Thomas's unsuspecting jaw. Thomas's head snapped back with the force.

He fell. Hard.

Once down, Dan straddled the dazed Thomas,

pinned his arms with his strong legs, and snagged him by the collar with both hands.

"C-can't breathe," snorted Thomas. "Get off me." The garbled words ran together, as blood trickled from his nose and out between his teeth.

"Shut up," ordered Dan, his own breathing clipped and jagged. "I'm doing all I can to keep from killing you, so you best keep your tongue under control!" Thomas stared in disbelief, but held his tongue.

Dan drew in a breath. "You okay, Callie?" he asked, venturing a quick look at her.

A smile played at Callie's lips, but she kept it contained, knowing the situation didn't warrant a smile. Still, seeing Thomas *under* Dan was a blessed sight.

"I'm fine," she managed.

"You sure? Your cheek is pretty red."

She brought a hand to the spot. "It's fine."

Dan glared down at Thomas. "Didn't anyone ever teach you not to hit a woman?" he barked.

Thomas spat blood, narrowly missing his target, Dan's face. When he might have retaliated, two uniformed officers appeared in the open doorway, armed and ready. "What's going on here?" one asked.

Dan relaxed his hold and yanked Thomas up by the front of his shirt, preparing to explain the circumstances. At that juncture, Thomas wheedled out of Dan's grasp and dove for his gun.

Foolish move.

Callie screamed, and in the time it took for Thomas

to lunge across the room, one of the officers jumped Thomas from behind and knocked him to the floor. The other fellow snatched the gun up before Thomas had a chance to reach it, Thomas's slower-than-usual reflexes helping to fix the situation in record time. Of course, the act added fuel to the fire, not to mention years to Thomas's impending jail sentence. Resisting arrest, attempting to pull a weapon on an officer, threatening bodily harm, not to mention the threats he'd put on Callie's life—none was a casual offense.

No doubt about it, Thomas May was in deep trouble.

Chapter 22

As soon as the police left with Thomas, his hands cuffed and mouth spewing rage, Dan took Callie in his arms. He first stroked her hair, sweeping it off her brow so he could see her better. The red mark on her face had not yet vanished. Dan touched it carefully with his fingertips and bent to kiss it tenderly. "I can't believe he did this to you."

"It's over now," she mumbled into his shirt, not quite certain she could believe it.

"Yes, it's over, but are you sure you're okay?" he asked again.

"Quite sure," she answered, pulling away to get a better look at him. "What about you? You're still not fully healed from the fall you took. How in the world did you find the strength to do what you did?

"That? It was nothing."

She slapped him playfully. "I'm serious."

"Callie, it's amazing what a little adrenaline can do for the body, particularly when someone you love is in jeopardy. More importantly, it's amazing what a body can do with God Almighty at the helm. I stood outside your door praying that the police would come, and when they didn't, and I heard Thomas threaten you—imagined him with his hands on you—well, I knew I had to do something. I prayed a quick prayer for protection and courage, and I came charging in like a mad dog."

"You reminded me of that snarling dog that wouldn't let me get out of my car the other day. By the way, Thomas told me there are no vicious dogs in his dad's neighborhood. He figured I made the whole thing up."

"Maybe there aren't," Dan said, removing a few stubborn hairs from her vision and tucking them back behind her ear. "Maybe that one just happened to wander in. Then again, maybe he was on some kind of mission. Who knows? All I'm certain of is that God has had His hand in everything right from the very start. He is in control, Callie. Thomas is an evil man, but I think we can safely say he's going to be behind bars for a good long while."

"I know this may sound strange, maybe even preposterous, but in some ways I feel sorry for Thomas. He's so lost, Dan."

"He needs the Lord, but all we can do is pray for him. The rest is up to Thomas. He's made his choices. I know he had a poor upbringing and too few positive role models, but he's still the one responsible for his actions."

She nodded, grateful for Dan's wisdom, knowing

them to be true. "I—don't quite know how to thank you." The overwhelming reality of all that had transpired began to set in, and she trembled where she stood.

He drew her close again. "You don't have to. Just knowing you're okay and that Thomas won't be bothering you any time soon are all the thanks I need. I don't know what I'd do if anything had happened to you."

A dark expression washed across his face. She knew he was referring to his former losses. It had to be prominent on his mind. "Well, thanks to you, everything is fine."

"I prefer to give the thanks to God. Things could have ended so differently, honey. One of us could have been either seriously hurt or even killed. Who knows what that man is capable of doing? I'll admit, had I known he carried a gun, I might not have been so gallant in my rescue." He tweaked her nose and grinned. "Thanks for keeping that tidbit of information to yourself, at least while I was sitting on him. The scream? Now, that came in handy later."

She giggled and reached up to stroke his face, moving her hand to the gash above his cheek. He closed his eyes, allowing her perusal.

"Are you still in pain from the fall?" she asked, suddenly besieged with sentiment for the man who had risked his life for her. If she'd had any doubts before about how she felt, they had long vanished.

He eked out an exaggerated moan before limping

toward the sofa. "I think I should sit. And you should probably come with me. I need sympathy." He beckoned her with the curve of his finger.

She giggled and flopped down beside him, then discovered herself snuggling into the circle of his expansive arm, loving his strength, and relishing in his protective warmth. Comfortable, she tucked both feet under her.

"There's something I should tell you," she whispered while she fumbled with the hem of her sleeve.

"Yeah, what's that?" he asked, kissing the top of her head and then keeping his mouth there. His moist breath warmed her to her toes.

"I thought I should tell you how I feel about you."

"I think that would be good. Unless, of course, I'm not going to like it, in which case, I think you should keep your feelings to yourself."

Her laugh wavered shakily.

"Well?" he urged.

A tiny whimper came from the nursery. "Emily! I can't believe I didn't check on her earlier." She scooted to the edge of the sofa, preparing to leap to her daughter's beckoning.

"Uh-uh, lady," Dan said, grabbing her by the arm in just the nick of time and gathering her back to him. "You were about to tell me something."

"But Emily..."

"...will be just fine until you say whatever it was you had on your mind," he finished.

She took a deep breath. "I…"

"Callie, is it so hard to say that you've learned to trust me and that you want to love me, but you're still so scared? The way Thomas treated you was wrong, but it's time you released your heart, learned to love again. If you could just…"

She squelched his next words with her fingertips. "I'm not scared anymore."

"Would you care to expand on that point?" he asked.

She laughed. "Yes."

He pulled her more tightly to him. "I'm waiting."

Emily squealed again, this time louder and with more persistence. Callie bit her lip hard with regret. "I have to check on her."

Dan let loose of her. "I know. I'll go with you."

Emily was fine. Her foot had tangled itself in her blanket. Once Callie remedied the situation, the baby was all smiles, particularly when she discovered Dan.

In one hurried move, she pulled herself up with the help of the crib railing, tears still fresh on her cheek, but eyes beaming. Dan laughed and put his arms out to her. She flew into them.

"What are you doing?" Callie asked.

"I'm picking her up. Didn't you see that look in her eyes? She *wants* me."

"But she was in the middle of her nap."

"Nah, she's done napping. It's playtime."

"And I thought you wanted her to remain in bed until I finished what I was going to say."

"You can't say it in her presence?" The twinkle in his eyes filled her with enchantment.

God, can this be real? Is this truly happening to me?

"Open up your heart, My child; experience My forgiveness, My blessings, and abundant life."

If someone had told her mere months ago that she would find herself in love so soon after her divorce, she would never have believed it possible. But here she was—about to spill her heart at his feet.

She swallowed down a lump. "You know something?" she asked, unexpectedly timid, yet wonderfully sure of herself.

"What?" he asked, walking over to the changing table and placing Emily on her back.

"I never expected to feel....What are you doing?" she asked, suddenly stopping mid-sentence.

"What does it look like I'm doing? I'm changing Emily's diaper."

"*You're* changing her diaper?"

He glanced at her as if she'd just grown a second nose. "Don't you detect a rather strong odor?" He grinned good-humoredly.

"Yes, but..."

"I'm perfectly capable—and I've done it before."

"I know that, but to think that you'd actually, I don't know, do it without..."

"Being asked?" In under than thirty seconds, he'd

unsnapped her pants, released the Velcro tabs, and pulled the wet diaper out from under her.

"Yes."

He laughed and gave her a sideways glance while he reached for a fresh diaper. She was certain at that point that his ruggedly handsome face was melting her bones.

"I'm not entirely helpless, young lady. I was a parent once, and I never could understand why some men figured the job of changing diapers belonged only to the woman. If a guy wants to bond with his child, he has to help with the parenting."

The way his long, lean fingers carefully powdered the baby's bottom and capably worked the diaper was pure fascination. Every move he made was calculated and practiced, as if he'd done it all a hundred times before. Moreover, the fact it was her child that he lovingly handled captivated her even more.

"She really loves you, you know," Callie said, watching Emily cooperate as Dan slipped her pants back on and snapped them shut. And when he finished the job, the child stretched her arms up to him, all giggles, ready to be held again.

"And I love *her*—almost as much as I love her mother," he replied with a wink and a smile, scooping up the baby.

Unexplained tears formed in the corners of her eyes, probably a result of the unpleasant events of the evening, the toll they'd taken on her emotions.

"What's wrong?" asked Dan, brow furrowed.

He dipped his face low so that his eyes met hers head-on. Putting Emily down on the floor, he grabbed a couple of nearby toys and placed them at his feet. The child grabbed for them immediately.

Simultaneously, Dan pulled Callie into his arms. "I have a feeling you need some time to let things settle. You've been through a great deal these past days, not to mention what transpired tonight. It's a lot to take in."

How was it possible that he already knew her so well?

"I don't deserve you," she blurted.

"What? Who has spent the last few months of his life living a lie? It's no wonder you don't trust me."

"But I do trust you. That's just it. I didn't know that I could ever trust anyone again, or that it would happen so quickly."

He shook his head. "God's clock is different from ours."

"I've noticed that."

"Do you think I expected this to happen? Three months ago, I moved here with the sole purpose of dodging reality. Instead, I came banging right straight into it. I realized in short order that no matter how far or fast I run, I can't outrun God.

"When I lost my wife and daughter, I expected my own life to come slamming to a halt. I even prayed it would end. I felt I had nothing more to live for. Imagine if God had listened to me, or, worse, given up on me—or *you,* Callie.

"Aren't you thankful God is not like that? He just keeps on calling our names until we hear Him. He keeps on chasing and chasing—and chasing. He loves us that much.

"Three months ago I never would have expected to be holding you in my arms, especially not after that first encounter I had with you." He pushed back from her to peer into her eyes. "You were a feisty little thing."

His description tickled her. "You were an ornery coot," she challenged. "You made my baby cry."

"I did that?" Emily played contentedly at their feet. "She doesn't look any worse for the wear," he replied sheepishly. He stared down at the innocent child. "I'm sorry that Thomas was such a disappointment to you, that he wasn't even interested in his own child. That had to have hurt you deeply."

"Dan..."

"No, I mean it. You must have had high hopes for your future when you first married him. And then when you had his child..."

"He never wanted her. He figured I got pregnant to spite him. In fact, he never came to see her until she was several days old, and then it wasn't to see her at all; it was just to tell me he was moving."

"He's a fool."

"I see that now."

"The point is that people will disappoint us, Callie.

God, however, never changes. He is the same yesterday, today, and forever. We can count on Him to love us unconditionally, and most important, to forgive us our shortcomings. After all, He designed us.

"When I think of how bitter and angry I was toward Him for the accident, how I blamed Him, I'm amazed at His faithfulness. Don't think that I can now look back and comprehend why it all happened because I can't. There are some things in life we will never find answers for, but we still have to accept them as part of the bigger picture, His perfect plan. It's the trials and hardships we live through that make us strong.

"Dan Mattson, I love you." The words slipped past her lips without warning.

He sighed audibly, then smiled.

Standing on tiptoe, she cupped his face with her hands and simply studied him. "And I meant what I said about not deserving you." When he opened his mouth to protest, she shushed him with a kiss, taking the liberty to mold herself into his waiting embrace. The kiss was tender, a promise of things to come. Moments later, she pulled away to examine him more closely.

"What?" he asked curiously, refusing to let go of her.

"I believe you have the best eyes and the nicest smile I've ever seen. And your face ain't all that bad, either."

Holding her at bay, he exclaimed, "Why, teacher, your English needs polishing!"

She giggled. "Seriously, I've wanted to tell you that for the longest time."

"Then why didn't you?"

"I was afraid you'd think I was flirting."

He chuckled. "And no telling what might have happened next had I thought that. I might have ravished you on the spot."

"I was trying to be serious." She nudged him playfully.

He kissed the tip of her nose and then both her cheeks. The maneuver left her wanting more of his kisses. "And I'm serious when I say I love you, Callie Jacobs May. And one day soon I intend to give you a fourth name."

"You do?" His subtle proposal made her shiver with excitement. Was she living a fairy tale?

"Up!" Emily interrupted, pulling at the cuff of Dan's slacks until he released Callie to swoop her up into his arms.

"Did you hear that? She's never said that word before!" Callie exclaimed.

"A command, no less. And I'm honored to be the first recipient. Come on, sugar," Dan said to Emily, patting her diapered backside. "I'm taking you and your mommy out for a bite to eat."

Emily pulled back from Dan's embrace. "Ea!" she shouted enthusiastically, cupping both of Dan's cheeks in her pudgy hands and smiling widely.

"I don't believe it!" Callie said.

Dan met Callie's gaze. "What?"

"She's talking!"

He laughed. "It must be my power and influence over women. After all, look at the things I got *you* to say!"

Callie laughed and followed Dan and Emily out the door, shaking her head, her heart full of hope and wonder.

The long corridor was empty and quiet except for the sounds of teachers' droning voices and the occasional squeak of a chair. Dan checked his watch. *Perfect.* Callie would never expect him to show up at her first-hour class. He asked himself why he was doing this now and not over a romantic dinner, but there simply wasn't any way to answer except that he couldn't wait another second to claim her.

Walking several paces behind was the principal, Blanche Austin, someone he liked on the spot but wouldn't have wanted to be caught dead sitting across from as a teenager. She had a quiet, no-nonsense manner that Dan had no trouble detecting; yet, he knew instinctively she was fair-minded.

When Dan had spoken to her on the phone yesterday, he had someone altogether different picked out in his mind. That woman had been smaller in stature and presence. This woman, the one that followed several feet behind, was no slouch. He was convinced she would take him down if challenged, and he'd go without a fight.

He didn't know why she didn't walk beside him unless she thought he'd find her presence intimidating, which he very well did. He was nervous enough as it was without the high school principal breathing down his neck.

"I hope you won't mind if I listen in," she said.

Dan glanced back. "Not at all." Actually, he did mind. An audience of one more would just make him that much more nervous.

"I'll be just outside her classroom."

"Good. Principals do have a way of making me stumble over my words, particularly if I'm looking one straight in the eye."

She chuckled. "I'm sure you'll do just fine. Turn left at the end of this hallway. It's the fourth classroom on your right."

He glanced back again and found another woman rounding the corner. It looked like the school secretary. She was smiling broadly, expectantly, and carrying something over her arm. *A camera? Great.* This wasn't a school-wide event. Still, he couldn't exactly fault anyone. It wasn't every day that some fool came into the building to propose marriage to one of the teachers. He grinned to himself while he fought down more jitters.

What if she turned him down in front of a bunch of middle school students?

At the corner, he gulped down a breath of air, then brushed the dampness from the sleeves of his leather bomber jacket. It'd been snowing hard this December morning. He checked his pocket once more for the presence of a little box. Finding it, he breathed easier and forced himself to slow his steps. He didn't want to shock her with his entrance.

"Okay, gang, listen up." Callie's voice echoed through the hallway, and his heart leaped with anticipation. Counting down four classroom doors, he stopped a few feet short of hers. He couldn't see any of the students from his vantage point, but he heard the shuffling of papers and books and the occasional screeching of a chair leg. "I want you to apply some of the principles you've learned with regard to correct punctuation," she was saying. A low groan sounded from somewhere in the classroom, followed by a chorus of giggles.

"Take out your notebooks, please." *She sounds like a teacher,* Dan mused.

"Aw, Mrs. May, this stinks."

"We can do with fewer sound effects and complaints, Rob. Let's not encourage him, people." Callie's voice held a hint of humor.

"She's good," Blanche Austin whispered at Dan's side. He hadn't even heard the woman sneak up behind him. It made him wonder if she made a habit of checking on her teachers in the same manner.

"Do we need to review the rules before we proceed?" Callie asked.

The principal nudged Dan in the side. "Now?" he mouthed. She nodded.

Dan rounded the corner of Callie's classroom to

find her leaning on the front of her desk, legs crossed at the ankles, hands resting flat on her desktop. She didn't spot him right off, her gaze intent on her students instead, particularly the burly one at the back of the room. No one could have mistaken which was Rob. She had told him plenty about star athlete, Rob Rankin, the hard-hitting quarterback. He even thought he had pert little Kaley picked out, and maybe even Josh Hansen. This was her favorite class period; that's why he'd picked this particular one to crash.

A gasp of surprise flew out of some young lady's mouth when she spotted Dan in the doorway, causing Callie to turn her gaze. When she saw him, her eyes grew wide. "What…?"

Dan smiled, feigning calm. Maybe he would play the situation out. "Don't mind me, teacher. I've just come to pay a little visit. You don't mind, do you?" He started to head to the back of the room. "May I?"

Whispers of curiosity filled the room as heads of every color turned to one another in question. "Holy, red-hot tamales, Mrs. May," some little blonde urchin cried, "Who is this?"

"Daniel Mattson, what on earth…?"

"Mrs. May," Rob asked, "you need me to take him out?"

Dan maneuvered his way through the aisles until he came face-to-face with the gigantic teenager. Grinning down on him good-naturedly, he said, "I have no doubt that you could, but trust me when I say it won't be necessary. I am *not* the enemy." With that, he winked at the surrounding students, and everyone appeared to relax, as if they somehow sensed they were in for a show.

"Daniel Mattson there had better be a good explanation for this. I was just in the middle of..."

"Oh, there is," he said, nodding at her and grinning. To the classroom of onlookers he asked, "She always like this?"

"Yes!" they all chimed.

"She drives us into the ground," Rob said. "But she's okay—*most* of the time."

"Yeah," someone piped up. "Fridays are the best."

"How so?" Dan asked, curious himself.

"All the other teachers make us work our tails off, but she says weekends are for enjoying."

That particular comment came from a long-haired guy full of earring studs and holes in his nose and lip. It appeared to Dan he could *use* something constructive to do over the weekend.

"She also lets us spout off about stuff," said a petite little brunette in the front. Kaley? After listening to Callie talk about some of her favorite students, he thought he could pretty well handpick who was who.

"I'd say that's pretty generous of her," Dan said, catching Callie's eye and winking at her. The flustered look she threw him in return had him baffled.

"Hey, aren't you that guy from Fellowship Chapel?"

The question came from a young man in the back. "You're a youth worker or something."

"I've been helping the youth pastor, yes."

"I thought so. I saw you there. You're pretty good with a basketball."

"I know a few things," he admitted with a grin. Several of the jocks sat up straighter.

Since getting back to church, he'd found himself involved in a one-on-one study with senior pastor, Rich Borgman, also now a good friend. In addition, he and Callie were volunteering their time in the youth ministry on Wednesday nights. Someday he would discover God's leading in terms of full-time ministry, but for now, he was comfortable as an unpaid assistant. Maybe it would be enough, or maybe God would eventually open new doors of opportunity.

His job with Freeman Construction had worked well for him. The main thing was that he wanted to be prepared for God's leading. Moreover, he wanted Callie at his side while he waited.

Looking at her now, he wasn't sure how to read her. It was clear his presence had thrown her.

"Don't let me interrupt," he teased. "I'll just stand back here and wait until you're done giving instructions or whatever that was you were doing, something about punctuation, wasn't it?"

She cleared her throat, her visage going from curious to annoyed. He wondered if he'd pushed the envelope a bit too far. After all, this *was* a classroom, not the playground. She unfolded her arms and moved to the back of her desk to study something she'd written down.

"As I was saying, class," she started, clearly flustered, "the assignment will be..."

"Well, actually," Dan interrupted. Callie looked up, quickly refolded her arms, and proceeded to stare daggers into him. "Maybe it would be best if I just went ahead and, you know, stated my purpose in being here. I mean if that would be okay with you, *Mrs.* May. Then I could be out of your hair. I mean I'm sure these students are *very* eager to get back to their lesson, right, guys?"

"Nah!" They all echoed. "We'll be glad to wait."

"Yeah, this is getting good," a young lady added in a singsong voice, tacking on a high-pitched giggle. Several echoed their agreement.

"Yeah, someone pass the popcorn!" This remark came straight from Rob, who by now had settled back in his chair and stretched out his long legs as far as they would go.

Cheers of support applauded his suggestion.

Callie narrowed her eyes at Dan. "What is this about?" she asked, her words almost indiscernible above the sudden chatter of anxious students.

"Hmm, I suppose you do need an explanation."

"I suppose I do."

At that point, Blanche Austin and the camera-toting secretary poked their heads in the doorway. Naturally, they didn't want to miss a thing. Callie's dumbfounded expression grew.

His heart thudded against his chest as he prayed his words would come out the way he'd rehearsed them.

∾

Callie felt numb. Why was Dan standing in her classroom looking for all the world as handsome as a prancing stallion? His presence not only threw her, it disarmed her. One minute she was talking correct punctuation and the next listening to her students' opinions of her with Dan as the moderator. Somewhere along the line, she needed to gather her wits about her and take back possession of her classroom.

Blanche and Louise stood in her doorway with expectant expressions. She wasn't sure what they hoped to see, but the way Louise held her camera at the ready made her wonder what Dan had up his sleeve. A thought she dared not entertain crept in, but she tucked it far back in a corner of her mind. Surely, he wouldn't propose marriage in front of a classroom of students, her boss, and the school secretary!

They hadn't broached the subject of marriage since the night of Thomas's arrest, and then only subtly when he'd stated he intended to change her name one last time! No, instead, he'd been courting her—enticing her with flowers, chocolates, and tender kisses, all of which had proven effective in winning her over. As if he even needed to make the effort. She'd been captivated by his charm and wit long before he started wooing her. Still, she had to admit to enjoying all the attention.

One night he surprised her with dinner and a movie, even arranging for the baby-sitter. Another time, he ordered Chinese take-out and met her at her door with a Disney video! Almost every week he either delivered flowers to her door or had them transported by the florist. One night he even placed a dozen roses on her doorstep himself, rang her bell then made a beeline for his own apartment to watch her reaction through his peephole.

As if his pursuit of Callie wasn't enough, he had captured every last bit of Emily's heart, as well. Of course, she willingly gave it, her trusting little soul incapable of refusing his advances. Whenever she heard his voice, her eyes grew wide with hope and wonder, her face emitting pure elation. Moreover, since she'd started toddling around on wobbly legs, they carried her to wherever he was as fast as they could go. No doubt about it, she was *his* from the second he entered the room—and he was *hers*.

If anyone else had been thrilled with Dan, it was Elizabeth Jacobs. Hardly a day went by without her mother phoning to invite them over. Of course, he tended to her every need since emerging on the scene, so that could explain her bigger-than-life view of him. He oiled her squeaky doors, tightened her leaky faucet, and unclogged her slow drains. Next, he repainted her bathroom and hung new blinds. However, his last offer to replace her worn kitchen linoleum with bright ceramic tile had been the icing on the cake.

It was a pleasure and an inspiration to watch Dan's faith rise to new heights. Almost overnight, he assumed a leadership role in their relationship, insisting that they pray and study God's Word together. His former life as a pastor revealed itself in the way he pored over the Scriptures, pointing out passages of interest and challenging her thinking. On top of that, he initiated a men's Bible study for any fellow construction workers who wanted to learn more about the Christian faith. So far, three had expressed interest. It was a start, and she was proud of him for the stand he'd taken with his coworkers.

She suspected one of the reasons Dan avoided the subject of marriage was because he was eager to put the matter of Thomas behind them. They sighed with great relief when Thomas pleaded guilty to a number of charges. Interestingly enough, the Florida courts wanted him, too, for alleged threats he'd placed on his banker. No telling what his sentence would wind up being once the judge came back with his final decision. A minimum of fifteen years had been her lawyer's guess.

"Mrs. May, is he your boyfriend?" Kaley Robinson asked, breaking into Callie's thoughts and bringing her back to the present. The girl's admiring tone echoed through the classroom.

"He's—this is..."

"Yes, I am, as a matter of fact. My name's Dan Mattson. Sorry. I should have introduced myself earlier," Dan answered, saving her.

Recently, the newspapers had been full of reports about Thomas May's character, not to mention his scuffle with the law and assured jail term. Fortunately, no one had dragged down her own reputation in the process, and she wanted to keep it that way. Teachers had to be careful to maintain a spotless standing in the community. What would folks think if they discovered she'd fallen in love so soon after her divorce and Thomas's recent run-in with the law?

"Whew!" Kaley blew out a sigh and sat back prettily. "He's *nice*."

She let the boldness of her two-word statement float through the air like a song despite the principal's presence, and for an instant, Callie thought she saw Dan wince with embarrassment. *Good. It serves him right,* she decided, almost smiling.

"Actually, that's why I'm here," he offered, winking at Kaley.

The teen sat up a little straighter, as did several others. "You gonna lay one on her?"

"Kaley, for goodness' sake!" Callie scolded.

"What? I didn't mean anything by that. It's just a saying, Mrs. May."

"I know, but it sounds crude. I believe this has gone far enough."

"Now, *teacher*, you've just interrupted what I was about to say," Dan said, stepping over Rob Rankin's size thirteen shoes to approach her. Several students whispered back and forth, speculating.

"Dan, what…?"

"Patience, my dear," he teased, issuing a half-grin and managing to melt down the last of her resistance.

Out of the corner of one eye she spotted Karen Swanson, the history teacher whose classroom was across the hall, sidle up next to Blanche Austin. Apparently, she'd gotten wind of something herself. All three women looked about ready to swoon. Maneuvering his way past long-legged students, notebooks, school bags, and stray textbooks on the floor, Dan kept his eyes on her, and for just a moment, she forgot that thirty pairs of eyes rested on her.

Once he reached the front of the room, Dan turned Callie's body to face him. His hands slid down her arms to where her own hands dangled helplessly, and he clasped them both inside his bigger ones, and then brought them to his mouth to kiss.

Someone sighed, and Callie nearly swooned herself. If her heart didn't slow its pace, she was afraid she'd hyperventilate. Dan, on the other hand, was a picture of complete composure, and the simple fact quite threw her.

"Sweet," Kaley uttered in whispered tones, hugging her notebook to her chest. She seemed to be the only one who dared to break the silence.

Except for the squirming chair legs of a couple of jocks in the back, the roomful of students and the gathering adults at the door appeared awestruck.

"The reason I'm here today, Callie, um, *Mrs.* May, is to make my feelings and intentions known publicly."

She swallowed. "Dan," she whispered through her teeth. "What are you doing? These are very impressionable kids. What will they think?"

He threw his head back and laughed, the booming sound drenched in confidence. "I have a feeling these kids have been around the block a time or two, right guys?"

Cheers rose up and Callie managed a shaky smile.

"Yeah, Mrs. May. We know what's up. We also got a pretty good idea of what's comin'. Let the guy finish," Rob said.

Callie turned her gaze outward. "Why is it that I don't normally hold your attention this well?" she asked. Everyone laughed, including Blanche.

When the room quieted, Dan focused all his attention on Callie while her heart hammered away. "I think you've probably guessed why I'm here, right?"

She gave a slow nod.

He grinned and she giggled nervously, squeezing his work-roughened hands as tightly as possible. "When I first laid eyes on you, I knew I was in trouble. Somehow I felt like you would make me face reality, and I had come to Oakdale as a means of escape. I tried to close up my heart, but you somehow wheedled your way right inside." He made a fist and placed it on his chest.

"Awww...." The entire roomful of people, guys included, echoed the sentiment.

"I've watched you triumph in the midst of tragedy. At first, I admired you from afar, but not anymore. I want the world to know what a wonderful, caring, giving, and forgiving person you are—and just how much I love you."

"Dan..." A couple of tears slid down her cheek and she dabbed at them.

"Callie." If she could have gotten a sneak preview of what would come next, she still wouldn't have believed it. First, he knelt down on one knee in front of her students, God, and everybody. Next, he drew a tiny box from his jacket pocket and removed a sparkling ring. Startled, Callie released an unsuspecting squeal. "I am hoping that you will make me a happy man by agreeing to be my wife."

Gasps rose up around the room, as he slipped the ring on her finger then stood up to face her. "Callie, will you marry me?"

Suddenly, the room erupted, and then just as quickly grew silent, waiting for her answer, which, by the way, did not come directly. She was too busy trying to find her tongue and then the wherewithal to form the proper words. "It only requires one word," Dan whispered encouragingly, eyebrows arched, and for just a moment, his expression bore a look of anguish.

"Yes!" she burst forth. "Yes, yes, yes!"

He wrapped his arms around her waist to lift her off the floor, then kissed her hard on the mouth before spinning her around. Once he'd made her sufficiently dizzy, he placed her back on the floor and for the next several minutes, stepped back so she could accept the warm hugs of well-wishers. Most of the girls jumped out of their seats and surrounded her to gawk at the round, bigger-than-life diamond Dan had placed on her finger, while the fellows feigned nonchalance. Except for Rob, of course. He was there to give her a bear hug despite the ribbing he might take later.

"Wow, Mrs. May," cried Kaley, "your ring is beautiful!"

"Thank you, honey," Callie said, accepting the pretty girl's hug once Rob stepped back. Callie could hardly wait for the chance to examine it herself. She'd probably have to pinch herself a time or two in the act just to make certain she wasn't dreaming.

Others came to offer smiles and congratulations. Blanche Austin beamed from head to toe when she finally fought her way through the barrage of yakking females. "My dear, I'm very happy for you. You do know you're done for the day, don't you?"

Callie laughed. "I'm sure I'll be able to regain control."

"No, dear, I mean you're done. We have a substitute coming in."

"What?"

"It's all been arranged. Seems your young man wants to sweep you away for the day." The woman threw a glance in Dan's direction. He had the fellows' full attention back in one corner of the room, demonstrating some kind of basketball toss and entertaining them with his banter. "He does seem to have a way with words. I thought I would faint from the suspense of it all."

Callie's heart filled to overflowing. "So you knew about this?"

"Of course. I thought the whole idea too romantic to pass up."

By now, several other teachers had gathered at the door to offer their smiles and best wishes. It seemed the principal's presence wouldn't deter anyone from temporarily leaving his or her classroom. Blanche turned her attention elsewhere when someone called her name.

"Callie." She turned to discover Jerry Watson standing behind her. My, how news traveled. His smile was genuine if not a trifle guarded. The episode at her apartment still made things awkward between them, but she'd long since decided to put it behind her. She hoped he would do the same and that in time they would establish a friendship of sorts. Rather than offer a hug, he extended a hand. "I see you've decided to marry the bodyguard after all." A friendlier tone replaced his earlier bad-tempered one.

She managed a laugh. "Yes, I have," she answered, sensing Dan's presence at her side.

"Dan," Jerry said, extending his arm for a handshake. "Congratulations, man. You've got yourself a prize."

Dan plastered a smile on his face and extended his hand, then put his arm around Callie's shoulder to draw her in. She sensed the ownership of his embrace and relished in the feel. She belonged to him, and the realization rocked her to the core. *Thank You, Lord,* she prayed inwardly while blocking out all other sounds.

Dan and Jerry talked for a moment. "Well, Watson, sorry to cut this short, but I must take *my* prize." He pulled her closer, his possessive tone sending a pointed message to the male teacher. Jerry nodded sheepishly, forced a smile, and stepped back.

Dan ushered her toward the door. "Get your coat, pretty lady," he whispered. "I want to get you out of here so I can lay one on you."

She laughed. "Daniel Mattson, you are a sneaky, shrewd character." The grin he returned was "divinely" impish.

Just then the school bell sounded, bringing those students who weren't already standing to their feet to gather up belongings and head for their next class. Everyone issued farewells, and just before the next batch of students arrived for class, Dan escorted Callie out the door and down the hallway toward his waiting car.

"What have you got up your sleeve?" she asked while dodging boisterous students, smiling and waving at those she knew.

He took her elbow to steer her out of the way of a couple of high-speed athletes.

"Well," he finally answered once they made it through the pack of lively teens and it looked like they were on the homestretch.

When the hallway was quiet and they'd passed the office and the media center, he finished what he'd started. "What I have up my sleeve is a whole lot of things, but first we're stopping by your mom's place for breakfast."

"Does she know about this?" She extended her left hand to study the shimmering new ring that fit her finger so perfectly. How had he pulled everything off so flawlessly?

"She sure does, and she can't wait to see you," he answered, holding open the heavy glass door for her. She slipped past him, only to be shocked by the frigid December air. She pulled her woolen scarf more tightly around her neck.

"What about my car?" she asked.

"We'll stop by for it later."

"Just what do you have planned, Mr. Mattson?"

"*Mr.* Mattson? I'm afraid that tone of voice calls up some rather bad memories of our shaky start," he teased.

She laughed at the memory. With his car in view, they hurried their steps. The icy temperatures played no favorites when it bit its ugly teeth into her face. Surprisingly, though, her heart was aglow, and the burning embers of love served to keep her warm from head to toe.

Once they situated themselves in the car and he'd started the engine, he turned to face her.

"I love you, Callie." It was a simple admission.

"I love you," she said with as little effort as it took to breathe.

He bent to kiss the tip of her nose, then moved his lips lightly over her face until he reached her waiting lips. The tender kiss evolved until their arms moved freely, almost hungrily, around the other, scarves and heavy coats a barrier for their bodies but not their hearts.

When he finally pulled away, it was to catch his breath. He chuckled and then righted his body. "There won't be many more kisses of that nature until we're married. I want to remain alive for our wedding night," he teased. "And speaking of wedding, what's say we make it soon?"

Her giggle welled up from nowhere as well as an outrageous thought. "How about the weekend after next? I'll be on Christmas break."

His eyes filled with wonder. "I'm game if you are, but are you sure?"

She sat back on the seat and thought of all the places she'd been in her life. All of a sudden, the realization of God's love slammed against the walls of her heart. She'd known pain at its worst, physical and emotional, but God had been there in the midst of it.

When difficulty had hit her on all sides, and the mountains of life were insurmountable, He'd carried her over. In darkness and light, in sorrow and joy, He was there, always had been, always would be. It didn't matter the circumstances; He had a perfect plan. She'd only needed to trust Him.

The verse from Romans 8:28, *"We know that in all things God works for the good of those who love him, who have been called according to his purpose,"* washed over her. God could take a broken heart and make it whole; a meaningless life, and give it direction.

Thoughts of Dan's past filled her mind. He'd lost his purpose and direction, even doubted God's very existence for a time, but God refused to let go. No, He'd chased him down, as an earthly father would run after his toddler who was ambling toward a busy intersection. It took a crisis to awaken him, but often times, God uses crises for that very purpose.

So here they were—two people whose lives had crossed over from pain to wholeness. For a time, they had tried to discount their feelings, even run from them. God, however, had His purposes to work out, and it would seem He had wrapped the two of them together in that perfect plan.

Just where that journey would take them was yet unclear. One thing was certain, though: Callie wanted to take the journey with Dan Mattson.

"Oh yes, I'm very sure," she answered, her heart too full to say much beyond that.

He planted one last hasty kiss on her lips, smiled, and then put the gearshift into place.

Then, hand in hand, heart in heart, they began their journey together.

Sharlene MacLaren's first Whitaker House title

ISBN: 978-0-88368-746-8
Tradepaper • 368 pages

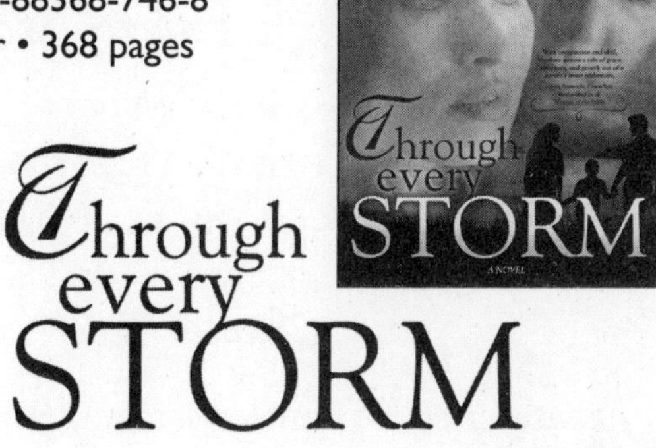

Struggling through the tragic loss of their child, Maddie and Jeff Bowman experience the immense pain and grief caused by a broken heart and a marriage so severely strained that a divorce seems imminent. Will life ever be normal again?

While still overwhelmed with feelings of complete hopelessness and loneliness, they are additionally faced with having to care for a precocious little boy. Then, Maddie slowly realizes how to let God be in control. The love that she discovers gives her the hope and strength to go on.

Maddie and Jeff must learn how to overcome their problems. But together they may find a joy and happiness that they had never known before.

www.whitakerhouse.com

Selected Excerpts from

Through Every Storm

Finalist,
American Christian Fiction Writers
Book of the Year 2007

Chapter Two

A baby cried, its muffled screams pulling at Maddie's senses. "Go to sleep, Emma. Mama's tired," she mumbled groggily, pulling a pillow over her head.

But the haunting cries continued, interrupting her sleep-drugged state, gnawing at the corners of her consciousness. Was this reality or another nightmare? These days, it was hard to tell the difference.

"Jeff," she whispered, "Emma's crying." But he slept soundly, their romantic evening having brought them both a sense of completeness, anesthetizing him to the point of oblivion.

The chilling cries rose in decibels, evolving into shrieks, then just as suddenly stopped, too abruptly.

She should have jumped from her bed right then and there. But she didn't.

Instead, she tossed from side to side, throwing covers and sheets away from her sweat-soaked body. Swiping at a tear, she suppressed a groan and thrashed about in search of air. Her chest felt heavy, immobile. Was this what death felt like?

Suddenly, her eyes flew open. In quiet desperation she searched for something familiar, some piece of certainty. She reached for Jeff, then realized he no longer shared her bed. Lying still and unsure, she stared at the ceiling.

She could have sworn she'd heard a baby—her baby. Did she dare hope it could be true this time?

Leaping to her feet, she ran the length of the hallway, threw open the door to the nursery, then heaved a sigh fraught with disappointment.

Sobbing, she fell in a heap beside the empty crib.

Chapter Fifteen

...In his usual morose mood, Jeff headed back to the bank after a meeting with one of his clients. His mind was a muddle of thoughts, mostly of Maddie and her decision to become a Christian. He wasn't quite sure why it bothered him so much. Others could claim a personal relationship with God, but when it came to his own wife, well, that was altogether different. He'd been downright rude to her lately, ignoring her attempts at conversation. No way did he want to risk finding himself in the middle of another religious dispute. *God can help you—just as He's helped me,* she'd said. Those words had dug a hole in his head and planted themselves there, messing with this thinking, reminding him that he and Maddie were miles apart. Where once she'd seemed so hopeless in her outlook, it now appeared she'd started to find a pathway through her grief, and something about that provoked him, made him feel like the loser.

To make matters worse, Christmas was coming, a holiday that served only as a reminder of happier days. And what of the annual trip to Arizona to visit his folks? Before Emma's accident, visiting his parents had always been a highlight of the season. But no more. Last year had been disaster enough. No way could he handle two years in a row. Therefore, thinking to ease both their minds about the matter, he'd told Maddie she didn't need to go this year. He couldn't tell if she was relieved or angered by the offer, but he figured if she'd wanted to go with him, she would have said.

As if all this wasn't enough, the face of Tracey James kept interfering with his sanity. She seemed relentless in her quest to break him down, visiting his office twice in the last few days—to drop off papers, she'd said, but he suspected it was more than that. She was in desperate pursuit of his attentions. And the very idea that he could fall into an affair with her scared the daylights out of him.

As he headed back to his office, he passed the mall on his right and made a quick U-turn. On the chance that Maddie had bought him something for Christmas, he wanted to be prepared. A small token gift couldn't hurt, could it?

The first flakes of winter batted against his brow as he made his way to the nearest entrance. A storm was brewing. Gray, threatening clouds loomed overhead, rolling in like a raging locomotive. Tugging his coat collar close around his throat, he bent his head down to face off the worst of December's bitter winds. At least, Timmy would be happy about the white stuff, he mused. The kid had had his eye out for the first signs of snow in the way a hunter waits for his first glimpse of a whitetail on the opening day of deer hunting season. He was going to miss the little whippersnapper when he went home to Seattle. It would devastate Maddie.

The mall was crowded with busy shoppers. He headed for the toy store with Timmy in mind. The boy had begun talking nonstop about his newfound interest in dinosaurs and mummies, an odd combination. Ever since visiting the museum he'd acquired what Maddie termed an unhealthy interest in strange-looking creatures.

Piped in Christmas music played above the hubbub of seasonal shoppers. Jeff closed his eyes and ears to everything else and focused instead on fighting the masses. On his way to the toy store, he passed Branson's Jewelry and, on a whim, spun around and walked inside. He knew Maddie loved jewelry, and he happened to have overheard her tell her mother at Thanksgiving that one of her favorite gold chains had recently broken. Would buying her a gift help to ease the guilt that pecked away at the walls of his heart like some willful woodpecker?

It was worth a try.

About the Author

Born and raised in west Michigan, Sharlene MacLaren attended Spring Arbor University. Upon graduating with an education degree, she traveled internationally for a year with a small singing ensemble, then came home and married one of her childhood friends. Together they raised two lovely daughters. Now happily retired after teaching elementary school for thirty-one years, 'Shar' enjoys reading, writing, singing in the church choir and worship teams, traveling, and spending time with her husband, children, and precious grandchildren.

A Christian for over forty years and a lover of the English language, Shar has always enjoyed dabbling in writing—poetry, fiction, various essays, and freelancing for periodicals and newspapers. Her favored genre, however, has always been romance. She remembers well the short stories she wrote in high school and watching them circulate from girl to girl during government and civics classes. "Psst," someone would whisper from two rows over, always when the teacher's back was to the class, "pass me the next page."

Shar is an occasional speaker for her local MOPS organization, is involved in KIDS' HOPE USA, a mentoring program for at-risk children, counsels young women in the Apples of Gold program, and is active in two weekly Bible studies. She and her husband, Cecil, live in Spring Lake, Michigan, with their lovable collie, Dakota, and Mocha, their lazy fat cat.

The acclaimed *Through Every Storm* was Shar's first novel to be published by Whitaker House, and in 2007, the American Christian Fiction Writers (ACFW) named it a finalist for Book of the Year. The beloved Little Hickman Creek series consisted of *Loving Liza Jane*; *Sarah, My Beloved*; and *Courting Emma*. Shar's new trilogy, The Daughters of Jacob Kane, will be released in 2009.

To find out more about Shar and her writing and inspiration, you can e-mail her at smac@chartermi.net or visit her Web site at www.sharlenemaclaren.com.

Little Hickman Creek Series

by Sharlene MacLaren

Loving Liza Jane

Liza Jane Merriwether had come to Little Hickman Creek, Kentucky, to teach. She had a lot of love to give to her students. She just hadn't reckoned on the handsome stranger with two adorable little girls and a heart of gold that was big enough for one more.

Ben Broughton missed his wife, but he was doing the best he could to raise his two daughters alone. Still, he had to admit that he needed help, which is why he wrote to the Marriage Made in Heaven Agency for a mail-order bride. While he was waiting for a response, would he overlook the perfect wife that God had practically dropped in his lap?

ISBN: 978-0-88368-816-8 • Trade • 368 pages

Sarah, My Beloved

Sarah Woodward has come to Kentucky as a mail-order bride. But when she steps off the stage coach, the man who contacted her through the Marriage Made in Heaven Agency informs her that he has fallen in love with and wed another woman. With her usual stubborn determination, she refuses to leave until she finds out what God's reason is. Rocky Callahan's sister has died, leaving him with two young children to take care of. When he meets the fiery Sarah, he proposes the answer to both their problems—a marriage in name only. Can he let go of the pain in his past and trust God's plan for his life? Will she leave him or will they actually find a marriage made in heaven?

ISBN: 978-0-88368-425-2 • Trade • 368 pages

Courting Emma

Twenty-eight-year old Emma Browning has experienced a good deal of life in her young age. Proprietor of Emma's Boardinghouse, she is "mother" to an array of beefy, unkempt, often rowdy characters. Though many men would like to get to know the steely, hard-edged, yet surprisingly lovely proprietor, none has truly succeeded. That is, not until the town's new pastor, Jonathan Atkins, takes up residence in the boardinghouse.

ISBN: 978-1-60374-020-3 • Trade • 384 pages

www.whitakerhouse.com